Moments of Truth

by Sandra D. Bricker

Bling!
Romance
Lighthouse Publishing of the Carolinas

MOMENTS OF TRUTH BY SANDRA D. BRICKER
Published by Lighthouse Publishing of the Carolinas
2333 Barton Oaks Dr., Raleigh, NC 27614

ISBN: 978-1-941103-95-1
Copyright © 2015 by Sandra D. Bricker
Cover design by Kim Killion, The Killion Group
Interior design by Karthick Srinvasan

Available in print from your local bookstore, online, or from the publisher at:
www.lighthousepublishingofthecarolinas.com

For more information on this book and the author visit: www.SandraDBricker.com

Brought to you by the creative team at Bling! Romance:
Sandie Bricker, Managing Editor, Bling! Romance
Jennifer Harshman, Proofreader

Library of Congress Cataloging-in-Publication Data
Bricker, Sandra D.
Moments of Truth/Sandra D. Bricker 1st ed.

Printed in the United States of America

PRAISE FOR *MOMENTS OF TRUTH*

"With every new release from Sandra D. Bricker, I think she can't improve; but *Moments of Truth* is even better than her previous books. I love the way she weaves in the stories of five different women who meet for "book club," which is just an excuse to talk, eat, and interact with each other's lives in a meaningful way. The romance is stellar! I promise you'll fall in love with all the characters. Highly recommend."

~**Barbara Scott,** author and editor

"Sandra D. Bricker has done it again! Her fun, ultra-contemporary style adds a breezy element to everything she writes—even when the characters are faced with serious challenges. As I read this book, I became so emotionally involved that I felt as though I was in Regan's pocket, living her life as she did, laughing with her, crying with her, and experiencing all of her emotions. *Moments of Truth* is one of those stories that will stay with readers long after they finish the book … and send them running to the nearest store to purchase another Bricker book."

~**Debby Mayne, author of the BELLES IN THE CITY series**
—*Trouble in Paradise, One Foot Out the Door,* **and** *Can't Fool Me Twice*

"*Moments of Truth* is aptly named as you follow the characters through the ups and downs of life. With characters that are relatable and well developed, the reader is drawn into a group of friends and captivated by a range of emotions from sadness to laughter to cravings for some seriously delicious desserts!"

~**Janese Lopez, Loving Life in Pink book reviewer**

"*Moments of Truth* is about girlfriends. BFFs. It's about the moments that hold us together and the memories that will always inspire us. *Moments of Truth* is the kind of book women will read and cherish because it's the story of our lives."

~**Eva Marie Everson, author of** *Five Brides*

"The characters in *Moments of Truth* by Sandra D. Bricker are some of her best. It's a story of women helping each other through life's messes. I loved these gutsy ladies, and the not-quite-so-gutsy as well. There are moments when you'll reach for your box of tissues and others that leave you laughing out loud, but you'll remember Bricker's characters long after you close the book.

~**Ane Mulligan, president of Novel Rocket**
and author of *Chapel Springs Revival*

DEDICATION

This book would not have been written without
the encouragement of *Rachelle Gardner*.
Thank you so much for everything you've done for me
and for the many shoves toward chasing my dreams.

Eva Marie Everson, you are the jelly
to my peanut butter. I couldn't have done
this without you.

Marian Miller, you have the heart of a cheerleader.
Thank you so much for your love, support,
encouragement, and personal chef duties.
I love you.

And thank you to *Eddie Jones* and *Shonda Savage*
for welcoming my girls to the Bling! party
with such enthusiasm and grace.

Welcome to VERTICAL MAGAZINE

Moments-of-Truth.net

Moments of Truth aren't limited to standing at the foot of a giant with nothing more than a sling and a stone. As women, we face Moments of Truth every day through our daily choices.

How am I ever going to survive his betrayal? ... Is this new guy worth dating? ... What does this outfit say about me, and do I really want to speak that to the world?

I believe when women join forces, they become like a superpower! So join me regularly on this lifestyle blog as we explore the everyday Moments of Truth. Grab your capes and let's fly together.

Regan Sloane

Chapter 1

Eight years of marriage. No kids. She got the house.

Regan felt as if those words might make a great tattoo—assuming she were inclined to get a tattoo, of course—maybe right across her forehead. Anything to keep from explaining it time after time. With the long bangs she still wore acting as a curtain of sorts, when someone inquired yet again, she could just lift them with the back of one hand, give the inquirer time to read her forehead, and be on her way. Story told. No muss, no fuss.

No muss, no fuss.

The words made her chuckle as she stirred vanilla creamer into her morning cup of bold roast. Had she ever had a muss- or fuss-free day in her life?

Regan twisted her long dark hair into a knot at the top of her head. She pushed her brown-rimmed glasses up the bridge of her nose before snapping the lid on her travel mug and padding, barefoot, across the cold stone tile of the kitchen. She climbed the oak stairs to the loft and pushed the large window wide open, stopping to inhale the salty Pacific Ocean in the distance. She flopped into the creamy Italian leather chair in front of her desk, flicking the power button on her laptop as she did. It wasn't much of a commute to work, but she set the alarm every morning, showered and dressed, and filled her travel mug with coffee before setting out across two thousand square feet of house. It made her feel as if her role as blogger for *Vertical Magazine* carried more importance than a simple lifestyle blog for women might tend to hoist. Regan knew a little something about the challenges of remaining spiritually vertical, after all, especially in the face of adversity.

It didn't pay much, but her one lone skill for putting words on the page combined with an abundance of random opinions on just about any topic concerning women made the job a good fit for her now. She'd almost thought it was a joke when Vertical's senior editor called.

"I ran across your blog this morning," said Delores Cogswell. "And I was so drawn to it that I spent hours reading the archived material. This is really something special, Miss Sloane. The way you tie your friends and your life with the lives of your readers. Oh, and I love how you refer to your ex-husband as 30-Watt."

Actually, it was 40-Watt; a metaphor for the realization that his 100-watt smile—the one promising a shiny future together filled with wonder and joy and children—soon grew dim in the face of reality.

"Anyway … You have a very *in-your-face* writing voice that I really appreciate," she went on. "Would you consider writing it for Vertical?"

Seriously? Regan had only just found her so-called *in-your-face* style in recent years. Since Craig left.

"You're like a mousy little bombshell," Craig had told her when they first started dating. If only she'd have paid closer attention. When a man referred to a woman as mousy right out of the gate, she later realized, that might be a sign their foundation lacked what was needed for him to stick around.

She'd started MOMENTS-OF-TRUTH.NET on a whim; an outlet for venting the steam of her own white-hot shame and niggling perplexity over the end of her marriage. Surely there were other abandoned women out there, married one moment and single the next, who might relate to what she had to say.

"Miss Sloane?"

"I'm sorry. Could you repeat that, please?"

It wasn't like she hadn't already thought about going back to work. She couldn't just sit on her duff and do nothing but collect a meager monthly alimony, after all. But Regan had spent the last four years of her eight-year marriage trying to get pregnant. It seemed like an important focus at the time—fertility treatments, about three hundred sharp kicks in the fanny with a hypodermic needle, ovulation calendars and lunchtime rushes to the bedroom, Craig's conference room, even the back seat of the car on one occasion. Anywhere they could find to seize those opportune moments for baby-making. But those experiences had resulted in nothing to show beyond the occasional breathless satisfaction. Not a baby, and not even her husband and the potential father of said baby sticking around.

Those years of frustration and failure didn't exactly bulk up a resume. Out of nowhere, however, this phone call from Delores Cogswell had solved the problem. Someone out there saw the only thing she had left with any value, and liked it enough to offer her a job.

So, what? A few years of working from home for Vertical during the healing process, writing her little blog and connecting with women just like her suited Regan just fine; despite that irritating little flutter in her gut lately, the one that poked her and whispered it might be time for something more. The one she worked hard to ignore because change struck her as quite terrifying in light of the fact that she'd only just begun to feel sure-footed on her own.

Regan drew in a warm gulp of her coffee and sighed, opening her inbox as she did each and every morning. She skimmed the first few emails there:

A collection of column suggestions from her editor;

A funny picture of Iris and Lynette in front of a truly hideous old hutch—the latest in a line of thirty or more of them Iris had considered in her consuming quest to redecorate the dining room;

An abrupt message from Delores Cogswell:

Please mark your calendar. I would like a conference call with you today at eleven o'clock sharp.

As Regan added the appointment to her online calendar, the fleeting thought that Delores might fire her pierced the nerve behind her left eye. She quickly checked the site meter on her blog, and the numbers soothed her fear; but only slightly. She'd been holding steady at around ten thousand page views per day for the last month since that oddball reviewer took notice and gave her blog a mention; this week had seen an increase to twelve thousand. Then again, maybe Delores wanted to offer obligatory congratulations rather than fire her.

The next email in the list bore the FEEDBACK label, telling her it had come through the blog site from a reader. A woman named Bristol, 26, recently abandoned by her husband.

"I've been reading your blog for a year now, and I know you've been through the same thing," Bristol wrote. "How did you ever manage to get out of bed again? I've never even considered the option of divorce, and I didn't think Neal had either, but three nights ago he left me. I feel like I've been hit by a freight train."

Regan couldn't really say she'd *never* seen the train barreling down the tracks before Craig came back from his monthly business trip to Atlanta and packed two large bags instead of unloading his carry-on.

She'd heard the *clomp-clomp-clomp* of the wheels as he rolled the suitcases from the hall carpet and across the tile in the foyer. Drying her hands with one of the soft organic dishtowels she'd bought that afternoon while shopping with Abby, she strolled out of the kitchen and spotted his things parked at the front door as if waiting for a bus to come along.

"What are you doing?" she asked him. "You have another trip?"

He hesitated. "N-no." It wasn't like Craig to stammer. Or hesitate.

"Then where are you going?"

"Here's the thing. I got a place in the Gaslamp Quarter," he stated. "It's close to the office, and it has good natural light ..."

Regan didn't remember much of the other details about her husband's new downtown abode, but two days later he returned with three generic strangers and cleared out his side of the closet, his office in the loft, and more than half of their modest wine collection to take to that new well-lit place of his.

On his way out the door, Craig had handed her an envelope she couldn't bring herself to open until the weekend. After she'd skimmed his petition for the dissolution of their marriage, Regan poured a large glass from the open bottle of merlot on the counter and downed it; then she calmly collected the four new organic dishtowels she'd bought—two with the tags still attached—and tossed them into the trash. They'd read warm and homey to her when she bought them; but Craig's packed bags at the door while she cluelessly dried her hands with one of them ruined the appeal. She didn't ever want to feel their lying softness again.

She put together three different links to past blog posts about recovering from or preparing for divorce, and she added a note to her reply.

"Hang strong, Bristol," she typed. "Take deep breaths and remind yourself that this isn't your fault. I know this for certain—"

Really? she asked herself. *For certain?*

"—sometimes the most desperate of situations will suddenly transform into something unexpected and wonderful."

She *mostly* believed that to be true. Although she'd really only experienced the UNEXPECTED part with Craig's abrupt departure from their life together. The dry, hollow sting still pinging inside her served as a reminder that she still awaited her serving of WONDERFUL.

"I want to say encouraging things to you like, *You can do it. Just hang in there and down the road, you won't regret it.* But here's the truth: This really stinks. And it's only going to get worse from here. You'll have weeks of feeling useless and shell-shocked—"

And lonely. Sex-deprived. Betrayed. Abandoned.

"—and your friends will get so sick of hearing about your trauma that they'll probably want to scream. And then one night they'll order Chinese takeout without even warning you. They'll bring you some chocolate fudge brownies, a bottle of Pinot and two boxes of tissues, and they'll sit on the floor flinging those same platitudes I mentioned above until you finally realize … *they're truth.* And you'll get up and shower and comb your hair. And—"

And maybe you'll manage to stop imagining his touch in the middle of the night, yearning for his fingers raking through your hair, wishing he'd storm through the front door and wordlessly take you one more time before declaring what a fool he'd been to ever stray...

"—before you even realize what you're doing, you'll start to breathe again without his touch or his dumb socks balled up in the corner of the bedroom. And as a personal aside, you might think about getting a dog like my French bulldog, Steve. He's great company, and he hasn't left toothpaste spit drying on the bathroom sink even once."

Regan pushed her glasses up her nose again and stared at the message she'd typed. When she finally blinked, her eyes stung and she realized she'd unexpectedly misted over with sharp emotion. Leaning back into the soft leather of her chair, she sighed. Iris, Abby, Celia, and Lynette had been leading her along through the healing every week since she'd heard the still-echoing door that slammed behind Craig when he left. She never could have come through that first year without them.

She glanced at the calendar in the corner of her screen. Only Wednesday. She wished it was Thursday and clicked over to the next day.

Thursday night—Iris's house—7 p.m.—Bring dessert

She'd been waiting for it all week. Thursdays had become her saving grace because of the circle of women forming one all-inclusive life preserver around her for so long. Before hitting SEND on the hopefully-soothing reply to Bristol Somebody, she made a mental note to pick up five of the ooey-gooeiest pastries they had at Woolman's Bakery on her way to Iris's the following night.

Regan noticed the file marked READERS, and she opened it as Steve toddled over to the foot of her chair.

"Where have you been this morning, huh?" she asked, scratching him behind the ear.

Steve nuzzled close to her leg for another few seconds before heading to the overstuffed emerald bed angled between several high stacks of novels that had exceeded her shelf space in the loft.

As she suspected, that file on her screen bulged at the seams with reader emails she'd found interesting enough to set aside. She clicked through them quickly, one after the other, until she decided on the six she would use for her weekly vlog post, and she printed them out.

After taking down her hair and combing through it with her fingers, she removed her glasses and hung them over the side of the desk lamp. She quickly applied a light coat of cherry lip gloss with the tip of her pinkie and wiped off her finger with a tissue so that she could rake her thick hair again with both hands. She glanced at her reflection in the small mirror positioned just above the webcam before activating the camera and raising the corners of her mouth into a relatively happy smile.

"Hi, everyone. Regan Sloane here for Vertical Magazine and MOMENTS-OF-TRUTH. NET," she told the silver eye of the small round camera. "I've really enjoyed hearing from so many of you this week. April from Buffalo, New York, writes, 'Regan, I'm new to the meat market again after twelve years of marriage, and I'm wondering if you have any advice for me about whether or not to try online dating.'" Regan grinned.

"Well, April, I can tell you this: I've always shied away from online dating myself, but one of my best friends—whom you all know as *Annette*—tried TAKETWO. BIZ about a year ago after her divorce. Three months ago, she married the second guy she met there, and they're now raising a large blended family—the two of them and five kids—under one roof. So there are success stories out there. I just suggest you employ a specific strategy about what kind of man you're looking for this time around, and stick to it. Keep us posted on how it goes, okay?"

Less than an hour later, Regan had completed filming and editing the vlog and posted it to the site. She leaned back and closed her eyes, willing away the annoying memory of Craig's fiery touch that she'd let wriggle back into her thoughts. In many ways, his touch had been more difficult to let go than Craig himself.

Regan smiled when her gaze landed on Steve, snoring carelessly in the corner, his little beige body and head stretched across the cushion, and his short white legs and undercarriage moving a-mile-a-minute as he raced across some unknown dreamland meadow. His beautiful brown eyes remained clamped tightly shut, and the black fur mask that surrounded them both wrinkled with adorable consternation.

Regan picked up her phone and snapped a quick picture, knowing she'd become one of *those* dog owners, but not caring in the least as she posted the photo to her Moments of Truth Facebook page, commenting, "Come on. Is there a cuter guy on the planet? I've found my soul mate."

She swept her hair into its familiar knot and replaced her glasses, and at eleven sharp—just as Delores's decree had demanded—Regan dialed the Vertical offices.

"Hi, Shell. It's Regan Sloane for Delores."

"I'll put you right through."

Delores never bothered much with greetings, so it came as no surprise when the line opened again to the booming voice she'd come to know so well. But what she said didn't exactly compute for a moment.

"Regan, I'll get right to the point. Valencia Publishing wants to give you a book contract, and I want you to say yes."

"I ... I'm sorry. What did you say?"

Chapter 2

"This has been just great. I'm so glad we could do it."

Iris's heart stopped at the words. She clamped her eyes shut for just a moment, suppressing the groan bubbling up inside of her.

"Maybe we can make it a regular thing. I've got lots of recipes to try out on you all."

She pasted a smile on her face and nodded as the conflicting vow resonated in her head.

I'd almost rather lie down in traffic than do this again.

The type of cuisine Trish had served had never set particularly well on Iris, but at fifty years old—and right smack-dab in the middle of The Change—Iris just couldn't tolerate the effects of ongoing dinners like this one anymore. What Trish had called coq au vin turned out to be nothing more than chicken stew with bacon grease frosting, and the espresso she'd served with that horrendous fruit tart had the consistency of a mud pie. Iris had barely survived the meal, a fact that had nothing to do with the violent inner reaction to making it "a regular thing." She had all the *regular thing* she needed with Regan and the girls, a fact which Iris felt almost certain had garnered this invitation.

Trish had been vying for a spot in the book club for more than a year. Iris had explained to her that they didn't even read the books anymore, so they couldn't even call their weekly meetings literary. Unfortunately, it seemed to make Trish all the more intent on joining them.

"Ready to go?" Dean asked her, but the words hardly reached fruition before his eyes popped open in reaction to the pained expression on his wife's face.

"I can't," Iris whispered.

"I know. It was a little heavy. I'll stop at the drugstore on the way home for some Maalox."

"No. Dean. I can't go."

He shot a quick glance at the others, all of them on their feet, in various stages of thank-yous and good-nights as they headed toward the front door.

"Iris, what is wrong with you? What do you mean you can't go?"

"I can't," she told him through tight lips. "I can't *get out of this chair.*"

"What—"

"I'm stuck." She rocked from side to side, taking the narrow chair right along with her. "I'm wedged into this thing, Dean. I can't get up."

His effort to hold back laughter only made it worse. A sort of screech escaped through his nose, followed by a bit of a raspberry from between his lips.

"Stop it. I'm mortified. What do I do?"

"Try turning sideways," he offered, pushing at the pocket of hip flesh trapped beneath the squared arm of the chair. "Then kind of wiggle out."

Iris knew there would be no wiggle wiggly enough to liberate two feet of fanny from one foot of chair.

"Man, you're really stuck in there, aren't you?"

His powers of observation were staggering.

"Yes, honey. I'm really stuck."

He pushed at her derriere as he pulled at the chair arm. With the sudden *crack!* of wood, Iris belted out a shriek.

"Holy moley, it broke," he cried.

Their eyes locked for a split second before Iris popped to her feet, tearing the hem of her dress on the splintered wood of the dangling arm.

She scurried toward the doorway, her husband's hand pressing against the small of her back. When a sudden notion tickled the underbelly of her brain, Iris stopped and considered it for a moment. Without a word to Dean, she circled him and returned to the dining room. Grabbing her chair's back, she dragged it away from the table and glanced over her shoulder quickly before plucking another chair from its spot and switching the two.

"What are you doing?" Dean asked her in a desperate whisper.

"I'm putting the broken one down where Jim was sitting," she revealed, sliding the unbroken chair into place where she'd been seated for dinner.

"You're framing Jim?"

"You bet I am."

And with that, Dean yanked her by the elbow.

A short time later, Iris dropped to the side of the canopy bed in their master bedroom and stroked the tear in her new dress. "Oh, this just makes me sick. I only got to wear it once."

Dean stood in the doorway to the bathroom in t-shirt and boxers, squeezing a line of toothpaste onto his bright red brush. "Can it be mended?" he asked before poking it into his mouth.

"I don't think so, unless I hem it into a mini dress."

"I like your legs," he managed past the foamy toothbrush.

"There's no accounting for taste," she joked, holding inside the gratitude that—after seeing his increasingly-round wife trapped between two chair arms—

he could still find something to appreciate about her.

Dean grinned and returned to the bathroom while Iris hung the dress over the fold of the closet door and pulled a clean pair of pajamas from the bureau: pink and gray flannel Capri-length pants that tied at the waist, and a short gray tagless tee. With a pair of polka-dot socks in hand, she grabbed the bottle of lotion from the dresser and returned to the bed. She pumped a dollop into her hand and rubbed it into her foot before covering it with one of the socks. She'd just begun working on the other foot when Dean walked out of the bathroom.

"Poor old Jim Swanson," he sang, shaking his head. "Framed for the cut-throat murder of Trish and Ed's dining room chair."

"You know how Jim rocks on the back legs of the chair all the time. Did you see Trish eyeing him when he did that all through dessert? When I saw the arm of my chair, hanging there by a thread, wobbling in the breeze, I just—"

"—thought you'd blame Jim."

"Yes," she admitted.

"Isn't Trish one of your best friends?"

"One of my best *charity work friends*," she clarified. "And only that until my big butt is responsible for breaking her Cindy Crawford chair."

"Cindy Crawford. Isn't she that model with the mole?"

"She also designs furniture."

"Sure she does."

Iris pulled the sock over her foot and slipped her legs under the sheet. "Anyway, it wasn't premeditated. It was a completely spontaneous reaction."

"That you could easily make right tomorrow when you call her and confess."

"Why would I do that?"

"Because it's the right thing to do?"

"Says who?"

"Says *thou shalt not lie*, that's who."

"Now you sound like my friend Abby! And I didn't lie. I didn't say a single word. I just innocently moved a chair."

"Innocently?"

"Well, I moved a chair. I didn't lie about it."

Dean chuckled. "Goodnight, you rogue."

"Can I have a kiss?" she asked.

When he moved toward her, Iris leaned forward in anticipation. She loved the way Dean smelled before bedtime; a combination of minty fresh and spicy all-male. Just the scent of him brought all of her nerve endings alive, and she tingled with a cruel mix of familiarity, desire, and resignation.

Tilting her head up toward his face, she smiled. "Will you still love me if I don't confess, and I just let Jim take the heat?"

"Only if you promise we never have to accept another dinner invitation from Trish and Ed."

"Oh, wasn't that chicken just awful?"

"That was chicken?"

"I think so."

"I'm guessing she failed her *Things To Do With Chicken 101* course?"

"If she didn't, they must be grading on a curve."

"Pretty big curve."

Iris giggled as Dean pecked her lips with a kiss goodnight.

"At least Trish is chasing her dreams," she said, returning her attention to the polka-dot socks. "You have to give her that."

"Cooking school at fifty? Who starts a whole new career at that age?"

"Trish is forty-three, Dean. And I think it's adventurous. She's always loved cooking, so—"

"Was she always this bad?"

"—now she's turning that love into a reality. Her plan is to open her own restaurant by the time she turns fifty."

"Do you have any idea how much work that is? Even at thirty, it's an undertaking. But at fifty? The sheer physiology of it makes it a ridiculous idea, Iris."

Iris grimaced. "Fifty is the new thirty."

"Says who?"

She pushed herself upright and glared at him. "Look at my sister! Are you telling me she was too old to start a whole new life at age fifty?"

"Barb fell in love with a doctor, Iris. She moved to Florida, married John Beckham, volunteers in a local clinic, and spends her weekends out in the Gulf with John and his boat. That's nothing like starting a restaurant from the ground up—"

"It's all the same concept," she told him. "It's never too late to do something really exciting, to chase down your dreams."

"What if my dream is to spend the first years of my retirement working in the garage and watching the Discovery Channel?"

Disappointment simmered in the pit of her stomach as she replied, "That didn't used to be your dream."

"I'm retired, Iris."

"Retired from being an architect," she pointed out. "Not retired from life entirely. What happened to all of those plans we made? I mean, the whole idea of working so hard for you to be *able* to retire at fifty-five was having that time to spend together."

Dean ran a hand through his thick mane of wavy salt-and-pepper hair and narrowed his steel-blue eyes at her. The lines at the sides of those eyes took the shape of smiles. "We're not together?"

"What happened to seeing Paris? And Greece? What happened to going on safari in Africa?"

"I can see all those places from the comfort of the sofa in the den, at a fraction of the cost."

Iris sighed. She slid her arm under her pillow and lay down with her back to him.

"Can't we see those places next year?" he asked as he leaned over her. "Or in five years?"

"Sure, honey. Maybe we can order some more cable channels in the meantime."

"Funny you should mention that," he said as he headed into the hallway. "I saw a commercial for a satellite dish you can get instead of cable. You get over a hundred more channels, and—"

"Goodnight, Dean."

"Night."

Iris ran her hand over the sheet before snapping off the light and turning onto her back. She leaned across the lavender-scented 800-thread-count top sheet. Her eyes went to the door leading to the hallway, the one through which her husband had just abandoned her. Again. The one leading to the guest room where Dean had slept for the past few years. Every night.

Every. Single. Night.

Well, nearly.

She'd purposefully put 180-thread-count sheets on "his" bed, hoping to draw him back to the pleasures of the master bedroom, but it hadn't seemed to faze him. And, oh how she'd grown tired of making up a second bed in the mornings. She came to hate the guest room the way a jilted wife hated the mistress about whom her husband thought she remained in the dark. She tried to mentally calculate how long it had been since she and her husband of twenty-four-and-a-half years had slept side-by-side in their king-sized bed.

Seven months?

Dean had never been much of a drinker, but he'd made an exception the night of his sister's wedding—her third in ten years—and Iris had snatched the keys and played designated driver. With his arm around her shoulder, he'd allowed her to lead him up the stairs and straight to their bed. Hopes of anything more out of him in that state were just ridiculous, she knew. But she'd nudged him into their bed and fell asleep in his arms. The next morning, however, she awoke alone again and found him sprawled across the bed in the guest room.

Yes, Jennifer and Clayton had married seven months back in an intimate ceremony on the lawn at the Grand Hotel resort on Mackinac Island. Iris had hoped she and Dean might rent a suite for the night and do a little sightseeing the next day, but he hadn't been the least bit interested. Instead, she drove him back across the border to Ohio—snoring like that hibernating bear he'd become since retirement—and helped him inside when they reached home.

The shrill ring of the phone cut her ponderings short, thank goodness.

"Iris!" Dean shouted, as usual. "Phone!"

"If you pick it up and say hello, you might also know who's on the other end," she grumbled as she stretched across the bed to answer it.

"Hello?"

"Iris? It's Celia."

"Hi, Celia. What's wrong?"

Her younger friend on the other end of the line launched into an emotional tirade—nearly all of it in Spanish—which, of course, Iris didn't speak.

"English, honey."

"Ah. *Siento*," she replied. "I forget. Did I wake you?"

"No, we just got home. Tell me what's wrong."

Iris sat upright and perched on the edge of the enormous bed and listened as Celia unloaded a musket full of ammunition aimed squarely at herself.

"I don't know why I am this way," she summarized. "*Ay carumba, Keffin* is such a good man, Iris. Why can I not trust him when he's never given me any reason not to? He says I make him sorry he tries so—"

The familiar click of another call cut through Celia's words.

"Are you coming tomorrow night?" Iris asked as she checked the screen on her phone.

"*Sí*. Yes. I may be a little late leaving the restaurant. But don't eat the dessert without me. Who's bringing it this time?"

"Regan. Listen, honey, my daughter is calling on the other line. I'd better get it."

"Ah, okay. Regan will bring something from Woolman's, yes?"

"Most likely."

"Maybe I'll call her now. I like their éclairs."

"All right." The click sounded a second time. "I'll see you then. And Celia?"

"Eh?"

"Remember to breathe in and out a few times. Slowly. We'll talk it through tomorrow night, but until then you need to keep breathing, all right?"

Celia chuckled. "*Gracias, mi amor.* See you later."

As she flashed over to the other call, Iris glanced up and saw Dean standing in the doorway looking at her. His hair needed a trim by his standards, but she loved it when he didn't get to it right on schedule and that wavy shock of thick hair grazed his forehead.

"Everything all right?" he asked.

"It was Celia," she whispered. "But it's Candace now." In a higher pitch, she greeted her daughter. "Candace? Honey, you don't usually call this late."

"Mom, hold on, okay?"

Iris sighed. Shrugging, she updated Dean. "On hold."

"Tomorrow's Thursday," he commented as he folded down to the edge of the bed.

"Just like last week this time. Would you prefer we met at Panera instead?"

She often offered, but he'd never once taken her up on it. Iris thought he just liked to be asked.

"Nah. Maybe I'll take a ride over to the club and hit a bucket of balls or something."

"That's a nice idea. I wish I could join you."

Another offer he never took her up on. Not anymore.

"Mom," Candace said before Iris even realized she'd returned to the line. "Is Daddy home?"

"He's right here with me."

"I didn't wake you then."

"No. You didn't wake us. What's wrong, honey?"

Dean had long ago coined the term MOMDAR for that familiar feeling of dread Iris often battled when a big shoe prepared to drop. And the imagined shoe overhead was a big one.

"You'd better put Daddy on the extension, Mom."

"Oh-boy."

"What's wrong?" Dean interjected.

"Go pick up another phone," she told him. "She wants you on the line too."

"Oh-boy," he echoed. Dragging to his feet, Dean headed for the doorway and muttered, "This oughta be good."

Chapter 3

"Do you have a problem with me, Abby?"

Abby tossed Nate a cursory glance over her shoulder. "This is hardly about you," she replied coolly. "I'm just concerned about the shower drain. Is your contractor still around?"

"What, you want to boss him around now too?"

Architects. Every one she worked with required hand-holding and finesse when trying to communicate even the slightest difference of opinion. And Abby didn't feel much like having to hold Nate Cross's hand today.

Well. Maybe she felt *a little* like holding his hand …

"Look," she said, wiping her palms on the front of her jeans as she straightened and faced him, "it's nothing personal. But when the homeowners ask why I let you finish over a raised tile basin, I'm the one who has to explain it to them."

"Or you could let my guy finish his job," he snapped back with a glint of amusement in his irritatingly blue eyes as he removed his hardhat. "Maybe then, the homeowners wouldn't even ask the question. That tile basin is sitting directly on the subfloor, and Chad's going to wield a three-eighth-inch notched trowel to apply some thin set before using a cement block to weigh it down overnight."

Oh, come on. This guy comes in here—with his perfect, cropped hair and metro-sexual good looks—and wants me to believe he understands subfloors. Please.

"Tell me the truth. Do you even know what a three-eighth-inch trowel looks like?"

He appeared almost like he might strike back with an answer before he inhaled sharply and clamped his lips tight, glaring a hole straight through her. After a moment, he exhaled and said, "If you would have stopped by tomorrow like we agreed, the thing would be flush and this wouldn't even be a discussion."

Heat rose in splotches across her chest, up and over her throat, scraping her face with fresh, steamy self-consciousness. Abby wasn't about to confess it to him, but her early arrival had more to do with the possibility of seeing Nate than with overseeing the master bath in the Jensens' new build.

"Why don't you tell me what you're really doing here," he sort of growled, and Abby had to look him straight in the face to determine that he was teasing her. "Come out with it, why don't you. You couldn't stand being separated for another twenty-four hours, so you created a reason for your visit. Go on, 'fess up. That's it, right?"

Abby's heart betrayed her, pounding wildly against her chest wall. She felt almost certain he could see it.

Nate normally wore his sandy hair cropped short on the sides, only slightly longer on the top. He'd had a trim, she realized. Even the velvety softness of his handsome face seemed coiffed in its smooth perfection, all of it barely perceptible to anyone else, but clearly discerned by Abby. She wondered why that was. Had she really been watching him that closely?

"Why don't you have dinner with me tonight, Abby. We can talk about this obvious attraction you have for me and how we can address it. I suspect it's the hardhat I wear when I come to the site, isn't it? Don't feel bad, now. It's a common affliction." He tossed the thing into the air and caught it again. "Even straight-laced women like yourself apparently go nuts for a guy in a hardhat."

"Straight-laced," she exclaimed, then chewed the corner of her bottom lip. That's how he saw her? Was she wearing a neon sign? Swallowing her embarrassment, Abby snatched her composure and shot him a disapproving frown. "Over-confident much?"

Instead of a reply, Nate tipped his head back and roared with laughter. She found it both melodious and galling.

"The glass tiles I ordered arrived today," she said, turning her back on him to inspect the shower drain again, "and I don't want to leave them in the back of my truck overnight. While Chad does his thing, why don't you make yourself useful and unload them for me. That way, you can be rid of me and I'll come back when—"

"Rid of you is really the last thing—"

"I'm parked right out here," she cut him off.

Shoulders back and head high, Abby stalked across the skeletal form of the 2,800-square-foot job site. She reached her light blue Forester out front and lifted the rear hatch door before she ever looked back to find Nate trailing her. Abby leaned inside and smiled at Regan—still lounging in the front, glasses on and laptop balanced on her knees—before she dragged the sealed boxes of tiles toward her.

Animated, Regan asked, "Is that him?"

"Shh," Abby replied with a nod.

Nate nudged her aside and grabbed one of the heavy boxes. "Just the two?"

"Yes. Master bath only," she called after him as he headed into the open garage.

"You're moving boxes dressed like that?" Regan asked him.

16

"She's a taskmaster."

"I've labeled them," Abby said, scowling back at Regan as she told him, "but put them somewhere safe, will you?"

Nate emerged quickly from the garage and jogged back to the SUV, shaking his head. "You just can't help yourself, can you?" Before she could answer, he added, "Who's your friend?" He hunched down and leaned in through the back. "Hi. Nate Cross."

"Regan Sloane."

"So I guess you're the reason Abby won't have dinner with me?"

"Well, I don't know," Regan retorted. "Maybe. But I don't know you well enough to determine that one way or the other. You should probably ask her why she won't."

When Nate looked back at Abby with a grin, she pushed his arm toward the second box of tiles.

"Okay, okay," he said. When he hoisted the box onto his shoulder, his bicep flexed and pushed against the long sleeve of his black knit Henley. "I guess I'll see you tomorrow afternoon. And Regan, pleasure to meet you."

"You too, Nate."

Once he'd gone, Abby slammed the hatch and slipped behind the wheel. She turned the key and waited for Regan to finish stowing her computer and secure her seatbelt.

"Ooo-kay. So."

Abby sighed. "What."

"So that's Nate."

"Yep. That's him."

She shook her head. "Shew! It's really no wonder."

"What do you mean?"

Regan grinned, still staring straight out the front windshield. Abby had known her since college, and this was vintage Regan; pleased with herself as she considered her next witty barb.

"What?" Abby pressed. "No wonder, what?"

"It's no wonder you're off your game," she said. "He's off-the-hook adorable, Abbs."

Abby retained her poise momentarily before wilting into a sigh. "I know. Right?" Twisting in her seat to face Regan, she groaned. "What am I going to do?"

"Uh, you could try accepting one of his invitations and actually go out with this guy with the magical power to reduce you to befuddled."

"I am not *befuddled*," she objected. "I'm … I'm …"

"Befuddled."

"No. Anyway, I can't go out with him, Regan. You know that."

"No, I really don't. I'm pretty sure you're the only one who thinks she knows that."

With a soft grumble, Abby shifted out of PARK and backed out of the makeshift driveway.

"You should bring it up with the girls," Regan commented as she tuned in a radio station. "You know you can share anything there. And they might have some insight for you that I don't."

Abby actually had been considering talking to the others about this semi-secret crush she'd developed on Nate Cross, but she supposed the saying-it-out-loud part was what deflected her from actually doing it. It wasn't like they didn't already know about her provocative past ... or that she'd made a decision to deviate from it in future relationships by developing a more chaste and honorable progression of rapport. She'd tried it the other way for too many years to count, always ending in the same result. Why not try something based more on mutual overall chemistry than on sexual attraction? Regan's term for it had been as straightforward as Regan herself.

"So you'll be like a born-again *virgin!*"

It sounded so lowbrow. But accurate. Abby wanted a fresh start, like her faith always promised was available to her, and so she had adopted a credo of abstinence. Since that time, three potential partners had dropped by the wayside between the third and seventh date in the direct light of this new philosophy, but she hadn't really cared too awfully much. None of the three presented a challenge to adhering to the commitment she'd made to herself and God.

But then she met Nate. Six feet and a couple of inches of protest against her newfound course. Tidy cropped light brown hair ... barely perceptible lines placed perfectly around symmetric and fetching dimples on both sides of his ridiculous, coercive smile ... blue eyes sparkling with equal amounts of mischief and magnetism. In one meeting between the homeowners, their architect, and their newly-hired designer Abby Strayhan, armor had been dented, pierced, and crumpled as easily as a foil paper around a stick of gum. Nate Cross had been keeping her awake at night and breaking her focus most afternoons ever since. From the instant his arm brushed against hers on that first day, she'd battled ignited flames.

"Breathe." Regan's soft, sweet reminder lifted the corners of Abby's mouth into a smile. "In with the good air, out with the bad. You're going to be okay."

Unsure, Abby nodded anyway.

"Once you made your decision, a Nate was bound to come along to test your resolve."

Test. Cajole. Annihilate.

"Did you remember dessert for book club?" she asked Regan. "It's your turn, right?"

Regan nodded.

"And why do we still call it book club?" Abby rambled. "We haven't read and discussed a book in nearly a year."

Regan chuckled. "We're like the speakeasies of the Prohibition era. From the outside, we look like a perfectly acceptable social gathering. Then you get inside where all the secrets are out on the table and you find out how gritty and scandalous we really are."

Abby reached over and shook her friend's arm. "I like that. We should have a password or a secret handshake."

"We have a password," Regan teased. With a narrowed covert expression, she lowered her voice and muttered, *"Pass the chocolate."*

The cars parked in Iris and Dean's circular driveway told Abby that she and Regan were the last to arrive. She loved the way she still fluttered with excitement as she headed up the stairs to the front door. These women had become a lifeline to her in their consistency and support.

When the massive double doors opened, instead of the lady of the house standing on the other side, Celia was there, her hand on one hip and her beautiful dark hair falling around her shoulders like a brunette cloud.

In full Latina attitude, she exclaimed, *"Chu* two are late. Did you bring the éclairs?"

Regan held up the box from behind Abby, and Celia immediately reached past her and grabbed it.

"Okay then. *Chu* can come in."

Celia led the way into the kitchen, and simmering fragrances greeted them at the arched doorway.

"Italian?" Regan asked as she rounded Abby and headed toward Iris at the center island.

"Lasagna, garlic bread, and mixed green salad," she replied before they hugged.

"Dessert first," Celia reminded them, flailing her arm to call them to the marble-topped table in the adjoining nook.

Abby shared a chuckle with Iris as they embraced, and she moved on to squeeze Lynette's outstretched hand before sitting down next to her. Once the wine was poured, the dessert box opened, and everyone was seated in their regular spots, Celia propped up her elbow and rested her chin on her fisted hand.

"I go first," she announced. *"Keffin* might be going to leave me."

"You always say that," Abby pointed out. "If you want first dibs on dessert, you'll have to do better than that."

"But this time he is the one who says it," she argued. "I found a parking *tee-kit* stub on the dresser—"

"On the dresser or in his wallet?" Regan clarified.

"No, out on the dresser in plain sight," she said, drawing a large X across her heart with two fingers. "I just wanted to know why he didn't mention he went downtown. That's all."

"Celia, girl," Lynette said, shaking her head full of twisted braids. "You've got to loosen the leash on that boy. You've got a good one, but you're going to lose him if you don't get this under control."

"I know, I know," she said with a sigh. "He tell me this morning I am *volviendo loco*. Making him ..." She tapped her temple several times while she searched for the word. "... *cray-see*."

"My turn," Abby piped up. "I've met someone." She waited for one of the women to comment but was met instead with wide-eyed disbelief all around. "His name is Nate. He's the architect on a design job I'm working."

"And he's adorable!" Regan chimed as she lifted her glasses and used them like a headband to hold back her long brunette hair.

"And he's adorable," Abby repeated with reluctance.

"*Chu* meet him?" Celia asked.

Regan nodded. "Just a few minutes ago. He's very ... coiffed. Like Ryan Seacrest, only more ..."

"I kind of think he reminds me of Bradley Cooper," Abby said with a timid smile.

"That's it," Regan exclaimed. "He's a real Bradley Cooper. On the red carpet. But without the tux."

"Ooh, I like him," Iris piped up. "He's young enough to be my son, but still."

"I prefer a more chocolaty man," Lynette added. "Like Denzel."

"Does Trevor know?" Sofia clucked.

"Oh, Denzel is universal," Regan said. "Doesn't matter the age or ethnicity, Denzel is just plain delicious."

"*ANY*way," Abby interrupted. "Back to me? Nate has asked me out several times, but I'm just—well, you know."

"Girl, it's just a date," Lynette said, and she reached over and rubbed Abby's arm. "You'll never know if there's even anything to worry about until you spend some time with him."

"But what if there is something to worry about? What if I fall hard, and then he's not patient enough to see it through because I'm not going to sleep with him? What then? You remember what happened with Dylan."

"Yes," Regan cut in, "but Dylan was a very specific case of LOSER."

"If you like him, and he's *caliente* ..." Celia said.

"Oh, he's ..." Abby nodded vehemently. "He's *caliente*, all right."

"Then see what is next."

"But what if—"

"Stop now," Celia insisted. "You throw yourself off that bridge when you get to it, eh?"

"Fine." Abby shrugged before turning to Lynette. "And you? What's your bid for the first éclair?"

"I haven't had sex with my new husband in three weeks."

"Three weeks!" Celia blurted. "No. You've haven't even been married for *un año!*"

"Six months since the wedding. But between my two kids and his three, there's not a moment alone. By the time we get into bed at night, we're both so tired that we just drift off to sleep." Lynette looked at Abby. When she tried to smile, it didn't reach her beautiful cocoa eyes. "We're practically newlyweds. And Trev is one of the most desirable men I've ever known."

"I like his accent," Celia cut in, and Abby chuckled. Trevor's British dialect made just about everything sound more interesting ... but having it pointed out by Celia—her Colombian friend with a thick accent of her own—amused her somehow.

"We shouldn't be able to keep our hands off each other, right?" Lynette continued.

"Well, a new blended family with five kids," Regan summarized. "That's a pretty big obstacle all on its own. Then he had to go back to England for two weeks, his youngest was sick for so long. I think it will just take some time for everyone to get into the groove."

"I thought I was prime to *get my groove back*, not have to carve out a whole new one."

Regan snickered. "Well, at least you have a love life to worry about nurturing. Mine is non-existent. A big snooze-fest. But I do have something to tell that I hope you'll all find interesting rather than cause you to turn on me like a pack of wild dogs."

"Must have something to do with your column," Iris interjected. "Don't tell me. You're going to reveal some more of our secrets?"

"Well—"

"Oh, no you don't," Iris cried.

"I've been offered … a book deal. And they want me to write about the five of us."

Abby's stomach lurched. "Are you joking? Why didn't you tell me that?"

"I'm telling you all now. Together."

Lynette shook her head, slowly at first, then more adamantly. "No. No, Regan. You can't just—"

"How about we table that part of the discussion until after dinner," Iris broke in. "And let me just interject that my husband hasn't touched me in seven months, I have gained a grand total of thirty-nine pounds and actually *broke a chair* at a friend's house for dinner. My dining room remodel has been ruined because the table I wanted to focus the room around has been discontinued. And—new development—my twenty-year-old unmarried daughter has a bun in the oven."

Celia crumpled her face and cocked her head. "What does this mean? She is baking something?"

"Candace is preggers," Abby interpreted.

"Pregnant," Regan clarified, her face curled up like a raisin. "Of course she is."

After several moments of screaming silence, Celia reached out and pushed the bakery box at the center of the table until it came to a stop in front of Iris.

"That does it. First pick on dessert is yours," she declared. "I don't think any of us can top seven months with no sex when your *hija* is *haffing* so much of *eet*."

Welcome to VERTICAL MAGAZINE
Moments-of-Truth.net

BLOG POST: REGAN SLOANE

It's that time of the month, readers. The update on the continuing saga of my book club girlfriends in a nutshell:

Annette and her new husband, James Bond, are still having trouble finding a time and place for sex because of five kids, two careers, and one roof. But if I know Annette, she's sure to keep trying. Let's all continue rooting for her.

Gabby is still holding fast to her "born again virgin" makeover. New development: An interesting, perspiration-inducing male—we'll call him Bradley Cooper—has crossed her professional path, and that stance is challenging her more than she'd anticipated. He's really handsome, and he's asked her out about thirty times now. I'm betting she'll give in soon. If not, though, I think a gift certificate for some therapy might make a great Christmas gift this year.

Maria has skimmed an all-new low in driving Pretty Boy even farther away from her. I know what you're thinking, readers. How can someone so gorgeous have so little self-esteem? But as each of us no doubt has learned by navigating our own roads, fear and anxiety know no boundaries.

And Irene? No movement on the Family Man front, I'm sorry to report. I just hope he comes around before she starts believing the dark voices whispering in her ear about her own lack of appeal. Sometimes those voices are all-too-easy to believe.

And me? What I lack in relationship possibilities, I make up for in general ones. Possibilities, that is. For instance, I may have some news to share soon about a book deal! Stay tuned, readers.

Chapter 4

Lynette barely had time to adjust the turban she'd worn to bed to keep her cocoa braids intact. She made a quick sidestep into the steamy bathroom and grabbed the robe hanging on the back of the door as one of the children called out to her again from the hallway.

"Lynette?" one of the children called from the hallway. "Clayton's trying to make coffee again."

Trevor's shape behind the frosted shower door drew her gaze and locked it there as she blurted, "No. You march down to the kitchen and tell Clay to keep his hands off the new Keurig. Do you hear me?"

"What did you say, Love?" her husband called from underneath the hum of running water.

Trevor's youngest, nine-year-old Margaret, groaned from the other side of the bedroom door. Through the last lingering remnants of the British accent she shared with her father and two teenaged siblings, she whined, "Yeah, I hear you. But he's not going to listen to me. He never does."

"Tell him anyway, Margaret. Right now."

The slow thump of her feet hitting the stairs told her the girl was in no hurry to confront her brother, which made Lynette move even more quickly. The last time 14-year-old Clayton had tried to make coffee, his twin sister Felicity's help had necessitated the purchase of a brand new coffeemaker.

"How hard can it be to slip a K-cup into the machine, lock the handle, and press a button?" Trevor had asked her that night after the children had retired— at last!

"You're asking the wrong person," she'd said as her head finally hit the pillow. "I only entered in time for the smoke to clear. What happened before that is above my pay grade."

As Trevor stepped out of the shower, he wrapped a beige-and-white striped bath towel around him, knotting it low on his waist. "What's going on?"

"My new Keurig is in jeopardy."

He grinned. "Maybe we should get something cheaper and let Clay think it's our primary means for morning caffeine."

"Like a dummy coffee pot, you mean? Set a Mr. Coffee on the counter, and hide the Keurig up here in the linen closet?"

Trevor stepped behind her and slipped his arms around her, sliding one hand inside the terry robe she'd just fastened shut. Lynette sighed and closed her eyes, leaning into him as he stroked her skin. When she opened them again, she watched their reflection in the mirror as he traced the curve of her neck with his lips.

"Don't start something with me you're not prepared to finish, Professor Parker," she warned with a smirk.

"Oh, I'm prepared, Mrs. Parker."

"Mom," Shaaron shrieked from her bedroom down the hall. "I can't find my chem notes."

"On the coffee table downstairs," she called, leaning back into his eager embrace. Softly, so only Trevor could hear, she added, "The one I'm ready to beat my head against."

He chuckled.

According to their tag line, the TAKE TWO dating website Lynette had reluctantly tried after a couple of years alone following her husband Lamar's death specialized in second chances. Too bad they didn't provide instructions on how to juggle one after you got it.

"My last class ends at three," Trevor said. "Meet me in my office on campus at 3:05."

In their six short months of marriage, they'd had to resort to making love behind the locked door of Trevor's office on more than just a few occasions. With their active, blended family of seven under Trevor's too-small roof, meeting on campus had become their only hope of time alone. Of course, they'd been interrupted there several times by Trevor's students, so Lynette had come to accept that there was really nowhere to hide.

"Mom, my chem notes aren't on the coffee table," Shaaron shouted from the bottom of the stairs.

"Yes, they are," she returned. "Look again."

Shaaron grumbled as she stomped away.

"Three o'clock, you say?" she asked Trevor by way of their reflection.

Trevor turned her around to face him and held her face with both hands. "It's going to get better," he promised. "We just need to give it a little time."

"Isn't it a little early in our marriage to begin lying to me?"

He didn't answer before pressing his warm lips against hers. When they parted, he leaned back in for a quick nibble.

"I'll get dressed," he said in a low growl. "You save the Keurig."

When Lynette reached the kitchen, all five children were there; Margaret still in her Hello Kitty pajamas. Felicity stood over the girl and untangled Margaret's bright orange curls using her fingers as a comb, and Lynette's boy Jamal watched as Clayton doctored a cup of creamer with a dash of coffee. Or vice versa.

"*Some*body moved them," Shaaron announced with all the flair of a 13-year-old drama queen.

"Moved what?" Lynette asked, her eyes glued to the very white brew in Clayton's cup.

"My *chemistry notes?*" She groaned. "I swear. You never listen to me."

"There's no swearing in this house. I did listen, and I'm glad you've found your notes."

"Yeah, but now I'm probably going to be late. Will you write me a note?"

Lynette glanced at the clock. "You still have thirty-five minutes before the first bell. If you hurry, you won't need a note."

"*Mo-om.*"

"Get a move on, all of you," she declared. "I'm in no mood for this today. Clayton, take your coffee-flavored milk and lead Felicity and Shaaron out the door. I'll deal with Margaret's hair before the bus comes."

"What about me?" Jamal piped up.

"Oh, are you still here?" she teased. "You get your books. Mrs. Donnelson will be here in ten minutes. Has everyone had something to eat?"

"Cereal," Felicity sang. "Everyone but Clayton."

"Coffee's all I want."

Lynette crossed to the refrigerator and grabbed a tub of cream cheese from inside. "You know what's good with coffee?" she said, untying a bag of blueberry bagels and removing one of them. "A bagel." She quickly swiped it with cream cheese, wrapped the bagel in a napkin and extended it toward him.

"It's not even toasted," Clayton objected, staring down at her hand as if he'd never seen a bagel before.

"No time. Eat it or I'll chop it into small bites and feed it to you myself."

With one of those sneers he'd no doubt inherited from his mother, Clayton grabbed the napkin and stalked out the back door.

"Hey! Wait for me," Felicity called out as she scampered behind him.

Shaaron rolled her eyes at her mother as she followed them.

Lynette sighed. Grabbing a cup from the peg under the cabinet, she headed for the Keurig.

"Umm. What about my hair?"

She reeled around to find Margaret still seated at the table.

Leaving the cup behind, she crossed the kitchen and stroked the child's shoulder. "I'll fix it. Do you have a barrette?"

"No," the child chastised. "I wanna wear a headband."

"Do you have a headband?"

"No."

"So why don't you go upstairs and get one while I make your father and me some coffee."

"Okay."

Before Margaret had disappeared, Lynette added, "And do you think putting on some clothes would be a good next move?"

The little girl giggled. "Oh, all right."

Because Lynette hadn't mastered the art of arranging Caucasian hair, Margaret missed the bus that morning and had to be driven to school. Added to that, Lynette missed the turn arrow while daydreaming about meeting up with Trevor later in the afternoon, and Margaret acted as if the world had come to an end when the driver behind them lay on his horn. When she finally came to a stop inside the circle labeled STUDENT DROP-OFF and Margaret moseyed her way out of the passenger seat, it was all Lynette could do to keep from peeling out of the schoolyard.

She arrived at Trevor's office twenty minutes early that afternoon and let herself in. When he strolled in a few minutes after three, he had three students along with him.

"Hello, Love," he said, kissing her cheek. "What brings you?"

Lynette narrowed her eyes and glared at him, wondering if he'd actually forgotten the appointment that had dogged her all day long.

"Just joking," he said with a wink as he rounded his desk and opened the leather-bound calendar. "All right, let's see. I have office hours on Tuesday from four until seven. All three of you, stop in any time during those hours and we'll talk about your mid-terms."

He wasted no time in herding them out the door. Leaning against it, he grinned at Lynette as he reached behind him and turned the lock. "Alone," he announced.

"I live in hope," she replied.

Thirty seconds later, her husband pushed her down to the couch in the corner and yanked up her long skirt.

"If anyone knocks at that door, or your phone rings ..." she managed to growl, but her thoughts splintered. She couldn't think or speak. She could only feel.

Chapter 5

"I'm headed out."

Celia remained completely motionless on the sofa—her legs curled beneath her and her fingers aching as she clutched one of the throw pillows. Her eyes darted about, following Kevin as he moved around the room.

"*Chu* be back … when?" she asked as he dug his keys out of the large hammered copper bowl on the sideboard by the front door.

"I shouldn't be much later than eleven," he said, sliding into his black leather biker jacket.

When he picked up the motorcycle helmet stowed under the sideboard, Celia hopped off the couch and hurried toward him. "No, no, no, *Keffin*. I don't want you to ride the bike tonight. The weatherman say it might rain. Don't make me worry about *chu*."

Kevin slid his arms around her waist and smiled down at her, the dimples on both sides of that smile digging deep into her until her stomach wrenched.

"I love you," he said.

"I love you too," she admitted, pulling him closer.

When their lips met, Celia couldn't help herself. A hot flare went off inside, followed by a flow of warmth that caused her entire body to melt into it. She wrapped herself around him as she returned the kiss, and a guttural groan rose into her throat.

"Careful," he said with a chuckle. "I might have to call Baz and cancel tonight."

Would you? she pleaded inwardly.

But she'd gone to so much trouble already. As much as she dreaded the answer to her nagging questions, she simply had to know. And she'd arranged everything so she could find out at last.

"Sebastian will blame me," she objected. "And *chu* know he doesn't like me already."

"Come on, Baz likes you. He just doesn't understand why you can't seem to trust me after three years together."

Celia couldn't bear to beat that dead horse yet again, so she did the one thing she'd learned to do when the subject needed changing. Kneading her way down his back with both hands, she moved in for another kiss. When her fingertips reached Kevin's waist, she converged on him until not even a pinhole of light could have been detected between them.

"Baz can wait," he muttered, breathless.

"*Si.* Sebastian can wait."

Not a cloud in the night sky. So much for her lie about the possibility of rain. But she'd lied for a good cause, she reasoned.

Up ahead, maybe five or six vehicles in front of her, the Mustang with the broken taillight changed lanes. She waited several beats before she did the same. Buried somewhere in the massive list of tips on the CHEATER-CHEATER website, Celia remembered "Don't follow too close" as one of a few important take-aways.

Break the taillight on his car so it's easier to keep track of him from several car-lengths behind.

If possible, have a borrowed vehicle or a rental available so that he doesn't home in on the familiar.

Don't follow too close. If he changes lanes, wait a few seconds before you follow suit.

Celia counted three cars and an SUV between Kevin's Mustang and her inconspicuous rental. A twinge of remorse pinched her. Purposely destroying the taillight on her husband's beloved car seemed a little like pinching another man's *bambino* until it cried out in pain.

Celia had never driven an Accord before, but it had fairly good pick-up as promised at the Hertz counter by a middle-aged, balding man whose eyes had turned round as plates when Celia walked in the door. Nothing to write home about—she'd keep her little Fiat, thank-you-very-much—but the Accord served her purpose just fine.

Kevin made the turn on Majestic, and Celia followed. Where was he headed? This wasn't the way to Sebastian's place. Perhaps they were meeting somewhere in between.

She hoped.

When her cell phone rang, she tapped the earpiece already in place.

"*A-lo?*"

"Celia, it's Regan. Where are you?"

Her conscience rumbled slightly before she replied. "In the car. Why?"

"Abby and I are over at the Wayfair and they've got a Colombian guitarist playing in the downstairs bar. Do you want to meet us for a drink or some coffee?

He's really fantastic, and we thought you might like a little taste of home."

"What's his name?"

"Hector Something."

"Heh, I never hear of him."

"So come on over and meet us."

"That would be nice. I wish I could, *chica*. But I'm almost home and *Keffin* is waiting."

In that moment, she hated herself a little. But when the white-instead-of-red taillight of Kevin's Mustang blinked, she dismissed the guilt at laser speed.

"Okay. Call me tomorrow," she sang. "Have fun."

She didn't wait for Regan to respond. She quickly closed the line and made the turn behind the Jeep Cherokee, maintaining the barrier between them. When Kevin turned again—this time into a small parking lot next to a run-down diner and a sports bar—she sailed past it, only tapping the brake twice when Kevin parked and climbed out of his black Mustang. She cautiously craned to watch where he might be headed without giving herself away before she went on to circle the block.

Just before she reached the parking lot again, Lynette's sweet voice rang in Celia's ears and sent a flush of hot shame upward from her neck.

"Celia, girl, you've got to loosen the leash on that boy. You've got a good one, but you're going to lose him if you don't get this under control."

Could she ever admit to anyone—even someone as understanding as Lynette—everything she'd done in her effort to alleviate her own irrational fears?

She turned off the ignition at the other side of the lot, as far away from the Mustang as she could get. She leaned back into the unfamiliar soft leather seat with a sigh. If Kevin had come here to meet Sebastian, why wasn't his friend's beat-up old pickup truck parked there anywhere? Celia bowed her head, closed her eyes, and began to pray in a whisper.

"Por favor, don't let my husband be inside with some blonde *gringa* with the big boobs and Bambi-deer eyes. I need him to be the man he promised me he would be. It took two years of talking to me before I felt like I maybe could trust him not to sneak around on me like Fernando did. But now..."

A strange noise—rumbling and loud—drew her out of her prayer, and Celia popped open her eyes to find a familiar bright yellow truck idling next to her. Sebastian cranked down his window and propped his folded elbow on the opening.

"No, no, no." She cringed inwardly while making every attempt to return Sebastian's crooked little smile.

"I didn't know you were joining us," he said as soon as she opened her window. "Kevin already inside?"

She had no idea how to answer. Instead, she blew out a sigh in puffs, shaking her head and focusing on a streak across the top of the windshield.

"The thing is, Sebastian..."

What is the thing? There needs to be a thing!

"He doesn't know you're out here, does he?"

Celia dropped her face into both hands. Nowhere to hide. "No. He doesn't."

"And whose car is this?"

When she finally looked at him through open fingers, Sebastian scratched his scruffy cheek and bobbed his head, setting his unruly blond curls to motion on the night breeze.

"I'm gonna go park," he said, using his thumb to punctuate the declaration.

A boulder of acidic regret rolled over inside Celia's stomach, and she groaned as she raised the window again. A dissonant mash-up of next move possibilities clanked in her head, and as Sebastian stalked toward her car, she scrambled to grab hold of just one of them. When he tried to tug open her door, the lock prevented him and she reluctantly yanked on the handle and opened it herself. Her jittering legs almost wouldn't hold her as she slid out from behind the wheel.

"Talk to me," he said, and she sighed in reply. Sebastian stood next to her, his arms crossed over his chest. "Really. What are you doing, Celia?"

"I came to see if he was meeting another *woo-mun*." There. Like a sudden landslide, the truth had swept out of her and she left it sprawled there at his feet like a spilled bucket of needles, no idea how to recover them.

"You do know how insane you are, don't you?"

"*Sí.*"

"No, really. You're certifiable. You need to get some help, Celia."

"*Sí.*"

"So why don't you?" he asked as if he really wanted to know the answer. "Why don't you get some help before it's too late for you two?"

A mist of emotion stung her eyes, but words eluded her.

"He's not cheating, chica." It sounded strange when an *Americano* used the word. "He's devoted to you. You better get that through your head."

"Please don't tell him, Sebastian." She didn't mean to beg, but Celia reached out and grabbed his arm, knowing full well that the tone of her voice sounded like someone about to hit her knees and plead for mercy.

Sebastian gently removed her hand from his arm, letting a few seconds tick by before he spoke to her again. "And whose ride is this anyway? You didn't steal this car, did you?"

"Please," she repeated.

He fell silent again, and it seemed like an hour passed before he finally let a bitter chuckle pop out of him. "Go home, Celia."

Without another word, he turned and marched toward the building.

"Sebastian?" she called out to him. "What are you going to do?"

He'd almost reached the entrance of the bar when he finally halted and dug his hands down into the back pockets of his faded jeans. Without a glance back at her, he snarled, "Go home, Celia. I won't tell him."

"*Ay! Gracias*, Sebastian! *Gracias*."

He tossed one final thought over his shoulder. "But get some help, woman. You're all kinds of nuts."

The Accord screeched out of the parking lot less than thirty seconds later, and Celia's hands shook as she redialed the last caller.

"You changed your mind?" Regan answered without greeting.

"*Si*. Are you both still there?"

"There's a chair at our table with your name on it."

"I should be there in twenty minutes."

"Celia, is everything all right?"

She thought it over for a moment and chuckled. "I may have lost my mind, *mi amor*. I just need my posse."

"Uh-oh. What did you do?"

"I'll see you in twenty."

It only took fifteen minutes to cross town and take the dark stairs down to Wayfair's basement bar. A blackboard propped on an easel at the back of the stage introduced Colombian Guitarist Hector Santiago in bright, colorful chalk. The man himself sat on a barstool with a guitar, a bright yellowish spot illuminating the bald spot capping his straight dark hair.

"Celia. Over here."

Abby's soft voice drew Celia toward the small table in the corner. Twenty or so other tables filled the small, dark space, only about half of them occupied.

Celia kissed Abby's cheek when she reached her, then Regan's. "*Hola*."

"Sit down," Regan whispered. "This is the last song of his set. Relax, order a drink, and enjoy the music for a few. Then we'll talk."

Celia ran her hand over the silky waves of sandy brown hair at the back of Regan's head. "*Eres un tesoro*, my friend."

"*Tesoro*," Abby repeated with a grin. "That means treasure, right?"

"*Si*," Celia replied. "*Excelente*, Abigail."

The waitress took Celia's order for an espresso while Hector Santiago completed his set. The instant he propped his guitar on the stand in preparation for leaving the stage, Regan leaned toward her and arched both eyebrows. "Well?

Spill. What happened?"

Celia paused to take a sip from the small porcelain cup, and she sighed as she set it precisely on the mosaic tabletop.

"Celia," Abby pressed. "C'mon."

"Where were you, really? You weren't headed home to Kevin, were you?" Regan surmised.

"No. I was following him."

Abby fell back in her chair with a groan, and Regan gripped the edge of the circular table with both hands.

"Honey, no. Why?"

"He told me he had plans with Sebastian."

"His carpenter friend," Regan filled in.

"*Chez*. But there have been six hang-ups in the middle of the night this week, and Caller ID say every one of them is from private number."

"And this means he's cheating?" Regan clarified. "Celia, honey…"

"I know. I know. But that's not the worst part."

The acid started to churn in her stomach again as she replayed that moment when she looked up to find Sebastian glaring at her from the other side of the glass.

"Sebastian, he caught me."

Abby and Regan gasped in harmony. "No!"

"He drive right up next to my rental and—"

"Your rental?"

"*Si*. The website suggested borrowing another car or renting one so—"

"Celia. You're still going to that cheater website?" Abby cried. "Why do you do that? You're like an alcoholic, honey. Step away from the liquor store. Nothing good can come from going inside!"

The waitress delivered a tray of drinks to the table next to them before turning her attention to Celia and her friends. "Can I get you anything else? We have a two-for-one on wine and beer."

"I'll have another espresso," Celia told her.

"Nothing for me," Regan said.

"Maybe another diet Coke?" Abby answered. "And could we get one of those sampler appetizer platters?"

"Sure thing."

"Did he rat you out?" Regan asked Celia before the waitress headed back to the kitchen.

"He said he wouldn't."

"Do you believe him?" Abby interjected. "They've been friends since college, haven't they?"

"They have." She felt her entire face fall several inches. "I think he's feeling I might be having … what's the word?" She swished circles in the air with one finger.

"A mental break?" Regan piped up.

"*Si. Vuelto loco.*"

"It would almost be sweet if he wasn't so right," Abby cracked. "What's this Sebastian like, anyway? Can you trust him?"

Celia shrugged, and Regan answered. "He seemed like a really sweet guy to me."

"You've met him?"

"At Kevin's birthday last year. You were at that convention in Bakersfield."

"Boston."

"Right. Boston."

"Well, what's he like?"

"He's a carpenter, really cute if you like the looks of *Deeks* on NCIS."

"Which one?" Abby asked.

"Los Angeles."

"Ah. Single?" She shook her head. "Sebastian, not *Deeks.*"

"Yeah," Regan answered, and she looked to Celia. "Right?"

"*Chez.*"

"Wait just a minute," Abby exclaimed. "I'm an interior designer, and you know a carpenter who looks like *Deeks*, and you've never set us up?"

"Oh, I never …" Celia began. "I could set you up if you want me to, *chica*. Although I'm not sure Sebastian would take my word for the match."

"Nah." But she looked a little disappointed. "Never mind."

"*Keffin* could talk to him."

"Nah," she repeated, waving her hand. "I've got enough to worry about with Nate."

"Ohhh! How is that going with *Señor Caliente*?" Celia asked.

"One disastrous relationship at a time," Abby said. "Let's talk about how you're decimating your marriage before we get into my most recent relationship wipeout."

Regan couldn't help herself. When sleep evaded, the internet called like a song on the wind whispering her name. After surfing both her Facebook pages for interesting-but-typically-meaningless morsels, she hopped over to the To Catch a Cheat website—half-expecting to find Kevin's picture stationed there like a Wanted: Dead or Alive poster.

She retrieved a bag of Skinny Pop and a bottle of water from the kitchen before curling up in bed with Steve, who seemed inordinately interested in scoring some popcorn while she immersed herself in the dozens of stories there about straying husbands, shyster boyfriends, and all-around charlatans.

"Cut it out," she snapped, yanking the bag away from him just as he managed to wriggle his nose into it. "I'm not sleeping with your farts again, so just get the thought of popcorn right out of your dog head."

He smacked his floppy lips as if to cluck in irritation, and he rolled over to his side and bellied up to her leg like an overstuffed sausage link getting comfortable against a fluffy buttermilk biscuit.

"I know. I'm the wicked stepmother and you're poor, misunderstood, and deprived Cinderella. Waa-waa."

Steve snorted softly and closed his eyes.

"That's right. Get your beauty sleep."

And while he did just that, Regan clicked around the site. Nearly an hour into it, she hopped over to the *Have You Seen...?* page and scrolled through the photos and stories from wives and girlfriends—and even a few husbands—who believed their mates to be cheaters.

Regan gasped, slapping her hand over her mouth as she did.

"Celia, no."

Third picture down in the second column. Kevin, in all his handsome, dimpled glory, atop his beloved motorcycle, smiling at her with his helmet tucked under one arm and a leather jacket folded over the handlebar. A thick font spelled out his name in block lettering beneath the picture: **Kevin**.

Regan chomped down on the corner of her lip as she clicked on the hyperlink.

"Kevin is a videographer who looks more like one of the actors he shoots," Regan read aloud. "Well, that's the truth, huh?"

Celia's profile of this presumed cheater read more like an ad to get him a date than a *Have you seen him out there messing around?* inquiry.

Twenty-eight years old ... a hair under six feet ... dark hair, dark eyes ... his first love is his Honda motorcycle.

Regan glanced at the clock on the nightstand. Too late to call anyone but Abby. She picked up her cell phone and typed in a quick text.

U awake?

A minute later, her landline rang and Regan snatched up the handset. "Hey. So I guess you're up."

"I can't sleep."

"Do you know why?"

"Yes," she whined. "I'm getting it together for a walk-through with my clients in a couple of days, and I'm just ..." Her words trailed away on a cloud of steam and embarrassment.

"Why is this one different than any other walk-through?" Regan asked. But realization dawned before Abby had the chance to reply. "Ohh. Nate will be there."

"Yes, all right," she snapped. "He makes me perspire."

"Perspire," Regan said with a chuckle. "Is it like Scarlett O'Hara when she gets *the vapahs?*"

"Oh, hush up," Abby cracked. "He's just ... irritating."

"And hot."

"He thinks he's God's gift."

"And he's hot," Regan repeated. "Admit it."

"Yes. Okay? He's aesthetically pleasing to the eye of a woman. Any woman. Not just me."

"*Aesthetically pleasing,*" Regan sputtered. "You kill me."

"Are you calling for a purpose?" she asked, irritation spilling over into the tone of her voice.

"You're not going to believe this. Are you near your computer?"

"It's in my hand."

"I'm sending you a link. Hang on." A short minute later, Abby gasped. "You've seen it."

"Oh, Regan. This is horrible."

"She's out of control."

"She's out of control," Abby repeated as if it was an original thought. "How did you find this?"

"I was surfing."

"Do you think she needs an intervention?"

"At least."

"You know, I'm taking Iris to the design center tomorrow afternoon. She wants to look around and get some ideas for the dining room. Why don't we call Lynette, and the four of us will meet for an early dinner to talk about it."

"If nothing else, it's a good reason not to cook for one," Regan said.

"When was the last time you cooked?"

Well, she has me there.

Chapter 6

Iris tipped her head to one side and folded her arms as she stared at the strange reflective chandelier before her.

"I know," Abby commented softly from beside her. "Some of it's really awful, isn't it?"

"*Really* awful. I've never been here before. I didn't really realize the design center is a whole center of stores. I guess I thought it was just one massive showroom or something."

"It's a good place to come when I have a client who wants something right on trend," Abby said. Tucking her long, orange-red locks behind one ear, she wrinkled her freckled nose and gave Iris a quick smile. "There's a handful of furniture stores, a place for custom window treatments, even a place specializing in outdoor living. I get inspiration here." She leaned closer to Iris and whispered, "And then I go try to find it somewhere else for half the price."

"Yeah, things look pretty pricey here," Iris remarked.

"They can be. But there's a pretty good representation of a full cross-section of styles."

"Listen to you," Iris teased. "You sound like a full-service interior designer."

"That's me," she said, pressing the crisp front pleat of her high-waisted trousers.

Iris' gaze was drawn to Abby's fair, porcelain skin. It had been a good many years since she had seen such a luminous complexion in her own reflection, if she ever had.

"Do you see anything here that inspires you?" Abby asked.

"Sort of."

"Yes?" she brightened. "What is it?"

"I think I may look into a facelift."

A surprised chuckle popped out of Abby's mouth and she shook her head. "Anything for the dining room?"

"Oh, that. No. Nothing jumps out at me. At least not in a way that makes me want to put it in my new dining room and look at it every day."

"Okie dokie then. Shall we head down the street to meet the girls?"

Iris sighed. "I think so."

"Walk or drive?"

Walk? Please.

"Let's drive. Do you mind?"

"Not at all. We can go together in my truck and I'll drop you back here after."

The sudden recollection of the last time she'd tried to scale Everest and hoist herself into the passenger seat of Abby's SUV pressed the air out of Iris's lungs.

"Sounds good," she said. "Except let's take my Volvo. I didn't wear my climbing clothes today."

Abby chuckled and led the way toward the door.

Regan had already scored a table next to the half-wall of stacked stone separating the open kitchen from the dining area, and Iris gave her a quick hug before she and Abby sat down across from her.

Glancing at the open chair beside Regan, Iris asked, "Is Lynette coming?"

"Yeah, but she'll be a little late," Regan replied. "One of her two dozen kids has a something-or-other and needs to be dropped off. Or picked up. I can't remember which. Anyway, she said to go ahead and order without her."

"She likes that penne dish with the hot sausages," Abby announced.

Iris scanned the open restaurant until she spotted a waiter. He headed in her direction, and she asked him, "Can we get some bread, please?"

He nodded. "I'll tell your server. She should be with you directly."

Iris felt her friends' eyes on her, and a blush of warmth moved up her neck and spread out over her face. "I didn't have lunch and I'm half starved."

"So did you get a chance to look at the cheater page on Kevin?" Regan asked without comment on her bread fetish.

"I did," she replied, shaking her head. "She's out of control."

"She is out of control," Abby repeated to the rhythm of a slow and deliberate nod.

The pubescent waitress arrived at their table with a bounce in her step and an iPad in hand. "My name is Sunny and I'll be your server today. Are we ready to order?"

An amused smile crept up on Iris, and she couldn't help herself. *Sunny.* It fit.

"We have a friend joining us in a bit," Abby told her. "Can I put in her order now?"

"Of course. What can I get for her?"

"You know that penne dish with the spicy sausage and the red bell peppers?"

"That's our Zesty Penne. Can I add a salad?"

"No. Just the pasta. And a—"

"Do you think we should?" Regan interjected. "You know Lynette's life lately. We might be lucky if she even shows up."

"I guess that's true," Abby told the waitress. "Better wait on that, if you don't mind."

"Of course. What can I get for you then?" Sunny asked with a jubilant, blinding-white smile.

"I'd like the antipasto salad," Abby replied. "Hold the banana peppers, dressing on the side. And an iced tea, no lemon."

Sunny redirected her white-hot spotlight on Regan.

"I think I'll have the Skillet Eggplant Pizza and a glass of merlot."

When it was Iris's turn, she didn't even have to glance at the menu she'd never opened. "Mushroom ravioli and a house salad with ranch dressing."

"To drink?"

"Iced tea. Thank you." As the waitress took the first step in leaving the table, Iris quickly added, "Oh. One more thing. Can we get some bread?"

"Of course."

Sunny scampered off toward the kitchen, and Iris leaned forward to ask the girls, "How old do you think she is?"

"Twelve," Regan replied without missing a beat.

Iris loved that about Regan, right from the first. She'd never been a laugh-out-loud kind of smart-aleck; instead, her surprisingly quick wit came across as smart, dry, and somewhat tongue-in-cheek.

"So what's going on with you today, Iris?" Regan interrupted her thoughts so sharply that Iris's mouth drooped a little, partially open.

"What do you mean?"

Regan brushed her bangs from her eyes and pushed her brown-rimmed glasses upward on the bridge of her nose. Behind them, her chocolate eyes narrowed into razor-sharp attention aimed right at Iris.

"The bread," she said. "What's going on?"

"What? I'm hungry."

"Yeah. Okay. But what's going on?"

Iris leaned in and smiled. "Sometimes bread is just bread, Regan."

"Not with you."

"She's right, Iris," Abby piped up. "Whenever you've got something weighing on you, you turn to carbs."

"Where's the bread?" Regan imitated her. "I asked for bread. Where is it?"

"I did not say it like that."

"Fine. You're right, we're wrong. Now get over yourself and tell us what's up."

Sunny returned with a basket of fresh and fragrant bread and set it down in front of Iris. "Your drinks are coming right up."

Iris casually removed one of the warm hunks of bread from inside the linen napkin and bit off a corner of it. The moment the buttery, garlic- and herb-infused manna hit her happy taste buds, she closed her eyes and moaned softly. When she opened them again, the focus of both her companions rested directly on her.

"Okay," she said, dropping the bread to the plate, "maybe I'm redirecting my fears into this bread. But it's *really good* bread."

Regan leaned on both elbows and stared at her. "What fears?"

"I think Dean might be having an affair." The instant the words crossed her lips, she scrambled to pull them back. "I mean, I don't have any proof of that at all. He's always where he should be, and I haven't caught him crooning at someone on the phone or anything. It's not like I'm going to hit up the cheaters website or follow him or anything. It's just a feeling, I guess."

"Based on?" Abby asked.

"Based on nothing, that's the thing. He's just ... stopped ... *seeing me*."

"Who has?" All three of them looked up in unison to find Lynette standing at the edge of the table in a short-sleeved colorful and flowy blouse, the thin material lightly smocked at the top. She wore her long braids twisted neatly atop her head, and a stack of wooden beaded bracelets partway up her arm. "What're you all talking about?"

"Dean doesn't see Iris anymore, and she thinks there's another woman," Abby recapped.

"Of course, she's wrong," Regan added. "But that's how she feels."

"And apparently those feelings have morphed into garlic bread," Iris said, straight-faced. "Do you want some? It cures whatever ails you."

"Or maybe just masks it in buttery comfort," Regan cracked, and Iris suddenly wasn't loving that wit of hers so much.

"I could do with some buttery comfort," Lynette said, and she slipped into the chair next to Iris and snatched a chunk of the bread from the basket in front of her. After she took a bite, she turned to Iris. "So who's the bimbo you think Dean's with?"

Lynette's words crushed Iris a little. "Could we please quit analyzing my inability to resist bread and remember why we're here?" She looked from face to face. "Celia?"

"Fine," Regan said. "We'll table your issue for a minute."

"What are we going to do about Celia?" Abby asked them, wide-eyed.

Lynette finished her bread and nodded at Iris in appreciation for it before asking them, "Is it really our job to do something about Celia? I mean, haven't we always known she's a little nuts when it comes to '*Keffin*'?" She air-quoted the name. "He's younger than she is, and the Lord knows he's hot."

Iris nodded. "He is that."

"I do like that dark, brooding thing he has going on," Abby said, squinting and doing her best imitation of a smoldering Kevin. "And then you talk to him and he's just as sweet as he could be, right?"

"So we pull her back a little this time," Lynette continued. "Won't we just find her crouching behind bushes again next week? That's what she does."

The four of them looked from one to the other, their gazes bouncing like a ball across and over the table.

"I see our fourth has arrived," Sunny chimed in. Beaming down at Lynette, she asked, "What can I get you?"

"Just an espresso, thanks."

"Good thing we didn't order your meal," Abby remarked.

Lynette nodded. "Trev has a faculty thing tonight, and there will be food there."

"Coming right up," the waitress sang as she departed.

Once she moved out of earshot, Lynette asked them, "Good grief, how old do you think she is? Twelve?"

And Iris popped with laughter.

"You know, I have an idea about Celia. Tell me what you think ..."

"I'm thinking of adding something new to the menu," Celia said without looking up from her work over the enormous commercial-sized sink.

The kitchen at *Latina* had become her kingdom, one of the only places where she felt completely in control and utterly at home. If only the rest of her life could be so easily diced, sliced, and corralled. She'd started there as a sous chef and, within two years, replaced her boss. She'd run the active kitchen for three years now, proud of her role at one of the most popular ethnic restaurants in the greater San Diego area.

Marabel, her young sous chef for the last eighteen months or so, stepped up next to her and wordlessly began scrubbing the potatoes in the enormous bowl.

"I laid awake last night," Celia told her. "I got to thinking about my mama's *asado huilense*. It took a while, but I found her recipe, and I thought we could try it out as a special one night this weekend."

"Pork, right? What else is in it?"

"Marinate the pork in beer and sour orange juice with *vegetobbles* and herbs." Maribel chuckled the way she always did at Celia's pronunciation of *vegetables*.

"Then you slow-bake under a covering of banana leaves. Very traditional Colombian fare. Very popular at *Las Fiestas de San Pedro*, a religious celebration that dates back in my country to the Spanish conquerors."

Before Marabel could say it, Celia chuckled and said it for her. "I know, I know. Always a lesson in Colombian *heestory* from me, *chez*?"

"It's your heritage," Maribel said with a shrug. "If you ever want to know about Mexico, I'm your *chica*." She didn't look up from the potato she scrubbed as she added, "Want me to take over here?"

"That would be great. I want to see to the produce order for tomorrow before we have to get started. When you finish with the potatoes, start on the plantains, heh?"

"You got it."

Celia grabbed a nectarine from the bowl on the prep table on her way to the back of the kitchen and into the office tucked into the corner across from the pantry. The first bite squirted the front of her apron with golden-orange juice, and she dabbed it with a wad of tissues she yanked from the box on her desk.

When her cell rang, she quickly made a nest of tissues to cradle the half-eaten fruit before she picked up the device and held it with two fingers. She checked the screen before pressing the button to answer the call.

"Regan. *Mi amiga dulce. Qué pasa?*"

"Hiya, C. How are you doing today?"

"You mean have I fallen over the deep end of the ocean yet today?" she teased.

"Gone over the deep end," Regan corrected with a grin.

"Not yet, but the day *es* still young, no?"

Regan gave a hearty laugh, and it lifted a broad smile to Celia's face.

"I have a favor to ask," she said.

"Okay. Tell me."

"It's nothing huge. I just need to get a phone number from you."

Lynette barely had time to get changed before driving out toward campus to meet up with Trevor. The hall overflowed with people, all the way out into the vestibule, and it appeared as if the program had already begun inside.

Slipping out of her wrap as she hurried toward the open double doors, she said hello to several familiar faces without names that came to mind. She glanced down at the note Trevor had left her that morning with the table number scribbled at the bottom corner.

Table 12.

She draped her wrap over the arm already strapped with her oversized bag and hurried through, scanning the numbers posted at the center of each table until she spotted number twelve. She placed her bag on one chair and hung her wrap over the back of the chair next to it before turning and looking around the room for her husband. When she finally spotted him, he saw her at precisely the same moment.

"Excuse me, there's my wife," she heard him say to the small group around him, and the grin that belonged to her alone as he made his way toward her made Lynette a little weak in the knees.

He wore no jacket, but he'd rolled the cuffs of the dress shirt that topped his favorite jeans nearly all the way to his elbows. He'd chosen that silk tie she'd given him for his birthday, but tied it all wrong so that it hung low and crooked beneath the collar. When he reached her, she immediately reached up to straighten it as he pressed his lips against her cheek.

"Your tie is catawampus," she said, turning her head to kiss him on the lips.

Tina Dudley and Ray Something—colleagues of Trevor's in the Arts & Humanities department where he taught—wandered toward them, interrupting the private moment.

"Lynette," Tina called to her as they approached.

"Tina. Ray. Good to see you both again."

"Hey," Ray Whatever-his-name-was exclaimed, "did you get any use out of that pottery my wife bought you for your wedding? I told her it didn't seem like your style, but—"

"Oh, not at all," she interrupted. "We have it displayed in the dining room and used it just last weekend for our family dinner."

Okay, so it wasn't so much a family dinner as pizza followed by an art project at the dining room table. Margaret had taken to storing her crayons and markers inside the ugly clay bowl that they hid behind the doors of the hutch.

"Really?" He seemed genuinely happy with her little stretch of the truth.

"Lynette, you must be so proud of your hubby here," Tina declared.

"Always," she replied. "But is there some specific reason this time?"

"I haven't told her yet," Trevor cut in. "I was just about to when you two walked up."

"Oh, oh, don't let us interrupt then. We'll get out of your way."

Tina tugged at Ray's arm and the two of them awkwardly retreated.

"Why am I proud of you today?" Lynette asked.

Trevor grinned, and his blue-gray eyes glistened as he did. "Well, Love. You are fortunate enough to be married to this year's Chancellor's Faculty Award recipient for Excellence in Undergraduate Teaching."

"Seriously?"

"Aye."

"Well, I don't know exactly what that means," she stated with a smile, "but it sounds like something worth celebrating."

"And celebrate we shall."

Trevor took two steps closer until their bodies pressed together. He slipped his arms around her waist and pulled her closer still.

"I don't think the Chancellor would appreciate our celebrating right here in the hall, do you?"

"Probably not. But we could always slip away for a few minutes."

"How about we stick around and have something to eat," she suggested with the quirk of her brow. "Since I'm half-starved and all."

"I thought you ate with the girls."

"I just had a coffee."

"But ... couldn't we just ..."

"I don't think we should *just*, darling. But I'll indulge in all the *justing* you'd like after I find sustenance and we get home."

Trevor stared into her eyes so deeply that she wilted a bit under his gaze. "Eat fast," he whispered. "Then let's take a side trip to the top floor of the parking garage where no one will be parked at this time of the night. We don't want to take a chance on waiting until we get home for our *justing*. We never know what might greet us there."

A cacophony of children's voices, demands, and questions played like a familiar song in Lynette's mind. Not the kind one didn't mind humming for days on end when the replay got stuck. But the kind of earworm that drove a person halfway to batty. Like that song from *Frozen*.

"First we eat," she stated softly. "Then we *just*, and *then* we drive home to see what adventures await. It's a good plan."

"Good plan, indeed."

Welcome to VERTICAL MAGAZINE
Moments-of-Truth.net

BLOG POST: REGAN SLOANE

In chatting with Annette today about all the different ways and places she and the new husband (I like to call him James Bond because of his British accent and piercing eyes) have to try and fit in time together—intimate time—I started thinking about my own history with that sort of thing. Not that 40-Watt and I were so much in love that we resorted to desperate attempts, you understand. But for a very long time, we were trying to conceive a child.

Many of you have shared your own struggles with infertility here on the blog, so I know you'll understand. Taking your temperature, tracking your ovulation cycles, the injections and the monthly aching hope that's ultimately dashed by a blue minus sign on a stick—all of it rotating around scheduled sex in hopes of just one of those tiny, squiggling sperms swimming upstream and doing in you what they so easily do in every other Joanne on the street. Even though I grieve with sadness missing the baby that never quite made it to my arms, I certainly don't miss the work involved in trying to make something happen that was never going to.

I don't miss 40-Watt, either. But I'll tell you what I do miss. The Sunday mornings in bed, sipping coffee and sharing the newspaper. Those hours just after the occasional date night where we were together for no reason other than the simple desire to be. I miss him cooking because I can't ... and the two of us cleaning up the kitchen together afterward. The touch of his hand, the way he hummed with the radio when he drove, the foot rubs. Oh yeah, I'm swooning at the memory of the foot rubs. I wonder if anyone will ever touch these feet again. Aside from Jasmine at my favorite mani/pedi place, of course.

Underneath it all, however, readers ... there is still the very distinct hope of moments like that occurring once again. Moments of truth, just like the name of this blog. Touches, shared laughter, investment in one another's lives. It will come again for me one day, after the healing is complete. I have to believe it will.

And it will come again for you too. We'll ride it out together.

Chapter 7

"Regan Sloane. How are you?"

She grinned and tucked the temple of her glasses into the point of her V-necked shirt as she pulled the door all the way open and greeted Sebastian Jordan. Backlit by the sun, his shaggy blond hair glistened, and as he removed his dark glasses, his striking clear-blue gaze seemed to imprint on her. "Come on in," she managed to say. "It's good to see you again."

"Been a while," he said as he passed, and the spicy, fragrant scent of him wiggled its way into Regan's nostrils. "I was surprised to get your call."

"Well, Celia's mentioned several times that you're a carpenter and a builder, and I really need some help in that area. So I thought maybe you could take a gander and tell me if what I have in mind is even feasible."

"Let's have a look. Lead the way."

She guided him up the oak stairs to the loft, suddenly self-conscious about preceding him, worrying that if he looked straight ahead during the ascent, his face would be confronted by her ever-widening behind. The thought made her pick up the pace.

"Great loft," he said when they reached the top of the stairs.

"Thanks. It's a work-in-progress. But I find it's good for my creativity to work up here with the big windows and the skylight."

Steve looked up at them from his cushion bed, yawned, and laid his head back down to rest.

"I've never seen a dog that didn't bark when somebody came to the door."

"Yeah, Steve's pretty laid-back. He doesn't take the stairs unless he's really enticed to do so."

Baz laughed. "I know the feeling." He squatted down in front of Steve and stroked his ear. "I have days like that too, buddy."

Regan chuckled. "Don't we all."

"I can't remember," he said, his back still to her as he focused his attention on Steve. "What do you do again?"

"I'm a writer."

He surveyed the wayward stacks of books piled on either side of the dog, and Regan wished she'd have remembered to straighten them before he arrived.

"Novels?"

"No," she replied. "Well, maybe someday. But right now I write a blog called *Moments of Truth* for Vertical Magazine."

He stood and leaned most of his weight to one side. "I don't know them."

"It's a lifestyle magazine for women. The editor saw my blog when it was really small. I think about thirteen people read it on a regular basis. But she saw something in it and asked me to re-brand it for their readership."

"And it's grown?"

"Like crazy."

"That's great." He seemed aimless as he walked the circumference of the loft, sizing things up. "So what did you have in mind up here?"

She went to her desk and unfolded the magazine page she'd been storing there, ironing out the crease against the thigh of her jeans.

"I saw this and just fell in love with it. I wondered if you thought there might be a possibility of building it into that wall. I mean, I know the ceiling slants, so it might not even be possible, but I really love the idea of all that storage for books, and a little cubby built into it for Steve's bed."

Baz took the glossy page from her with a smile. "Steve," he repeated. "I like that."

He stared at the magazine page for a long few beats. Finally, he nodded tentatively but still didn't speak. He looked from the page to the wall, and back to the page again before he spoke up. "I think it's workable."

"Really? Would it be terribly expensive?"

"I could do it for under a grand. If you think that could work for you, I can put together some plans and a quote."

"Yes." She grinned at him and touched his arm. "Thank you. That would be so great."

"Happy to do it. I can be back in touch by the end of the week."

"All right."

Their gazes seemed locked together like some sort of pressure hinge, and Regan felt a film of perspiration spread out over the skin under her hair at the nape of her neck.

"Okay then," he said, slicing the connection with an invisible bolt cutter.

He moved slowly toward the stairs, and she finally managed to speak. "You know, Baz … there's something else I'd like to speak to you about if you have the time. Would you like to go downstairs for a cup of coffee?"

"Sure."

This time, Regan let him go first, and she followed him down the stairs, keeping her eyes trained on the ripple across his shoulder blades, and chastising herself for doing so.

"Have a seat at the counter," she said as she rounded it and crossed the kitchen. "I have every flavor of coffee known to humankind. Have a look in the K-cup dispenser and choose your poison."

Regan produced two cups from the multi-colored mug tree; an orange one and a blue.

"Crème brulee, caramel vanilla, chocolate glazed donut," Baz read from the coffees displayed on one side of the dispenser. "Have you never heard of just coffee?"

"Just coffee," she repeated dryly, retrieving the vanilla creamer from the fridge. "I don't think I know that brand."

"Seriously?"

She looked up at him—her heart thumping rapidly when their eyes met—and smiled. "Turn it to the other side. The loser flavors are on the back."

He spun it around so that the wall of her favorite bold roast faced him. While he looked at it, she reached across the counter and plucked one of the K-cups for her own use.

"Having a loser flavor, are you?" he teased.

"Yeah. It's my fave."

Baz pulled another one out of the rack and tossed it to her. Regan pushed out a relieved puff of air when she caught it.

"Bold roast it is. How about some special creamer?"

He tossed his head back and released melodious, resonant laughter.

"Fine," she said over a chuckle. "You don't know what you're missing."

"I'm sure I'll kick myself later, but I think I'll go with just black."

She doctored her own coffee while brewing his, then slid a cup of black bold roast over the counter toward him. He took a sip and quirked a brow, nodding.

"Okay," he said. "That's really good coffee."

"Vanilla creamer only makes it better."

"Pace yourself. Let's save that for another time."

Her heartbeat thudded again at the mere mention of future shared cups of coffee.

"So what did you want to talk to me about?" He took another swig from the steaming cup.

Regan leaned against the counter opposite him, nibbling the corner of her lip absent-mindedly until it ached. She pressed her lips together for a moment before admitting, "It's about Celia."

The expression on Baz's face went from amused interest to irritation in nothing flat.

"She told me about you busting her when she followed Kevin."

He folded his arms on the edge of the counter and leaned on them. "Yeah."

"I'm just wondering—"

"If I told Kevin that his wife is a stalker? No, I didn't."

"Why not?" she asked, and his eyes registered clear-blue surprise. "Really. Why didn't you tell him?"

"Because she's his wife? His life? Look, your friend clearly has trust issues and could probably use a year or six of therapy, but the bottom line is that the best way to foul up a friendship is to poke your nose into it. And from the look on your face, you'd probably do well to glean the benefit of my wisdom."

The corner of her mouth twitched, and she willed it into submission. "Thank you, Obi-wan," she cracked. "The truth is you're my only hope."

"Look," he said, pausing to swallow another gulp of his coffee. "The way I see it … It's not my circus, and she's not my monkey."

Regan couldn't help the chuckle that slipped up and out of her without restraint.

"She's his crazy to solve," he went on. "It's not like he didn't know she wasn't ticking on time when he married her, but he married her anyway."

"What do you mean?"

Baz set the royal blue mug on the counter and stood. "There's not enough coffee or free time to cover it all. My advice to you, Regan Sloane? Steer clear of other people's marriages. No good can come from it."

He headed toward the front door, and Regan slid her cup to the counter and followed him. Just as she closed the gap between them, Baz turned around and faced her. He had a good six inches of height on her, and she couldn't help noticing his shaggy, disheveled hair. She resisted the surprisingly strong urge to reach out and run her fingers through it.

"So do you really want storage in your office up there?" he asked. "Or was that just an excuse to get me over here so you could talk to me about Kevin and Celia?"

"N-no," she blurted, her eyes so wide open that they stung. "I … I really do need the storage. I want to see what you come up with … if you're willing."

He lifted one shoulder in a partial shrug and turned back toward the door. Once he'd crossed the threshold, he glanced at her over his muscular shoulder.

"I'll be in touch then."

"O-okay."

She closed the door before he'd even reached the sidewalk, almost certain embarrassment—or whatever that was consuming her—might cause her to wilt away like the Wicked Witch did when splashed with water.

"Can we see the master bedroom?" Juliet Jensen asked, never slowing down long enough to hear the answer.

"Right this way," Nate said, and they filed out of the partially complete kitchen, first Juliet, then her husband Darren. Nate waved his arm with a flourish, allowing Abby to pass in front of him before he took the role of enthralling caboose.

"Oh, Darren, look at this," Juliet cooed as she peered around the studs of the doorway. "It's so spacious."

"Take a look at the master bath," Nate urged. "My contractor's guys finished the tiling job just this morning." Wielding a sharp glance at Abby, he added, "Check out that level basin floor, huh?"

"I never realized, as the architect, you'd be so active in the whole process," Juliet told him. "But it's been such a relief knowing you and Abby were keeping it all on track."

"That's why you pay us the big bucks," he replied, and Abby tried not to roll her eyes. "Everyone involved just wants to make sure you get everything you want."

"Ohh, Abby," Juliet sang as they filed through the doorway to the master bath. "You were so right about the glass tiles. They look amazing. It's so fresh and cool, like a spa retreat. Isn't it, honey?"

"Just like a retreat," Darren replied. Abby didn't catch him even turning a look toward the shower, but she'd already come to learn what Darren Jensen had no doubt known since the day he met Juliet—her opinion was the only one that really mattered.

"I returned the vanity lights," Abby told her. "And they're going to apply the cost to the new cylinder lighting you wanted. We should receive them next week."

"Good. I hope it wasn't too much trouble."

Only about twenty hours out of my day. No trouble at all.

"That's what I'm here for," Abby said. "To give you exactly what you want from a new build."

Nate stepped up next to her and slid his arm around her shoulder, smiling far too broadly as he added, "We're here for you. Team Jensen."

Abby's skin tingled strangely beneath his touch, and she elbowed him in the ribs before slipping out from underneath his arm. If she had any hope at all of maintaining her resolve to avoid sticky situations, the high-alert siren had better sound off, and quick. "I'm Team Jensen," she tried to joke. "I don't know who *he* is."

"Oh, you two are adorable," Juliet said. "When you're building your own dream house together—Nate's designing it and you're styling it, Abby—you can both credit Darren and me for bringing you together."

"If you think that's getting us a discount of some kind, darling," her husband remarked, "I'm afraid I only have to look at Abby's face to know how disappointed you'll be."

She tried to chuckle good-naturedly, but it might have come off like a snicker and a sneer. The idea of anyone thinking she and Nate were going to get together ...

"I'm partial to the La Jolla area, dear one," Nate said, and he moved so close to her that she could feel his body heat radiating on her skin. "Do you have a preference about where we live?"

"La Jolla is just fine," she said, turning away. "For you. I'll be out in Old Town."

"Darren, why don't we round up the children so they can see their rooms, and leave these two to work out the details of their hot date for tonight."

Abby snorted, more out of astonishment than amusement, but Nate laughed unabashedly with delight and lifted his palm into the air. Juliet slapped it as she turned to leave.

"Do you get the feeling they've been conspiring?" Darren asked softly as he passed Abby.

"Ya think?"

Once the Jensens moved out of earshot, Abby glared at Nate.

"What are you going to do if your face freezes like that?"

"You are hard enough to deal with when we're alone, but I won't have you involving clients in your nonsense," she said, her feet planted firmly, her hands balled into fists at her side.

"Nonsense," he repeated. "Nice, Abby."

And with that, he turned and stalked away from her.

The imminent return of the Jensens hovered around her like a shroud, and the weight of it kept Abby anchored to the spot, despite the fact that she wanted to follow him, yank him back to make him look at her. Still, she remained stationed. Breathing. In with the good air, out with the bad.

"Hey, Abby!" Kym, the Jensens' thirteen-year-old, exclaimed as she appeared. "Mom says we can finally look at colors and stuff for my room."

She righted herself and inhaled sharply as she changed gears. "I brought along some pictures and swatches. They're in the kitchen."

"Which way is that?"

Abby pointed the way and followed the bouncing blond ponytail wrapped in a rhinestone band as Kym bopped along ahead of her. By the time she reached the kitchen, the young girl had already hiked herself up onto the marble-topped center island. She held Abby's project book nested in her lap and flipped through it.

"Here," Abby said, turning the plastic pages and opening to the tab marked with Kym's name. "Try here."

The instant the book fell open to the selection of "blingy lights" Kym had requested, the girl gasped and lifted the book into both arms. "Abby, you rule!"

"Yes, I do, but why don't you look at all of them before you put my crown in place. There are five choices, all of them with the bling you love."

Over the next few minutes, Kym was fixated back on the first chandelier—The Mod—varied lengths of mirrored rounds hanging from a platinum circle. And she'd chosen a purple fur rug, the Flower Power lavender bedding dotted with purple daisies, a dark purple accent wall, and, for the corner of the room, a swinging hammock trimmed with fur.

"When you said you liked sixties fashion, you weren't kidding," Abby said, grinning. "You have a very unique sense of style for someone your age."

"Yeah" was all she said, and she shrugged one shoulder as if she'd heard that observation a time or two already.

"Now I just have to find your brother and nail down his preferences, and get your parents' approval, and I'll get started on your bedrooms this week."

"Daddy said we might not get to move in right on schedule," the girl remarked. "What's up with that?"

"I don't know," she replied. "I'm on track, so you'll have to ask him what he meant."

"Is it my turn yet?" Fifteen-year-old Drew Jensen stood beneath the arched entry to the kitchen, a skateboard under his arm and wearing pants that hung low around his hips, the top of his boxers showing.

Nate stepped up behind him and tapped Drew on the arm. "This way, homie."

"Can I see Drew's room too?" Kym asked Abby.

"No!" her brother called back to her.

"Can I?" she repeated.

"Come on. Let's both go."

Abby found herself following the bouncing ponytail through the house again.

"One of my *mains* has these *tope* shelves for his collection," Drew told Nate as Abby and Kym reached them.

"What's tope?" she whispered to Kym.

"Like, cool. It means tight and dope," she answered softly.

"Ahh."

"They go from the floor up to the ceiling," Drew continued, "and every one of the openings is just the right size for one of his 'bots."

"Like cubbyholes," Nate commented.

"I guess."

"What's a 'bot?" Abby asked, and the two guys in the room turned and looked at her as if she'd just grown a third eye. "Seriously. What's a 'bot?"

"Drew builds these lame robots with his friends," Kym explained.

"They are not lame."

"They are so. They're like a foot tall and they're, like, bugs and animals and stuff."

"That doesn't sound lame at all," Abby told them. "You build them?"

"Yeah," Drew replied with a hint of bravado. "They come in a kit. The one we're working on now is a crab that slides sideways."

"Is it battery-operated?" she asked.

"Nah, they're all solar-powered. We started learning about renewable energy sources in science class, and then somebody mentioned these and we wanted to give 'em a try. You think I could get some cubby-things built into that wall over there for my collection?"

Abby glanced at the short wall next to the closet. "I'll have to discuss it with your mom. Then I'll take some measurements …"

"And yo," Drew interrupted. "I want some o' them swaggy details on it too. Like instead of rough edges, they're, like, carved."

"Can you get me some pictures?" she asked.

"Sho thing."

"Well, let me speak to your mom first."

"She'll say yes," Kym whined with the roll of her turquoise-blue eyes. "He gets anything he wants."

"Like you don't, *emo*?" Drew snapped.

"All right, all right," Abby said, lifting her palms toward them. "Enough of this. I'll go find your mom and we'll make some decisions once we get the approval. Fair enough?"

"Whatever."

"Fine. But make sure I get my fur rug, k?"

"I'll see what I can do."

"A fur rug," she heard Drew drone as she left. "What are you, a caveman?"

"It's purple, and it's really cool."

"Sounds it. A purple fur rug. I guess you'll be beating down the doors to get yourself one of those, won't you, Nate?"

Abby grinned as she heard him exclaim, "Hey. Don't drag me into this."

Chapter 8

"Iris. Honey. I'm not one to negate someone's feelings—*especially yours*—but I think you're spotting monsters where there is no basement."

Iris hadn't realized she'd been holding her breath until she exhaled, long and hard; the kind of exhale that made her chest ache. She closed her eyes for a moment, allowing the Pacific breeze to caress the frozen frown muscles working overtime in her face. Two young mothers ambled past, pushing strollers along the sidewalk behind where she and Lynette sat on a bench facing the usually compelling ocean waves. She hardly even noticed the water today, though. Instead, she yearned to dive into Lynette's confident words and swim around in them for a while. If only she could manage it.

"My husband has made a home out of our guest room. He hasn't touched me in months. And when I went into his room last night and slipped under the covers with him, he patted my hand and rolled over. Five minutes later, he was snoring like a leaf blower. He's a man, Lynette. If we women are sugar and spice and everything nice, aren't men testosterone and sex and all things complex? If he's not interested in pillaging his willing wife, where is he focusing all that ... *maleness*?"

Lynette stared her down for several beats before slowly repeating her words. "Testosterone and sex and *all things complex*? Did you just make that up?"

"No, my Aunt Reba used to say it to us girls." She lifted her hand and waved the rabbit trail away. "We're getting off track."

"Well, if Dean is so *complex*, maybe there's another reason behind his lack of interest, honey. Maybe he's just getting older and losing his sex drive. It happens, you know."

"He's fifty-six years old, Lynette. Not eighty-six."

"Can I just remind you of something you already know?" she asked.

"What's that?" Iris replied in monotone.

"Dean Kramer adores you. He always has, he always will. If he's not pillaging you, there's a reason behind it that has nothing to do with his affections being diverted from the woman he clearly loves."

Iris sighed. Her heart saw the truth in those words. But her brain had kicked into overdrive for the last twenty-four hours, imagining all sorts of uncharacteristic behavior from the husband she'd thought she knew so well.

"Do you want to grab some lunch?" Lynette asked her. "There's a wonderful soup and sandwich spot a short walk away."

Iris's heart tapped out a different idea. "You know what I'd rather do?"

"What's that?"

She dug into her bag and produced the folded sheet of paper she'd grabbed from the printer before dashing off to meet Lynette on the spur of the moment. "I want to go here," Iris said, handing it to her.

"Tony Broadway's House of Beauty?" Lynette chuckled. "Seriously?"

"It's a 50% off Groupon," Iris told her. "A complete makeover. Hair, nails, brows, and makeup. No appointment necessary. Will you go with me?"

"Oh, honey. I can't. I have a meeting this—" Lynette cut her own words in two, then she sighed. "Let me make a call. I'll move some things around, and we'll head over to"—she referred to the paper in her hand—"the *House of Beauty*."

Iris slid across the bench and tossed her arms around Lynette, yanking her into a hug. "Thank you. You're such a good friend."

Many hours later, Iris sashayed through the front door of her house with Tickled Pink fingers and toes, Va-Va-Red lips, and short, bouncy Golden Cinnamon waves. She could hardly wait to find Dean, a mission interrupted when she found the note on the kitchen counter in her husband's familiar scrawl.

Should be back around 7.

Iris glanced at the clock over the oven. That would give her an hour to stuff a couple of pork chops and whip up Dean's favorite scalloped potatoes, maybe steam some of that fat asparagus she'd picked up at the farmers' market the previous morning.

When her husband hadn't found his way home by eight, Iris called his cell. It rang in the den. He'd left without it. By 8:30, half starved, she sat across from Dean's empty place setting, lit the candles at the center of the table, poured a glass of chardonnay from the bottle she'd chilled in the freezer, and dined on the wonderful meal of Dean's favorite dishes that she'd prepared just for him. By 9:00, the leftovers had been neatly stowed, the dishwasher loaded, the counters wiped, and the *Va-Va* long since gone from her pursed lips.

Iris took a long, warm shower and turned up her nose at the coral nightgown—Dean's favorite color on her—she'd intended to wear. She stepped into charcoal gray sweatpants and an oversized pink t-shirt instead. While climbing into bed, she stopped to wiggle her Tickled Pink toes before groaning and yanking the covers over them. A few minutes later, six high-pitched beeps from downstairs—punched at a very familiar rhythm—told her the security system had been disarmed.

Well, at least he's home safe, she thought. And Iris rolled to her side, clutching the body pillow that had replaced Dean as her nightly companion, and she closed her eyes. One lone tear squeezed out from beneath her eyelid and dribbled down her cheek.

No use wasting a full stop at a red light, Celia rationalized, and she reached over to the passenger seat and slipped open the lid on the bakery box. She moaned softly at first sight. And when the chocolate aroma of the thick, rich brownies frosted with peaks of fudge slithered over and tickled her nostrils, she clamped her eyes shut and breathed in the moment.

Until the driver behind her blasted his horn and shouted something obscene through his open window.

"*Está bien, está bien,*" she yelled back at him. "I'm going."

But before her foot hit the gas pedal, Celia snatched one of the brownies from the box and took a bite big enough to cut it in half.

"Oh my," she exclaimed. "*Delicioso!*"

"Come on, *laaady.*"

"Yah, yah, yah. *Voy.*"

By the time she pulled into Iris's driveway, she'd licked the last of the fudge icing from her fingers and sealed the box again. The first dessert traditionally went to the book club member with what was unanimously deemed the saddest story. But with the telltale signs of her covert theft gone from her fingers, no one, she decided, had to be the wiser.

As Celia climbed from her car, Abby's SUV pulled up behind her. Celia glanced into the rearview mirror as she tugged her large bag from the passenger floor and tucked the bakery box into the fold of her arm.

"Hey, Celia."

"Hey, *chica. Cómo estás?*"

"It's been a very long day," Abby replied as she twisted her orange-red hair into a ponytail. "I am so ready to just kick back and relax."

Celia touched her friend's arm and took a closer look at the bottle of wine in her hand. "*Vino.* Good girl."

"And what did you bring?"

"Is a surprise," Celia teased. "But I think it will make you happy like a—" She thought it over for a moment before shaking her head. "Something about a cat and a bowl of milk."

"Well, I'll bet it's something chocolate. Am I right?"

"How did you know?"

Abby shot her an odd little grin. "My reasoning is twofold. Number one, it's your favorite. And number two, your face told the tale."

"My ..." Celia's hand jerked to her face.

"You have chocolate smeared all over your lips."

"Eh." She tried to laugh, wiping a smudge off the corner of her mouth. "I was hungry."

"And you couldn't wait the four minutes it took to reach Iris's house," Abby ribbed as she pushed the doorbell. "You know she always cooks up a feast."

"I know, I hardly can *stond* to see what she make tonight."

"You can't wait," Abby corrected playfully.

Regan flung open the door and greeted them. "Welcome to The Girl Zone. No boys allowed."

The scent of something Italian accosted Celia's senses. "Ah, it smells so good in here. What did she make?" she asked as she and Abby filed past.

"Salad," Regan replied.

"What else? I smell garlic. And *oree-gahno.*"

"Oregano," Abby deciphered.

"Yeah. About that." Regan touched both their arms and leaned in close when they stopped and turned toward her. "Iris didn't feel like cooking, so we ordered pizza."

"*Qué?*" Celia exclaimed.

"Oh, no," Abby chimed in. "What's wrong?"

"I know, right?" Regan said softly. "She's a mess."

"Well, let's pretend to give the first brownie to her then," Abby said. "No one has to know this one was covered in chocolate when she arrived."

Regan gave Celia's arm a gentle smack before grabbing the bakery box from her.

"What? I was hungry."

Just before they headed into the kitchen, Regan turned back and whispered, "And whatever you do, don't mention Iris's new hair."

"Why?" Celia asked. "Is it *aw-fill?*"

"No, it's not awful. It's cute, actually. But just ... just *don't mention it.*"

With that, she spun around and led them into where Iris and Lynette had already poured glasses of wine and settled into the nook. As they took their usual places around the table, Regan set the brownies atop the three large pizza boxes stacked at the center.

"We've all agreed that when you don't feel like cooking," Regan told Iris, "the world just doesn't sit right on its axis."

"*Sí*," Celia concurred. "You automatically get the first dessert." Abby shot her a crooked grin, prompting her to add, "Full *diss-closhure*, I did have one on the drive over here. Forgive me?"

As Iris tossed open the flap on the box, Celia checked out her new hair.

It's very becoming, she decided as Iris grabbed a brownie and bit into it. *Why not to mention?*

Once the chocolate comfort had the chance to do its thing, she closed her eyes and smiled. Over a full mouth, Iris crooned, "You're forgiven."

The others dug in, each of them grabbing one for themselves. Aside from the smacking of lips and the occasional soft moan of ecstasy, the room fell completely silent until Lynette leaned forward and collected the last crumbs from the bottom of the empty box.

"Can't let any of this go to waste," she said with a grin.

When she finished, Regan took the empty box and popped up from her chair. "Abbs, help me get the salad, and some plates and napkins?"

The two of them headed from the nook into the main part of the kitchen and busied themselves doing all the things Iris normally did; all the while, Iris leaned back in her chair and concentrated on guzzling the last of the wine from her long-stemmed glass.

"I brought merlot," Celia told her. "Shall we open it?"

"And I brought a gallon of my Aunt Midge's raspberry lemonade," Lynette piped up. "It's really wonderful. It has fresh berries in it. Why don't we switch to that with dinner."

Celia caught the flicker in Lynette's eyes as they diverted to Iris for one fleeting moment. She wondered how many glasses of that wine Iris had already downed.

"That sounds lovely," Regan said as she approached the table and set plates and napkins in front of each of them. "Let's switch to the lemonade."

Iris narrowed her eyes and glared at Regan before she sighed. "You don't have to hover. I'm not having any more wine."

Abby joined them with forks and a large green salad in a cut-crystal bowl as Lynette set about opening the pizza boxes.

"Looks like vegetarian," she said over the first one. "And ..."

"Pepperoni and mushroom," Iris told them. "And I think I got sausage and onion too. It's Dean's favorite, in case there's leftovers. I'm sorry, it's not much. I just didn't feel up to fussing tonight."

"As long as we're together—" Regan began.

"—and have a delectable dessert," Lynette cut in.

"Yes, and have dessert," Regan said with a laugh, "it doesn't really matter what we have for dinner, does it? Book club has always just been about being together."

"Well, it used to be about *books* too," Lynette said, and they all shared a laugh. Even Iris.

"So why don't you tell us what's eating you, heh?" Celia said.

Iris dropped her slice of pizza and locked eyes with Lynette for a long and lingering moment before she wiped her fingertips with a napkin.

"Does it have to do with—" Her voice turned to a whisper as she continued. "—*your hair?*"

"Celia!" Regan exclaimed. Looking to Lynette, she added, "I told her not to mention Iris's hair."

"You don't like my hair?"

"No, I *luff* your hair, *niña.*"

"Well, so do I," Iris said with a pout. "But my husband isn't attracted to me anymore. And I think he's seeing someone else."

If a pin had dropped in a house across the street, they might have all heard it through the squawking silence that followed.

"Iris, no," Abby broke through, and she draped her arm around her friend and kissed her shoulder. "Dean would never."

"That's what I told her," Lynette added.

"What makes you think that he is?" Regan asked Iris.

"He's started drifting away," she replied. "It's been getting worse and worse over time. He's so distant, and he's still sleeping in the guest room. And sometimes I have no idea where he is. Like the other night, he left a note saying he'd be back around seven. I made this great dinner and changed my dumb hair. He finally came home at nearly ten, and all he said the next morning was that he was *unexpectedly delayed.*"

"You should follow him," Celia told her.

At once—in three-part perfect harmony—Regan, Abby and Lynette sang, "*Nooo!*"

"Why not?" she snapped. "She needs to find where Dean go when he disappears." Turning her attention to Iris, she said, "I have a special pair of binoculars you could borrow. They have a button that records everything you see, in case you need it later for the divorce lawyer."

"The divorce lawyer?" Iris exclaimed. "What a terrible thing to say."

"Celia, really," Lynette chastised as she took Iris's hand between both of hers.

"What? *Chu* think she should just go along blindly, *beliefing* everything he does—or worse—*doesn't* tell her? These men, they can be *muy engañoso*, and we cannot let them get away with it."

"What's *engañoso*?" Iris asked the others.

"How you say it?" Celia asked Abby.

"Deceptive."

"*Chez*. Deception."

"Dean is not deceptive," Iris defended.

"No?" Celia asked, taking a bite from a slice of sausage and onion. "If he is seeing another *woo-man*, like you say, then he is deception, is he not?"

"Celia, really." Lynette scowled at her. "Dean is not cheating. He's probably—"

Iris turned and looked at her, first in hope, then in defeat as the buoyant belief in another explanation gave way to reality.

Her disappointment pricked Celia's heart, and she sighed. "Maybe you are right. Maybe he is planning a big surprise you can't know about. When is your birthday?"

"Three months ago."

"Oh. … Anniversary?"

"Celia," Regan barked as she refilled their glasses with the last of the lemonade and sat on the other side of Iris. "Enough."

"I'm just trying to help her *cara la realidad*. Face facts."

"Well, while we're talking about *facing facts*, there's something we all want to talk to you about."

"*Chez?* What's that?"

Abby reached for Celia's hand and tapped it. "You're out of control, honey. We're your friends and we love you, but you're completely out of control."

"What *chu* mean? Oh, the brownie? I only had the one. Well, two if you count the one I had here."

"Not the brownies, Celia," Iris stated. "This thing with Kevin. You're so far over the top that you're going to drive him away if you don't stop."

"*Keffin?*"

"Baz caught you stalking him the other night, Celia," Regan interjected. "He didn't tell Kevin, but it's only a matter of time before he lets it slip—"

"You think Sebastian will tell him? He promised me he wouldn't."

"Yeah, he told me that too, but—"

"You spoke to him about it?"

"He came over to look at the loft, remember?" Regan turned to Abby. "He's going to build those shelves, like the ones in the magazine."

"Oh, that'll look so good. Are you going to include the cubby for Steve?"

"I think so. He's putting together some plans, and I'm meeting him again to check them out."

"He's cute, is he?"

"Yeah, I guess so, but—"

"Hey," Celia exclaimed, pointing to herself in a "back to me" fashion. "*Chu* didn't tell him anything, did you, Regan? Why do you think he might slip and say something to *Keffin?*"

"No, I don't mean just that. But what about the fact that Kevin is a pretty smart guy? If you keep doing what you're doing, he's sure to catch on sooner or later, and Baz won't have to tell him anything. You have a really good thing going, Celia. Do you want to drive him away?"

"Of course not." She deflated. "I can't lose him."

"Consider this a friendly intervention," Lynette told her. "We don't want to sit back and watch you destroy your marriage."

Iris clicked her tongue and sighed. "While you still have one to destroy."

Regan slowed the car to skim the signs identifying the various storefronts in the long line of them. Her heart did a little flutter when Abby pointed at one of them and declared, "I think that's it."

"Yes, there it is. Jordan Designs."

She checked her hair in the rearview and blinked several times to get her contacts to slip back into the right spot. She didn't wear them much anymore, but she'd had the odd notion that she didn't want Baz to see her again with her glasses sliding down her nose.

"Contacts are just more glamorous," Abby had influenced her. "You can still wear your glasses for everyday, but contacts for special occasions." And like a gullible consumer, Regan had caved. Not that seeing Baz Jordan again was a special occasion or anything.

"He has his own shop," Abby commented. "I'm surprised I've never heard about him."

"It looks like a pretty small place."

Once she'd parked, the two of them grabbed their bags and headed across the lot. The beat of Regan's pulse kicked it up a notch as she pushed open the door and stepped inside. An odd and attractive combination of scents—wood polish, coffee, and cinnamon—caressed her senses as her gaze stroked orderly rows of chairs, dining sets, and coffee tables. Various styles of shelving lined the length of one wall, and Regan instinctively moved in that direction.

As she strolled along, she heard Abby's muffled voice behind her. She glanced over her shoulder to find her speaking to a pretty young sales clerk. She wondered for a moment whether HI. MY NAME IS DEVIN had a relationship with Baz beyond simply working in his store.

"All these pieces are crafted by the same designer then?" Abby asked.

"Yes. Mr. Jordan has a large studio where he designs and builds each and every item carried here. He's been at it for a decade now."

"He does incredible work," Abby remarked as she ran her fingers along the back of a wide rocking chair with clean, curved lines.

Regan imagined herself swaying gently—forward and back—in the outer corner of her glass-enclosed porch, sipping morning coffee with Steve snoozing at her feet while she dreamed up her next blog post.

"Regan."

Her heart flopped over and fell to the pit of her stomach at the sound of his voice. With a sharp intake of breath, she turned and smiled at Baz as he stalked toward her and took her hand. He didn't so much shake it as just ... *caress and release.*

"Good to see you."

"You too," she said, and she wondered if she'd actually croaked out the words like it felt she had. As Abby approached, she added, "Baz Jordan, meet my friend Abby Strayhan. She's an interior designer, and I thought she might enjoy seeing your work."

"Nice to meet you, Baz," Abby said, and he actually shook her hand. "Your store is exquisite."

"Thanks." He smiled at her before turning his floodlight back on Regan. "You ready to see some plans?"

"Absolutely."

"Can I see too?" Abby asked.

"Of course. This way."

They followed Baz to the back of the store, beyond the service desk, and down a short hall to a spacious office. An entire wall of windows across the back, valanced by blinds pulled all the way up, ushered in fat beams of sunlight across the oversized desk and the long brown leather sofa with platinum nail heads. The beacons puddled atop the room-sized merlot rug with contemporary beige designs stamped lightly over it.

"Great office," Abby commented as he invited them inside with the wave of his arm before closing the door behind them.

"Thanks."

The leather chair creaked as he sat behind the desk and rifled through neat stacks of paperwork. Abby and Regan exchanged mutual glances before parking in the two oversized, upholstered chairs angled at the two front corners of the desk.

"Oh, sorry," he muttered. "Have a seat. Can I get you something?" He shook his head as though wiping a slate clean. "I should have asked."

"No. We're fine," Regan replied.

When he seemed to find what he'd been searching for, Baz let out a sigh of sheer exasperation. "It's been one of those days."

Regan gave what she assessed as an awkward nod, willing herself not to stare at the man on the other side of the desk; but she couldn't manage to comply. His shaggy blond hair shimmered under the scrutiny of the afternoon sun, and his biceps pushed against the restraint of the long-sleeved knit shirt.

He is really ... beautiful, she thought, and Baz stunned her as he looked up at just that instant, folded his arms on the edge of the desk, and leaned on them with a smile.

Had he read her thoughts? Caught her staring at him like a love-starved puppy? Why was she suddenly aware of how long it had been since Craig left?

"Ready to see what I have for you?" he asked her, and Regan simply nodded, unsure if she could find her voice at that precise moment. "I have a couple of options for you." He flipped open a large sketch pad and turned it toward them. "This is the first one, based the most closely on the picture you showed me the other day."

Regan noted that Baz was something of an artist. She'd expected to see a far more technical image, perhaps resembling a blueprint. Instead, he presented her with a pencil sketch of floor-to-ceiling white shelves with clean, straight lips edging each of them. Directly in the middle, right at the floor, sat a square opening where he'd drawn a large blue dog cushion with Steve's name scrolled across the front.

"It looks just like the photograph," she said with a sigh. "It's lovely."

Baz picked up the sketchpad long enough to turn over the page. "Here's another idea I thought you might like." He stood the pad on its end, using his hand behind it like an easel for a better vantage point. Running his index finger down the side, he said, "This isn't too much different, but because of the great light you have in the loft, I thought we could close in a row of cabinets on either side of Steve's roost with beveled glass doors to catch the sun. It's a little more expensive, but not by more than a few hundred dollars."

"Oh, Regan," Abby breathed. "That would look so great in your office."

"It really would," she agreed. "But could we have the doors on the top row of shelves instead of the bottom?"

"Easy enough," he said with a nod. "Sure."

"I have this collection of teacups that belonged to my grandmother, and I have nowhere to display them. Right now, they're in a box in the garage collecting dust. But it would be nice to have a place for them, and I'd love to have them behind glass this way."

"Sure."

"Will there still be enough shelving to put away all your books?" Abby asked. Turning to Baz, she grinned. "Regan loves her books."

"So I gathered," he replied. "I saw the stacks." Turning to Regan, he said, "You want the finish painted white? Because I was thinking we could go with a fully-grained wood and just whitewash it so the grain shows through."

"Ooh, yes," Abby exclaimed. "That's what she wants."

Regan chuckled. "What she said."

"Whitewashed it is then."

"When can you get started?" she asked.

"How about next weekend?"

"Saturday?"

"Nine o'clock okay?"

She winced, not sure about getting contacts in her eyes at the crack of dawn. "How about ten?"

One corner of his mouth twitched slightly before he nodded. "I'll see you at ten."

Chapter 9

Lynette raked Margaret's bright orange mop of curls with all ten fingers, smoothing them toward the back of the nine-year-old's head.

She squirmed in the kitchen chair and asked, "Are you gonna make a pony again?"

"I thought I might."

"Make it a high one, k? Chester Keaton pulls my hair if the pony or the piggies are too low."

"Have you mentioned this to your teacher?" Lynette asked as she reworked the child's hair toward the top of her head and secured it there with a shiny sequined band.

"I'm no rat fink," Margaret bellowed. "Besides, I don't mind it all that much."

Oh, the justifications are starting early with this one.

"It's nice and high," she told her. "Now go put on your shoes."

Margaret scampered from the chair and bounced down the hall. "Hi, Daddy," she sang in mid-stride.

"Good morning, Sweet Pea."

Lynette turned toward her husband as he strode into the kitchen, and she stopped in her tracks when she saw him.

"Don't you look dapper this morning," she exclaimed appreciatively.

A lock of Trevor's dark, nearly black hair brushed his forehead, resting just above remarkable steel-blue eyes. He'd chosen to top his favorite black jeans with a black sport coat and charcoal tie; the knot hung loose around the collar of the matching dress shirt.

"What's on deck for your day?" he asked, and he brushed her arm with his fingertips as he passed.

"I've got the morning off for conferences with the teachers of four of our five children," she replied. "This afternoon, I'm training two new nurses on the joys of our computer system."

"Two more new nurses," he commented, brewing a cup of coffee. "The practice is certainly growing."

"Indeed it is."

The three oncologists who employed her to keep their professional worlds running smoothly had gained a stellar reputation in the San Diego community. Dr. Jarvis, in particular, had recently been gearing a good bit of time toward educating herself, her two partners in the practice, and even the eleven nurses and office workers in their employ on the most current and cutting-edge advancements in cancer research. Although Dr. Jarvis's specialty remained gynecological in nature, she'd attended a conference on breast cancer treatment in Dr. Beal's stead so that the information could be brought back to the group.

Lynette's early nursing training had served her well in her position of office manager for the three oncologists. And when she'd finally figured out that nursing wasn't her primary strength—but organization and office administration were—a casual meeting with Dr. Eleanor Jarvis while standing in line at Starbucks had been serendipitous … and had changed the entire course of her life. Twelve years later, she couldn't imagine a more fulfilling or satisfying job.

"Felicity, Clayton," she called out loudly as Trevor placed a warm cup of coffee into her hand. "Shaaron, Jamal. All hands on deck, if you please."

"Jamal won't get out of the bathroom," her drama queen exclaimed from the top of the stairs.

"Then use the other bathroom," she hollered.

"*Everything* I *need* is in *this* one."

Lynette turned toward Trevor, and he shot her a kind smile.

"And everything *I* need is in another one; far, far away," she said softly. "Preferably on a desert island. Overlooking a pool. With no phone or Wi-Fi."

Trevor chuckled and brushed her neck with a kiss. "Are you saying you need a vacation, Mrs. Parker?"

"That depends. Are we talking a private getaway, just the two of us? Or a family trip?"

"Just you and me."

"Then, yes. That's what I'm saying."

"Let's give that some attention and see what we can figure out, shall we?" The British accent and the way he strung his words together caused her to grin while a deep warmth settled on her.

"Have I told you lately?" she asked him.

"Why, yes, you have. But tell me again."

She pressed against him and rubbed his cheek with her own. "I love you," she whispered.

"*Mo-om.*" Shaaron broke through the momentary reverie with a shriek.

"What is it, my darling?" she called, her eyes still closed and her husband's face touching hers.

"Will you tell Jamal he *has* to get out of the bathroom?"

She sighed. Before she had a new breath on which to reply, Trevor's cell phone rang. He pecked her jaw with a kiss. "I'll take care of it." On his way out of the kitchen, he checked the screen of his phone. "It's the university," he told her before answering. "Hello?"

She eyed his muscular frame as he left the kitchen, appreciated the way his well-defined scapula strained against the shoulder blade area of his jacket. When they'd first met, the hair at the nape of his neck whisked his collar. Now, he wore it trimmed short, and she preferred it that way. Even as he walked away, Trevor Parker set her heart to pounding.

Lynette gulped down the last of her coffee on her way to the sink. After rinsing the mug with a quick splash of water, she set it into the last available spot on the top rack of the dishwasher. She grabbed the package of detergent pods from under the sink, dropped one in the dispenser, and locked the door. One flick of the dial, a push of another button, and the dishwasher kicked into gear to do its job. When she turned away from the sink, she gasped at the sight of Margaret—the spitting image of her mother with her bright orange hair and small, upturned nose—smiling at her from the doorway.

"What are you wearing?" Lynette asked with the shake of her head.

"I don't know. I just felt like a little color today."

"A little?"

The nine-year-old's high ponytail had slipped slightly, and she'd topped a bright yellow flared skirt with a teal t-shirt bearing her mirror image, the character with whom she identified because of her wild orange curls: *Merida* from Disney's animated movie *Brave*. Both forearms remained hidden by a hundred or so bangle bracelets of every color known to mankind, and her mismatched shoes— one pink sneaker and one orange—were both tied with purple glitter laces.

"Are you sure you want to wear every color of the rainbow, all in one ensemble?" Lynette broached.

Margaret's pale, freckled face curled up like a withering melon as she considered the question. After a moment, she nodded confidently. "Yes. This is what I'm wearing."

"Okay then. Come here so I can fix your pony."

Margaret skipped over to the chair where she'd been seated earlier and allowed Lynette to remove the shiny blue scrunchie. She slipped it onto her wrist as she reworked the girl's hair.

"I wish I had hair like yours," Margaret stated through the traces of British accent still left in her, and Lynette grinned.

"Oh? Why's that?"

"Then I could wear it in lots of braids like you do. When I braid mine, it just sticks out every which way, cattywampus. Daddy says that's because of your lovely brown skin. People with brown skin have hair you can braid."

"That's true," she said, wrapping the band around the ponytail at the top of the child's head. "Is that too tight?"

"No. It's good. Thank you."

"You're welcome." Margaret turned on the chair and pushed up to her knees as she faced Lynette. "I'm glad you wanted to be my mother."

"Are you?"

"Yes. Very. Felicity and Clayton are glad too. They just don't have the good sense to show you on account of they're teenagers."

A laugh sneaked out of Lynette like a snicker, and she stroked Margaret's fair-skinned cheek with her thumb. "I love you very much, you know."

"Yes. I know. I'm glad." She grabbed Lynette's hand and brought it up to her face for closer inspection. "I'd like to have a silver ring for my thumb like yours."

Lynette inspected the engraved sterling ring she'd picked up somewhere. She couldn't remember where. "Maybe we should get you one."

"Really? That would be lovely."

"Sunday after church. We'll go—just you and me—in search of the perfect thumb ring for such a tiny thumb."

"Just us?"

"Just us."

"Can we get ice cream?"

"I think ice cream is always a fine idea when combined with a shopping expedition."

Margaret extended her hand toward Lynette and looked her straight in the eyes until Lynette finally shook it.

"It's a deal then." Margaret sealed it with one sharp shake.

"Deal."

"What's a deal?" Shaaron asked from the kitchen doorway.

"We're going to buy me a thumb ring like the one Mama wears. And we're going to have ice cream."

"*What?*" Shaaron exclaimed, indignant. "You're buying her a ring. *Without me?* When?"

"Sunday, after church," Margaret told her.

"Oh, fine," she snapped. "You do that. Have a great time with your *replacement daughter.*"

Lynette groaned as Shaaron flung herself into an about-face and stomped down the hall, passing Trevor as she headed back up the stairs.

When their eyes met, Lynette shot Trevor a lopsided frown.

"Whatever it is, she'll survive," he told her before rubbing Margaret's shoulder. "Go on upstairs, Love, and finish up."

"Daddy, I'm gonna get a thumb ring just like Mama's."

"Won't that be something?" he replied. "Now go on. Upstairs with you."

The instant Margaret scurried from the kitchen, Trevor turned to Lynette with one of those serious, we-have-to-talk expressions she'd seen occasionally during their short time together.

"What is it?"

"You better sit down, Baby. We have to talk."

Uh-oh.

Iris winced as Candace's grip on her hand tightened. "Honey. There are bones in there."

"Sorry."

She sighed with relief when the grip loosened. She gazed at Candace's pretty face and couldn't help thinking how old she suddenly appeared. Hadn't it just been a few months ago when she'd sent her only daughter off to kindergarten in pigtails and a frilly blue dress? Now a junior in college, unmarried with no prospects, and her *baby* had a baby of her own onboard. In the shadow of that very serious revelation, Iris still couldn't help but experience a swoon of giddy wonder at the prospect.

"This will be a little cold," the doctor said as she applied a thick glaze of blue gel to Candace's exposed belly.

Her blue eyes grew wide and moist, locking onto her mother's gaze as she pressed her lips into a thin, terse line.

"Let's just have a look."

The warbling black and gray image on the monitor thrilled Iris to no end. It seemed to fascinate and horrify Candace in equal parts.

"The black bubble you see here," the doctor pointed out, "is the amniotic sac. The slight flicker here—at the bottom of the sac—is the fetus's heartbeat."

Iris squeezed her daughter's hand and suppressed a squeal of joy at the rapid *tap-tap-tap* of her grandchild's pumping heart.

"At about six weeks, your baby is nothing more than a peanut. His or her fetal development is only just beginning to show. Have you given any thought to what you'd like to do about the pregnancy?"

Candace's mouth gaped open into a perfect round little O. Her blue-green eyes darted back to Iris.

"What do you mean?" Iris asked her.

"Candace indicated this pregnancy was unplanned."

Candace pushed out a harsh chuckle on a puff of air. "To say the least."

"And she said the father is not in the picture."

"No. He's not."

"In cases like this, many women will opt to end the pregnancy in the early stages."

"No," Candace and Iris sang in two-part harmony.

"If you have any questions about the process, I can certainly explain what it entails. In this day and age, about one in three women in the United States will have had at least one abortion before she reaches middle age—"

"Doctor," Iris sliced her explanation with a clean, sharp blade. "An abortion is *not* part of the plan."

"Then you have one."

"I'm sorry?" she replied.

"A plan," the doctor clarified.

Candace's sniffling drew Iris's attention, and she noticed that her daughter's face had curled up like an old plum on a windowsill, red and crumpled. Tears squirted out of her clenched eyes, and clear wet snot puddled at the edge of one nostril.

She resisted a strange, defensive urge. "Make no mistake, doctor, this has taken our family completely by surprise," she articulated slowly. "My daughter still has a year and a half to go before she finishes her degree. To be sure, it's going to be a challenge. But we're going to handle it the way we handle every challenge that faces us." She glanced at Candace and smiled. "Head on, and together."

"Mom, I'm so sorry," she whimpered.

"Stop it, Candace," she said, taking her hand between both of her own and shaking it. "There are no apologies and no regrets. This is what we're facing, plain and simple. We'll get through this."

"But ... Daddy ..."

"You let me reason with your father until he comes around. But don't think for one instant he would expect—or even tolerate—the idea of aborting your baby."

"Th-thank y-*ooou*," she howled.

Iris and the doctor exchanged knowing glances, and she figured the doctor must be a mother herself.

"So why don't you tell us what we can expect, Doctor Ruskin," Iris suggested as she dabbed Candace's eyes and nose with a tissue.

"My nurse will give you some literature when you check out about what's ahead in your first trimester," she said, nodding. "But as an overview, I can tell you that the changes to your body will occur very quickly. Hormones will trigger your body to begin preparing to nourish your baby. You'll probably experience morning sickness—"

"And if you're anything like your mother," Iris teased, "it won't be isolated to mornings."

"Quite right," the doctor concurred. "The nausea during the first trimester stems from a rise in estrogen and progesterone. Your sense of smell will be heightened, so aromas like sizzling bacon or your favorite perfume, for instance, might not be so pleasant anymore."

"When I carried you," Iris told her, "I couldn't bear the taste or smell of toothpaste. I'd gag every morning."

"Oh, no ..."

"If it becomes terribly uncomfortable, call my office and we'll try some remedies to help you cope until you can progress into your second trimester. After you review the literature we send home with you, write down your questions if you have any. My nurse will schedule you for some tests, just to screen for any chromosomal abnormalities, and get you started on prenatal vitamins and nutrition. I'll want to see you again in four weeks."

Twenty minutes later, mother and daughter sat across from one another at a charming bistro table, a latte and a mug of hot chocolate between them, along with half a dozen brochures about early pregnancy.

"It says here," Candace said, a blob of whipped cream from her hot chocolate dangling from the tip of her nose, "my peanut's skin is still translucent, and his little brain and spinal cord are visible through it."

Iris reached across the table and wiped the cream from her nose. "You said *his little brain*. You feel like you want to have a boy?"

Candace looked up and her expression froze for an instant. "Oh. I don't know why I said that. I was kind of hoping for a girl, actually."

"Well, we'll know soon enough," she said. "My face grew round as a plate when I was pregnant with you. They say that doesn't happen with a boy. Their tell is a perfectly round basketball stomach."

Candace smiled at Iris and reached for her hand. "I don't know what I'd do if you weren't my mother. With all the trouble I've caused you and Daddy, have you ever wished I'd never been born?"

"Never," she replied in earnest. "Not even once."

"Mom, what am I going to do about school?"

"You're going to finish out this semester," she stated with far more confidence in her voice than in her heart.

"What then?"

"I don't know. But you, your father, and I will figure that out together."

Candace seemed to draw a lot of comfort from her words, and she returned her attention to the hot chocolate and brochures before her.

"Mom, listen to this. The first trimester ends at fourteen weeks, and ..."

Iris didn't hear the rest. She couldn't, over the thundering sound of her own inner voice bouncing about inside her head. It wasn't until a familiar voice—one she knew well, but that didn't fit into the location and moment—broke through that she tumbled back to the moment and skimmed the other occupants of the café in search of the source.

"Thank you. I think I'll just have a chicken walnut salad and a nonfat cappuccino."

"Mom, there's Lynette," Candace voiced just as Iris caught sight of her. "Lynette. *Hi.* Come and sit with us."

She lifted her eyes, and Iris immediately recognized something was off. Lynette touched the waitress on the arm and nodded toward their table before standing slowly and gathering her things.

"Well, this is a surprise," she said as she settled into the chair next to Candace, across from Iris. "What are you two up to this afternoon?"

"I just had my first OB appointment," Candace piped up. A blush of pink rose from her neck as she added, "Did Mom tell you?"

"She did, and you and the little one are in my prayers."

"Thank you." Candace used both hands to rein in the overflow of brochures and paperwork across the tabletop. "There's a lot to learn."

"So what did the doctor say?" Lynette asked, her gaze locked strangely onto Iris. "Everything on track?"

"Looks like," Iris replied.

"We heard the baby's heartbeat," Candace gushed. "It was really ... surreal."

"I remember the feeling."

"Do you want to see the pictures?"

"You have pictures," Lynette stated, and a smile wound its way across her lips.

As Candace rooted through the paperwork, Iris caught Lynette's eye again and mouthed, "Are you okay?"

She lifted one shoulder in half a shrug which said it all.

"Here. It's that little peanut right here."

Lynette considered the sonogram photo for a moment before nodding. "I see the resemblance," she teased. "Quite a beautiful smile."

Candace giggled. "Well, you two talk among yourselves. I'm going to make a pit stop before we go."

Iris didn't know if her daughter actually had to use the restroom or if she simply sensed the two other women at the table needed a few minutes to themselves. In any case, the moment she left them, Iris reached out and touched Lynette's hand.

"What?"

She shook her head emphatically without answering.

"Lynette. I can see something's—"

"I have a sex tape," she blurted, and Iris gasped, her eyes bulging.

"Come again? … Lynette Burris Parker. Are you joking?"

"If only." Her friend's normally radiant dark brown face appeared ashen and serious as she rubbed her forehead and groaned. "Did I mention to you that Trevor received the Chancellor's Faculty Award for Excellence in Undergraduate Teaching?"

"Um," Iris said, regrouping. "That's … wonderful."

Lynette nodded. "It really is. I'm so proud of him."

"And?"

"Oh, right. Well, they had a big to-do at the university. Remember? After we got together to talk about Celia."

"O-kay."

"Well, afterward … we snuck away to a place we like to go sometimes."

"What place?" Iris inquired, trying to imagine.

"See, the top floor of the parking garage is almost always empty when classes aren't in session, and sometimes we park up there and … you know … have a little private time."

Iris bit down on the corner of her lip, trying not to laugh.

"We go there all the time. I never even *imagined* …"

She tried to urge Lynette along. "Someone filmed you?"

"Yes. I mean, no. Not someone. Some*thing*."

Iris considered her words carefully, but … "What does that mean? What some*thing*?"

"It turns out the university has security cameras all over campus."

Iris gasped again, this time covering her gaping mouth with her hand. "No."

"Oh, yeah. A young woman was assaulted in the parking garage last year, so they doubled the coverage by installing more cameras."

Almost afraid to ask. "How did you find out?"

"Trev is friendly with one of the security officers. He called earlier—which is pretty unusual, to call Trevor at home—and he told him he'd left a CD on his desk. Then he said, 'Just so you know, there are a lot of cameras around this place. You might want to have a look at it sooner rather than later.'"

"Oh ... dear."

Lynette chuckled. "I think stronger language is required here, girl."

So Iris gave her what she wanted, and Lynette laughed all the harder.

Welcome to VERTICAL MAGAZINE
Moments-of-Truth.net

BLOG POST: REGAN SLOANE

After my post a couple of days ago, I was so touched by the volume of replies and emails I received from all of you. Sometimes it's easy to forget that another blog post published doesn't add up to words just entering some swirling void somewhere … but it's actually taking my thoughts and observations and opinions out to you, readers.

A message from Miranda from Newark stands out in my mind among so many others that touched my heart, and I thought I'd share it with all of you:

"After reading your blog about your friend Irene learning that her unmarried college student daughter is unexpectedly pregnant, I really felt your pain. So many years of trying everything you could to make a baby of your own with 40-Watt, someone in your life randomly turning up pregnant probably seems like an injustice. I used to think that way too, until I learned from my mother over the summer that I was an unexpected turn of events myself. She told me I'm her own living proof that we just never know what God has in mind, who He'll use, or how He'll do it. I hope you'll take heart, Regan. Even when we don't understand the journey we're on, I've come to believe it's a waste if we spin our wheels trying to change it rather than enjoying the ride."

Wiser words I've rarely read. Going forward, I'm going to make a concentrated effort to try to enjoy the ride more. How about you, readers? Share a cab with me?

Chapter 10

"I have to admit it," Abby said as she inspected the built-ins the crew had constructed in Drew's bedroom. "They're really beautiful."

"You think the boy will like them then," the chief contractor said.

"I do," she said, nodding.

She turned to give him a smile and found Nate standing behind her as well. When he didn't back away, she swerved around him and headed for the doorway.

"Thank you. I'll get my phone and take a few pictures to send over to the Jensens."

The contractor nodded and left them alone together.

"Why do you always do that?" he asked her, and she glanced at him over her shoulder.

"Do what?"

"Run away from me."

Abby absently tried to toss her hair ... before remembering she'd swept it all to one side and fastened it into a ponytail that hung over the slope of her shoulder. She covered by running her fingers through it.

"I am not ... *running away from you*. Sheesh, center of the universe much?"

Nate took several long strides toward her and came to a stop mere inches away. "What are you trying to say, Abigail?" His silky voice took on a far more sensual tone than the words conveyed. "You don't think the world revolves around me?"

"Don't call me Abigail," she said, flinging the words at him like a wadded sheet of paper.

"Sorry. *Abby*."

"And stop it, *Nate*."

"Stop what?" he asked, and it infuriated her.

Twisting her hands like a couple of used rags, she pushed out a sigh. "This whole flirting-but-not-flirting thing you like to do," she blurted. "I'm not into it. Will you get that through your head? Not. Interested."

"Except that you are."

"See!" she exclaimed, taking a leap backward into the hall. "That's what I'm talking about. Why can't you understand? I am not going to date you or sleep with you or whatever else it is you're looking for. So just stop it."

Abby spun around on one heel and stalked down the hall, through the house and out the back door, struggling to regulate her breathing the whole way. Despite her efforts, by the time she reached her Forester, she found herself panting softly. She tugged the door open, and let out a tiny shout as it unexpectedly flew from her hand and slammed shut. It took a moment to process, but Nate had followed her and pushed the door closed before she could climb behind the wheel.

"What do you think you're doing?" she snapped.

"Simmer down, Sparky. I just want to talk to you."

She groaned. "Really? Are you seriously this impaired?"

He grinned, and its embers ignited a flush of heat that raged through her. She fought against slapping the self-serving, smug smile right off his face. That perfect, clean-shaven, silky smooth face.

"Abby," he said, and the sound of him speaking her name set her heartbeat to thumping double-time. "I'm not trying to push you into anything, all right? I'm not interested in making you uncomfortable—"

"All evidence to the contrary," she cut in, and he placed one finger over her lips.

"Would you please just hear me out? Give me two minutes to express myself without interpretation or assumptions?"

She sighed through her nose, nodding beneath the warmth of his determined index finger.

"Thank you." He removed it, and she pursed her lips in an effort to remain silent. "All I want to say is that I don't have any ulterior motives here. No hidden agenda. I'm attracted to you, yes. But all I really want is to take you to dinner. Maybe have a little mutual conversation where we learn a little something about one another and see if what I suspect is true. That we have a lot of common ground. Is that too much to ask?"

His clear-blue eyes bore into her brown ones, making them sting.

"Is it?"

Abby sighed again. "I'm just not interested. I'm sorry."

"Are you committed elsewhere?" he asked. "Have I misread you that badly?"

"Yes," she said. It was only a partial lie. "I'm committed elsewhere."

He narrowed his eyes, concentrating the intensity of his scrutiny. "Really."

"Really."

"There's another man keeping you from the possibility of getting to know me better."

"Yes."

The weight of his engrossment pressed in further before he said, "Name."

"What?"

"His name. What is it?"

She gulped down an air bubble. "You'll laugh."

"I won't laugh."

"You will. Believe me, you will."

"Try me."

"His name is ... *Jesus.*"

And even though she'd predicted it, Abby nearly drowned in her own astonishment when Nate erupted with unabashed laughter.

After a moment's recovery, she yanked her door open and fell into the SUV. She pushed the keys into the ignition and turned over the engine before she even pulled the door shut behind her.

"No, no, no." He reached past her, twisted the keys, and tugged them out before she could stop him. "Wait a minute, wait a minute. I'm sorry. I shouldn't have laughed, but I'm not laughing *at you*—"

"You're laughing *with me,*" she nearly spat.

"Kind of, yeah."

She swiped for the keys, but he was faster and lifted them into the air over the roof of the truck. "Give those to me."

"I only laughed out of ..."

"Amusement," she finished for him. "Oh, the Christian girl, she's so, so funny, right?"

"Not at all," he said.

When he shook his head like that, shining his sweet, crystal blue gaze at her, he looked almost ... sincere.

Still.

Abby saw her opportunity as he relaxed a little and draped his arm over the open door, and she seized it, grabbing her keys out of his hand.

"Step back or I'll drag you alongside," she warned him. "Your choice."

A flicker of disappointment flashed just before he raised both hands in surrender and took two steps away from the SUV, allowing her to start the engine again and peel out of the driveway.

"I need an update, Regan. Let's talk about the book. And have you signed the contract yet?"

Acid churned in Regan's stomach every time her boss reminded her of the book Valencia Publishing wanted her to write. She'd stared at the contract for three days before she finally forwarded it to her divorce attorney who had promised to have one of their contract attorneys look it over.

"Take your time," she'd said, and she meant it. Because once they came back and said there wasn't a thing wrong with the contract, she would have to sign it. And then she'd have to begin actually *writing the book.*

"My attorney is looking it over for me," she told Delores. "I'll check back to see where we stand."

"Good. Now let's talk specifics. Have you decided on your slant?"

"My slant?"

"What do you have in mind?" she clarified, and Regan recognized the flicker of irritation at the base of her words.

"Well," she said with a sigh, leaning back into the corner of her oversized chenille sofa. "I was thinking of using my columns as a sort of blueprint for the story and—"

"And fictionalizing it," she interrupted. "That's where my mind has been going too."

"I've never written anything that's—"

"Fiction, yes. I realize. But you're a very good writer, Regan. I can't imagine why Valencia wouldn't go for it."

"My only concern," Regan interjected, "is an article I read earlier this week about how fiction is—"

"A tougher sell in the marketplace." *How does she DO that?* "I saw that article too. But let's put together a proposal for them, Regan. You send me your thoughts and I'll work on tweaking it so we have something in hand once the contract is finalized. They love the way you've used your friends as the backdrop for your column, and I think this could be a great tie-in."

The sudden roar of power tools from up in the loft sliced the conversation with a clean chop.

"What is that?" she shouted through the phone. "What are you doing?"

"Oh, that's my carpenter," she said with a sly smile. "He's putting in some shelves for me in my office in the loft."

"It's giving me a headache over the phone line. I can't imagine working in that racket."

"I have my next two columns written already," Regan reassured her. "And after he leaves, I'll shoot the next vlog post. Nothing to worry about. Everything's on track."

"Well, go sit in Starbucks if you have to," she replied. "But put together your proposal notes for me by the end of the week."

"I will."

"And follow up with the attorney. We want to get that signed contract to them sooner rather than later."

"Got it."

"This is going to be good for us both, Regan. For you and for Vertical."

Before she could reply, Delores abruptly said good-bye and ended the call. Regan found herself thinking of Judy Garland's *Dorothy Gale* and her observations of Oz.

"My! People come and go so quickly here."

Not that Delores Cogswell could realistically be compared to *Glinda* by any other stretch of the imagination, of course. In fact, with her sharp features—made sharper by benefit of Skype, the only manner in which Regan had ever seen her face-to-face—and pale yellow complexion, she seemed more like *Dorothy's* broomstick-riding, green-faced nemesis than sweet *Glinda*.

Regan dropped the handset to the coffee table before climbing the oak stairs to the loft, Steve shuffle-clomping behind her all the way. When she reached the top, she found Baz leaning over the large red toolbox he'd carried upon arrival a couple of hours prior. When he looked up and caught her staring at him, the corner of his mouth twitched with the hint of a smile.

"Do you mind if I just grab a few things from my desk?" she covered.

"No problem. I'm getting ready to take a break before I haul in the last section."

She crossed the loft and stood in front of the skeletal beginnings of her new built-ins.

"I can almost see the finished product," she commented, and he stepped up next to her and looked on. "They're going to be beautiful, Baz. Just what I had in here." She tapped on her temple with two fingers. "You were so right about the whitewash. It looks really pretty."

"It'll look even better after tomorrow when it's glazed with the protection coat."

"Oh," she remarked, making every attempt at remaining casual. "You'll be back again tomorrow?"

"Is that a problem? If you have something else to do—"

"No. No, no, that'll be fine."

"I thought I'd get the bottom section installed today and get the protective coat on. After it has a couple of days to set, I'll come and put on the glass doors so you can be done with me."

Like she wanted to be done with him?

"I'll even help you start putting your books and teacups where you want them. It will be like they've always been here."

She hadn't noticed she'd been staring a hole through him until he smiled and stepped closer. Before she knew it, he'd lifted a finger toward her face and gently pushed her glasses up the bridge of her nose.

"I could adjust those for you," he said. "So they won't slip so much."

Regan instinctively plucked her glasses off and pushed them into her pocket. "Yeah, they do slip a lot."

Baz held out his hand, open palm facing up as he nodded at it.

"Oh. Okay." She pulled the glasses from her pocket and set them into his hand. "Uh, did you want to have some coffee? Or something cold? You said you were going to take a break."

"Something cold would be great. I'll just get my kit and be down in a minute."

Regan tapped her thigh, and Steve followed obediently as they headed down the stairs. Scrambling around the kitchen, she pulled together a plate of butter cookies and a small bowl of freshly washed cherries. By the time he joined her and sat at the counter to work on her glasses with the tiniest little screwdriver she'd ever seen, she'd poured two tall glasses of lemonade over crushed ice and set one of them in front of him. Instead of taking a drink from the glass, he stood and rounded the counter, stopping just inches away from her. As they stood there, facing each other, Regan felt her mouth go instantly dry.

What the ... What is he doing?

As if answering the question pinging around in her head like a small metal pellet inside a tin can, he lifted her glasses and slowly set them into place on her face.

"How's that?" he asked.

She bobbled her head, side-to-side, and then forward and back. When her glasses didn't slip, she grinned. "Better." She tossed her head again. "Much better, actually."

He adjusted the temples with his thumbs and smiled. "Good."

The room felt suddenly stuffy. Warm and humid. Regan blew upward, and her long bangs crested the puff of air before wafting down into place again. Baz muttered something that she didn't quite hear over the rush of wind in her ears, but it sounded strange ... like ... *Let me. You should.*

She stepped backward with a start. "Let you do ... *What?* What did you say?"

"The lemonade," he said with a nod toward the counter. "It looks good."

"Uh ... oh. Yeah. It's ... let's have some."

"So this is the grandchild, huh?"

Iris chuckled at Dean as he inspected Candace's sonogram photo, now preserved within two sheets of plastic.

"Yep, that's our grand-peanut."

He set the photograph on the dining table and collapsed against the chair back with a rumbly sigh.

"You go through your life feeling pretty good," he said. "A little arrogant maybe, about what a great job you've done raising your kid. She goes off to college and you feel like, okay, we can breathe, the worst is over, and …" He ran his hand through his hair and groaned. "Where did it go off the rails?"

Iris crossed from the kitchen to the dining room and stood behind him. With a sigh, she wrapped her arms around him from behind and kissed the side of his face.

"The job of a parent doesn't end when they leave home. It just changes."

"I guess you're right. But I wish I knew what to do next."

"I've been thinking about that," she said, pausing to press her lips together. She'd wanted to talk to him about an idea that had crept up on her overnight, but she hadn't had time to prepare the most gentle and effective way to suggest the solution. "You know how we used to talk about doing something with the little house behind the garage?"

"The pool house?"

"Yes. What if—while Candace finishes out the semester—we take the money we set aside to redecorate the dining room and guest bath, and we convert the pool house into a little cottage with a nursery where she can live until after she has the baby. She'd have her daddy and mama nearby if she needs us, but not so close that she wouldn't feel like she was still on her own."

Dean took her hand and guided her around to the front of the chair. When he tapped his thigh as an invitation, Iris felt her forehead instinctively move into a curious sort of frown.

"Really?" She hadn't meant to say it out loud, but the two short syllables just sort of slipped out.

"Come here," he said.

She hesitated. It had been a long time since Dean had invited her to sit on his lap. At least … *thirty pounds ago?*

He placed his hands over her hips and urged her toward him until she finally gave in. Still, she used every remnant of core muscle she had left to keep from dropping her full weight to his lap.

"Stop it," he said with a grin.

"Stop what?"

"Stop trying to suck it in and hold it up."

"Please." She snorted. "I'm not doing that."

"You are."

And before she even knew it, all the pretenses dropped from her face to her toes; with it, her full weight pressed down on her husband's legs. Not to mention the poor old chair legs straining beneath them.

"I think it's a good plan about the pool house," he told her.

"You do? She's coming home this weekend, and we can talk to her about it then."

"I'll let you handle the details. But it's a good plan."

As Dean moved his hands smoothly over her waist and hips and down the sides of her thighs, Iris dipped into it and closed her eyes. As she tilted her head back and enjoyed the moment, his lips skittered down the side of her throat.

"Let's go upstairs," he whispered.

Her eyes popped wide open as she perused the beginning of their day, wondering what he might have forgotten up there. Surely, he didn't mean—

"Come on," he said, nudging her upward. "Let's go upstairs."

Iris resisted the urge to take off at a full run before he changed his mind. And out of all the reactions that could have plagued her mind just then, it was Celia's thickly accented voice that clanked through her thoughts.

"Girl," she'd exclaimed over cannoli and wine at that very table just a few weeks prior. "You better start shaving those legs whether you think he's coming for you or not. Men don't need no forewarning and they come at you out of nowhere. You don't want him thinking you're cultivating a darn jungle when he's not around, do you? Because those are some hairy legs you got poking out from the hem of those pants."

Despite the regret spurring beads of perspiration over every square inch of her neglected too-round female body, Iris wasn't about to put a halt to things now in favor of a quick visit with a razor. As she and Dean tumbled to the bed they hadn't shared in such a very long time, Iris threw caution to the wind— and all thoughts of hairy legs and unlotioned arms as well—and gave in to her husband's surprising and glorious advances.

Chapter 11

"You told him *what?*" Regan exclaimed. "You told him the other man in your life—the one who is the reason you can't go out with him—is … *Jesus?*"

Abby wilted into her chair and groaned as the other women at the table dissolved into various levels of amusement. Iris snickered and Celia cackled outright. Lynette clicked her tongue and tossed her long braids over her shoulder, shaking her head.

Regan clucked once, then again, and a stream of others followed. "Oh … Abby," she managed, breathless.

Dropping her face into both hands, Abby whimpered. "I know. Don't you think I know?"

"Did you at least explain to him what you meant?" Iris inquired.

She didn't want to admit it, but finally she raised her eyes and peered at them over her fingers.

"No?" Regan clarified.

"Uh-uh." Abby folded her arms and dropped her head, face down, into them. "I just drove away."

"What?" Iris asked the others. "What did she say?"

"She *yust drofe* away," Celia said.

"Ohhh."

Abby felt Iris looking around at the others bordering her table before she asked them, "That's not good, is it?"

"No," Lynette declared. "It is not."

When Abby finally lifted her head again, Celia was the first to catch her eye.

"*Yust* to recap," Celia said, "Lynette has shown the *geefts* God gave her to the maintenance staff at the college."

"The security guard," Lynette corrected.

"Eh," Celia said with a shrug. "I have been eaten alive with suspicion and drive my husband away—"

"What else is new?" Lynette said with a dry smile.

"*Si.* And Regan, the worst thing she can come up with is that she's finding herself *attrocted* to Sebastian, of all *peoples*, and let's face it—a woman could do much worse than him, no?" Celia's dark eyes followed her thoughts toward the ceiling for a moment before she continued. "Iris, she has a pregnant daughter moving in, but then she's finally been laid after *enorme* dry spell, so we can't really feel too sorry for her."

Their mutual glances intersected and crossed one another, but no one replied.

"But Abby, she has turned down a flesh and blood, *magnífico* man and she use Jesus as her *ree-sun*."

Without a moment's hesitation, Celia slid the plate of oversized cinnamon rolls at the center of the table toward Abby. "I think you *haff* earned the first dessert tonight, *chica*."

The others nodded in agreement and Abby unapologetically lifted one of the gooey, icing-laden delectables from the large platter and dropped it to the small matching plate before her.

Licking her fingers, she smiled at them and lifted one shoulder in a shrug.

"Who wants what to drink?" Iris asked. "I have wine, mineral water, and coffee."

Once the orders had been placed, Regan stood and hurried into the kitchen to lend a hand in filling them. "So what are the plans for Candace?" she asked Iris. "She'll just move back into her bedroom?"

"No," Iris replied, and a long pause followed. "No. She's going to move into the pool house, actually."

"You have a pool house?" Celia exclaimed.

"Well, it's really nothing more than a structure next to the pool," Iris said with a chuckle. "But we're going to cease fire on the dining room remodel and put it toward giving Candace and the baby their own space. Which brings me to …"

When her words trailed away, followed by silence, Abby glanced up from her cinnamon roll and caught Iris' expectant gaze. "Sorry. What?"

Iris smiled. "I was hoping you might know a designer with a kind heart who works cheap for her friends."

"Ah." She chuckled and licked the last of the icing from her finger as she nodded. "I see. What kind of timeline would this sucker designer have to do the job?"

Iris cringed comically. "By the end of the semester? … In a few weeks."

The others laughed, and Abby slapped a faux frown across her face. "Weeks?"

"I know. I'm sorry. We only just decided it's the best option for everyone to have their own designated areas."

"Especially since Iris and Dean are doing the mambo again," Celia teased.

Iris smiled slyly. "Well, there is that. But it's also important for Candace to feel like she's able to handle things on her own without us looking over her shoulder every minute—"

"Even though mama and papa are *steel* paying," Celia clarified.

"—and yet if she needs us, we'll be just across the patio."

Abby stood and carried her gooey plate to the sink. When she turned around, she touched Iris on the arm. "Why don't we let the others finish making dinner, and you and I go for a walk across your backyard?"

"Thank you." Iris started the microwave before turning to Regan and tapping the outside of the oven door. "The asparagus is steaming, and the chicken and potatoes can come out of the oven to rest. There are biscuits on the sheet under the hand towel on the counter. They can go into the oven for about twelve minutes."

"Chicken out, biscuits in," Regan said with a nod. "Is it just me, or does everyone else feel like dinner with Iris is the only actual nutrition you get all week?"

"Oh, it's not just you, girl," Lynette chimed in. "I'll set the table. Celia, you clear."

"I eat okay," Celia said. "But I like when somebody else cooks the meal."

While the three of them set things into motion, Abby followed Iris through the back door and to the cobblestone path that curved around the patio and the pool. Tucked into the corner of the property behind the garage sat a small white cottage in need of some serious tender loving care.

Iris pushed open the dark teal front door, and Abby noticed the chipped paint and loose knocker as she followed. Inside, the place looked more like a storage unit than a cottage; however, part of Abby knew that her character as a designer came with an innate ability to see past furnishings and boxes to the true potential of a space. In this case, she knew it might take a little extra effort, but the pool house had … hope.

"There's a small kitchen around the corner," Iris said, and she waved her arm for Abby to follow. "I think there's enough room there to make it into an eat-in, don't you?"

"Sure," Abby said, looking around. "Maybe build a bankhead into the corner."

"And there's a small room through here that could make a bedroom for her."

Abby followed, her gaze drifting back to the living area as she did. Crossing through the doorway to the stark, empty bedroom area, she scanned the space and landed on a good-sized nook that would convert to make a wonderful walk-in closet.

"There's a fairly big bathroom, all things considered," Iris told her. "It has a tub *and* a shower. Maybe the small nook there that could be converted to a nursery area."

Abby chuckled. "I was thinking about all of Candace's shoes. But I guess an area for a crib and a changing table would probably be a much better idea than the closet I had in mind."

Iris rubbed Abby's arm briskly and smiled. "You have an excuse. You haven't started a family yet."

"No, but I have a lot of shoes."

They shared a laugh as Abby took a slow walk around the perimeter of the room and headed into the bathroom. No joke about the size of the bathroom, either. This little cottage had a bathroom bigger than the one in her apartment.

"Depending on what you have to spend," she said as Iris stepped up behind her, "we could put a pretty good closet on the left side of the entrance to the bathroom."

Iris hesitated for a moment. "Well, she has to have a closet. Can you draw up some plans and give me an idea of what you'd charge us? I mean ... do you think this place will work for Candace and the baby?"

"There's some promise lurking here, absolutely," she said, nodding.

"Will we have to take out a second mortgage?"

Abby grinned. "I'll come by tomorrow and take some measurements and make some notes, and I'll put together some preliminary plans over the weekend. Okay?"

"Thank you," Iris said, and she squeezed her arm.

"I'll keep the cost of expenses as low as I can, and my own fees are on the house."

Iris gasped. "Abby. No."

"It's my gift," she interrupted. "For Candace and the baby."

When she faced Iris, she noticed that her eyes had turned glassy with tears. Moving forward, Abby slipped her arms around her shoulders and pulled her into an embrace.

"Thank you so much," she muttered into Abby's neck.

"Besides, you can think of it as partial repayment for all the amazing meals you've made for me," she said with a giggle.

"You're such a good friend."

"And you," she answered, "are a wonderful mother. I hope you know that."

Iris pulled back to look Abby straight in the eyes. "Oh. I know," she stated.

Abby giggled, and the two of them locked arms and headed back toward the house to join the others for dinner.

Latina was humming, even for a Friday night, and Celia's falling arches had been throbbing since eight o'clock. Just about the time she'd started to look forward to the task of closing down the kitchen for the night, the door burst open. Stella, the willowy hostess, stepped in like the manifestation of a designer breeze.

"The couple at Table Twelve would like to meet the chef," she announced. "They both had the *Asado Huilense*, and I'm fairly certain they're going to ask you for the recipe."

"Not going to happen," Maribel said from behind Celia without looking up from the pan she scrubbed in the large sink.

"I guessed. But I thought I'd give you the warning."

Stella's thin, sky-scraping heels hardly made a sound on the tile floor as she left the kitchen. By the time the swinging door whooshed to a close behind her, Maribel had grabbed a stiff, clean apron from the pantry shelf, handed it to Celia, and helped her tie it into place before she pushed the door open again.

Table Twelve's occupants looked in her direction expectantly as she approached, and Celia broke into a broad smile when she recognized them. *Mary and Gary Somebody.* Gary worked with Kevin at the ad agency.

"Gary, how are you?" she said when she'd almost reached the table.

He stood and touched her elbow as he gave her a peck on the cheek.

"You remember my wife, Maryann."

Maryann. Mary. I was close.

"Hello, *Maryonn.* How are you both?"

"Better after having tasted your asado huilense," she said with a shiny white smile.

"Ah, you like it. I'm glad to hear it. It's my *abuela* Inez's recipe."

Maryann looked to her husband. "*Abuela?*"

"Oh, so sorry. *Myyyy* ... grandmother."

"Of course. Well, it's exquisite. I've never tasted anything like it."

"Have you all had dessert yet?"

"Oh, no. I couldn't."

"Of course you could," Celia teased. "I'll send over some *enyucado* for you to share, *sí?*"

Gary folded to his chair again as he asked, "What's *enyucado?*"

"Another of my *abuela's* recipes," she told them. "You'll love it. A cake made from shredded yucca, a little cheese and coconut, some star anise seeds and butter, sugar. Very sweet and delicious."

"That sounds fantastic," Gary said for them both.

"And some café," she said. "I'll have it sent right over."

"Thank you, Celia. That's very generous." Gary wiped the corner of his mouth with his napkin before asking, "Tell me, how's Kevin feeling?"

"*Keffin*? He is good. Why do you ask?"

"He couldn't make the photo shoot the other night because of his flu. I've never known him to postpone a shoot, so I figure it must have been pretty bad."

Celia's heartbeat increased steadily in a matter of seconds, from a soft rhythm to a thunderous drum. Recovering, she nodded. "Oh, he's feeling much better. I'll tell him you asked about him."

She numbly excused herself and made her way back toward the kitchen.

"They wanted the recipe, right?" Maribel asked as Celia stumbled to the stool in the corner. "Celia? Are you okay?"

"No," she stated frankly.

"Can I get you something?"

"A gun," she replied. "But first send an *enyucado* and two cafés to Table Twelve. Then get me the gun."

"You're not going to shoot customers, are you? Because I *really* need this job."

Celia inhaled as deeply as she could stand and held her breath for as long as it would stay in her throbbing lungs. When she finally exhaled, she felt like its power propelled her to her feet.

"You close up the kitchen, yeh?"

"Sure."

"I'm going."

"Uh, okay. See you tomorrow."

She'd meant to say something halfway friendly on her way out the back door. Instead, she sort of grunted, tore off her apron, and tossed it at the open hamper.

Celia wasn't entirely sure she'd taken more than three breaths all the way home, but she suddenly found herself hyperventilating as she pushed open the door between the garage and the kitchen.

"Hi, Baby." Kevin greeted her without looking up from his laptop at the kitchen counter. "How'd it go tonight?"

"Busy."

"Friday night, my wife in their kitchen," he said with a shrug. "*Latina's* the place to be."

She hung her purse on the hook by the door. "It sure is."

"How'd the—"

"Where were you Wednesday night?" she blurted.

Kevin looked up from his work and removed his glasses. "Wednesday? I told you. I was working."

"Where, exactly?"

He leaned against the wrought iron back of the counter stool and grimaced. "What's this all about, Celia?"

"You know who came into the restaurant tonight, *Keffin*? Gary Something, from your agency."

"Gary Sheldon?"

"Yes. With his chunky wife Mary."

"Maryann."

"Stop correcting me like I'm a handicap," she shouted.

"A what?"

"He said you called in sick with the flu on Wednesday night and never even went to the video shoot. Where were you, *Keffin*? Because you weren't here with no stinking flu."

"Not this again," he enunciated.

"*Si.* This again. Where were you?"

Kevin closed the screen on his laptop and slid away from the stool before stomping across the room and grabbing his jacket from the arm of the couch.

"Are you going to answer me?" she exclaimed.

"No, Celia. I'm not going to answer you."

"Why not?"

"Because I'm tired of answering you. Again and again and again. Answering you is getting really old, and I'm not going to do it anymore."

"*Keffin*, just tell me where you were."

He stood there staring at her for an eternity before he said, "I got one of the other guys to cover for me on the agency job. Doug called when his videographer bailed at the last minute. They had the location prepped and the actors already arriving. You know I wanted a chance to prove to Doug what I can do, and he got me in as DP on a thirty-second spot for the city. A DP is the Director of Photography on a commer—"

"I know what a DP is, *Keffin*," she snapped.

"Well, I jumped at it," he said. "You know how long I've wanted to show Doug what I can do. I really think this could lead to something, Celia. It should come as no surprise to you that I would be all over a chance like this one."

Wait a minute. Wait. Just ... Let me think—

"Why would you do that and not tell me about it?"

"You were working, Celia. Do I need to call and ask for permission before

I make any changes to my schedule now? Check in with you every hour on the hour so you know exactly where I am and who I'm with?"

"No, I just ..." Her words trailed away, and she couldn't seem to get a deep enough breath to fuel them again.

"You have got to get yourself together, Celia," he said. "I am not going to live like this the rest of my life."

And with that he left, slamming the door so sharply she jumped.

Regan's enviable morning commute took her from the bedroom to the kitchen, the kitchen to the loft, her fanny to the desk chair. Her daily routine amounted to a short checklist of preparations for the day ahead:

Wash face and swipe with tinted moisturizer;
Floss, brush teeth, and swish around some mouthwash;
Dab lips with balm, elbows and hands with lotion, glasses with cleaner;
Push glasses into place for purposes of seeing;
Comb hair and secure with scrunchie/band/clips;
Find a loose top, clean yoga pants, and fresh socks.

The car didn't have to be gassed and she hadn't tuned in to a traffic report in two years. Still, on this particular morning, she set the alarm for an hour earlier than usual ... filled her travel coffee mug ... twisted her hair into a scrunchie ... and sank into a steamy lavender bath for a nice, long soak.

After about twenty minutes, she opened her eyes and lifted her toes just above the crest of the water to inspect last night's pedicure. She wiggled Flirty Coral enamel toes and sighed. She closed her eyes again and lowered into the bath water until it caressed the slope of her shoulders.

Regan hadn't spent so much time getting ready for a day at home in ... well ... Okay. She'd never spent so much time getting ready for a day at home. Period. It wasn't lost on her that Baz's expected arrival might play a significant role in the extra time and care, but she decided not to dwell on that fact and chalk it up instead to simple courtesy. Didn't everyone make themselves more presentable than usual when someone—anyone, really—planned to stop by?

Baz was set to perform one last task. Today, he would install the glass doors on the shelving unit. But after that ...

Will I ever see him again?

That now-familiar jolt of electricity shot through her ... the one elicited by the mere thought of Sebastian Jordan. She'd spent an inordinate amount of time over the previous week wondering what his messy blond mop of hair would feel like between her fingers, if his lips were really as soft as they looked, and how strong his arms would feel wrapped around her. Each time, though, she sliced the thoughts cleanly with the recollection of Craig's departure; she tied up the two chunks with imaginary burlap sacks made of logic and reasoning—*It's been a long time since I've been held or kissed or even close to a man. This is just my body responding to the closeness, the obvious attraction. It doesn't mean anything*—and then she buried the imaginings with thick shovelfuls of dirt. And reality.

That is, at least until they dug their way out again like an undead zombie from a horror movie she'd seen as a teen. The one where the corpse in the backyard clawed its way through the earth and took revenge on everyone in its far-reaching path.

An hour later, Regan—in full make-up, hair straightened and flowing, wearing contacts instead of glasses, jeans instead of stretchy pants, and actual shoes instead of fluffy socks—responded to the knock at the front door and grinned at Baz who stood on the outside of it.

"Good morning," she said, beaming. And she knew she was beaming because she'd rehearsed it in the mirror before he arrived.

"Morning," he said. And she thought she noted a flash of appreciation for the way she looked in that split second before he removed his sunglasses and passed her at full stride.

"Would you like some coffee?"

He tucked the glasses into the pocket of his denim jacket as he turned and lifted the Starbucks cup in his hand. "Got some, thanks."

"Oh." So much for the bold roast she'd picked up in hopes that he'd want some. "Okay then."

"I'll just get started upstairs."

As she watched Baz climb the stairs to the loft, Regan felt a little like an over-inflated balloon with a miniscule pinprick that slowly expelled her excited anticipation of his arrival. By the time she heard him working, the last bit of her enthusiasm went reeling around the room until it smacked into the wall and fell to the floor. Empty.

She thumped down the hallway and into her bedroom, grabbed a scrunchie from a basket she kept on her dresser, and tied her hair into a messy knot at the top of her head. She stepped into the bathroom long enough to remove her contact lenses and dip them into their saline encasements, kicked off her shoes at the doorway, and grabbed her glasses from the nightstand on the way out.

After she headed up the oak stairs, she paused at the top, standing back to watch Baz set the glass doors into place with a battery-operated screwdriver. When he sensed her presence and glanced at her, his blue eyes flashed with surprise.

"I'm just going to grab my laptop," she said on her way to the desk. "I'll be working downstairs if you need me." She gulped. "Anything. If you need anything."

"If you stick around a couple of minutes," he said, interrupting her mission, "I can help you place your books and those teacups you mentioned."

"Oh, you're almost finished then."

"Just about," he replied without looking away from his work.

Regan dropped into the desk chair and clutched the arms, digging her fingernails into the grooves.

"It looks really nice," she told his back. "You did a great job."

"Thanks."

When he finally turned around, he didn't even glance her way. He just set about packing up his toolbox, leaving Regan feeling strangely like a dangling cord with no power source in sight.

"Do you want the books sorted on the shelves, like by theme?" he asked when he straightened. "Or alphabetized?"

She blinked as she thought about his question. Pushing her glasses up the bridge of her nose, she shrugged one shoulder. "I hadn't thought about that. I guess by theme would be good." She stood and joined him in front of the largest pile of books leaning against the wall beneath the window. "I have more fiction than anything else, so let's put those in the center section. Then maybe … I guess, biographies on this side and self-help on the other?"

"Here's a cookbook," he commented as he picked up a large selection. "Where does that go?"

"The Smithsonian?" Regan clucked out a sharp chuckle. "My friend Lynette gave that to me for my birthday a few years ago. I don't think I've ever cracked it open."

"Not much of a cook?"

She hesitated before admitting, "Not so much."

He inspected each book before loading it onto the proper shelf and, after a few seconds, he commented, "Well, you have a really nice kitchen for someone who doesn't use it."

"That's why it's so nice. It gets no use," she said with a giggle. "Craig was the cook out of the two of us. He spent a fortune on the appliances, and two months after he left I started using the oven to store my sweaters."

He turned toward her and quirked a brow. "You're joking. So you eat takeout every night?"

"Not *every* night. Sometimes I hike down to the farmers' market and buy fresh things for a salad or a stir-fry, or some eggs for scrambling."

His expression stopped her for a moment.

"Have you ever been?" she went on. "North Park's farmers' market is world-famous."

"You don't say."

"But ... well, yeah. I do eat a lot of takeout."

"Salads, stir-fry, scrambled eggs, and takeout."

"I don't think I've used my oven twice since he left," she admitted.

"How do you—" He cut himself off with a chuckle. Changing gears: "So if I went downstairs right now and opened your oven, I'd find sweaters inside."

"Folded nice and neat on both racks."

"Do you have a closet?"

"Sure. And it's a good size too. But there are no shelves big enough for my bulkier clothes."

He smiled and went back to the job of sorting her books.

"I know a good carpenter who could help you with that," he remarked a moment later, and Regan's heart lurched slightly, as if it had been charged with an electrical current. "And if you play your cards right, he might make you an actual meal that doesn't come wrapped in paper or in a foam box."

"Ohhh," she replied, mock-serious as if truly considering the ramifications. "Like what Iris makes on Thursdays. Right here in my own home, you say. That would be ... an adventure."

"What do you say," he suggested as he placed the last of the books on the shelf. "Let's roll out the adventure tomorrow night."

"Sure. That'll give me time to move my sweaters."

"Please."

Chapter 12

Abby had completely forgotten about her monthly commitment to join her singles group in stocking the food pantry at her church. The nine o'clock meeting time felt especially stark after a very late night of leaning over the drafting table in her home office sketching some ideas to share with Iris about her pool house makeover. Inspiration had slipped into her semi-conscious brain after Jimmy Fallon had bidden her goodnight and closed out another episode of The Tonight Show. The morning alarm had sounded minutes after her head had finally dropped to the pillow; at least it had seemed like only a few minutes.

"I'm so sorry I'm late," she said by way of greeting as she hustled into the vestibule to the pantry, taking note as she dropped her jacket and bag that only two others of their six-member team had apparently shown up. "Where is everybody?"

"Jamison had to work," Becky announced from atop the stepping stool while turning cans of vegetables label-out on the highest shelf. "McGee and Miller are on loan to the cleaning crew in The Kid Zone."

Abby scanned the dozens of plastic bags scattered around the floor in piles, all of them emblazoned with the logo of their very successful semi-annual food drive. "How are we going to get all of this organized?"

"The cavalry is on its way," George stated from his spot on the floor, fenced in by a circle of boxed potatoes, rice, and pasta. "The earthquake last month did some structural damage over at Cornerstone Grace, so they're going to send people to us while the repairs are underway. Their church van is on its way now with pantry staples and the contents of their clothes closet, and they'll stick around to help us unload and organize."

"Outstanding," Abby exclaimed. "Where should I start until they get here?"

"Gift cards?" Becky asked George, and he nodded. "In that shoebox on the counter. We got close to a hundred gift card donations. If you can get them filed with the others, that would really help. Do you know the system?"

Abby grinned. She should know the gift card filing system since she was the one who set it up. With a nod, she simply replied, "Yep," and climbed on the stool behind the counter to sort the cards by redemption amount.

Ralph's cards abounded, as did Food4Less and Albertsons. They didn't see

Walmart cards very often, but there were several of those as well.

"This last food drive was ridiculous," she said with a grin. "We'll easily feed people who come on Thursday nights, and then some."

"Love it when a plan comes together," George commented.

Abby had filed the last of the cards—those with $100 value—when a ruckus from the church lobby announced the arrival of their visitors and temporary benefactors.

"That must be them," Becky said. "Abby, can you greet them while I finish up the last two bags?"

She hopped off the stool and yanked on the waistband of her old jeans. "Sure."

Abby pulled the scrunchie from her pocket on the way toward the wall of glass doors at the front of the lobby and twisted her hair upward into a haphazard knot, tucking the ends beneath the band.

"You must be our friends from Cornerstone," she surmised as a middle-aged man with a well-worn cardboard box in his arms shot her a grin.

"We are indeed," he said. "I'm Vince, and the woman following behind me covered in plastic bags would be my wife, Jean."

"Good to meet you. I'm Abby."

"Where would you like the clothes portion of our program, Abby?"

"Straight down the wide hallway to the left. The boutique is at the very end."

"The boutique," Vince repeated as he headed in that direction. "I like that." Over his shoulder, he called out to his wife as she pushed through the front door and groaned. "Jean, meet Abby."

"Hi, Abby."

"Hi. Is that food or clothing?"

"Food."

"Down the hall, first room on the right."

"Got it. The guys on their way in are Bill and Nate. They're food too."

Nate.

She hardly had time to yank the scrunchie and give her hair a fluff when she spotted him.

"Abby? This is a surprise."

"Isn't it, though," she stated. With a tiny gulp, she diverted her attention to the other end of the box he carried. "You must be Bill. I'm Abby, and the food donations are down the hallway, first room on the right."

"Got it. Nice to meet you, Abby."

"You too."

As he passed her, Nate's very-blue gaze remained locked to her average-brown one like a magnet latched on to a metal bar.

Taking a moment to regain her composure, Abby pushed the scrunchie into her pocket again and gave her hair a more thorough rake with the fingers of both hands. She tried to catch her reflection in the glass doors, but daylight prevented a good look. One last toss of her hair and a deep inhale of fresh oxygen, and she felt as ready as she might ever be. As she reached the pantry, however, Nate stood there, his arms raised to casually lean against both sides of the jamb so that he filled the entire doorway—smiling one of those annoying smiles of his—and knocking the wind right out of her.

"Excuse me," she said, but he made no move to let her pass.

"Interesting coincidence, don't you think?" he muttered.

"More like ... *odd.*"

"You say tomato," he said with a shrug.

He always thinks he's soooo charming.

"Can I get in there, please?" she asked.

"Of course. In just a minute."

"Nate—"

"I just wanted to say something to you." He dropped his arms to his side and glanced at his shoes, the first glimmer she'd ever seen of him losing a bit of his swagger. "The other day. You remember when you said what you did? And I laughed?"

"Yes," she stated. "I remember."

"Well, I wasn't laughing at you, Abby. I was laughing because it was ..."

She waited, but his words trailed away from him and didn't show signs of circling back. "Because it was funny?" she helped him along.

"No," he answered, shaking his head. Then, more sternly, he repeated, "No. It wasn't funny." Waving his arm with a flourish, he said, "This. I mean, now I get it. But then I just thought it was quite a ..."

"Joke?"

"*Coincidence.*"

"Oh? You're dating Jesus too?" she quipped.

He surprised her when he replied, "Well. Sort of, right?"

His eyes turned into deep blue glitter as he grinned at her, and she almost couldn't help herself as she returned the smile.

"I guess so. Yes."

"Look," he said softly, leaning closer. "I don't meet a lot of women of faith out there in the marketplace. You took me by surprise. But does being a believer mean you *can't date at all?*"

Abby swallowed around the large lump in her throat as he continued.

"After all, if believers don't date, they don't marry. And if they don't marry, they don't have kids. No kids and … in one generation, there goes the church!"

When the snickers caught her attention, Abby glanced past him to find they had quite a wide audience looking on—but pretending not to. "This isn't exactly the best place for this conversation, is it?"

"No. You're right."

She sighed in relief, but its reach only extended about two seconds out.

"Abby's going to help me fetch the last few bags from the van," he announced over his shoulder. "Okay. Be right back."

And without a moment's hesitation, he grabbed her arm and led her down the hall, across the lobby, and through the glass doors.

When they reached the church van parked in the loading zone out front, Nate released his soft grip on her arm and moved his hand to her shoulder. She looked up at him, meaning to say something—she wasn't sure what exactly—but she got caught in the crosshairs of his blue eyes again and fell uncharacteristically silent instead.

"Abby. Just have dinner with me," he said. "We'll have a whole table between us, and all we'll do is exchange some dialogue, get to know each other a little better. If you do that, and there's no interest or spark or anything, then I'll leave it alone."

"Why can't you leave it alone without that?" she asked him. "Just because I'm asking you to."

"Because now I think I get it. I think you're asking me to leave you alone because you think there isn't a man out there that you could be attracted to, but who will understand your desire to remain pure. Isn't that right?"

A flush of heat washed over her face and neck, and she diverted her eyes. Softly, she admitted, "I'm not *pure*, Nate."

"No?"

"Well." She lifted her eyes to meet his again. "I am now. But I haven't always been."

Nate blocked her words with one finger to her lips. "Abby."

"Hmm?" she hummed into his finger.

"We haven't even had our first date yet. There's no need to explain anything so personal to me. But I want you to know … I get it."

"Yeh?" she asked his finger.

"Yes. I don't want anything more from you than a chance for us to get to know each other. Can you do that?"

She nodded, smearing her lip gloss on his finger as she did. He removed it, inspecting it for a long moment before he smiled. "Not my color," he cracked, then he wiped it on the pocket of his jeans.

"Good then. After we finish up here, you'll give me your phone number and address. I'll call you tomorrow and we'll set some plans in stone. You'll dress up in something nice, and I'll shave and shower and do the same. Then I'll pick you up and we'll have a date. Any questions?"

She shook her head. "Uh-uh."

"Good. Now let's grab these bags of food and get to work."

Iris stood back, flipping through Abby's sketch book page by page, while Abby zipped her trusty measuring tape from one wall to another and back again. One of the pages in particular caught her eye, and she ran her finger across the swatch of light brown chenille marked with a handwritten title: Café au lait.

"Oh, I love this fabric," she said, holding it up to Abby. "What did you have in mind for this?"

"A sectional sofa for that corner," she said, pointing at the living room. "It has a beautiful rocker-recliner built into one side of it that would be perfect for her and the baby."

"That sounds lovely. And Candace loves blues. Can we work in some blues?"

"Turn the page," she replied with a grin.

On the next page, Iris found suggested paint colors stapled to the heavy paper. The one marked Living Area was a cool slate blue.

"How did you know?"

"She mentioned it once," Abby remarked without looking up from the spiral notebook where she recorded her measurements. "I remembered."

Iris propped her elbows on the tall kitchen counter and watched her young friend. The sunlight snaking through the window blinds ignited her knotted nest of red hair with flames of orange-gold, making her fair skin all the fairer.

It had been a lot of years since Iris had the figure for jeans like those Abby wore, but when she caught sight of the frayed, torn knees that had come back into fashion, she wasn't all that sorry. Even though she'd been considered young enough when the trend came around the first time, she'd never felt compelled to wear torn clothing, no matter which designers deemed it the cool thing to do. No, she'd dressed a little more mature than her age for most of her life. It was only recently that she'd begun considering younger trends; but still, ripped knees and plunging cleavage would never make their way into her modest closet.

Speaking of clothing...

"Have you decided what to wear to dinner?" she asked.

Abby had hurriedly recounted the morning's events on the walk across the backyard, already regretting her agreement to date the young, handsome architect who'd been pursuing her for weeks on end.

"No," she whimpered. "I'm thinking of backing out of it."

"You'll do no such thing. Every man you meet is not *Dylan*, Abby."

"I know."

"Do you?" Iris crossed the room and stood in front of Abby. "You let your guard down, and he hurt you."

"The last three guys I dated did the same thing, Iris. A few weeks went by, they were perfectly respectful about where I stand. And then BAM!" Iris jumped slightly at the volume. "I was suddenly a prude and they weren't going to stick around and wait for me to get over it. Gone. Just like that."

"And have you learned anything from them?"

"Yes. I've learned dating is not for me."

"No. That is *not* what you've learned."

"No?" Abby asked sarcastically.

"No. What you've learned is that you have to go slowly before giving your heart to someone who doesn't deserve it. And you've learned that a shared faith is one of your deal-breakers. So you go to dinner, you chat and have a nice time, and you see if you want to proceed. If you have enough in common to proceed."

Abby shrugged.

"Now you said he told you to dress up. So what are you thinking of wearing?"

"You?"

Iris chuckled. "You can't wear me."

"Why not? Will you come along?"

"No. I will not."

"Then I don't have a thing to wear."

"Yes, you do. What about that color-blocked dress you wore to Dean's birthday party? The black and royal blue. You looked so pretty that night."

"Hmm." Abby shifted her weight to one leg and balanced her notebook on her hip. "I just picked that up from the dry cleaner. I guess I could wear that … with those strappy black shoes. The heels are really tall, but Nate is over six feet so I won't have to worry about that."

"Now you're cooking," Iris congratulated her. "I'm proud of you."

Abby sighed and stared into Iris's eyes for a moment. "Thank you," she said, and with no forewarning at all, she tugged Iris into her embrace and rocked her from side to side. "Thank you so much."

"Call me afterward and tell me all about it."

"I will."

Just as they finished looking through Abby's sketches and made some decisions about furnishings, Candace called out from the main house, "Mom? Are you out here?"

"She's home for the weekend," Iris warned. "She doesn't know anything yet. Dean and I are going to talk to her today."

"Then we have a lot to talk about after my dinner with Nate," Abby teased. "I'll call you when I get home and you can let me know if I'm still remaking the pool house."

Iris placed her hands on Abby's shoulders and looked at her squarely. "Have a good time. Relax and enjoy yourself."

"Thanks. I'll try."

Abby tucked everything away into a large leather case and zipped it shut before the two of them headed across the yard.

"Oh. Hey, Abby. How are you?" Candace asked when she saw them.

"I'm okay. Congratulations, by the way."

"Oh. Yeah. Thanks."

"Iris, I'll speak to you later."

Abby followed the path around the side of the house and through the gate to the front, so Iris took the opportunity to give Candace a nod.

"It's such a pretty afternoon, honey. Do you want to sit outside for a while?"

"Not really. I'm feeling a little queasy today, Mom. I kind of just want to take my stuff upstairs and lie down. Do you mind?"

"Not at all." *That will give me time to strategize about our conversation with your father.* "I'll bring you some tea."

"No, don't bother. I really don't want anything right now."

"Okay. I'll check on you before dinner then."

Candace disappeared inside the house while Iris sank into one of the cushioned lounge chairs next to the pool. She kicked off her shoes and propped her feet on them, crossing her legs at the ankles. As she gazed at the rippling blue water, it struck her that, since Candace had gone back to school, no one had been swimming at all for months on end. She suddenly entertained visions of a grandchild splashing around in the pool with his or her mother, streams of sunlight—just like this day's—illuminating new life coming back to the Kramer house again, and her pulse quickened at the thought, then squealed to a halt.

We'll need to put a security fence around the pool. Not tomorrow, of course, but soon.

When Candace had revealed her pregnancy, Iris's initial reaction had been one of dread. Regret. Self-chastisement at having failed her daughter in some way. But everything had changed somehow, and now she could hardly wait for her grand-peanut to grow healthy and strong, and to reach out for its grandmother with little pink fingers.

And with that, the thought dropped on her with a clunk.

Would her grandchild actually have *pink fingers*? Or another color entirely? Had she really never asked Candace one question about the father?

Regan stared at her reflection curiously. She hardly recognized herself. Abby had come by to help with her makeup—and stayed long enough to straighten her hair and help choose her outfit for a casual evening with Baz. But now as she inspected the final results, she couldn't help wondering if she'd overdone it. When her eye began to twitch a little, she had to force herself not to rub it for fear of smearing black mascara into a raccoon's mask. Not to mention the rogue contact sure to end up on the top of her cheek like some sort of optical road kill. And when she took one more sip from the hard plastic straw protruding from her travel glass with the screw-on lid, a ring of dark pink gloss remained behind. She wiped it with a tissue, wondering what poor Baz might look like if he decided to give her a kiss at some point during the evening.

A fresh film of perspiration appeared on her upper lip and between her shoulder blades. Just the thought of kissing Sebastian Jordan flipped a dormant switch inside her.

It's just a friendly dinner, she reminded herself for the two hundredth time that day. *There will be no kissing going on. Just. Dinner.*

But when the doorbell rang and she nearly jumped straight out of her skin, Regan's thoughts of dinner, kisses, and anything else fell to dust at her feet as she stepped into strappy sandals with three-inch heels and clomped toward the front door with Steve in tow.

Deep breath in. Slow, deliberate exhale. Okay. Now open the door.

Baz greeted her from the other side with a smile—and a scratch behind the ear for Steve—before lifting a brown shopping bag with double handles that bore the Trader Joe's logo. "I come bearing food prep. Is the closet free for cooking?"

"All the sweaters moved and accounted for."

"Let's get at it then," he said as he passed through the doorway. She nearly slammed right into him when she closed the door and turned to find him standing at a surprising halt.

"Go ahead into the kitchen," she told him with a nod, but he just stood there. Hovering. "What?" she added when he made no move to follow her instructions. "What's wrong?"

"Where are your glasses?" he asked.

"My ... I'm sorry. *What?*" An unfortunate snort squeezed out through her nose.

"Glasses. You're pretty cute in your glasses."

And with that confusing declaration, he turned away and headed for the kitchen, leaving behind traces of his unique spicy scent.

And Regan's bewilderment.

"So you're saying you *prefer* me in glasses," she clarified, stepping up next to him at the counter as he unloaded the contents of the shopping bag.

"I wouldn't put it that way. I just think you look even cuter when you don't try so hard."

Try so hard.

"What's that supposed to mean?"

"The glossy hair and all the makeup and ... presumably contacts?"

She blinked. "Yes."

"And the fifty-foot shoes. Don't your arches ache already?"

She paused, wondering if she should admit that he'd straight-up hit the nail on the head.

"Of course they do," he answered himself. "I need a colander and a cutting board." As she went about retrieving them, he added, "Why don't you kick those things off and just go barefoot? Or grab some sneakers and be comfortable. ... Do you like pasta?"

"Uh—"

What was it about this guy that made her lose whatever dribble of cool she might actually have had?

"Pasta?" he repeated.

"Yes."

"And your shoes? Admit it. You don't enjoy wearing shoes like those."

Regan looked up at him—all shaggy and blond, and with that funny little smirk on his stubbled face—and a chuckle rolled out of her. "Not so much," she admitted, and she kicked them off.

"That's the spirit. Why don't you get a pot of water boiling on the stove. I'll heat the pesto."

Her eyebrow quirked into a tall arch. "You bought pesto?"

"I *made* pesto. What, you don't like it?"

"No," she said, lifting her hands with a giggle before retrieving a large pot. "You're just a very unexpected person, Sebastian Jordan."

"In a good way," he deduced.

"In a *curious* way."

She set the pot into the sink and ran water into it. When it was full, she had just touched the faucet to turn it off when Baz stepped up behind her and slipped his arms loosely around her waist. She wondered if he could hear the drumbeat of her pulse as it thundered in her own ears.

"What are you doing?" she asked, miraculously without flinching.

He buried his face in her hair and nuzzled the nape of her neck for just a moment, the rough bristles along his jaw scratching her. Regan felt like her knees might give way beneath her. Clutching the edge of the sink, she resisted the cacophony of sudden urges dancing around her mind.

Baz inhaled deeply. "I love the way your hair smells," he growled.

Straightening, she summoned every ounce of resolve she could find. "You don't know my hair well enough yet to go around smelling it. Step back, please?"

She thought she heard the trace of a snicker before he complied. "You know," he said, "you are so right. Let's get that water on the boil, shall we?"

Regan closed her eyes for a moment before lifting the pot from the sink and turning to set it on the range. Baz had already turned on the burner and moved to chopping elements for a salad.

"You still have a stereo," he noted, nodding across the counter toward the stereo in the living room as he dumped a bag of pasta into the pot. "Not just an iPod with downloaded music. Whatcha got in there?"

"Do you have a preference?" she asked, relieved for the gear shift. If there was one thing Regan could contribute to a home-cooked meal, it was background music. As she padded toward the stereo, she told him, "I've got country, pop, old-school rock. I even have Beach Boys for the chef in my kitchen who looks a little like someone who might like them."

Baz laughed. "Not a big fan of pop," he told her. "Otherwise, anything sounds good. I like classic rock, some of the contemporary country artists. You choose while I preheat the sweater drawer."

Regan chose an array of her favorites from the hundreds in the cabinet. Van Morrison. Keith Urban. Billy Joel. Maroon 5. Seger. By the time she'd set them up and invited Van Morrison to kick things off by crooning *Crazy Love*, she returned to the kitchen and found Baz placing little clumps of dough on a cookie sheet he'd found all on his own.

"What is that?" she asked.

"Garlic knots," he replied, slipping the sheet into the oven. "This is a pretty great kitchen, Regan. You might think about using it more often."

"I guess I just got tired of the smell of burnt food," she joked. "It takes so long to air the place out afterward."

"Come here."

Suspicion pushed a frown to her face. "Why?"

Baz chuckled and reached for her hand. "Come here."

Her racing thoughts didn't match her slow, deliberate approach as she timidly slipped her hand into his and allowed him to lead her to the counter. He peeled back the lid from a plastic container to reveal a fragrant green concoction inside.

"My pesto is basic. Basil leaves, fresh garlic, olive oil, salt and pepper, pine nuts, and Pecorino cheese. You could do this, I guarantee it. It only takes about five minutes to—"

"Pine nuts?" she interrupted.

Baz smiled at her. "You'll love it. ... Unless you have a nut allergy I don't know about. In which case, you will not love it and I can make something else." Looking to Steve—curled up under the adjacent dining room table—he added, "She allergic to nuts, buddy?"

When the French bulldog simply yawned noisily and tucked his chin between his paws, Regan replied, "I'm not allergic. I just ... Does all pesto have pine nuts in it?"

"I've had it with walnuts too. But pine nuts just taste better."

He dipped his index finger into the sauce and offered her a taste. Regan's eyes widened until her contacts felt as if they could drop right out.

"No?" he said with a shrug. "Okay." And he licked his own finger. "You don't know what you're missing. But it's better warm anyway. I'll heat it up and you'll see."

There's certainly no lack of heat in this kitchen right now.

When he turned away to check on the boiling pasta, Regan sighed and leaned against the counter for support.

Welcome to VERTICAL MAGAZINE
Moments-of-Truth.net

BLOG POST: REGAN SLOANE

Prepare yourselves, readers! Wait for it … Last night, I had my first real date since the end of my marriage. It was a pretty simple plan: I would move my sweaters out of the oven where I store them, and he would use the space for other purposes; namely, baking buttery mounds of deliciousness called garlic knots. He made pasta with pesto sauce (Did you know there are pine nuts in pesto? No, neither did I!) and a salad of greens and tomatoes and gorgonzola with balsamic dressing. A rugged, sweet, funny guy who can wield a hammer as well as an oven. Great music. A little wine. It all seems very civilized and healthy, doesn't it?

Yeah. That's where the supposed-to-be ends and reality comes into play.

Every song on the stereo transported me back to my days with 40-Watt. Even though I was the one who chose the music, songs I've listened to a thousand times without any sign of PTSD suddenly swooped over the crest of our dinner in the form of me-seeking missiles. And although I've been more attracted to Carpenter Chef than I've been to anyone in years, our date was choked by dim 40-watt memories I couldn't seem to shake.

Despite a close encounter in the kitchen at the first part of the date, there was nothing physical. Aside from his assessment of my appearance, that is. Turns out he prefers Writer-from-home Me to Best-foot-forward Me. Lose the heels, makeup, and contacts in favor of bare feet and glasses. Perhaps this was the moment when my world turned on its ear? 40-Watt was always willing to wait an extra hour if it meant I decorated his arm a little better. What is this "You look cuter in your glasses" of which you speak? I don't understand.

Anyway, there was no goodnight kiss to write home (or readers) about—just a warm peck that lasted about half a second and smelled of too much dinnertime garlic —and instead of taking thoughts of this new man with me after closing the door, I went to bed with a French bulldog, thinking about my many failures over eight years of marriage.

Is it really so bad to be alone a while longer? Or for the rest of my life, if that's what seems right and comfortable to me? Of course, I have no answers to any of these questions, but I pose them to you, readers. Let's talk first dates.

Chapter 13

One of the most difficult things about Lynette's job—the part she tried never to carry home with her or even talk about with anyone—involved moments like these. Becoming personally involved with the cancer patients treated by the doctors at the practice was almost unavoidable. When they survived and picked up their lives where they'd left them at the time of diagnosis, it was a bittersweet celebration as they left her behind. When they didn't—or when they weren't expected to—survive, their memory left her heart scorched; a wound that never really healed.

She stared down into the small box on her desk. Satiny mounds of ice blue fabric cushioned the somewhat massive chandelier earrings constructed by a pyramid of steel circles fastened together with gunmetal rings. She lifted one of them out of the box and held it in front of her for closer inspection.

"They're so light," she remarked, then glanced up at Peggy Downton as she stood on the other side of the desk. "From the look of them, I'd have expected a lot more weight. And you made them."

"It's what I do," Dr. Jarvis's patient told her. "I design jewelry. And you've been so kind to me that I wanted to create something especially for you. Something no one else will have. It's just a small thank-you."

Lynette gingerly returned the earring to the box before she stood and rounded the desk with open arms. Peggy stepped into her embrace, and she burst into tears as the circle closed around her. Lynette's heart sank like a stone.

"Dr. Jarvis says we'll need to start another round of chemo next week," she whimpered. "It's beyond me how ovarian cancer can return once they've taken your ovaries and everything else."

Lynette rubbed her back and held her close. "I'm so sorry, Peg. Is your sister still staying with you?"

"No. She went home after the last round."

"Do you have anyone to take you for your treatments?"

"I ... hadn't really thought about it."

Lynette pulled away and looked into Peggy's weepy hazel eyes. "I don't want you going alone. You call me if you don't have anyone to take you, and we'll make a plan. Do you hear me?"

The woman chuckled. "Thank you."

"Meanwhile," she said, and she reached across the desk and picked up one of the earrings, "I'm going to wear these and say a prayer for you every time I do."

She removed the long beaded earrings Iris had picked up for her at a craft fair the previous autumn. "I think they go with your tribal vibe," her friend had said with a straight face. Words which—coming out of Iris—made Lynette laugh every time she remembered them.

"Lynette?" The receptionist poked her head through the door of Lynette's office and smiled. "Dr. Eisen would like to see you when you're free."

"Tell him I'll be right there."

Once the girl had gone, Peggy smiled and released a heavy sigh. "I'll be going."

"Promise you'll call and update me."

"I promise."

Lynette walked her out to the front desk and gave her another hug before they parted ways.

"We have two sales reps in the waiting room, and your husband is holding on line three," the receptionist announced as she passed.

"Ask him to keep holding a minute longer?" she called back. "I just have to check in with Dr. Eisen."

"Too late. He's on a conference call now."

Lynette stopped for a moment before changing gears and turning back toward her office. When she saw all the lights blinking on the phone, she hacked through the overbrush of her busy morning trying to remember which line had been relegated to Trevor.

"Was it two or three?" she asked aloud. Taking a chance, she answered line three. "Lynette Parker."

"Good morning, Lynette Parker. You sound hot. Are you up for some dirty phone talk?"

"I can pencil you in sometime next month."

Trevor chuckled, and it sounded like music. "I won't be home for dinner." And there went the music.

"You're joking. I had plans to take Margaret shopping for a thumb ring."

"I know. Which is why I have made reservations for a very elegant supper with Shaaron."

"You have?"

"It's either that or have Margaret deported back across the pond," he said.

"And I've grown so fond of her."

"I thought it might help her realize we're one big clan now, and she's still the senior daughter in the village."

"Good thinking," Lynette commented with a smirk.

"Jamal is all about the idea of being in charge of the twins—" *Despite the fact that he's a year* younger *than Clayton and Felicity.* "—and I've left him with cash and the phone number for pizza delivery. The children will be fine until we get home. I'll meet *you* in the shower … say, eight-thirty?"

"Earlier if I can manage it."

"Don't start without me."

"I can't make any promises."

Trevor's tell-tale soft, throaty moan sent warm ripples down Lynette's limbs. "I love you, my darling," he added softly.

"Talk is cheap," she replied. "See you tonight."

As she hung up the phone, Lynette's eyes landed on the computer screen before her. The very full calendar of appointments and reminders mocked her momentary visions of a leisurely shower—or *anything* really—with her husband. That beckoning steamy shower disintegrated into a quickly-forgotten mist between the lines of appointments and reminders about pharmaceutical reps, payroll records, invoices, and timesheets.

When the end of her day finally clunked at her feet, the last thing on earth Lynette wanted to do was walk through a mall alongside a tiny British child in the guise of an investigative reporter. The *who-what-where-why-when*s of nine-year-old Margaret Parker twisted and turned like those crazy orange curls of hers.

And yet, tired as she was, Lynette couldn't think of a single thing that seemed more important. They hadn't made it to the mall on Sunday as planned, so this was the day. Ready or not.

Abby folded her hands and planted them in her lap atop the linen napkin, the edges of which she clutched with two fingers. Not that a napkin would keep her grounded, but she needed something to hold on to and it was handy.

Nate sat across the table from her, chatting with the waiter about the best appetizer to pair with the pork tenderloin dinner-for-two they'd just ordered. He looked so dashing in his dark charcoal suit that it pressed in on her throat like two stiff thumbs. He certainly looked like no other architect she'd ever met … with his cropped light brown hair and his dazzling blue eyes … his square jaw and just-right pinkish lips … And what about those perfectly-shaped symmetrical ears of his? She didn't remember ever noticing a man's ears before, but Nate's were somehow noteworthy.

And he was Christian too?

There has to be something wrong with him, right? Something? Anything?

When his gaze drifted back to her, Abby felt the immediate pull. Like a shark yanking her beneath the surface of the water. She could hardly breathe.

"Does that sound right to you?"

She choked back a gasp. "Sorry. What?"

"Crab cakes?"

"Oh. I love crab cakes." She smiled at the waiter. "That's wonderful."

"Very good. I'll bring you some warm rolls in just a moment."

She felt strangely exposed when he walked away from their table, leaving her there with just Nate and no one else in the entire room.

Abby glanced around the restaurant decorated in rich jewel tones and noted that not a single table was actually unoccupied. So, okay … maybe she and Nate being alone in the room was a stretch. But it still felt that way.

"How long have you been attending Cornerstone Grace?" she asked before taking a deep sip from her glass.

"About five years. You?" He shrugged. "I mean, how long have you been at your church?"

"Just a couple. I'm a sort of … newbie. I mean, I was raised in the church. But when I went away to college, I slipped away from it. I found my faith again about two years ago."

"That's great," he replied as the waiter set down a hunter green basket overflowing with bread and rolls. "What was the turning point?"

He lifted the basket and offered it to her. Abby plucked a warm slice of bread from it and smiled.

"I think I just got really tired of living my life the way it was going, if that makes sense. Just sort of drifting, you know?" she asked, and he nodded. "Something just wasn't right. I couldn't put my finger on it, but I just knew I wasn't content and I needed a change. After I finished a big redesign for a client in Balboa Park, they invited me to dinner—the big unveiling—and I was seated next to her father."

One corner of Nate's mouth twitched, and flickers of amusement danced in his eyes. "Her father was…?"

"The pastor of United Community Church," she replied with a chuckle.

"Ah! The plot thickens."

"By the time we finished coffee and dessert, he'd invited me to visit his church the next weekend, and I've been going ever since."

Nate delayed taking a bite out of the large roll in his hand for just one long and lingering moment. Then he nodded and smiled—he undoubtedly understood.

"I've always been a believer," he declared before taking a large bite of the bread. "Went to church every Sunday morning and Wednesday night of my life, even attended Christian camp every summer with my friends."

"So why aren't you happily married to one of your kind by now—your childhood sweetheart, or someone named Pam or Emily—popping out babies and living in a house you bought with the intention of flipping but which Emily fell in love with and begged you to stay?"

Nate chortled with amusement. "Carrie," he stated.

Her heart twittered slightly. "Carrie?"

"The girlfriend from junior high through graduation. The day I left for college, she dumped me and, by Christmas, she was shacked up with my best friend." An invisible dart poked him in the center of his chest and he playfully nursed it.

"I'm so sorry. You must have been devastated," she said with a grin.

"I'm still getting over it. But I'm confident you'll help me forget, won't you?"

Abby tucked her hair behind one ear as a flush of heat rose from her chest and scorched her cheeks.

"The truth is … I've been waiting for the right woman to cross my path," he said, and his blue eyes darkened with serious undertones. "It's been a pretty long wait."

"I know what you mean," she muttered.

"But things are looking up." He lifted his glass in a toast and grinned at her.

She wondered if the brown of her eyes had actually turned blue when they fell into his, or if it just felt that way.

"Here we are," the waiter announced upon arrival at their table. "Dinner for two." Abby struggled to strip her gaze away from Nate's as the waiter set two domed plates in front of them. "Roasted pork tenderloin seasoned in fresh rosemary and garlic with our brie mashed potatoes, steamed asparagus with pearl onions, and baby maple-glazed carrots. Can I get you anything else?"

"It looks perfect," she told the waiter.

"Thank you, sir," her date added.

And just before Abby took her first bite of the fragrant feast before her, Nate stood, rounded the table, and knelt next to her chair.

"What are you doing?"

He took her hand and caressed it softly. "I'd like to get something out of the way so we can enjoy our meal."

She arched a brow. "You're not proposing, are you? Because if you are, that's where I draw the line."

"Sort of," he said, leaning closer. "I'm proposing we get a kiss out of the way. Like in some areas of the world, they eat dessert first in an effort to fully enjoy the meal."

Abby was no stranger to the concept. "We do that at Thursday night book club."

"Good. Then you're in agreement."

"Not necessarily."

Her words were swallowed as Nate's lips touched hers in a warm and tender kiss. Several seconds later, it was a somewhat reluctant parting.

"Thank you," he whispered. "Now we can enjoy our dinner."

Oh. Is there a dinner?

"Celia, what have you done?" Regan exclaimed.

Celia's temper flared like a rocket, and she tossed her arms into the air. "Why do I need always hear that from you women, heh? Celia, what have you done? Celia, have you *vuelto loco*? Celia, you need a visit to the funny farm."

Abby laughed and smoothed Celia's hair with her palm. "I think she means the chocolate cake, honey."

Celia's eyes darted to the luscious dessert sitting at the center of the table. "Oh." Did she say chocolate cake? "Oh, no. *No es el chocolate*. It's *torta negra*. A … how you say? … block cake."

"Block cake?" Lynette repeated.

"No, no," Celia declared. "A *block* cake!"

"She means a black cake," Iris interjected from the other side of the kitchen.

"*Sí*. This what I say. A *block* cake."

"No chocolate?" Regan clarified with a disappointed wince. "It looks like chocolate."

"*Chu* will like it just as much. *Es* a tradition in Colombia. It wasn't a birthday or wedding or anniversary without the *torta negra*. Grab us some tools and plates, I cut it for you."

"What's in it?" Regan asked as she sat across the table from Celia and inspected the cake.

"Eggs and flour and *cee-nuh-moan*," she answered.

Iris whispered a translation to Abby. "Cinnamon."

"Nutmeg *y* cloves *y* baker's caramel. A lot of flavor," she told them. "The cakes are brushed with port wine and rum, *yust* to … enhance the flavors of the figs and the fruit."

"It's a fruitcake?" Lynette asked her.

"No. It has fruit in it, but *es* not a fruitcake." Celia grew frustrated and sighed. "Just taste it. That will explain what I cannot."

They gathered around the table as Celia cut fat slices for each of them. When she slid a plate toward Abby, she noticed her friend's nose curl up oddly.

"Are those prunes?" she asked.

"It has prunes in it, *si.*"

Abby and Regan exchanged telling expressions of terror mixed with disgust.

"It sure does *look like* chocolate, doesn't it?" Regan muttered.

"*Yust* taste it," Celia exclaimed. "Taste the darn cake, *wouldchu?* I make for the restaurant, and my customers they love it. You love it too."

Lynette was first to poke her fork into the slice of cake, but she froze as Abby shouted, "Wait!"

Celia's hand flew to her heart in surprise as Lynette's fork clattered to the table. "What is it now?"

"We didn't decide who gets the first dessert. We always tell our stories first."

Regan giggled. "She just wants everyone to hear that she doesn't have a horror story to tell. Abby has been *kissed by a boy.*"

They sang in unison. "Oooooh!"

"Abby, tell us," Celia encouraged. "You and the *Brodley* Cooper?"

She nodded, grinning from one ear to the other and blushing deep crimson. "And his name is Nate Cross."

"Get to the kissing part," Lynette teased.

"Well, you all know he's been asking me out for quite a while now," she began.

"And he's *muy caliente,*" Celia threw in.

"*Si,*" Abby said with a chuckle. "He is that."

"So you finally say yes?" Celia asked.

"I did. We just went to dinner, but we stayed there for hours. Just talking, and eating the most marvelous meal. We had this wonderful caramel cheesecake for dessert—"

Regan elbowed her playfully. "Tell them how he kissed you." Turning to the others, she added, "This is so adorable."

"Well, we'd just ordered our meal when he stood up and walked around the table toward me," she said, her flickering cocoa eyes darting from one of them to the other. "And he kneels down and says he wants to get the first kiss out of the way so we can really enjoy each other's company."

"And he kiss you right there in the middle of the *restaurante?*"

"In front of God and everyone," she answered with a nod.

"And?" Lynette prodded.

"And it was ..." She ran a hand through her copper hair and sighed dreamily. "Amazing."

"So we know Abby is *not* getting the first taste of the dessert tonight," Iris declared. "What about you, Regan? Any sad story to tell?"

"Not from all I hear," Celia told them. "*Keffin* say Sebastian finish the bookshelves, and now he's making her a closet."

"Not to mention cooking for her," Abby told them.

"Dinner?" Iris exclaimed, her eyes bright and shining with questions.

"Well, I think it was more about proving that my kitchen appliances are in working order," Regan joked, pushing her glasses up her nose. "But yes, he made a fairly spectacular dinner."

"This is an interesting development," Iris said. "Lynette? What's your bid for the first slice of cake?"

"Well, I hate to win by default," she replied. "I mean, if I'm going to win, I'd like it to be because I trumped you all, not because I'm the only one with a desperate, sad story."

"Oh, you're not," Celia cut in.

"Do tell."

"Ah, I make the egg face again," she said, closing her eyes and shaking her head. When she opened her eyes, she spotted the others holding back their laughter. "What?"

"The egg face," Regan sputtered, and they all guffawed.

"What? That's not the right way to say?"

"Well, I'm not sure," Lynette replied. "Tell us what you're trying to say, and we'll tell you how close you are."

"Like if I get the egg," she said, making circles around her face with one hand. "You know, like a fool."

"Egg on her face," Iris told the others. "Embarrassed?"

"*Sí.*"

"Ohhh." They exchanged nods of understanding.

"Anyway, one of *Keffin*'s colleagues come into the restaurant, and he say *Keffin* called in sick with the flu, but I know he don't have no flu. Long story shorter, he had good explanation, but I jump all over him and he's still *ongry* with me."

Lynette cringed for a moment before turning to Iris. "Whatcha got?"

"I'll see your jealous streak and raise you a sob story," she cracked. "Dean finally got his groove back, and five minutes later our grown daughter agreed to move back home. I'm pretty sure we may never have sex again."

"But she will live on the other side of the pool, yes?" Celia encouraged. "There will still be some privacy. You and Dean can *groove some*." And she did a little dance in her chair to punctuate her meaning.

Iris shrugged. "I really do hope you're right." Turning to Lynette, she quirked a brow. "You?"

Lynette leaned back in her chair and crossed her arms. "Five kids and two adults under one roof makes for very little alone time for us. But hey, we've learned to work around it. We've managed to forge out time together, but it hasn't been easy."

"Or private," Iris teased.

"Well, it's only going to get less private from here," she told them. "Trevor's mother is coming over from England for a visit."

"Oh ..."

"And she's staying for three months."

Without another word, Iris simply picked up Lynette's previously dropped fork and handed it to her.

"Yeah. I thought so," she said, taking it.

After the girls had gone their own ways, Iris spent a few minutes cleaning up the dishes and storing the leftovers. By the time she made her way upstairs, Dean had already retired to the guest room. She checked the opening beneath the closed door and saw the flicker of the television cutting through the otherwise darkened room.

"Honey?" she said, giving the door a timid knock. "Can I come in?"

"Sure," he said. When she opened the door, she found him in bed in underwear and an open robe, propped by pillows as he watched television. "What's up?"

She walked across the room and sat on the edge of the bed.

"The girls gone?"

"Yes," she replied, hoisting her legs up on the bed and stretching out next to Dean, close enough to share his stash of pillows. "Celia brought a cake she makes at her restaurant. I can't pronounce the name, but I think it means Black Cake. It was surprisingly delicious. Considering it has prunes in it."

"Prunes," he exclaimed.

"I know. But I think you'll still like it."

"I'll pass."

Iris chuckled as she wriggled closer and laid her head to rest on the slope of his shoulder. "What are you watching?"

"News report," he said as he lifted his arm and wrapped it loosely around her. "More shenanigans in Washington."

Tilting her head back, she looked up at him. The bluish reflection from the television shadowed his handsome face in ebbs and flows.

"Dean," she muttered.

"Mm?" he softly grunted without looking down at her.

"Kiss your wife."

"Huh?"

"Dean," she said less tenderly, and he glanced at her.

"What?"

"Kiss me." She lifted her hand and tenderly stroked the line of his jaw until he quickly pecked her lips. "Not like that," she told him. "Like this."

Iris placed her hand on the back of his head and gently pressed until their lips touched again.

"Come to our room, honey."

"Not tonight," he replied, and the too-familiar cold blanket quickly dropped.

"Why not?"

"I don't know," he answered with a shrug. "Just not tonight."

She pushed upright and turned to face him. "Dean, what's going on? I thought we got past this the other night."

"Got past what?" He groaned. "I mean, we did. That doesn't mean I'm—" He groaned again and pushed off the bed and stood next to it fastening the belt on his robe. "Just not tonight, Iris. That's all."

"Dean, what is going on? Don't you find me attractive anymore? Is it the weight gain? Because I thought the other night was really wonderful."

"It was," he said, lifting and then dropping his arms at his side. "What do you want me to say?"

"I want you to say you still love me." The words had fallen from her lips without warning.

"Of course I still love you." Dean walked around the bed and sat on the opposite corner with his back to her. "Don't be ridiculous."

"But you don't ... *want* me."

Dean raked through his hair with both hands and sighed. He dropped his head and stared at the dark floor as the local news anchor reported from the scene of a robbery outside the convention center.

"The truth is," he began, then he fell silent.

"Please. *What is* the truth?" she prodded.

"I've been seeing a doctor, Iris."

"A doctor?"

"There may be something wrong with me. It's too early to get all worked up about it, but—"

"Dean." She hurried from the bed and rushed around it. Standing in front of him, she used both hands to gently lift his chin until he returned her gaze. The torment simmering there broke her heart, and Iris pulled his head to her chest and smoothed his hair as she held him. "Why didn't you tell me about this?"

"It's probably nothing," he muttered, wrapping his arms around her thighs. "But ... it might be *something*."

Her heart dropped as she plunked to the bed beside him and stroked his hand. "Start at the beginning and tell me everything."

"It's not like I'm not aware ... you know ... about how much time passes ... in between. I mean, I'm a guy."

She grinned. "I am aware."

"But you just choose not to think about it, I guess. Until other things ..."

She held her breath, waiting. But Dean simply sighed and fell silent.

"Honey. *Please*. You're scaring me."

He groaned. "I started noticing some other things." He turned suddenly and looked straight into her eyes. "Do you know I've gained twenty pounds in three months?"

Iris suppressed the chuckle threatening to creep out of her. Twenty pounds seemed like nothing to her. Inconsequential in comparison to her own weight gain.

"Honey, that happens when we get older."

"In three months, Iris." He shook his head, and she could see that he wanted to give up on the conversation.

"Well, that is unusual for you, I guess. Was there anything else that led you to the doctor?"

"Some headaches and unusual fatigue. This nagging pain in my lower back."

"Are you still struggling with that?"

"Almost every day. And I can't sleep for more than a couple hours at a time. I get up and wander around, get something to eat—" *Which might explain the weight gain.* "—watch some television. But when it felt like it was escalating, and I was having trouble concentrating, I figured I'd just go see Dr. Renner so he could give me something to get some sleep. Instead, he asked a lot of questions and started connecting the dots ... Anyway, it ended up with him sending me to see this new guy, Dr. Lotus."

"Lotus?"

"Nice guy. About my age, trained in the UK—"

"What kind of specialist is he?" she interrupted.

"Urologist. Anyway, he did a complete work-up with an exam, and he ran a bunch of tests. He said he'd call with the results, but instead his nurse called and said he wants to see me. I have an appointment Tuesday afternoon to talk about the results and find out what he thinks."

"Tuesday. Did he give you any indication?"

"Nothing solid. We talked about a host of things that can cause some of my issues. Anywhere from male hormones all the way to cancer—"

"Cancer! Dean."

"That's worst-case scenario," he said, squeezing her hand. "I didn't want to tell you any of this until I had some sort of resolution."

Anger with him for holding back this secret wrestled her deep love and concern, and the latter won out. Iris slipped her arm through his and nudged closer, nestling her head into the crook of his neck. "We should have gone through it together," she told him. "I don't just want to hear the resolution. I want to know what you're dealing with along the way. That's who we've always been, honey. It's always been you and me against the rest."

"So I guess cancer isn't too much worse than no more sex drive, huh?"

"It is infinitely worse, you idiot," she said, shoving him gently. "I can live the rest of my life without sex if I have to. What I cannot live without is *you*."

"Here's hoping," he remarked, his tone dark and gravelly. "But he mentioned cancer more than once during the appointment."

"I'll go with you on Tuesday. And whatever it is, we'll handle it together. Do you hear me?"

He nodded and sighed. A moment later, Dean slipped his arm around Iris's waist and drew her close to him. After a deep kiss, he lowered her backward to the bed. A rush of warmth coursed through every square inch of her body as he planted kisses on the side of her neck and worked his way down her throat.

When the kisses stopped, Dean looked up at her, and she spotted the flicker of sadness in his eyes. "I'm sorry," he said, and he pulled away and rolled over to his back.

"What are you apologizing about?" she reassured him. "Have you had a shower?"

"Just a little while ago."

"Good. Then let's get you into bed, and I'll rub your back for a while. It'll help you relax and maybe get a good night's sleep."

"Iris—"

"For the purposes of relaxation only," she said, grinning at him. "Then you can come to bed with me. Unless you think you'll get better sleep alone in here?"

"I'm sorry. I do."

"Then I'll tiptoe out and let you drift off if you can. The lack of sleep isn't helping anything at all."

"Well, that's the truth."

"Then come on. I'll turn off the television and you shed your robe and lie on your stomach."

"You don't have to do this," he said as he complied.

"You withdraw when you worry," she reminded him. "I nurture."

He chuckled. "Yes, you do."

"So hush up and let me nurture."

After about twenty minutes of silence in the room—aside from the occasional soft moan out of Dean in response to Iris's massage—she noticed his breathing grow deeper ... then deeper still ... and then the soft snoring began.

She carefully stood, maintaining the rhythm of her hands' work, slowing gradually until she lifted them and waited to make certain the little snores continued their sleepy cadence. When she felt assured, Iris tiptoed toward the door and winced as she drew it open. On the other side of it, she pulled it shut only as far as she could without the click of the latch.

In her room, behind the closed door, she perched on the very edge of the bed, still and erect, frozen by her own fears and imaginings. It wasn't as if she'd never before imagined a life without Dean in it. The day that phone call had come from the ER saying he'd collapsed on the golf course, she'd been inundated with anxious *WHAT IF?*'s that plagued her long after she'd been allowed to bring him home that evening. That same salty, convulsing fear invaded her now. With an added course of nausea on the side.

Iris glanced at the clock. Nearly midnight. She couldn't very well follow her inclination to phone Lynette and take a chance on waking the kids. Instead, she deep-breathed her way through preparations for bed. Ten minutes later, sitting in the same spot—except now dressed in a cotton knit gown and thick socks slipped over freshly lotioned feet—she imagined this might be what it felt like at the beginning of one losing their mind.

On impulse, she picked up the phone and dialed. On the third ring, a sleepy voice answered.

"He—llo?"

"Abby, I'm so sorry to call so late."

"Iris?"

"Yes. I'm—"

"What's wrong?"

"It's Dean. We won't know until next week what the doctor has found, but I have this terrible feeling inside."

"Um. Iris? What are you talking about?"

"Aren't you listening? There's something wrong with Dean. He doesn't follow up with the doctor until next week, my heart is telling me it's going to be horrible news."

"That's your fear," she said. "Try not to listen. What can I do?"

The reply sat on the very tip of her tongue, and her own mind taunted her about actually speaking the words. She didn't know if she could. At least not with a straight face.

"Iris?"

"Yes. I'm sorry. I … was thinking maybe …"

"Do you want me to pray for you?"

Relief flushed over and through her like a waterfall. "Yes. And for Dean."

"Just sit back and relax. Take deep breaths and close your eyes. I'll pray."

Iris lifted her legs to the bed with a groan and pushed back against the pillows. "Okay," she said. "I'm ready. Thank you, Abby."

With no additional reply, Abby's soft, sweet voice soothed Iris's aching heart with the balm of petitions for healing and comfort and peace. Still, Iris couldn't help feeling like a bit of a freeloader sitting there wrapped in a blanket of someone else's faith, but it was all she really had at the moment. And she couldn't give up the cozy warmth it provided, so she simply fell backward into it and sighed.

Chapter 14

"I really don't know how to thank you two," Lynette said, still holding Abby's hand between both of hers. "Really. I just—"

Abby giggled. "Will you stop it please? This is what friends do."

"Oh, I don't know. I've had a lot of friends in my lifetime, Abby, and this isn't what any of them have done."

Abby shook her head. She found that very sad.

"Trevor's mother arrives next week, and we've simply got to have some alone time before that happens." Lynette released her hand and headed into the kitchen. Abby trailed after her. "It's a miracle we were both able to clear the whole weekend at this late notice, but we've booked a suite at The Horton Grand Hotel for three whole nights. We'll be back on Monday morning ..." She turned and frowned at Abby. "...assuming there are no earth-shattering emergencies to call us home earlier."

"If there's blood, unconsciousness, or broken bones, we'll call you," Abby vowed. "Otherwise, I feel confident that Regan and I can handle things for three nights."

"The kids' schedule is on the fridge," she said. When she crossed to it, Abby followed. "Margaret has art class Saturday mornings at ten. The address is on the card next to the calendar. Jamal likes to go with her and stick around. He says it's so she won't get scared being there alone, but it's really because the instructor lets him help hand out supplies and act like an assistant."

Abby chuckled. "Okay."

"Oh, that's not all," Lynette warned. "Shaaron, Felicity, and Clayton have a school dance party tomorrow night. Nothing formal. They can wear jeans or whatever. You'll want to watch Shaaron closely. Even if she's dressed like a normal girl, look twice to make sure she isn't hiding a Miley Cyrus outfit underneath. There's a flyer here behind the calendar. One of you will have to play chauffeur to pick up Clayton's two friends on the way. Felicity's best girlfriend will come here to the house in the afternoon so the girls can all get ready together. After that, you can drop them all at the same time and pick them up ..."

Stomping, screeching mayhem interrupted them as Regan galloped down the stairs and into the kitchen with red-haired Margaret riding on her back shouting, "Giddyup!"

"Margaret Parker," Lynette exclaimed, "get down from Regan this minute. She is not your personal equestrian center."

"She'd make a good one if she was," Margaret declared.

"Thank you very much," Regan chimed in.

"When you pick them up after the dance," Lynette continued telling Abby, "it will just be the girls. The boys will go with Tyrone's mom and spend the night there. Clayton may need a ride back here on Sunday."

Pausing, she tried to sort out the jumbled details clunking around in her head. Had she forgotten anything important?

"Are you still prattling on?" Margaret teased as she jumped to the floor. Turning back to Regan, she rolled her eyes. "There are pages and pages on the refrigerator, on the calendar, on the counter over there. It's like she thinks we need step-by-step *instrunktions*."

Regan pushed her glasses up on her nose as she giggled and exchanged a glance with Lynette. "Moms are like that. It's how they let you know you're loved."

"Hey!" Margaret said, jumping toward Abby. "Wanna see my new thumb ring?"

Abby inspected it carefully, nodding. "That's pretty spectacular. Do you think I could borrow it sometime?"

"It won't fit you," she stated. "Besides, it's just mine. I ain't never taking it off."

"Try again," Lynette said.

Margaret thought it over, looking at the ceiling as if the answer might be hiding there. "Oh. I'm not gonna take it off."

"Better. A little."

"Her English accent is adorable," Regan muttered to Lynette.

"Let's see if you feel that way at the end of the weekend after listening to her chatter eight hundred miles an hour without stopping."

Regan squeezed her arm and chuckled. "Try to just have a good time. Don't think about anything here at home. Abby and I will have it all under control."

Lynette groaned. "Promise?"

"Yes. Go. Enjoy your husband while you can."

"Oh, I will," she assured her before calling out toward the stairs. "Trev? It's time to go."

"Thirty seconds, Love," he answered. "Meet you at the front door."

Lynette planted a warm kiss on Margaret's porcelain cheek and the little girl took her hand. Looking down at their clasped hands, Lynette thought the paleness of Margaret's small hand inside of her larger, dark brown one looked almost artistic. She wished she had a photograph of it to keep with her all the time. Margaret adjusted her own thumb so that it fell right next to Lynette's, their two thumb rings right up against each other.

"I know you'll have a really good time," the child told her. "But I'll miss you when you're gone."

"I miss you already," she said, and she kissed her orange curls. "You keep the bigger kids in line for Regan and Abby, will you?"

"You can count on me. I mean ... I'll try. But they don't often listen."

"I hear ya, sistah."

Margaret's giggles rolled out like a bouncing ball.

"Paging Lynette Parker," Trevor called out. "Lynette Parker, please meet your party at the escape hatch."

Lynette grabbed her bag, tucked her cell phone into the outside pocket, gave Margaret's hand a final squeeze, and hurried down the hall. When she reached the front door, she noticed something out of the corner of her eye. She turned back to find Shaaron perched on a lower stair looking about as sour as sour could be.

She walked over to her and cradled Shaaron's chin with one hand. "You are so beautiful," she said.

"Mother. Spare me the guilt compliment."

Lynette felt her blood pressure spike straight through the top of her head. "Shaaron—"

"I thought we spoke about that," Trevor said from directly behind her, and she—surprisingly—watched her daughter's face soften considerably.

"Sorry."

Lynette turned her head slowly, stopping it before it spun completely around, landing on her husband who smiled at her.

"You knock 'em dead at the dance party," Trevor said, and he reached past Lynette—frozen to the spot by sheer astonishment—and shook Shaaron's entire arm by the wrist.

"Thanks," she replied. And then she did something Lynette hadn't seen her do in six months of Sundays. She ... *smiled.*

"We'll call you tomorrow," Trevor told her, despite the fact that they'd agreed to forget they had children for three days, barring emergencies. Lynette's heart felt like warm wax had been poured over it as she stepped aside and allowed Trevor to kiss his stepdaughter's cheek. "We'll want to hear all about it."

"Have a nice time," Shaaron told them, even allowing her mother to benefit from a trace of that bright-white smile Trevor had conjured.

"You too," she said.

"And thanks for the earrings," she added, and the words flew right over Lynette's shoulder, straight to Trevor.

"I'm glad you like them. I wasn't sure."

"They're dope."

"And that's a good thing."

Shaaron chuckled. "Very."

"Excellent."

The moment the front door closed behind them, a stunned Lynette turned to her husband and grabbed his arm.

"I just have to tell you about this dream I had last night. In fact, I may still be asleep right now because … imagine my surprise when my daughter in this dream actually *smiled at me.*"

Trevor laughed. "C'mon. Let's get in the car before you wake and ruin everything."

The car waited for them in the driveway, all packed up and ready to fly away. Trevor tugged open the passenger door for Lynette.

"You bought her earrings?" she asked before sliding into the car.

"Yeah," he replied with a shrug. "It's her first school dance."

Shame washed over Lynette in hot, damp droplets. It had completely escaped her that Shaaron had never gone to a school dance before.

"How did you know that?"

"She told me when we went to dinner the other night. There's a boy named Vincent that she sort of fancies, and he asked her if she was planning to go. As girls often do, I believe, she said yes as if she'd even considered it."

Lynette chuckled and leaned forward to kiss his warm lips. "I love you," she said when they parted. "Have I told you that enough lately?"

"Not nearly," he answered. "But I'll give you a detailed rundown on how you can make it up to me on the drive over to our hotel."

As Abby grabbed the poker to stoke the fire in the massive stone fireplace in Lynette and Trevor's great room, Regan prepared two cups of pumpkin spice coffee with heavy cream from the other side of the kitchen island. She might not be a chef like Baz, but she knew how to prepare a great cup of coffee. She sprayed spirals of whipped cream over the top of each beverage. Holding the handles of both cups with one hand, she used the other to grab the platter of snacks Abby had put together after the shuttling of children had been completed: a circle of crackers, a pile of huge strawberries, a wheel of brie, and two red velvet cupcakes topped with heaping mounds of cream cheese icing.

"This looks so good," she said while Abby replaced the poker in the rack next to the hearth.

The two of them fell to opposite ends of the plump brown sofa, and Abby yanked the coffee table closer before accepting her cup from Regan. A moment later, she descended into giggles.

"Regan, you have whipped cream all over your nose and upper lip."

She laughed and used her sleeve to wipe it off. "I was eager." Picking up a cupcake, she offered it to Abby. "Dessert first?"

"Of course."

The two of them silently dug into their cupcakes, moaning with pleasure in perfect unison, then cutting up with laughter.

"So tell me about Baz," Abby said, pausing to lick frosting from her finger.

"Funny you should ask as you did that," she replied, pointing at her friend's hand. "He actually offered me a taste of pesto off his finger."

Abby's eyes flickered with amusement, then narrowed with questions. "Did you?"

"No," she declared. "I don't lick *my own* fingers. I'm going to lick his just because he can cook?" She grinned. "And let me tell you, the boy can cook."

"So you mentioned."

"It's worth repeating. Craig was pretty great in the kitchen … not as great as he *thought he was*, but still. I don't remember ever enjoying anything he made as much as that meal with Baz."

"That's because you like him more than you liked Craig."

Regan chuckled. "I liked him very much when I thought he was faithful and genuine."

"Until he wasn't."

"And then I didn't." Regan finished her cupcake, then offered a finger smeared with frosting to Abby, who gave her a face full of Blue Steel.

"Are you serious? I'm not licking your finger."

Regan shrugged and grabbed a napkin. "This is what I'm saying. Even best friends don't lick each other's fingers."

Abby turned the platter and dove into the crackers and brie. As Regan followed suit, Abby said, "Terrible about Dean, isn't it?"

"I can't imagine what Iris is going through. She must be losing her mind."

"She even asked me to pray with her."

"Did she?"

"Yeah. We were on the phone for nearly an hour." Abby shook her head.

"She loves him so much."

"They're like yin and yang. I can't even visualize one without the other, can you?"

"I won't even try. I'm not going there," she said. "I'm just going to keep praying that we still have him for a long time."

"Well ... sometimes—"

Abby held up her hand between them and croaked out a strange noise that seemed like a warning. "Don't," she exclaimed.

"Don't what?"

"Don't go into your Negative Nellie about prayer, Regan. Let's just keep a positive thought and let God do the rest."

Regan sighed. There was just no talking to Abby when she went off on this rabbit trail. "Fine."

After a few more silent bites of brie and crackers, a strawberry or two ... "I know you don't believe like I do," Abby said softly. "But can't you just concede that I might not be a complete crackpot?"

"I don't think you're a crackpot. I just think you're ..." She couldn't finish it. Every word that came to mind felt like a label or an insult.

"Naïve?" Abby finished for her.

"Maybe a little," she admitted.

"Okay. I can live with naïve." An ember of levity flickered in her brown eyes. "I love you anyway."

"Well, good."

"Speaking of. I'm going to church in the morning, and I thought I'd take along any of the kids who want to go."

Regan shrugged. "Yeah. Okay."

"Or we could all go as a group."

"Oh, Abby ..."

"Come on, Regan. The building won't fall down around you. I think it would be fun for us all to go together." She twisted a strawberry in her fingers until it danced. "And we can go to brunch at Lael's after," she sang. "You *looove* their *omelet bar.*"

Bribing me to church with the promise of eggs and a waffle. Shameless.

"Yeah, okay. We'll talk to the kids in the morning," she surrendered. "But if they don't all want to go, I'm hanging back. Maybe we can meet you afterward at Lael's."

"Oh, no you don't. No church, no omelet bar."

Regan snickered and popped a berry into her mouth. "So tell me about you and Nate. What's going on there? Anything new to tell?"

Abby's face flushed with deep crimson, and her brown eyes glazed with a mist of emotion.

Regan straightened and stared her down. "There is. There's something to tell?"

Abby's eyes darted away, focusing somewhere on the floor beyond the coffee table. When Regan touched her arm, she jumped slightly.

"What's going on?" she asked. And the intensity with which her friend stared back at her sent a shot of adrenaline through Regan's entire body. "Abbs?"

Abby blinked and a single large teardrop burst from her eye and ambled down her cheek.

"Oh, no. What happened?"

She shook her head and wiped away the stream of moisture left on her face. "No, it's not ... We didn't ..."

"Abby. Talk to me."

She tried to smile, but it didn't quite reach her eyes.

"Did he do something to hurt you?"

Abby snickered and shook her head. "No. Not unless you count—" She interrupted herself with a chuckle that came out like a cluck. "He didn't do anything to hurt me."

"Then what's going on?"

Regan's pulse up-shifted, and she could feel the bass drum of her heartbeat in her limbs, hear it thumping in her ears. She couldn't even begin to imagine what could have happened to make—

"I'm in love with him," she whispered.

—make Abby cave under it this way.

"Wait. What?"

"I love him," she repeated, an octave higher. "I know, right? How is that possible? But I do. I'm sure of it. I'm in love with Nate Cross, Regan."

"In ... *love* ..."

"Yes. Soul-stirring, life-changing, not-a-doubt-in-my-mind love."

The two of them sat there staring at each other in silence for several seconds before Regan finally blew out a puff of air. "Wow."

"I know."

"What are you going to do?"

"No clue."

"Does he know?"

"I haven't told him ... but I get the feeling he knows," she said. "It's like he knew it all along, even before I did." Abby leaned forward and their eyes locked so tightly Regan could almost hear the CLICK! "It's like I have no secrets from him, you know? Or ... like I don't even want to. Do you know what I mean?"

Regan nibbled on the corner of her lip. She felt pretty sure she'd never felt that way about anyone in her life.

Before she had to admit it out loud, Abby continued. "He gets me. I never even had to tell him about my choice to ... you know. Change. In fact, *he* told *me.*"

"And he doesn't mind?"

"Not only does he not mind, but he *supports it.*"

"Seriously?"

Abby nodded. "And get this. Even though I'm happy to be here with you, spending a whole weekend together ... I find myself ... Well, I can hardly stand not being *with him.* I miss him. I want to be with him, hear what he has to say, see his smile. He has the most amazing smile." She leaned forward for emphasis. "Regan. He's *the one.* I know it."

If she were a praying person, Regan thought she might say a prayer just then. A prayer for her friend's heart, that it wouldn't be broken. That her desperation to find someone who understood her choices wouldn't overpower her good sense.

"He's a good guy," Abby reassured her, as if Regan's concerns had manifested in words clearly scrawled across her forehead for her friend to read in crystal detail. "You're going to love him, I promise."

Regan tried to swallow around the lump in her throat so she could speak. "If you love him, I love him."

Abby's face ignited with a smile. "Then you're nuts about him," she said, followed by a melodic—and relieved—laugh. Tossing herself at Regan, they fell into a clumsy embrace as Abby exclaimed, "It feels so good to say it out loud. It's like a pile of bricks lifting off me."

Okay. You win. Uncle. And Regan sent a quick prayer sailing toward the ceiling. *Don't let him break her heart. Please.*

Welcome to VERTICAL MAGAZINE
Moments-of-Truth.net

BLOG POST: REGAN SLOANE

I've been thinking a lot about love lately, readers. Not the spread-the-love kind or the general peace-and-love kind, but the deep life-changing kind of love that alters everything. After spending the weekend with Gabby—You remember her, right?— and hearing how, after about twenty minutes, she feels more certain that she's met The One than I felt after a few years of marriage to 40-Watt ... I'm a little haunted with questions and wonderings. And worry.

If you've read this blog for very long, you know that my friend Gabby made a decision a while back. After spending most of her life kissing the wrong men and falling into the wrong beds—her words, not mine—Gabby experienced one of the worst break-ups any of us could imagine. In fact, for three years, every time we thought it was over, that relationship circled around like a maniacal serpent and bit her on the fanny again. As a result, Gabby—in desperation—turned to a childhood faith in God. And it changed her. Among many other adjustments and shifts in her life, my friend made a commitment to behave in a very different way when it came to dating. I've teased her often about trying to become a "born-again virgin" and un-ring the sexuality bell that had clearly clanged loud and often. But to her credit, her pledge hasn't wavered in the least since the day she told me about it.

Don't think Gabby hasn't paid the price for that change, either. Let's face it, there aren't many men out there without expectations of ably penetrating our varying walls of abstinence, right? I once heard a single buddy of 40-Watt's joke that he could "scale that wall within three dates, max." And if not, he declared, he would simply move on. No harm, no foul. He'd just find another wall to scale around the corner. I hoped that wasn't true and that this dimwit was just a pompous fool. But Gabby—a stunning redhead with chocolate-gold eyes and a pretty great rack—since her resolution to remain pure until marriage, has engaged in a seemingly insurmountable ongoing quest for the elusive fourth date. I guess Dimwit wasn't as foolish as I'd thought ... as I'd hoped ... because as fabulous as she is, men give up if they don't see any signs of crumbling resolve.

My latest concern on the topic: Gabby believes the new guy—the one I call Bradley Cooper because of his crazy delicious appearance—is The One. Even though she's known him for quite a while, they haven't even reached the third date end zone, and yet my friend Gabby turned to me over the weekend and dropped this unbelievable declaration into my lap.

Tell me, readers, what am I supposed to do with that? Do I prick the bubble of her realized dream with the first pin of reason I can find? Or is my perspective of ever even finding true love just so skewed that I can't make a reasonable assessment? Perhaps I just quietly begin setting the net into place to readily catch her when she inevitably falls … while hoping against hope that it doesn't actually happen. Please, Bradley Cooper, surprise me.

Is the authenticity of Gabby's kind of conviction about a man even possible to attain? Let's hear what you have to say, readers. What's your take on True Love?

Chapter 15

Celia set the basket at her feet so that she could press the button on the panel for the sixth floor and stepped back to lean against the wall.

"You're Kevin Hake's wife, aren't you?"

She took a good look at the man in the suit, the one she'd hardly noticed when she boarded the elevator car.

"*Chez*. Celia Sanchez. You are…?"

"Rick Hudson," he replied with a smile. "I work at the agency with Kevin."

"Ah. We met at the Christmas party, no?"

"We did." She nodded, not sure of what to say next.

Hudson leaned over and peered at the basket on the floor. "Whatcha got there? … Is Kevin even in the offices today? I didn't see him earlier."

Celia's heart dropped a few inches with a thump. "I hope I didn't misunderstand. I thought he was going to be here into the evening, so I brought him a little something to eat." She nodded toward the basket at her feet, trying to remain casual. Rick Hudson didn't need to know she'd spent hours preparing Kevin's favorites.

"I can't remember the last time my wife did something like that," he said as the car came to a bumpy stop on floor six. "Hake's a lucky man."

"Thank you."

He stood back, holding the door open with his hand as she passed. The two of them walked side-by-side, saying nothing, down the hall and through the large glass doors of Momentum Advertising. As Celia stopped at the tall reception desk, Hudson gave her a nod.

"Have a good day now."

"You too." She smiled, her heart slamming around in her chest as she asked Molly, "Is *Keffin* around?"

"Hang on," the blonde said, her index finger in the air as she pressed a button on the phone. "Is Kevin Hake with you all?" An hour passed in those few seconds before she added, "Tell him his wife is at the front desk?"

Celia inhaled sharply, and the oxygen stung. *He's here.* The thought of another lie … of discovering once again that he wasn't where he said he'd be … she just couldn't take it.

"Celia?" She turned around, and a flush of hot relief nearly overwhelmed her at the sight of Kevin's approach. All she could see was him, and everything else blurred behind him.

"*Hola, mi amor,*" she said, hurrying toward him, but her warm greeting was stonewalled by Kevin's stern silence.

Finally, he asked her, "Celia. What are you doing here?"

"I have the night off from the *restaurante*. You said you have a long day of it, so I thought I'd bring you some *dee-ner.*" She held up the basket, feeling the need to prove her words.

"We're in the middle of a meeting."

"You don't have to eat it now," she said. "Just take it, and it will be there when you get hungry." He gave her a somewhat blank look as she handed off the basket. "I make some of those sausages you like. The ones with the *poof* pastry around them. And some rosemary *cheekin* with honey-glaze carrots. Maybe need to warm that if you wait too long. Some *cucomber* salad and a little caramel cake."

"Seriously?" he said with a grin, and Celia warmed with gratitude. Kevin hadn't smiled at her in days.

"*Chez.* There's enough to share, if anyone else is hungry." She squeezed his hand over the handle of the basket and kissed his cheek. "I love you."

When she turned to go, Kevin snatched her arm and gently pulled her toward him, wrapping her in his one free arm and planting a firm kiss on the side of her head. Celia closed her eyes and sighed.

"I love you too," Kevin said at last.

She looked up at him and, when she blinked, her eyes blurred. "I know I've been making you crazy, *Keffin. Por favor, perdóname, si?* Can we have a fresh start?"

He nodded. "Fresh start," he said, and he kissed her lips. "Why don't you stick around for twenty minutes, and we'll eat this together."

Her heart leapt. "Really?"

"Really." He turned back to Molly. "Would you set my wife up in the small conference room so I can finish the proofing with the clients?"

"Of course."

Celia couldn't help thinking how handsome he was as she reached up and wiped the smear of red lipstick from the corner of Kevin's lips.

"Go with Molly, and I'll be in as soon as I can."

"All right."

"And afterward," he said, his dark eyes flashing with deeper meaning, "we'll find somewhere private so I can thank you properly."

"I'll make it worth your while," she teased.

"You always do."

Celia's blood felt hot as it coursed through her. Relief pounded her limbs, and vibrating solace pressed hard on the deepest places of her body.

Voy a comportarme. Voy a salvar mi matrimonio.

She continued repeating promises to herself about behaving, about saving her marriage, all to the rhythm of Molly's shoes on the marble floor as she led the way to the conference room.

Abby dropped her purse to the kitchen counter before hoisting herself up on the island, her legs dangling over the side.

"You know, I have to admit you were one hundred percent right about this nanotech material for the counters," Nate said as he leaned on the corner of the island. "It's pretty spectacular."

"It is, right?" she replied with a joyous smile. "Anti-reflective, anti-fingerprints. Even though I had to really sell it to Juliet, I think it's a great durable choice for Team Jensen."

He grinned. "So how did your weekend go with your friend's gaggle of kids?"

"It was a good time. Until the brunch at Lael's, that is."

"Ah, I love that place."

"Yeah, Regan does too. So I used it as a bribe to get her to come to church."

Nate laughed. "Good for you. Got some butts in the pew, did ya?"

They shared a goofy high-five as Abby teased, "It's what we do."

"So what happened to ruin the fun?"

"One of the teenagers had a meltdown. Three of them went to an old-fashioned dance party the night before at their school, and it seems Felicity spent too much time talking in her irritating—and possibly counterfeit—British accent to the boy Shaaron is crushing on—"

"Crushing on," he repeated with a sly grin.

"—and Shaaron felt the right time to call her on it was while they were standing at the omelet bar. Between me and Regan, we managed to get it under control."

"Nobody went to the ER then."

"No, only one waffle was injured during the scuffle."

"Nice," he said.

"You know how I told you I'm helping my friend Iris prepare her pool house for her daughter?" He nodded. "I was thinking you might help me with the bones of it. I really want to get it right, and—"

"Happy to help in any way you need," he interrupted. After a moment's pause, he added, "About what you said before, speaking of girls who *crush on boys* ... I was wondering, Abby ... Is there any chance you're crushing *on me?*" Her heart stopped for a few seconds, but before she could think of a reply, he continued. "I only ask because I found myself inordinately distracted over the weekend."

"Oh?"

"Yeah." He moved closer and positioned himself against her denim-clad knee. "The truth is ... I'm finding I think about you constantly, Abby."

"You do?"

"What about you? Do you think about me?"

She shook her head seriously for a moment before answering. "Only all the time."

He rumbled out a sigh before giving her knee a playful slap. When their eyes met, Abby felt as if Nate had the strange power to hold her gaze. No matter how she tried, she couldn't manage to look away.

"You know, Abby ..."

His comment was sliced cleanly in two as the front door burst open and the rambunctious Jensen kids clanged into the kitchen.

"Hey, Nate," fifteen-year-old Drew exclaimed. "What up."

"Final walk-through," he replied, and the two of them exchanged a strange secret handshake.

Drew tossed a way-too-cool nod in Abby's direction when they were through. "Sup."

She almost giggled but Drew's younger sister strolled in, distracting her from it. "Hi, Kym."

"I kind of can't believe we won't see you any more after this, Abby."

"I know. But look what you get to take my place." She waved her arms with a flourish. "A fantastic new home."

"Still."

"Like she's your best friend or something," Drew cracked. "Lame."

"Don't even."

"*You* don't even."

Juliet Jensen stood at the edge of the kitchen and shook her head. "Go look at your rooms and give me some peace." As their father walked in, the two teens roared out. "Darren, those kids are going to be the end of me today."

He slipped his arm around her waist, smiling at Abby and Nate. "You two make a good team. The place looks amazing."

"Reserve that for after the walk-through," Juliet said, and she stepped out of her husband's loose embrace. "Shall we?"

"Absolutely," Abby said, and she hopped down from the island. "Let's start with the upstairs."

She led the way, and Nate and the Jensens followed. It was a slow amble through the new house. They took their time walking across the bamboo flooring, over thick-pile area rugs, and past oversized furniture, all blanketed in the rich jewel tones the Jensens loved so much. On the main floor it was more of the same, all of it cohesive and luxurious while still maintaining a family-friendly atmosphere.

"You have a gift," Juliet told her when they'd come full circle back to the kitchen. "Both of you."

"Like I said earlier, you work well as a team," Darren said.

"We do," Abby replied.

"Color her surprised," Nate added, and they shared a laugh.

"We could not be happier with the end result." Juliet ran her fingers over the stainless steel door of the massive refrigerator, and Abby said a quick prayer of thanks that she'd chosen to spend a little more on the model that didn't show the fingerprints. "I have a photographer scheduled for tomorrow afternoon to take some digital photographs. Would you like me to send you copies for your portfolio?"

"That would be wonderful," Abby exclaimed. "Thank you."

After saying their goodbyes to the kids, Nate and Abby left through the front door. When they reached Abby's SUV in the driveway, they stood back and took one last look at the Jensen home.

"It's a good house," Abby declared.

"That it is." Nate nudged her arm with his. "Why don't you follow me down to Seaport Village and we'll celebrate with lunch at Edgewater Grill."

"Really? That sounds great. It's a warm day. Maybe we can get a table outside."

"You've been then."

"A few times. I'm kind of a sucker for their shrimp mac and cheese."

"I've never had it," he told her. "I usually get the ceviche."

"I don't enjoy scallops. But if you're a very good boy, I may give you a taste of my mac and cheese."

Nate angled downward, and Abby's shoulder burned at the close touch. "I'm always a good boy. But I may have to order my own. Then we can split a margherita pizza, if you're up for it."

"That's a *lot* of cheese," she observed with a chuckle.

"Oh, well, we can—"

"No, no," she interrupted. "I'm all about the cheese." She climbed behind the wheel and Nate closed the door for her. Once she opened the window, he poked his head through it and kissed her lightly on the lips, sending a flame of emotion straight through her body.

"Want something to think about on the drive over?" he asked with a sly grin.

"Sure."

"I'm crazy in love with you." He kissed her again, then darted down the driveway toward his car parked on the street.

"We don't really know exactly why, but smokers are at the highest risk of this particular type of cancer," the doctor said. "On the forms you filled out, Dean, you said you smoked in excess of a pack a day for about fifteen years."

"He quit eight years ago," Iris interjected. "That should count for something."

Dr. Lotus stared blankly at her. When Dean squeezed her hand, it dawned. What a ridiculous thing to say.

"What do we do now?" she asked, and her voice broke in her throat. "What's our next move?"

"We'll schedule surgery to remove the tumor from the bladder with a transurethral resection," he explained. "Once that's done, we'll be able to tell more regarding the stage and grade of the tumor. From the ongoing duration of the symptoms, I'd say it's had a while to grow, so we'll just have to wait before planning further course of treatment. My nurse will call you once the arrangements are made, but do either of you have any additional questions for me?"

"I'm sorry to ask this," he said to Iris softly. "But I think we should know. Am I going to die?"

Dean's question splintered Iris's resolve, and she descended into sobs. She tried to absorb her own grief and be strong for Dean. But she didn't want to know the answer to that question just yet. She couldn't bear the possible answer.

"I'm going to do everything I can to make sure you live as long a life as possible," Dr. Lotus assured him, but Iris wasn't convinced.

This doctor surely looked the part of the genius he was supposed to be—despite his comb-over—but Iris knew firsthand how unreliable and volatile cancer could be. She'd sat at her mother's bedside just two months after being told her breast cancer prognosis looked pretty good ... only to watch her pass away in her sleep.

"If the tumor is low-grade and superficial," he continued, "treatment can be as simple as a couple of doses of chemotherapy. There's still a chance of recurrence, but not usually a progression to higher stages. If it's high-grade, however, we'll discuss additional options. Let's just get that tumor out, and then we'll talk again."

"Sounds like a plan," Dean said with a nod, and he sounded so certain and optimistic that Iris almost wanted to scream.

Bladder cancer.

The words echoed all the way home in the car, bouncing around like Candace's voice when they'd taken her to visit the Grand Canyon the summer before she entered sixth grade.

"I'm Candace Kramer," she'd shouted into the ravine, and it came back at her several times over. "Candace-andace-dace Kramer-ramer-mer."

When they pulled into the garage, Dean turned off the ignition and stared straight ahead at the boxes of Christmas decorations.

"Bladder cancer," he said aloud, and for a moment Iris thought it was her own inner voice still plunking around in her brain. "It's hard to …"

"Yes. It is," Iris whispered.

Dean looked over at her and sighed. "We'll figure it out."

That was Dean. Always the one to figure things out. When they were first married and about to be tossed out of their crummy garage apartment … When he'd been laid off from the first truly great job he'd ever had the very morning that Candace's impending arrival had been announced … When the car broke down on the Tijuana side of the border … It had always been Dean's fervent belief that they would somehow "figure it out."

"You always say that," she reminded him.

After a long few moments of silence, Dean smiled. "The thing is … I always say *we'll* figure it out. But it's always been you that did."

"Well, honey." Iris sighed. "Then I'm afraid we're in some real trouble now."

Dean chuckled, and it morphed into full-on laughter that resonated deep inside her. Iris leaned over and nudged his arm up until she could easily tuck her head under it. She pressed her ear to his chest, taking profound comfort in the steady beating of his sweet and melodic heart.

"I adore you," he whispered. "If I haven't made that clear to you over the years—"

Iris shushed him softly. "You've loved me well, Dean Kramer."

"If I did, it's because you taught me how."

She closed her eyes to hold back the threatening stream of tears. "Somebody had to."

And there it was. That laugh again. How she treasured the rhapsodic music of it. After a quick few words of a clumsy prayer asking that the music might not end, Iris straightened and opened the passenger door.

"Let's go in and call Candace."

"After that, I think I'd like to take a swim."

"I think I'll join you."

In a swim, and in every spare moment, at every possible opportunity, for however long I still have you.

Chapter 16

Regan touched the speaker button and set her cell phone on the bathroom counter. She was running late already and couldn't really spare the time for a chat, but the urgency in Abby's voice spurred her into multi-task mode.

"Okay, take a few breaths and then tell me again. What happened?" she asked, running a brush through her hair.

"We just finished our final walk-through with the Jensens," she said. "We decided to go over to Edgewater Grill for lunch."

"Oh, I love their ceviche."

"That's what he's having."

"Are you there now?"

"No," Abby told her as Regan scooped her thick hair and secured it with a scrunchie before twisting it into a nest at the top of her head. "He's in the car ahead of me. We're on our way there."

"So you haven't even gotten to the restaurant yet. What, you're afraid it won't go well?" She paused to gaze at her reflection for a moment. "I can't meet with my new publishers wearing a scrunchie, can I?"

"No. Wear your hair down. It looks pretty down."

Regan pulled the scrunchie out of her hair and tossed it into the copper container on the counter with a dozen other hair accessories and tools. "So you're following him to Seaport Village," she prodded.

"Regan, he said something before we left. Something so … unexpected. And confusing."

She waited several seconds, and finally picked up a tube of lip gloss—Pinky Nude—and applied it with the spongy tip. "Are you going to tell me what he said? My cape is in the closet, so my mind-reading super power isn't available right now."

"He said he *loves me.*"

Regan froze, the gloss wand suspended in the air as she stared into her own eyes through the mirror's reflection. "Repeat, please."

"He asked me if I wanted something to think about on the drive over. I said okay. And he said he's crazy nuts in love with me."

Regan picked up her phone, turned off the speaker, and pressed it to her ear.

"Then what happened?"

"Then he kissed me, and just … got in his car."

"And he's still in it."

"Yes. But we're pulling into the parking lot now. What am I going to do?"

Regan quirked a brow. "I don't follow you."

"How am I going to sit across the table from him and eat shrimp macaroni and cheese with that hanging in the air between us?"

Stepping into the chunky platform booties she'd ordered on the internet from Zappos, Regan shrugged. "You just told me over the weekend that you're in love with him, Abbs. Now he says he feels the same. This is not a disaster, you dope. This is a good thing. Go eat lunch. Take a walk on the boardwalk and look at the blue ocean. Tell him how you feel. Let him tell you again how he feels. Now if I don't get into my car and head for Los Angeles, I'm going to miss this meeting."

"What meeting?"

"My first one with Valencia Publishing. Remember? My book?"

"Oh. Right. Ask them if you can write it without the Gabby character."

Regan grinned. "But she's my favorite."

"Knock 'em dead."

"Yeah. You too."

"I can't breathe," Abby half-whispered.

"Yes, you can. Talk to him, Abbs. This is what you've been waiting for. *He gets you.*"

Regan heard muffled static, then—presumably—Nate as he asked, "Ready to go?"

"I have to go, Regan," she said. "Have a good meeting."

"And have a good rest of your life."

Abby immediately disconnected the call and Regan laughed as she tucked her phone into the small bag she'd readied that morning.

Credit cards … some cash … my phone …

She grabbed the lip gloss tube she'd used and pushed it into the inside pocket.

Okay. Tablet's on the kitchen counter. And … I'm ready to go.

She tossed the strap of her handbag over her shoulder, and the chunky heels of her shoes made a clomping sound as she hurried down the hall. Picking up the tablet, her stomach flopped at the thought of what lay ahead.

"We'll want to discuss the book in detail," her new editor's email had read. "If you can come prepared with a chapter-by-chapter outline, that will help us accomplish more."

A few minutes later—as she reached the edge of her neighborhood—Regan questioned whether she'd remembered to flick the button to close the garage, and she had to backtrack. Sure enough when she reached her driveway again, the open door to her garage offered gaping access to her home for any random passerby.

"Regan," she growled, pressing the button and waiting for the door to close before setting out a second time.

She punched buttons on the radio until the familiar loops of a bluesy acoustic guitar caught her attention. Her favorite classic oldies station playing a Rickie Lee Jones tune she remembered from her school days.

It might have been an oldie even back then.

Regan tapped out the beat and hummed the catchy tune. When the chorus surfaced, she changed the lyrics as she sang out with it.

"Ab-by's in lo-ove..."

"Iris, are you serious?" Lynette asked, her eyes so round and wide that it ached. But who could see a ten-foot cake at the center of a table and not react? "Did you make this or buy it?"

"I made it," Iris replied.

"How many layers is that?"

"Six."

"Six layers."

Lynette leaned in closer and examined the work of art.

"It's chocolate cake with buttercream, filled alternately with salted caramel and raspberry ganache. It took half the night."

"Iris ..."

"Oh, it's okay. I don't sleep much anymore."

"I can only imagine."

Lynette's heart squeezed at the thought. If she had to face life without Trevor, there wouldn't be a cake tall enough or a pastry sweet enough to ease the pain. She followed Iris to the kitchen and stood behind her for a moment before sliding her arms around her friend's waist and setting her chin on Iris's shoulder.

"What can I do?"

Iris clucked out a bitter little chuckle. "I wish I knew."

The front door whooshed open. "That'll be the girls," Lynette told her, and she kissed Iris's cheek just as Abby, Regan, and Celia filed in.

"*Ay carumba!*" Celia exclaimed when she spotted the cake. "*Es una obra maestra.*" She turned to Regan and asked, "How do you say that in English?"

"Honey, I don't speak Celia."

"*Es* a … masterpiece!" she declared once she found the word.

"It certainly is," Abby remarked. "Iris, I didn't think it was even possible, but you've outdone yourself."

"She couldn't sleep," Lynette told them, and she exchanged a quick message of understanding with Regan.

"What's in the oven?" Celia asked, seemingly oblivious. "It smell like heaven."

"Honey-roasted pork tenderloin, twice-baked potatoes, and broccoli casserole," Lynette announced as she gathered dessert plates, forks, and a cake knife.

"I brought some *kee-noah* salad too," Celia said as she set a large Tupperware container on the counter. "It has beets and oranges and avocados. I make it for *Keffin*, but he turn up his nose."

"Imagine," Regan said dryly. "He didn't want a quinoa salad."

"Is very healthy, *Mees* Smarty. They eat it in parts of the world like Colombia and Peru before it become *fushionobble* here. And I think we could all use some extra fiber, don't *chu*?"

"Thanks anyway."

Lynette chuckled as she quietly cut into the cake. "I might try it later," she told Celia. "I've never had quinoa." Slipping a large slice of cake onto the first plate, she said, "Come on, ladies. Let's gather around this amazing dessert, shall we?"

They slowly filed toward the table, and Iris was last to take her seat.

"I don't think we need a discussion tonight, do we?" Lynette asked them, and she pushed the first large slice of cake toward Iris.

"No, we do not," Regan agreed, and she smiled at Iris. "Dive into this wonder, my friend. Take solace in the comfort that is chocolate."

Iris grinned and made no show of objecting. She produced a chunk about twice the size of her fork and pushed it into her mouth, eyes closed. "Mm-hm," she hummed, nodding.

"While Iris is having an intimate moment with her cake, why don't we let Abby tell us her news," Regan suggested, and Lynette caught the flash of pink on Abby's face, clashing with her beautiful orange hair.

"You have news?" she teased. "Let's hear it, girl."

"Well …"

It appeared that her words had caught at the base of her throat, and Regan reached over and shook her wrist. "If you don't spill, I'm going to."

"Go ahead."

Never one to shrink away from a challenge, Regan boldly spilled it all.

"Abby's in love. And he says he loves her right back."

Iris tossed her fork to her plate with a clamor. "What!"

"I know," Abby said, tucking her hair behind her ear. "I already knew I loved him. I mean, I think I've known for a while. And then he said the words first."

"And get this," Regan chimed in. "He told her on their way to lunch, and then they went over to Seaport Village and ate their whole meal without either one of them ever mentioning it again."

Celia chuckled. "Everything about Abby *es* the G-rated version of everyone else, no?"

"Well, the kiss we shared in the parking lot after lunch was definitely *not* G-rated," Abby objected with a pout.

"Hah. PG-13?" Celia teased.

"He walked me to my car and said maybe we should talk about the elephant in the harbor."

"Cute," Iris cracked.

"And he said it again," Abby told them with a giddy grin. "He said, 'Abby, I know it hasn't been very long, and I realize I'm taking a chance on scaring you off. But I want you to know that I have no doubt about this. I'm in love with you.'"

"And what did you say?" Lynette asked, licking the salted caramel filling from the back of her fork.

"I told him it does scare me. In fact, I'm shaking in my heels. But I said, 'Nate, the truth is … I love you too.' He looked at me really … *strangely* after that. Like I thought he might faint or throw up."

They all chuckled at her telling of it.

"But then he got this really sweet look in his eyes, and he moved close to me and asked me to repeat it. I tried to, but before the words came out, he just grabbed me, lifted me right off the ground and laid one on me. I swear, I couldn't *even breathe.*"

"But in a good way?" Celia inquired.

"Very." Abby twirled a lock of hair around her index finger and blushed again. "A very, very good way. In fact, I don't think I've ever been kissed the way Nate kisses me."

"Uh-oh," Lynette teased with a chuckle. "I know that feeling. You're a goner, girl."

Abby looked around at each of them, landing finally on Lynette, and she smiled. "I really am. I think I'd almost marry him tomorrow if he asked."

Regan gasped. "You would?"

"Hardly a doubt about it."

"Good grief."

"What about you and Sebastian, Regan?" Celia asked. "Is it *love*?"

"Unlike my sweet redheaded friend here," Regan replied, "I have too much experience with the death of supposedly undying love to hand over my heart this quickly. Thank you very much, Craig Sloane."

"But you can see the maybe out there ahead, *chez*? Somewhere, with Sebastian?"

Regan shot her a sideways glance, and Lynette chuckled. "Celia, you're relentless."

"Yes, she is," Regan agreed.

"Easy to hush me," Celia told her. "*Yust* answer the question. Personally, I don't see the *attroction*. But if you do …"

Regan pushed out a heavy sigh. "Sure. Maybe. Somewhere out there, in the galaxy, behind a gazillion stars, *maybe* I can see the faint flicker of a possibility with Baz." She sighed again. "It's kind of surprising. I mean … we just seem to … *fit*."

"Hey, I forgot to ask," Abby exclaimed. "How did the meet go with your new publisher?"

Regan shrugged. "Everyone's very nice, especially the editor I'll work with. But I still feel a little weird about it."

"Imagine how we feel," Abby joked.

Iris left the rest of the cake on her plate as she pushed back her chair, stood quickly, and crossed to the kitchen. Lynette caught a quick glimpse of the pain on her friend's face, and it strangled her with emotion. She followed, standing beside her at the stove.

"Can I help with anything?"

"No. It's all … under … control …"

"Completely unconvincing," Lynette whispered.

"Yes? Well, it's all I got."

"I know."

In the next instant, Iris turned to her and moved into Lynette's embrace, sobbing against her shoulder. Before she even knew it, the others had gathered around to form a circle of support as Iris's sobs turned to wails. A solid five minutes passed as they all stood there like a big clump of ten arms, five bodies, and several gallons of liquid love for Iris.

Regan broke the circle first as she grabbed a roll of paper towels, tore one off, and handed the roll to Abby as she blew her nose. The others did the same in an effort to pull themselves together.

"I'm starving," Celia sniffled.

"Me too," Iris said with a smile. "You all sit down and I'll pull our meal together."

"No," Lynette said. "You sit down and *we'll* pull the meal together. Is Dean here? Should we send him a plate?"

"He's out to dinner with Candace," she said, heading for the table. "She came home early when she got the news. I said we'd save them each a slice of cake."

"We can try," Celia sang.

"And we're still on for the pool house remodel?" Abby asked. "Or will she want to stay in the house?"

"We discussed the ins and outs, and we all decided together to go ahead and let her have a separate space." Iris dried her cheeks with a second towel and dabbed at her runny nose. "We'll need to talk about how to get started. Maybe tomorrow?"

"I'll call you."

Lynette slipped her hands into oven mitts and removed the fragrant pan from inside, setting it to rest atop the burners on the stove.

"Oooh, look at that," Celia exclaimed.

When she reached for a taste, Lynette smacked her hand. "Hey. Why don't you set out some plates and silverware."

Celia tossed her thick black hair over her shoulder and shrugged before she obediently sauntered toward the cabinets, leaving traces of her sweet floral scent behind her.

"Spoil *spo-art.*"

She'd told her friends she had "hardly a doubt" about whether she'd marry Nate if he asked right now. The recollection tickled something at the back of her jaw, and Abby couldn't resist the broad smile that seemed to lift her entire face. They'd arranged to meet at Iris and Dean's to have a look at the pool house and collaborate on the plans to get things underway for Candace, and she could hardly wait to see him.

Abby lowered the window and shut off the air. No reason not to enjoy the ocean air if it happened to drift that far inland. And if it didn't, the blue skies of San Diego at this time of year were best enjoyed without barriers. When the left turn arrow ignited and the car next to her made no move to accelerate, Abby glanced over at the driver and noted he was too busy staring at her to realize he'd missed the light change. Her eyebrow quirked and she gave him a nod toward the stoplight. Startled, he jumped a little and shot her a quick grin before gunning into the intersection.

Abby couldn't help but chuckle. There she'd been, sitting behind the wheel of her car, grinning like a giddy schoolgirl, her happy face turned into the fresh air like a dog on an adventurous car ride. No wonder he'd been staring. She probably looked like a nut case.

I think I'd almost marry him tomorrow if he asked, she'd told her friends. But Abby knew—even in the very instant she'd uttered the words—there was no *almost* about it. Her feelings for Nate Cross had taken her over in an impetuous whirlwind that was so unlike her. After Hurricane Dylan, Abby had made a solemn oath. No MORE BAD CHOICES IN MEN. She'd turned to God and asked Him to cleanse her from her past and do what He did best: Make her new. Wise. Discerning. Give her a fresh start. And she'd felt His grace at work almost immediately, she really did.

So when had she slipped down the perilous slope from vehement denial about her attraction to Nate to ... to *this?* Daydreaming about him and—

The driver behind her blasted her horn, and Abby gasped.

—and missing the light just as the guy in the blue Accord had done?

"I'm thunderstruck, Lord," she whispered. "I hope You know what we're doing. Because I think we've clearly established that I don't."

Abby's pulse rate quickened as she turned onto Iris's street and noticed Nate standing out front. Dark blue jeans, a black shirt, and a tailored black sport coat. She hadn't noticed until she pulled into the driveway that he stood chatting with Dean.

Dean. He looks tired.

Abby slid out of the car and headed straight for him. Tossing her arms around Dean's neck, she pulled him into an embrace.

"How are you feeling?" she asked.

"All things considered," he replied as she kissed his cheek, "pretty peppy."

"Well, keep that up," she said. "I see you've met Nate."

As she and Dean separated, Abby reached out and squeezed Nate's hand. Wordless greetings passed between them, and her heart raced with the electrical current generated by the simple connection.

"Yeah, your architect and I, we were just talking about the pool house. Iris and I are really appreciative of what you're helping us do for Candace."

"Happy to do it," Nate interjected.

"Dean? When's your surgery?" Abby asked.

"Pre-op meeting tomorrow morning, surgery on Wednesday," Dean told them.

"Can we pray with you?" Nate asked, leaving Abby slightly stunned. Oh, to have that kind of boldness in her faith …

"It's been a long while since …" He stammered slightly before adding, "Yeah. Sure. I'd appreciate that."

Abby's eyebrows arched and a smile lifted. She hadn't expected that response at all.

Nate led them into a tight circle, and she couldn't help the way her heart soared at his authoritative demeanor. He placed one hand on Dean's shoulder and grasped Abby's hand with the other. She took Dean's hand and he squeezed hers in response. She closed her eyes and allowed Nate to lead the way. He prayed for Dean's well-being and health, for the wisdom of the medical professionals, for God's grace to rest upon him.

"Dean," Nate said when he'd punctuated the end of the prayer. "Do you know Christ?"

Abby inhaled sharply, and Dean dropped her hand. Her mouth went immediately dry as she awaited his reply.

"We were pretty good friends for the first part of my life," he replied candidly. "But we've lost touch in recent years."

Nate smiled at Abby. "Why don't you go ahead inside. We'll join you in a few minutes."

She hesitated for a moment, examining Dean's face for signs of agreement. As if he could read her mind, he grinned and shot her a nod. "Iris is in the kitchen."

"Of course she is," she joked. "See you inside then."

Abby tried not to look back, but couldn't resist. With her hand on the knob of the front door, she glanced over her shoulder, but when it turned and slipped out of her hand, she reeled to find Iris standing in the doorway.

"Good morning."

"Hi."

Gazing past Abby, Iris stepped just outside and asked, "Is that him? He's cute."

Abby nodded.

"What's going on there?"

The two women stood side-by-side, watching Dean and Nate, but unable to hear them.

"We were talking about the surgery, and Nate asked Dean if we could pray for him."

"And he said no," she said confidently.

"Actually, he said he wanted us to."

Iris paled. "He did? ... Are you sure?"

Abby chuckled and elbowed Iris's rib. "Yes. I'm sure. It was a very nice prayer."

"What are they talking about now?"

The two women watched the men for a moment before Iris gasped as Dean folded to the pavement beneath him, kneeling, his head bowed. Nate placed his hands on Dean's shoulders and bowed his head as well.

It wasn't until Iris slowly turned toward Abby—her eyes wide and round as glassy china plates—that Abby realized she'd cupped her hand over her own mouth in astonished joy.

"What just happened in my front yard?" Iris asked as her lips turned upward and her full cheeks plumped like red apples.

"Something wonderful."

"Better call that guy in Rome," her friend muttered. "We've just witnessed a bonafide freakin' miracle."

Chapter 17

Regan stared at the blinking icon on the laptop screen, wishing she had the words to send it on its way across the open document. Instead, she leaned back in her chair and closed her eyes. She could almost feel the floor shimmy as Baz and his power tools put together the last of her new walk-in closet directly below. In an effort to divert from the immediate reality of writer's block, she picked up the phone on her desk and keyed in Abby's speed dial number.

"Hi, Regan."

"Are you busy?" she asked.

"No, just in my car. What's up?"

"Have you been reading my blog?" Regan asked her, and she nibbled the corner of her lip awaiting the reply.

"Of course. I have to see what I'm up to. Why?"

"Listen … after meeting with my publisher, I realize this whole thing has … well, I never meant to cross any lines, Abbs. Not with you or the other girls. You guys know that, right?"

Abby chuckled. "Regan. When you started the blog—even before Vertical approached you—it was your life preserver after everything that happened with Craig. We all talked about it then, remember?"

She nodded, then realized it needed a voice. "Uh-huh. But now that it's grown so much, and there's going to be a book …"

"Remember what we said? As long as you changed the names to protect the innocent—"

"Or not-so-innocent," she interjected.

"Right. And after Vertical called, we discussed it again. We hate it, Regan. You know that. But at the same time, we kind of love that we're part of you creating this whole new life for yourself."

"And that hasn't changed?"

"You can bring it up again on Thursday if it will make you feel better. But as far as I'm concerned, nothing has changed."

Regan sighed. "I just wanted to make sure."

"You have writer's block, don't you?"

She clucked out a chuckle and lied. "No."

"Regan."

"Yes."

"I'm hanging up on you. Go write things."

"It's all the noise," she said with a groan. "Baz is finishing my closet, and I can't even hear my own thoughts."

"That's what that is? I thought we had a bad connection."

"No. It's my *closet connection*."

"Now that he's finishing the closet, what will you ask him to do next?"

"A dog house for Steve?" Regan teased, and they shared a laugh.

"Okay, I'm getting out of the car now," Abby announced. "I'll talk to you later."

Regan sighed and disconnected the call. A few minutes later, blessed silence fell over the house before the momentary peace shattered with the thump of approaching footsteps. Before she could turn her chair, Baz had crested the top of the stairs and stood in the loft smiling at her.

"Come see your closet," he invited her, all of his weight leaning on one hip, his hands stuffed down into the pockets of his snug, faded Wranglers.

She popped up with a grin. "Is it fabulous?"

"You be the judge."

She followed him down the stairs and across the hall to her bedroom. Steve lay sprawled across the center of her bed, his big droopy head resting on Baz's balled-up leather jacket.

"Oooh," she cooed when she spotted the unexpected whitewashed door on a rolling barn hinge. "That's beautiful."

"You like it?" he asked. "It's reclaimed wood from my ranch."

Regan chuckled. "Your what?"

"I have a small horse ranch up in Julian. We rebuilt the out-buildings last year, and we salvaged some of the wood. Including the old barn door."

She cocked her head, curious about how many other surprises this man held back.

"We?"

"Settle down. A group of buddies helped me out."

"Just checking."

"The closet. Have a look."

She grinned as she rolled back the door to reveal what seemed like a much larger space than before—cavernous in comparison, really—fitted with rods, shelves, drawers, and shoe cubbies.

"Well, I love it," she told him, struggling to cap her enthusiasm to somewhere between ALOOF and APPRECIATIVE on the Richter scale.

"That's it?"

"No," she said, tipping her head with a straightforward grin. "I *really love it.*"

"That's more like it."

Regan timidly touched his shoulder. "Okay if I hug you?"

"Be gentle with me," he teased.

On her tiptoes, she slipped her arms around his neck and pulled him close. "It's beautiful, Baz. Thank you so much."

"You're welcome."

He pulled away—only slightly—and peered down at her. A silver flicker of amusement danced in the rivers of his blue-gray eyes. He set his hands on both sides of her waist, then slid them around her.

"You know, it really begs for a closer look," he almost growled, and he guided her one step backward, then another, until they were both inside the closet, and he rolled the door shut behind them.

Standing there in the dark with Baz, nearly swooning over the spicy male—now very familiar—scent of him, Regan's senses stood at full attention, curious what he might do next. He broke the suspense and lowered his face closer to hers, scratching her cheek with his stubbled one.

"What are you doing?" she whispered.

"Giving you a closer look at your new closet."

"Uh-huh."

"Oh," he added. "And this."

Pressing her against one of the shelves behind her, he kissed Regan until her lips ached. Even at that, she hadn't had enough when he broke the connection. Reaching through the darkness with both hands, she clutched his shirt and yanked him back to her.

Lynette looked down at her dark brown hand clasped with Iris's ivory one before glancing over at her friend. Staring straight ahead, Iris's short brown waves—normally bouncy and light—fell tired and flat around her face. Mascara—smeared more from exhaustion than from crying—shadowed bloodshot eyes. On the other side of her, Abby held Iris's right hand. Beyond Abby sat Regan. And then Celia. The five of them, connected by so much more than just the steel-armed chairs along the slate wall of the hospital waiting room, had sat in silence for hours. There had been creamed coffee in thick paper cups, unappetizing snacks from the vending machines, and two updates from nurses that were really more like extensions of the waiting. It had still been hours of motionless, silent *waiting*—all of it punctuated by distinct, palpable waves of restrained torment swirling around Iris.

"It's taking too long," Iris said in a raspy voice that cut through Lynette's heart. When their eyes met, she asked, "It shouldn't take this long, should it? I feel sick."

Lynette caught sight of the worry in Abby's eyes as she caressed Iris's hand. "The last nurse said the doctor would come out as soon as he's able. Don't worry. He'll come around that corner any minute."

Celia stood and crossed to the window, pressing a cell phone to her ear and speaking in whispers.

"Weren't we supposed to turn our phones off?" Regan asked them. "I thought I saw a sign by the elevator." When no one replied, she shrugged. "I turned mine off anyway."

Lynette leaned forward to catch Iris's eye. "Do you want some more coffee? A cold drink?"

"I just want some good news. Do they have that in the vending machine?"

They shared a smile, Iris's looking half-beaten.

"Sorry, honey."

Abby's whispers drew her attention, and Lynette glanced over to find her head bowed, eyes closed, praying.

I send a big old AMEN to those prayers for Dean. Please, just let him come out fine.

Iris homed in and watched Abby, waiting until she opened her eyes and lifted her head again. "Thank you," she said softly, and Abby smiled warmly. To Regan, she added, "Thank you to all of you for being here. I don't know what I'd do without you today."

"Where else would we be?" Regan asked.

Celia tucked her phone into the pocket of her skin-tight jeans as she approached them and stood in front of Iris. "*Keffin* sends his love, *chica*. And I get *cufferage* for the dinner prep at the restaurant. I just have to get there by six."

"Mrs. Kramer?"

Iris bolted to her feet before even looking up, wringing her hands as she awaited the details the doctor came to deliver. Lynette, Abby, and Regan all stood as well.

"Dean came through just fine," he told Iris, and she released a relieved sob. "He's still in Recovery, but he should wake from the anesthesia very soon."

"Can I see him?" she asked, looking for all the world as if she might take off at a full run.

"You can sit with him, yes." He glanced at those gathered around her and added, "Just you, though."

"Okay," she said, nodding.

"Dr. Lotus," Lynette piped up, "I work for Dr. Eisen, and I'm a close friend of Dean and Iris's."

"How is Leroy?" he asked her. "Attending the symposium in Cleveland, no doubt?"

"He is. He'll be back in a couple of days." Lynette slipped her arm through Iris's and smiled at him. "Can you tell us what it looked like once you got in there? What's Dean's prognosis ... now that you've gotten a closer look?"

The doctor pressed his lips together and sighed, looking at his shoes for a long moment. When he glanced up again, his eyes met Iris's directly.

"Dean's cancer is advanced."

Iris gasped, and Lynette covered her hand with her own.

"It looks to have spread to the lymph nodes, as well as metastasized to his prostate and liver, and possibly further. We'll know more in a few days, and we'll meet to discuss next steps and possible treatment plans. Since your friend knows Dr. Eisen, you and Dean may want to consider a second opinion with him. At this moment, however, he'll need some time to heal from the surgery and get some strength back."

Lynette felt her friend deflate into her. She slipped her arm around Iris's shoulder and led her backward to the chairs where she collapsed.

"I'll look in on Dean in about thirty minutes," the doctor said. "You can go back whenever you're ready."

Lynette looked up and smiled at him. "Thank you, Doctor."

Abby sat next to Iris. Without a word, she took Iris's hand, bowed her head and began to pray again. Lynette watched streams of silent tears flow down Celia's cheeks as she and Regan embraced.

"This can't be happening," Iris muttered. "How will I tell Candace?"

"We'll tell her together," Lynette promised. "She's taking her final exam today, right?"

Iris nodded. "We thought it would be best if she went ahead and officially finished out the semester. She'll be back in San Diego tomorrow."

"All right then. I'll wait for you to see Dean, and I'll stay with you when you call her. Trevor knows I may stay overnight, so if you want me to be with you when you talk to her tomorrow, I can do that."

Iris nodded blindly. "First I'll see Dean. ... Just a few more deep breaths, though. I don't want him to wake up and see me this way."

Abby had stood and rushed across the waiting room before Lynette had even noticed. She caught sight of her as she flung herself into the arms of a handsome blond—hair cropped short on the sides and longer on the top, clean-shaven and dressed in jeans and a nice sport jacket.

"That's Nate," Regan told them.

"*Ay carumba*," Celia sang. "He really is a hottie, yeh?"

The way Nate held her—and how Abby clung to him—pinched Lynette's heart with a sort of sweet relief. As she watched them converse softly, she thought this boy looked every bit the part of someone Abby might love. They appeared to be a perfect match.

Iris stood and straightened her blouse before walking toward them. The moment she reached Abby, she stepped back and Nate opened his arms and embraced Iris. When they parted, he placed his hands on her shoulders and looked her squarely in the eyes. Lynette couldn't hear what he said to her, but she recognized the warmth and conviction of his tone. Iris seemed to sense the same thing as she kissed his cheek and gave his hand a quick squeeze before hurrying back to where the rest of them waited.

"I'm going to Recovery to sit with Dean. You go ahead and go home, all of you. I'll call you when I know more."

"What about Candace?" Regan asked. "Do you want one of us to call her?"

"I'll wait here for Iris," Lynette told them. Turning to Iris, she added, "Go see Dean and take as long as you need. I'll be here when you're ready to head home, and I'll go with you."

Iris leaned over and hugged her. "Thank you." When she straightened, she added, "Thank all of you."

"We love you," Celia said.

"Tell Dean we love him too," Regan added.

"I'll do that." Nodding to Lynette, she said, "I'll be back soon."

"Take your time."

Iris waved at Abby and Nate as she scurried away, then Abby led her new beau by the hand toward them.

"Girls, I want you to meet someone special," she said. "This is Nate Cross. Nate, you know Regan already." He smiled at her warmly. "These are my other friends, Lynette and Celia."

"Pleasure," he said, shaking their hands.

"We feel like we know you already," Celia gushed. "Abby speaks very kindly about you, Nate."

"Good to know," he teased, shooting a spark of a grin Abby's way. "She speaks highly of you all too."

"I have to go get ready for the dinner crowd at the restaurant," Celia said. "If you all want to come by tonight, I'll make sure you're fed very well."

Nate looked to Abby. "Are you up for a meal? Maybe relax a little?"

She nodded. "Sure." Looking to Regan, she asked, "How about you?"

"I was going to have dinner with Baz tonight. I'll see what he thinks and maybe we can meet you and Nate around seven?"

"Sounds good," Nate said. "What about you, Lynette? Can you join us?"

"She's staying the night with Iris," Abby told him.

"You have our numbers," he said. "If either of you needs anything, just give us a call."

"I'll do that," she replied. "Thank you. Why don't you kids go ahead and have a good time."

"Can we get you something before we abandon you?" Regan asked her.

"I'm fine. I'll call you later."

"I've never seen Iris like this," Regan said. "In all the years I've known her."

"She's never had to face something so horrendous," Kevin replied. "She's reeling. Watching someone you love go through this kind of thing can be life-changing."

Regan glanced across the table at him and smiled, wondering what he'd endured that ushered such understanding about Dean's illness. She could see it in Kevin's dark brown eyes and in the lines beside them; he identified somehow with Iris.

"Listen to this," Abby said softly to Nate. "*Aguapanela con Queso.* It's a drink. Served hot, made with cane sugar and soft Colombian cheese. Have you ever heard of this?"

"No. Let's try it," he suggested.

"It's very sweet," Kevin told them. "A little rich for my tastes. Especially after the meal we've just had."

Regan couldn't help noticing the waitress—her uniform just the slightest bit too tight—hovering next to Kevin, basically ignoring everyone else at the table while hanging on his every movement.

"I agree," she said, leaning over his shoulder.

"I'll just have the *tinto*," he told her. Turning to the others, he added, "One hundred percent Colombian. Black."

"Make that two," Baz chimed in.

"Three," Regan added.

"We'll have two of the *Aguapanela con Quesos*," Nate said.

"Do you have any of that rice pudding?" Regan asked her. To Baz, she added,

"It's so good. Creamy. With cinnamon."

"*Arroz con Leche*," the waitress said with a nod. "How many?"

Everyone except Kevin raised their hands.

"Oh, by the way," Regan said, trying to sound casual but suspecting she'd already failed miserably. "Could you tell Celia we're here? The hostess said she'd tell her, but we haven't seen her, and this is *her husband*, you know." She waved her hand in Kevin's direction, and the waitress straightened. Her face dropped as she took one step backward.

And I don't think you want someone like Celia to discover you've been fawning over her man all night, do you?

"Yes, I … know. I'll be happy to tell her right away."

Regan shot Abby a grin as the waitress hightailed it toward the kitchen. A fraction of a moment later, she happened to catch the end of a look passed between Kevin and Baz, and Regan leaned over and asked, "What was that?"

"You didn't have to do that," Baz said with a grin. "He's a big boy."

"Yes, he is." When she noticed Kevin paying attention to their exchange, Regan smiled. "If you're going to be married to Celia, maybe you should think about uglying it up a little."

Kevin chuckled. "Like that would change anything? She'd still think I was screwing around."

"Probably," she said with a nod. "But maybe the women wouldn't flock the way they do. You're just too adorable, Kevin. Maybe get some glasses and a flannel shirt or two." She pushed her own glasses up the bridge of her nose for effect.

"I'll work on that."

"Yeah, tone it down over there, would you?" Baz joked with his buddy. "Give Nate and me a chance to be noticed." He looked across the table at Nate and mugged, "Nobody puts Nate and me in a corner."

"*Dirty Dancing*," Regan said, nodding and grinning at the reference. "Nice."

"All right, all right," Kevin groaned. "Enough already."

Baz leaned close to Regan. "Think he'll lead all the kids in the merengue?" he muttered.

Regan snickered. "Now you're just showing off."

Celia emerged from the kitchen just then and scurried across the restaurant to their table. Regan couldn't help noticing that her friend looked fresh as a summer flower, her thick, dark hair twisted back just so, her bright-white smile beaming. She certainly didn't look like a woman who'd spent the last few hours over a kitchen stove.

She planted a kiss on Kevin's cheek from behind him, then massaged his shoulders as she greeted them. "I didn't know if you all decide to come or not. You enjoy your meals?"

"So good," Abby exclaimed. "I had the tilapia with shrimp—"

"*Tilapia en Salsa.*"

"Yes! Those creamy little onions are so delicious. Sometimes I forget how magnificent you are in the kitchen."

Celia rounded the table and hugged Abby from behind her chair. "*Gracias por decirlo*, Abby." She reached over and squeezed Regan's shoulder before leaning down between her and Baz. "*Buenas noches*, Sebastian."

"Hola, Celia."

She snickered before nodding at Nate. "And what did you have for *deener*?"

"I had the marinated steak with the little yellow potatoes."

"*Sobrebarriga a la Plancha*," she replied. "And?"

"And … it was *amazing*. Abby said you're quite the chef, but I had no idea. I think I could eat here every night of the week."

"This is what we like to hear," Celia told him. "Abby, Señor Hottie, he is a keeper, *chez*?"

"*Chez*," she mimicked.

Regan laughed out loud before shifting the gears of the conversation. "Hey, guys. Baz and I were talking on the way over here. What would you all think about trying to break away for a couple of days and heading up to his horse ranch in Julian?"

"Celia can't do anything on the weekends," Kevin interjected. "She can't get away from the restaurant."

"No, but I can go early in the week," she said. "Monday and Tuesday, maybe?"

"You have a horse ranch?" Abby asked in surprise.

"It's nothing much," he replied, "but it is beautiful country up there."

Celia hurried around the table, back to Kevin's side. "This would be good, no? Let's make *plahns* to go." When he didn't answer right away, she slid her arms around his neck and leaned in close. "Come on, my darling. Let's get away from the city, *chez*?"

"I can try to get a couple of days," he conceded, and Celia bounced excitedly as she kissed his temple.

"What about Iris and Dean?" Abby said. "And Lynette. Should we invite her and Trevor?"

"They won't be able to leave the kids again so soon," Regan remarked. "Anyway, she'll want to stick around for Iris. But I don't think we'd be terrible friends if the rest of us went for just a couple of days."

Abby leaned in closer and asked Regan, "How big is the house? I mean, are there enough ... *bedrooms?*"

"It has five bedrooms and two baths," Baz answered for her. "Plenty of room for this group."

"Baz said he'd give the master to you and me," she told Abby. "Then he'll take a guest room, one for Nate, and one for Kevin and Celia. Then there's one to spare in case you snore."

Abby cackled before assuring Nate, "I do *not* snore." When he grinned at her, she sighed. "Separate bedrooms. That's okay, right? Do you want to go? It might be fun."

"I'd love to. We can sneak away one afternoon and maybe spend some time working on the final details of the pool house project for Iris and Dean."

"Perfect," she exclaimed. "We're in."

"Monday and Tuesday then?" Regan asked. Nods and agreements all around. "Excellent."

"I'll call the Fosters and let them know we're coming," Baz said.

"The Fosters," Regan said, turning to Abby, "are the married couple who live on the ranch and take care of the horses and stuff when Baz isn't there."

"They can get the rooms ready and stock the fridge," Baz added.

Regan noticed that his focus seemed fixed on Kevin as he spoke, and she followed his line of sight until she landed on Kevin, straight-faced and serious. He'd agreed to come along, but Regan could see he wasn't exactly excited about it.

Welcome to VERTICAL MAGAZINE
Moments-of-Truth.net

BLOG POST: REGAN SLOANE

I've given a fair amount of blog time here over the years to my friend you all know as Irene, and to her husband whom I call Family Man. So it seems appropriate to share with you that Family Man has taken quite a hit recently with an unfortunate diagnosis, subsequent surgery, and a lot of questions in the balance like hanging bats in a dark cave. Irene is reeling, of course. And the rest of us ... well, our hearts are breaking.

Chinese philosophy teaches that Yin and Yang are polar opposites, and yet completely complementary at the same time. Yin isn't Yin without Yang, and vice versa. This is how I see Irene and Family Man, and so this whole idea of our mortality has really been weighing on me as I try to be the best friend I can be without infringing—or interfering, if that makes sense—with this private magnetic connection between them.

I can't stop thinking about how certain people flow with the current, into our lives and then out again, while others whoosh in with the tide and organically take us with them when they go. Irene, Gabby, Annette, and Maria—they are the ones who happened in at various times, each of them attaching to a certain part of me. What if I'd never met them? Who would I be now? And my Carpenter Chef ... without Maria and Pretty Boy, we might never have met.

Gabby and her Bradley Cooper are the praying kind. They latch onto a thread of hope as they surrender their fears and concerns to Someone in the air. I don't think I'd even know how to begin doing something like that. Annette—she has this inner strength to rely on. Sometimes I watch her closely as she leans back into it, drawing from a wellspring of wisdom that I know I certainly don't possess. And Maria is another story entirely. She's a passionate lit fuse who somehow manages in her own chaos to find comfort in the belief that, no matter how dire things become, they will always unfold into destiny's hand. Everything happens for a reason, and all that. The fact that she struggles so hard to orchestrate destiny is one that I choose to ignore at the moment.

But me—I don't have anything like that to prop up this fear and—Yes!—anger. I'm angry that a sweet guy like Irene's Family Man would be randomly crushed by an enemy as indiscriminate as cancer at the very moment that his genealogy lives on in the grandchild growing in the belly of his daughter. I find myself questioning, imagining, writhing under the crashing waves of this diagnosis and its possible outcome. Not just for Family Man ... but for Irene.

I know there are praying folk among you, readers, so please keep them in your prayers. And the rest of us too, come to think of it. I love this precious platinum circle surrounding my life, and the prospect of finding it broken is almost more than I can bear to think about.

What challenges like this have you faced out there? And how did you manage to overcome?

Chapter 18

Iris set Dean's cell phone on the nightstand and smiled. "I have mine in my pocket," she told him, tapping her sweater. "If you need anything at all, just jingle."

"Will do."

"I'll come and check on you before dinner. How's chicken and dumplings sound?"

"Like a piece of heaven."

"Oh, good. Because that's what we're making. Your daughter's idea."

"Lynette still here?" he asked, pulling the quilt up to his chin.

"For a bit."

"Good. Thank her for me, will you?"

"I shall."

She leaned over him and kissed his forehead, her eyes clamped shut tightly as she did. With one last stroke to his hair, she turned to leave, and she closed the door softly behind her.

"Mom, get this," Candace said as she walked into the kitchen to find her daughter's sweet face and the front of her blouse dusted with flour. "Lynette's granny used to make chicken and dumplings too. It's comfort food for all of us."

"Is that a fact?"

Iris suddenly felt as weary as she'd ever been, and she climbed onto one of the tall stools tucked under the short end of the island where Candace busied herself forming lumpy balls of dough into dumplings. On the other side, Lynette wore a bibbed apron and chopped onions, carrots, and celery.

"How's Daddy?" Candace asked her.

"He's resting."

"You look like you could use a little of the same," Lynette observed. "Why don't you head back upstairs and take a nap. Candace and I can take care of dinner, and we'll wake you when it's ready."

"Oh … no … I couldn't do that."

"Of course you could," Candace said. "Go on. It's been such a long couple of days, Mom. Take advantage of a chance like this one. We're *cooking* here."

Iris let out a tired little chuckle. "Anything from the girls?" she asked Lynette.

"Abby texted half an hour ago. They arrived safely and are planning an early dinner."

"Just like us." Candace smiled at her mother and nodded. "Now go dream things."

"Really?"

"Really, Mom. Go on."

Iris slid down from the stool and leaned on the counter. "Will you still be here when I get up?" she asked Lynette.

"You're joking, right? I plan to help you eat this feast before I head home."

"Promise?"

"You have my word." Lynette and Candace shot twin we-mean-business expressions at her, and Iris laughed.

"All right, all right. I'm taking a nap, and I don't want to hear another word about it."

She dragged up the stairs, willing the creaking floor of the landing to be silent for a change. Instead, the boards enunciated her every step.

"Iris?"

She froze. Had Dean called out to her?

"Iris, is that you?"

She crossed to the guest room door and turned the knob. There was certainly no doubting the kinship of the architectural details of her house, the floors and the doors all creaking with the same familial pitch. As she poked her head through the opening, she spotted Dean propped up in bed by pillows, the television whispering softly.

"Do you need something?" she asked him.

"Yeah. I do." She waited for him to identify it, but he just smiled.

"What can I get you?"

"My wife," he replied. "Come and sit with me awhile?"

Thoughts of a nap soared off her shoulder with wings spread wide as she rounded the bed and gingerly climbed in next to him. Dean winced as she took her place beneath his open arm, and they settled into place.

"I thought you'd be sleeping," she told him.

"I'm not?"

Iris chuckled. "Maybe we both are."

"Better wake me up. I don't much like the turn this dream is taking."

Me neither.

Angling her head to look up at him, she sighed. "We're in this thing together."

"Yeah," he replied, the tone of his voice about three octaves lower than normal. "Sorry about that, kiddo."

A day with you is better than a thousand somewhere else.

Where did she know that quote from? It had just popped into her mind out of nowhere. Poetic in nature, she figured it had to be Elizabeth Barrett Browning … or maybe John Keats? A distant memory left over from her college infatuation with the greats.

Well, whoever wrote it must have had intimate knowledge of what it meant to truly love another person.

Regan sipped her hot chocolate, trying not to betray her eager anticipation of Baz's answer to the universal question Kevin had posed: *Your ideal man or woman from the movies or television.*

Baz set his coffee on the table in front of the sofa to pay closer attention to Steve, who had whimpered, pressed himself against Baz's leg, and gone directly to sleep. "I guess if I had to choose, I'd go old school and pick Julia Roberts. She's cute, girl-next-door, but with an edge. I do like a good edge." He scratched Steve behind the ear and sighed. "Besides, I'm a sucker for the wild hair."

Regan chuckled, quirking a brow at Abby before telling him, "We can see that."

"What do you—" And then he figured it out. Scowling, he ran both hands through his own shaggy blonde tresses. "Hey, don't mock the hair."

"You have to admit … You do rock the wild mane."

"It's not wild," he defended with a grin. "It's unencumbered." Baz leaned into the corner of the sofa and narrowed his blue-gray eyes at Regan. "What about you? Who's yours?"

"My what?" she teased.

He soured comically. "Come on. Spit it out. What's his name?"

"Well … he's not in the movies or on television, per se," she said, grinning. "But I do have a celebrity crush."

"Spill."

Regan opened her mouth to speak his name, but Celia and Abby beat her to it in two-part harmony. "Keith. Urban."

"Keith Urban?" Kevin exclaimed. Darting a glance at Baz, he declared, "Man, you two are made for each other."

"What do you mean?" Baz snorted. "I'm nothing like Keith Urban." Turning to Regan, he added, "I can't sing a note, and I wouldn't know an F string from an H on the guitar."

"*Chez,* but we *establish* you have the messy blond hair thing going," Celia pointed out. "And I suppose you have some degree of attractiveness …"

"Gee, thanks." Baz picked up his coffee, careful not to disturb the sleeping dog at his thigh.

"I just mean, you aren't *my type* … but you are a handsome man, Sebastian."

"Okay, Celia. This I gotta hear. Your turn. Who's your ideal?" Baz prodded.

"I don't need no celebrity crush," she said seriously. Waving her arm at Kevin, she added, "Look who I married." Groans sounded all around, and she shrugged. "I can't help *eet*. I married my ideal man."

"What about you?" Nate asked Kevin.

He paused for several beats before offhandedly replying, "What she said."

"Oh, come on," Celia said. "You can tell them. I'm not bothered."

"Celia," Abby piped up, "take the win."

Regan giggled. "She's right."

"No, I already know *Keffin*'s celebrity crush. He loves Mila Kunis."

Both Nate and Baz nodded as if approving his choice.

"Yeah, I guess I knew that," Baz commented.

"Now you two," Celia directed at Nate and Abby. "We know Abby's crush, but Nate, you *haff* to play too."

Nate turned to Abby. "They already know your crush, huh?"

She shrugged. "Taye Diggs."

Baz and Kevin both leaned forward and belted out hoots.

"Didn't he help Stella get her groove back?" Kevin joked.

"He's done a lot of wonderful work since then," Abby defended. "I don't know. I just think he's dreamy."

"Dreamy," Nate repeated.

"Yes. In a hypothetical world. Now you. Who's your crush?"

"I can truthfully tell you," he said, turning serious, "that I haven't thought of another woman for two seconds since the day I met you."

The room fell completely silent, and Regan's heart pounded wildly. That kind of romantic statement was sure to reel Abby in smoothly.

As expected, Abby reached over and touched Nate's hand. "What a lovely thing to say."

Kevin groaned, and Celia shook her head and leaned into him.

"But hold the sugar coating," Abby added with a pragmatic stare. "'Fess up."

A sly smile crept over Nate's face. "Well, it used to be Sandra Bullock," he said. "But recently … I've started to notice Jessica Chastain."

Celia cackled. "The redhead. Just like Abby."

"Did you see *Zero Dark Thirty*?" he stated. "She was kind of brilliant."

"I liked her in *The Help*," Abby said. "But she was a blonde in that one."

Nate twirled a lock of Abby's red hair and remarked, "I prefer a redhead."

Regan thought she felt Baz's gaze on her, and she confirmed it with a smile.

"Want to take Steve for a walk?" he suggested softly, and they both glanced down at the sleeping dog. "He looks like he's eager to get outside."

Regan chuckled and nodded. "He does, doesn't he?"

Baz shook the French bulldog by the scruff of the neck. "Settle down, boy. Be patient."

They both stood, and Baz lifted Steve from the sofa and set him down on rickety paws.

Celia asked, "Where are you two going?"

Baz took Regan's hand and led her toward the door without reply. After he helped her slip into her jacket, she latched the leash to Steve's collar. She handed it to Baz, shot Abby a grin over her shoulder, and followed Baz out the door in silence. She closed it behind them and they took the stairs leading off the porch. Their arms crossed in the back as they simultaneously slid them around each other's waists. The wide rock driveway—flanked on both sides by soft yellow torch lamps—crunched under their feet as they followed it, Steve trailing a couple of feet behind.

Regan angled her head toward Baz as she stared at the night sky, black as ink except for the spray of silver stars twinkling like pinholes of light peeking through a velvet canopy.

"It's so beautiful up here," she commented.

"It's hard to get over, right?" he asked her. "I can never stay away for long."

She understood why. "I didn't think it would be so chilly. I might have under-packed."

"It'll be in the seventies by mid-morning. I thought we'd go riding. You like horses?"

"Oh, yeah. Me and horses, we go way back." *Way back a decade, which is the last time I've been within three miles of a horse.*

"Why don't I believe you?"

"I guess you're just the suspicious type," she teased.

When Baz laughed, Regan thought it sounded like music threading its way through the low-hanging branches of the trees. He took her off guard—the stones beneath his leather high-tops grounding out the sound of his sudden halt as he turned—and he took her into his arms, lifted her right off her feet, and kissed the breath right out of her.

Regan couldn't even think, and her attempts to do so reeled in upward spirals, weaving in and out of those platinum stars in the overhead sky, leaving one fragmented thought behind.

It's ... too ... soon ...

Regan pressed against his shoulders with both hands until he set her down; then, breathless, she grabbed his jacket for balance when her wobbly knees buckled.

"I ... I'm sorry," she sputtered. "It's just ... too soon, Baz."

He rubbed her hair back from her face with his thumb and looked down into her eyes without speaking.

"I *l-like* you," she said. "I really do. But I'm just not ready to dive into something. I haven't finished paying the consequences for the last time I did that. And I'm not willing to relive—"

"Forty-watt," he muttered.

"Yes." Her heart stopped. "Wait. You read my blog?"

A crooked grin lifted one side of his lips. "I do."

"Oh ..."

Her racing heart had only just begun to slow down. But only for an instant. Shreds of her writing pierced her brain like clean slices taken from a firm pie.

It will come again for me one day, after the healing is complete. I have to believe it will...

And although I've been more attracted to Carpenter Chef than I've been to anyone in years, our date was choked by dim 40-watt memories I couldn't seem to shake ...

Her throat actually ached, warm dread parching her as the recollections rolled like a bulldozer.

"Now I know how the girls feel," she muttered, feeling so completely exposed by her own self-indulgent admissions. Did she dare ask him to stop reading it? To avoid the Moments of Truth URL like a debilitating first-century plague? To even forget what she did for a living?

"It's easy to forget that another blog post published doesn't add up to words just entering some swirling void somewhere," she'd once written, *"but it's actually taking my thoughts and observations and opinions out to you, readers."*

"Regan," he said, taking her hand. "If you're not ready for me yet, I get it."

"I'm ... sorry."

"Don't apologize to me. Don't ever be sorry for your feelings. Own them."

"Baz ... when you kiss me ... I almost feel like I could—" A spontaneous sob choked back her words, and tears rolled out of her eyes before she'd even known they were there. "I'm so messed up ... completely defective, Baz. Run. Run like the wind. Save yourself from me."

"Thanks," he replied with a smile, so sweet, soothing, and warm, like honey melting down the inside of a teacup. "But I think I'll take my chances and stick around awhile."

Regan turned away, her back to him as the tears continued to flow. "Why would you do that? Why ... would you *want* to?"

"I'm not sure yet," he said. "Can I get back to you after I figure it out?"

A soft snort escaped through her nose, and she gazed at him over her shoulder. "You know what, Baz? You may be more messed up than I am."

"Nah. Nobody's that bad."

"Hush."

"Make me."

She turned around and tucked her fist on her hip as she grinned at him. Baz took two cautious steps toward her and lifted his hand, nodding as if to say he came in peace this time. He used the pad of his thumb to gingerly wipe the tears from her cheek, then he kissed the top of her forehead.

"Let's just have some fun these next couple of days, shall we?" he suggested. "Forget everything else and just enjoy ourselves."

"Can we do that?"

"I think if we set our minds to it, we can muddle through."

"No, really," she clarified. "*You* can do that? ... With no expectations?"

"I'm amazing like that," he stated.

Regan sighed, and a mound of tension left with it. She extended her hand toward him. "Finish our walk then?"

"With no expectations beyond another cup of decaf when we get back."

"You should try the hot chocolate Abby made."

"Maybe I will," he answered as they continued down the stone drive.

Everyone else had gone to bed, but Nate and Abby decided to spend a little more time together in front of the roaring fire enjoying another hot chocolate. Abby made a mean hot chocolate, sure; but she knew—and suspected Nate knew as well—it was more about having an excuse to extend their time together side-by-side on the loveseat than about the refill of chocolaty goodness in their cups. In fact, it was her third mug of the night, and Abby wasn't entirely sure she even wanted to finish it.

"My thoughts keep drifting back to Iris and Dean," she told him as she settled beside him and stared into the flickering flames.

"Mine too," he replied, and the bass beneath his words rumbled through his chest and against the back of her head where it rested against him. "I've prayed for them several times in the last few hours."

Abby smiled. "I have too."

"The look in her eyes at the hospital haunts me," he said.

"She was pretty torn up. We have a tight circle, and she's closest to Lynette, but ... Dean is Iris's best friend. The thought that ..." Tears sprung to her eyes and the emotion strangled away her words.

Nate stroked her hair and planted a kiss on the top of her head. But as an acidic heat churned inside her stomach, Abby considered whether to put words to the thought that had replayed in her heart and mind, plaguing her for most of the day.

"I hope this doesn't sound awful," she began, then she sighed.

"Go on."

"I mean, I hate to even say it out loud, but ... I have this ... terrible feeling." She stopped; she couldn't give voice to such a horrible thought.

"I know," Nate whispered. "I feel it too."

His words catapulted her forward, and she spun around to look at him squarely. "You do?"

"I know," he replied, shaking his head. "I don't want to say it either. But I feel like God reveals these things to us sometimes so we'll know how to pray. And that's what we need to do. We'll continue to pray for Iris, and for Dean."

He nudged her back into place, and her head came to rest against his chest. A moment later, she drew a long sip from her cup.

"I'm so happy you were there at the house that day, Nate." She closed her eyes and listened to the rhythm of his steady heartbeat. It brought her comfort somehow, like a familiar song whispered in her ears. She felt him nod and—eyes still closed—she sighed.

Before they said their goodnights and went their separate ways, Abby and Nate sat upright on the edge of the loveseat cushions—hands clasped and heads bowed—and prayed together for Dean's health and faith walk ... for Iris's strength and comfort ... for blessings on Candace and her baby ... and for their own roles in supporting this family they'd both come to love so much.

Regan was still awake reading—Steve curled up beside her with his head on her pillow—when Abby eased open the bedroom door, prepared to tiptoe into a dark room.

"Oh, you're still up," she said. "I thought you'd be sound asleep by now."

"I meant to just read one more chapter," Regan replied, nodding at the book in her hands. "But that turned into two, then to three."

Abby pulled her pajamas out of the overnight bag in the corner and began changing into them while Regan told her all about the novel's plot.

"So how was your walk with Baz?" she asked, sliding beneath the blankets on the other side of the king-sized bed.

"Enlightening."

Abby rolled to her side and leaned on her elbow to look at Regan more closely. "Oh?"

"Well," she said with a grin, dragging one of the extra pillows to her and wrapping her arm around it as though she needed it for support. "The guy kisses like no guy I've ever known, Abbs. Seriously. It's ... epic."

"Better than Joe DiMirro?" she teased.

"Even better than Joe."

"Was that the enlightening part?" Abby asked.

"No. That was the delightful part."

Abby chuckled. "Go on."

Regan slipped a bookmark between the pages of her book and set it on the nightstand. "You know, the words came out of my mouth before I even really realized it's how I feel. But I told him I'm not ready yet to get involved in something with him." Abby rubbed Regan's arm swiftly and smiled at her friend. "I know Craig's been gone a long time—long enough, right?—but I'm still so messed up over everything and how it happened. Do I want to carry it into a new relationship? I mean, I'm still so ... *angry*. Maybe I need some therapy or something."

"What you need is time," Abby told her. "Only you'll know how much time that is."

"I don't want to miss out on someone as great as Baz just because of timing."

"If he's as great as you say, he'll wait on you. What did he say when you told him you aren't ready?"

Regan blushed and grinned. "He said he'd wait."

"Well, there you go."

"I asked him why he'd want to, and he said he has no clue."

They shared a laugh, and Regan tossed her head back against the pillow, sending Steve straight up to all four paws.

"Sorry, boy. Sorry. Go back to sleep. It's just Mommy being dramatic."

Abby scratched the side of the dog's face. "You should be used to that by now, buddy."

Once they all three settled down again, Regan flipped off the light. Just about the time Abby closed her eyes, Regan whispered, "What about you and Bradley Cooper? What—"

"Regan, don't call him that. This is real life. He has a name out here in real life."

"Fine. Nate. What were you *and Nate* up to all this time?"

"Sitting by the fire," she replied. "Sipping hot chocolate."

"How many of those things did you have?"

"Three."

"What else? Any explosive kisses for you guys tonight?"

"A few."

"Anything more?"

Abby turned her head and stared into the darkness between them.

"I can feel you glaring at me over there."

"Well, you earned a glare from me," Abby told her. "You know nothing more is going to go on with Nate until we're married."

The bed jolted, and she realized Regan had shot upright. "Until you're married. You said that so matter-of-fact. Abbs, did he propose to you?"

"No."

"Did he?"

"No," she exclaimed. "Lie down and go to sleep."

"Would you tell me if he did?"

Abby chuckled. "I tell you everything. You think I could keep that from you?"

Silence. And more silence as Abby waited for Regan to consider her words.

"No, I guess not," she finally replied, falling back to the pillow again. "I just have this feeling about you two."

"You do?"

"Let's go to sleep now."

"In just a minute," Abby said. "First I want to hear about this feeling you have."

"Didn't you ever just get one of those premonitions about something where you just absolutely know it's going to happen at any time?"

She thought back to her conversation with Nate about Dean. They both had one of those feelings Regan referred to. Not about a happy turn of events, but still.

"Yeah. I've had those."

"Then you know."

"I guess. Go to sleep."

Several minutes passed before Regan broke the screaming silence again. "G'night, Abbs."

"Goodnight, Regan."

The *tick—tick—tick* of the clock on the other side of the room seemed amplified.

"Night, Steve."

"Regan."

"Sorry."

Tick—tick—tick.

"Was that you?"

"Regan, for crying out loud. Was *what* me?"

"Never mind. It was Steve."

Moments later, the evil stench of salty, rotting garbage confirmed for Abby that Steve had been the culprit.

She hoped.

Chapter 19

Lynette's nostrils tickled with delight as she sat there at Iris's kitchen table soaking up the lovely fragrances.

"I made a triple batch of this, by the way," Iris told her. "There's a whole pot of it for you to take home and serve your brood. It's only missing the pasta, which you add when you heat it up. Just let it simmer about twenty minutes."

With everything on her plate, Lynette wondered how on earth her friend managed to march on in such a spectacular way. She imagined her own reaction to the challenges of an unmarried, pregnant daughter and a husband with cancer. It certainly wouldn't involve cooking meals for others, of that she could be sure.

"I also wrapped up two loaves of French bread for you. It was my mother's recipe, and it's amazing with this soup. You'll just keep it in the foil and put it into the oven for about ten minutes at three twenty-five. There's also some garlic butter in a small container."

"You're amazing." Lynette walked over to the stove and stood beside Iris. "It smells incredible."

"Another of Mama's recipes ... one of Dean's favorites. It's called Italian Wedding Soup—"

"Italian soup, French bread," Lynette cut in with a smile. "You're all about the diversity, aren't you? I'd like to think having a black best friend has something to do with that."

Iris chuckled. "You're a nut."

Lynette leaned over the simmering pot and inhaled deeply. "Exquisite."

"The little meatballs are made from a combination of ground pork and beef. I like to make extras and freeze them for other recipes at a later date."

"You really do excel at highlighting the inadequacies of the rest of us, don't you?"

"Stop." Iris popped open a tall stainless steel canister and produced a handful of fettuccini noodles. "Mama liked to drop orzo pasta into the soup at the last few minutes, but Dean likes the thicker ones like these."

"You've been cooking for us every week for I don't know how many years. Why haven't we ever had this before?" Lynette asked as Iris stirred the uncooked pasta into the pot with a large metal spoon.

"Haven't you?"

Lynette grinned. "I would have remembered."

"I hope your family enjoys it."

Iris set the spoon into the curved ceramic spoon rest, placed both hands on the edge of the stove ledge, and stared into the pot. Her worry became a palpable thickness in the air around them.

"What can I do?" Lynette asked. "Anything at all."

Iris lifted her head. "You've done so much." She turned to Lynette and sighed. "I don't know what I'd have done without you. But go home to your family, and go back to work tomorrow."

She'd called the office that morning and said she wasn't sure how many more days she might need. "Are you sure?"

"I'm sure."

Lynette wrapped her arms around her, and Iris turned into it. "I love you so much," she whimpered.

"Back atcha, sistah." When they parted, Lynette told her, "I'm going upstairs and pull my things together."

Iris nodded, and Lynette kissed her plump cheek. "We'll get through this."

Iris balanced the tray with one hand while she turned the doorknob to the guest room—*Dean's room*—with the other. He looked up from the open book in his lap as she entered and gave her a weary smile.

"Are you hungry?" she asked.

"Not especially."

"How about if your loving wife spent most of the afternoon making Italian Wedding Soup and warm French bread with garlic butter?" she sang. "Would you be hungry then?"

"Famished."

She grinned at him as he closed the leather book and slid it to the bed beside him so that she could set the tray on his lap.

"I brought iced tea, but if you want something different to drink, I can—"

"Tea is great." Dean looked up at her, his gaze fixed on her for several beats before he finally broke the connection and checked out the meal before him. "Sit with me while I eat?"

"Sure."

She dragged the wingback chair in the corner closer to the bed and plopped into it. Dean closed his eyes for a moment, and it sent an arrow of adrenaline soaring straight through her. When he opened them again, he smiled at her, and she noticed the usual light in his eyes had dimmed somewhat.

"What are you reading there?" she asked with a nod toward the book next to him.

"Bible," he muttered before dipping a chunk of bread into the broth of the soup and pushing it into his mouth. "Mm," he said, nodding. "Good."

"You're reading the Bible?"

"Yeah."

"I didn't even know you owned a Bible."

"It was Mother's. I thought I remembered seeing it on the closet shelf under her hat box."

Iris swallowed around a lump of dry emotion at the back of her throat.

"It's pretty good stuff," he said.

"Well, I remembered it's one of your favorites, and I haven't made it in a while—"

"Yeah," he interrupted, "the soup is great. But I meant the Bible. Pretty good stuff."

If there was an expected or natural response to that, Iris couldn't imagine what it might have been.

"Here," he said, picking up the worn leather Bible and handing it to her. "Why don't you read it out loud while I eat. We can both benefit."

She accepted it from him with the quirk of a brow. "Are you serious? You want me to read to you out of the Bible."

"You don't have to. I just thought it might be nice."

At first, she simply folded her hands and stared at the book. Then she glanced up at Dean—oblivious to her puzzlement as he spooned soup into his mouth—and almost laughed out loud. At second thought ... *What could it hurt?* If Dean wanted her to read to him—out of the Bible or pretty much any other book—what harm could it do?

As she opened it, Dean gave her a nod. "There's a receipt marking the page where I left off."

She opened it and laid the book's binding flat on her open palm. "Psalms?"

"Yeah. Where the chapter continues on the last column."

"Uh ... okay." Iris scanned the double rows of small print. "That's Psalm 84." She cleared her throat before beginning to read. "Hear my prayer, Lord God Almighty; listen to me, God of Jacob. Look on our shield, O God; look with favor on your anointed one. Better is one day in your courts than a thousand elsewhere; I would—"

The words stuck at the back of her tongue, and she read over them again in silence.

Better is one day in your courts than a thousand elsewhere.

"Lose your place?" he asked, and he bit off a chunk of bread.

"No. I thought of those words just the other day, and I couldn't place where they were from. I thought it was poetry."

"What words?"

"I remembered it something like ... *One day with you is better than a thousand somewhere else.*"

Dean noisily slurped a spoonful of soup. "It does sound poetic, doesn't it?"

Iris laid the Bible to rest on her knee and watched her husband as he dunked a piece of bread into the broth and popped it into his mouth. When he noticed her watching, he smiled.

"This is your best yet."

"I'm pretty sure you say that every time I make it."

"Always improving," he said, returning his attention to the bowl.

Iris sighed. She'd wasted so much time feeling alienated from Dean, wishing he wanted her the way she wanted him, thinking she'd have time to seduce him back to her. It all seemed like such nonsense to her now. No, now all she wanted was to make a better batch of his favorite soup ... to see the lines at the side of his eyes deepen when he smiled ... to take stock of the silver threads that had worked their way into his temples and eyebrows sometime when she wasn't looking closely.

Why hadn't she looked more closely?

"Iris? Where did you go?"

She shook her head and smiled. "I'm sorry."

"What are you thinking about?"

"How much I love you," she admitted.

Dean looked up from his nearly empty bowl and pushed the tray away slightly. "Seriously. What were you thinking about?"

"Seriously," she exclaimed with a chuckle. "That's what I was thinking."

Dean leaned back into the pillows and closed his eyes. After a few moments of quiet contemplation, he said, "I think we've wasted a lot of time, Iris."

"I think so too."

He lifted his head and opened his eyes. Blinking, he told her, "I'm sorry."

"I'm sorry too."

"No." He slid the tray to the bed beside him and turned toward her seriously. "You have nothing to apologize about. You're what's made my life worth anything. Without you ... I'd be nothing."

"You couldn't possibly," she replied frankly. "I'm so blessed to have found you."

"Come here."

Iris stood and set the closed Bible on the nightstand. After moving the tray to the dresser by the door, she climbed across the bed and settled next to Dean. He wrapped his arm around her shoulder and urged her closer, pressing her head to his chest. She could hear his heartbeat beneath her ear, and her breathing conformed to the rhythm of its pulsation. Unaware that she was so easily drifting to sleep, Dean broke through the cadence of the melody of their alignment.

"Iris," he murmured.

"Hmm," she hummed from the edge of slumber.

"One day with you ... is better than a thousand anywhere else."

Iris smiled as she gave in to the exhaustion and let sleep claim her for what felt like the first time in days.

Regan's limbs throbbed, and she found herself wishing she'd just done like the anti-drug advertisements advised and just said no. But with her arms tightly wrapped around Baz's waist and her face planted against his back, she clenched her thighs around the massive animal beneath her and tried to remember to breathe.

"How you doing back there?" Baz called over his shoulder.

"Oh ... just ... great. When are we stopping again?"

"Just over the hill. You've got to see this view."

Regan peeled her face away from his soft denim shirt and glanced around. Nate and Abby rode up ahead—Abby had been brave enough to mount her own shiny brown horse instead of clinging to Nate's back like a frightened wuss occupying half a saddle—but she saw no sign of Celia and Kevin.

Her left thigh tightened and Regan whimpered.

"Regan?" Baz shouted.

"Fine. I'm fine."

But she wasn't fine. She was one massively painful muscle cramp away from fine. As the inside of her thigh seized, she cried out, impulsively banging her fist against Baz's shoulder blade as she did.

"What are ... you ... doing?" he exclaimed.

"My leg. My leg. It's ... My leg!"

Baz eased back on the reins. "Whoa. Whoa." When the horse came to a halt, he dismounted smoothly and extended his arms to Regan. "It's just a cramp," he said. "Come on."

She tried to relax her legs, releasing the grip they had on the saddle, but her left leg refused to comply. With his arms tight beneath hers, Baz slid her down from the horse and tried to set her right on the ground. Fortunately, he was quick enough to catch her when her legs wouldn't hold her at first.

"I don't know what happened," she whined.

"Tension," he said. "It's a new move for your thigh muscles. Like when you get back to the gym after staying away for too long."

"Right," she said. As if she'd ever had a gym membership. "Any chance we could walk up this hill of yours?"

Baz chuckled. "Sure. Come on."

Nate circled back, his horse stopping in front of them. "Everything all right back here?"

"Yep," Baz told him. "We just decided to take it slow. Maybe walk the rest of the way."

Nate's gaze skimmed over Regan before he laughed. "Got it. We'll meet you up there."

"Where's Kevin and Celia?" Regan asked him.

"They made a pit stop," Nate answered with a sly smile. With a nod, he added, "Back that way."

Just about that time, their two friends rounded the corner of the trail sharing one horse, Celia's dark, wavy hair dancing on the breeze. Kevin's too, for that matter.

"What happened to the other one?" Regan asked Celia when they reached her.

"Oh, sorry," Celia said, directing it at Baz. "He wander off when we weren't watching. We try to find him, but *Keffin* say he probably wander back on his own, yeh?"

"More than likely," Baz said.

"Sorry, man," Kevin added with a grin.

As the horse galloped up the hill, Regan noticed the layer of grass coating the back of Celia's jacket and poking out of her hair.

"Oh," she said, realizing what their "pit stop" had entailed.

Baz shook his head and laughed as he wrapped the reins around his fist. Guiding Regan on one side and their abandoned horse on the other, they started their hike up the hill. Using her hand as a visor, she peered into the distance and noted that their four friends had already crested the hill without them. Measuring the pain in her thigh against the idea of saddling up again, she groaned.

"Yeah, I'm going to keel over if I try to walk it," she admitted.

"Want to climb back onboard?" he asked her.

"Onboard you or the horse?"

"Either."

She clicked her tongue and sighed resolutely. "You think you can get me back up there?"

"I'm pretty sure I can."

Remembering that he'd provided a step stool when she originally made the climb, she stopped in her tracks, the two of them just staring at each other.

"Today? Or do we plan on sticking around for tomorrow's sunset?"

"We didn't bring the stool."

The corner of Baz's mouth twitched. "Come on over here."

Regan approached the horse with caution, gingerly patting the side of his neck. "Okay, horsie. How ya doing?"

Baz twined his fingers together, creating a sling. "Step up with one foot, then put the other into the stirrup."

"Simple."

Her quivering thigh muscles threatened to betray her, but she followed his instructions. First one foot, then the other; then with his hands cupping her derriere, Baz shoved her up and over the saddle while Regan released a shrill screech. Once he climbed in front of her and the two of them had settled into the saddle, she slapped his shoulder.

"Quick. Tell me something you stink at so I can put you to shame."

He laughed and shook his head, gathering the reins and kicking the horse's side with one foot. "Hah!"

Regan screamed into his ear and buried her head against his shoulder blade again as the animal trotted the rest of the way up the hill.

"Seriously," she said, her eyes clamped shut tight and the fingers of both hands clutching his shirt. "What can't you do? Roller skate? Disco dance? Name something I can make you do and then laugh at your efforts."

A moment later: "Have a look."

The horse came to a complete halt, and Regan pushed her eyes open. Nate and Abby had climbed down from their horses and stood in front of them while Celia and Kevin remained in the saddle. An explosion of vibrant color served as the backdrop to their silhouettes—cobalt blue swirled with a kaleidoscope of lavender, pink and gold—and Regan gasped when she saw it.

After a few moments of the group's silent admiration—untethered by unnecessary words—Baz glanced over his shoulder in Regan's direction. "Do you want to get down?"

"Unless you're going to leave me to sleep on this hill, I'll just stay right here until we head back down to the house."

He snickered. "Fine. But it's pretty amazing, right?"

"*Ay carumba, Sebastian,*" Celia breathed. "*Es espectacular.*"

"Baz, I'm so glad you brought us up here," Abby called back to him. "It's beautiful."

"The best view for fifty miles."

The jingle of Regan's cell phone went off, and the horse jolted underneath her. When she pulled it out of her jacket pocket, she saw Lynette's name on the screen.

"Lynette," she quickly answered. "You wouldn't believe what we're looking at right now."

"Regan." The alarm in her voice gave Regan a chill.

"What's wrong?"

"Come home."

"What? Why?"

As Regan's gaze met Abby's, she almost heard the *click!* as they locked.

"Dean's gone. Trev and I are here with Iris."

"What? What do you mean he's *gone?*"

Lynette sighed. "She fell asleep next to him, and when she woke up ... he was gone."

"He died in his sleep?"

Abby gasped and moved into Nate's open arm. "No," she cried.

Celia began whispering in Spanish under her breath.

"We can leave within the hour," Regan said.

"Wait until the morning," Lynette suggested. "I'm with her and Candace now."

"I'll call you from the road when we're on our way. We'll come straight to the house." Regan gulped back the tears as she added, "How is she?"

"Inconsolable."

"Lynette, what happened? They said the surgery went well, and the chemo treatments are scheduled to start in two weeks. I don't ... understand."

"We'll know details later. It just happened. He just passed away in his sleep; that's all I know. I need to go. See you in the morning?"

"Yes. Tell her we love her."

"I will."

"And ... that we're all ... so ... *sorry.*"

"She knows."

"Love you," Regan added.

"You too. See you tomorrow."

Once she'd returned the phone to her pocket, Regan pressed her forehead against Baz. Without a word, he yanked the reins and guided their horse into a u-turn. The two of them reached the stable first, and the others followed right behind. Barely five words passed between the six of them until after they'd returned to the house.

"Celia and I will get some food started," Kevin announced, and the two of them headed inside.

Baz rubbed Regan's arm briskly and asked, "Do you need anything? What can I do?"

She couldn't think of one thing to say and, when her eyes met Abby's again, the two of them moved into an embrace with the force of a magnet and steel. The instant their arms closed around one another, they both broke down into tears and sobs.

"I can't believe it," Abby cried.

"I can't either."

"Poor Iris."

"I know."

When they finally let each other go, Nate and Baz had gone inside the house. Despite the fact that the chill in the air had Regan trembling, she and Abby climbed the stairs and sat down side-by-side on the bench swing secured to the porch rafters by heavy chains.

Abby slid her hand into Regan's, and the two of them sat there, staring straight ahead without speaking.

Abby finally broke the silence. "I'm going to pray now."

"Yeah. Good idea."

Welcome to VERTICAL MAGAZINE
Moments-of-Truth.net

BLOG POST: REGAN SLOANE

I'm saying goodbye to a dear friend today, readers, and I'm really struggling with it. I almost feel like, if I don't show up to the memorial, he won't actually be gone. Like if I sit here long enough studying the nuances of the unique markings on Steve's fur, the horror of the moment will pass and I won't have to participate in the awful chore of facing it.

He's gone.

But he shouldn't be.

It's not like we didn't know the time might come. We just didn't imagine it would come so quickly.

My amazing friend Irene—asleep in the arms of her precious Family Man— awoke to find that he'd slipped away. Not just from her, but from all of us. From the world. And none of us have had time to even consider what a world without Family Man might look like.

Here's what I know for sure: It will be far less kind. Less understanding. Less accepting. These are the things I always found in him, without question. And now we all face a new world, one where those familiar, comforting blue eyes aren't there to anchor us. A world where—most devastatingly—Irene has lost the pillar that moored her. IreneAndFamilyMan. They've been one word to me for such a very long time. I wonder how she'll manage. In fact, I'm plagued with this incredulous and inescapable mountain ahead of her as she figures it out.

A poem hangs on the wall of my friends' home, framed in burnished copper. Irene told me once that it defined her relationship with her husband.

> He's more myself than I am.
> Whatever our souls are made of,
> his and mine are the same.

"Emily Bronte may have written it," she once told me. "But I feel the words. All the way to my soul."

I can't imagine how that soul will ever flourish without him. How any of us will. These are the Moments of Truth upon which this blog is based, and yet I have no answers for my friend today. All I have to offer is love.

Chapter 20

Nate turned off the ignition, and Abby flipped down the visor to check her reflection in the lighted mirror. She produced a tissue from the pocket of her coat and dabbed at the mascara smeared beneath her eyes.

"I look a mess," she muttered.

"You're beautiful."

She sighed and gave him a weary smile. "I wish I knew what to say to Iris."

"You do know." He took her hand and rubbed it with his thumb. "You tell her you love her ... that you're here for her, whatever she needs. You tell her how you felt about Dean, and how much you admire the connection they were able to maintain over so many years. You tell her you hope to have that yourself someday."

Abby nodded. Nate always knew just what to say. One of the ten thousand things she loved about him.

"She called me this morning," he said, and it took Abby a few seconds to process his words.

"Who did? Iris?"

"Yes."

A flock of sensations pinged, each of them with a question attached, leaving her uncertain about which to address first.

"What did she say?"

"She wanted to know more about that afternoon when we prayed with Dean."

Abby wiped the smudge from beneath one eye and then the other.

"She found him reading the Bible the night he passed away," he continued. "I think she was just looking for some confirmation that he was at peace. I told her Dean knew where he was headed next, no question."

A rush of emotion raged through Abby as the realizations dawned. Dean had only just taken a knee to the sovereignty of God that recently. What if Nate hadn't been there that afternoon? What if she'd simply prayed *for Dean* instead of *with him*? What if—

"Abby?"

She shook her head. "Sorry. I'm lost in all the might-have-beens."

Nate lifted her hand to his lips and kissed it. Clutching it to his chest, he smiled at her. "Things happened as they were supposed to happen," he whispered. "We know that, don't we? Even when life is at its most confusing, we have assurances others don't. But we know."

She nodded. "It's just so ... hard to think about what ... Iris has to—"

"I know. But in the same way that Dean met his Savior at just the right time, Iris will find the road to healing in her time as well."

Abby's heart seized, and Nate kissed her hand again before releasing it.

"You're always so sure of things," she remarked. "I wish I was more like you."

"Iris said something else to me," he said. "She talked about all the time they may have wasted. She called it a trap."

"She's so right. We have to live every day to the fullest," she said, tucking the wadded tissue into her pocket for its inevitable use throughout the day.

"I'm glad to hear that."

When she glanced back at him, Nate had shifted in the driver's seat and sat facing her, holding a small hinged box in the palm of his hand. Her lips parted, but she didn't speak. She couldn't. She just stared at the tiny box, then at Nate, then back at the box.

"What ... is that?"

"You know what it is," he replied. "Open it."

She started to take it from his hand, then stopped. "Nate, what are you doing?"

"I'm taking Iris's advice and not wasting time," he said. "You're the one, Abby. I know it. And so do you. You are the love of my life and we both know we belong together. Let's not squander a single moment of this extraordinary blessing we've been given. Marry me. I love you, and I'll spend the next sixty years showing you how much."

Heart pounding, pulse racing, her mouth went instantly dry and she felt like she couldn't breathe. When she finally found her voice, she sputtered, "You ... you just proposed in the ... in the ... the parking lot of *a funeral.*"

"It will be an epic story to tell our grandchildren," he told her with a grin. "We'll say we were just about to get out of the car to honor a friend and celebrate his life ... along with all the other people who loved him ... and while we were still in the parking lot we realized time is precious, not to be wasted. We'll tell them, 'When you know, you *just know,*' and we'll encourage them to always listen to their hearts." He removed the exquisite diamond ring from its box—a couple of princess-cut carats, a simple platinum setting—and he slipped it onto the ring finger of Abby's left hand. "And we'll show them this ring, and give it to our oldest grandson so he can present it to the love of *his life* as a symbol of time not wasted."

She stared down at her hand. There wasn't much sun in the sky that morning, but what little there was managed to form a sort of beam aimed directly at that diamond, casting prisms of light at the dashboard and across the fabric of her full skirt. She wiggled her fingers to set the luster to motion.

"And you know what they'll say?" she said in a raspy, strained voice.

"What will they say?"

She locked her gaze with his. "They'll say, 'But grandpa. You *proposed at a funeral.*'"

Nate tossed his head back against the headrest and laughed. A full laugh. One of those across-the-spectrum, completely unencumbered laughs that bubbled over with unavoidable contagions.

"So for the sake of our grandchildren," he said with an added chuckle, "are you accepting my proposal to spend the rest of your life with me?"

Abby grinned. "I am accepting, yes."

Nate's eyes lifted toward the roof of the car. "Thank you, Lord."

"But—" she said, and Nate cried out as she removed the ring from her finger. "*Buuut* … let's wait on telling everyone. This day just can't be about anything except Dean and Iris. It wouldn't feel right."

"Agreed," he said on a sigh.

As she removed the long chain around her neck and slipped the ring on it next to the small silver locket she'd decided to wear that morning, a few thousand butterflies took flight, their wings fluttering softly against the inside of her stomach.

"No giving that back, either," Nate warned.

"Why would I do that?" she asked as she replaced the chain and dropped the locket and ring inside her blouse. "The man I'm supposed to marry just proposed to me. Even if you don't see it there for a while, that ring's securely on my finger, buddy."

"No doubt about it?"

"Not a single one."

Nate caressed her cheek with two knuckles and guided her face toward him. "I adore you," he said, and his lips felt hot against hers as he kissed her.

Celia absently tapped her fingernails on the door handle as Kevin steered into the parking lot of the funeral home and cruised the rows for a parking spot.

"The place is jammed," he remarked. "Do you think they're all here for

Dean, or do they have more than one service going at one time?"

"If you wouldn't have picked me up more than thirty *meenutes* late, we would have beaten them all here and had a place to park," she barked.

"I said I was sorry," he said. "I just couldn't get away as fast as I thought I could. Then there was the back-up downtown—"

"There's a place right over there."

The instant the Mustang stopped, Celia yanked on the handle and threw open the door. "We're already late," she told him. "I'm going to run in and find us a place to sit, yeh?"

"Fine. I just want to call the office and I'll be right there."

"*Keffin*. You just left the office. Now *chu* are going to call them? This is Dean's funeral, Baby. It's … how you say? … a … *una cosa de una sola vez* … *chu* know? A one-time thing."

"Go on," he said, nodding toward the entrance. "We're already late. I'll be right behind you."

Muttering, she pushed the door shut—"*Santo cielo! Si no es una cosa, es otra!*"—and trotted across the parking lot to the huge double doors at the end of the carpeted walk. Hurrying beneath the awning, she yanked the ornate metal handle and rushed inside.

Strains of music met her in the vestibule, and white block letters spelled out Dean's name on a standing portable sign placed outside another set of doors. Celia stopped to scribble her name on the guest book before dragging open the door and scurrying inside while a young woman at the front crooned a version of *Amazing Grace*.

Nearly every one of the chairs was filled. At the front, Lynette and Trevor sat on one side of Iris with Candace on the other. She spotted Regan and Abby—flanked by Sebastian and Nate—in the third row. Abby waved her toward two vacant seats in front of them that they'd apparently reserved for her and Kevin. As she excused herself and made her way down the row, Nate removed the jacket he'd draped across the chair backs.

"I'm so sorry I'm late," she whispered over her shoulder. "*Keffin* got tied up at the office."

"Is he here?" Abby asked softly.

"Yeh," she replied, pointing toward the back of the room. "On his way in."

When the music ended, the funeral director—who looked every bit the part with his smart black suit, red tie and comb-over hair—stepped up to the podium and thanked everyone for coming. Celia craned to see the door with no sign of Kevin's entrance just yet.

She reached forward and placed one hand on Iris's shoulder, touching

Candace's arm with the other. Iris glanced back at her, and Celia took the opportunity to kiss her cheek. As she leaned back against the padded chair, Kevin made his way toward the one next to her and dropped to it.

Several of Dean's chums took their turns at the podium speaking about their friend's infectious sense of humor, devout work ethic, and his devotion to his wife and daughter. Iris—last to walk to the front of the room—blew a sweet kiss toward the large framed photo on the easel next to her before addressing those in attendance. She spoke for several minutes about her "lifelong love affair," and Celia could hardly hold back the tears. Kevin slipped his arm around her shoulders as sniffles and sobs popped from various spots throughout the room behind them.

"In closing," Iris told them, "I just wanted to share with you all that Dean had become quite spiritual at the end of his life. In fact, a few hours before he passed away, I found him quietly reading his Bible. And I'm really glad I did because it gives me an odd sort of comfort on this otherwise horrifying day. After he left us, our new friend Nate said something very ... well, I found solace in his words." Tears streamed down her cheeks as she smiled in Nate's direction through them. "He told me Dean knew what was ahead of him ... where he was headed ... that he was safe there. Thank you for that, Nate. I hope you won't mind ... Would you come up and lead us all in a prayer for Dean's safe travels?"

Nate stood and headed toward her, and the spark of hope she saw in her friend's otherwise grief-stricken demeanor sent Celia's composure reeling. She folded in half at the waist, dropped her face into her hands atop her lap, and tried in vain to quiet her wails of sadness. Kevin pulled her toward him and surrounded her with his arms as she cried, accompanied by Regan's muffled sobs from the row behind.

Regan allowed Abby to load her arms with layers of casserole dishes and salad bowls before she headed out of Iris's dining room and carried them from the makeshift buffet table into the kitchen. Abby collected random plates and napkins and filled several glasses with the utensils and quickly followed. Iris and Lynette hurried toward them to help with the unloading process.

"When I think of how preoccupied I became with the idea of remodeling that room," she said, nodding toward the dining room. "It all seems like such balderdash now."

Regan stroked Iris's arm. "Only you can say a word like *balderdash* and make it seem charming."

Iris chuckled. "And *only you* would notice me saying a word like balderdash." Turning to Abby, she said, "By the way, I wanted to speak to you and Nate about the pool house. Is it too late to put those plans on hold for a bit?"

"Of course not," Abby replied.

"I'd like to have Candace here in the house with me now that …" She fluffed her hair and allowed her words to trail away.

"I think that's a wonderful idea," Regan told her. "For you and for her."

Iris nodded thoughtfully. "We talked about it last night, and we both feel like it's a good move. At least for a while. Later, if we find she and the baby need their own space, we'll revisit the plans. I think Dean would like the idea of us sticking close, don't you?"

Regan nodded. "I do."

"If you have everything under control here," Abby said, "Nate and I are going to drop Celia home and be on our way."

"Where's Kevin?" Regan asked her.

"Oh, he had to check in on a project at the office. We said we'd take her."

As if on cue, Celia hurried into the kitchen to join them, balancing a stack of empty plates. "Iris, the last of the guests are *leafing*. I don't remember her name, but the woman with the tall blue hair wants to see you before she goes."

"Celia, what a thing to say," Lynette said, relieving some of the load.

"Oh. That's Regina Wood. She's a friend of Dean's sister," Iris told them on her way out of the kitchen. "I'll be right back."

"Regan," Celia said. "*Keffin* forgot his jacket and it's getting chilly outside. Sebastian say you will drive right by his office building on your way home and can drop it off to him. I left it on the banister by the door. Don't forget it, heh?"

Regan nodded. "Okay. We should probably head out too." To Lynette, she asked, "Are you staying?"

"Trevor's already gone home to rally the kids and get them to bed. I'm going to stay the night with Iris and Candace."

Regan hugged her. "You're a good friend."

"Oh, I'm good at lots of things," she cracked.

Regan leaned close to Lynette and quietly asked her, "Hey, do you think it would be okay if I snagged some of that lasagna to take with me? There's a boatload of it left, and I love eating it cold for breakfast."

"That's disgusting," Lynette chastised. "I'll get a container together for you."

"See? You're a good friend."

"Mm-hmm."

Regan busied herself with loading the dishwasher while Lynette scouted out a plastic container and spooned a good-sized chunk of lasagna into it. While she dried her hands, Baz appeared in the doorway and smiled at her.

"Ready to go?"

She nodded, and Lynette handed her a plastic bag, the top of it tied in a bow. "Thank you. Call me tomorrow, will you?"

Lynette nodded and squeezed Baz's arm as she passed. "Take care."

"You too," he said. Then, as he spotted the bag in Regan's hand, he asked, "Taking home a doggie bag? Really?"

She grimaced and stuck out her tongue. "I like cold Italian for breakfast. And there was so much of that lasagna left over that Iris and Candace wouldn't be able to finish it in a year's time. Do you have anything to say about that?"

"Not a word," he replied, waving his arm for her to precede him through the doorway.

"He's smarter than he looks, ladies and gentlemen."

He laughed as he followed her down the hall. When they reached the door, Regan grabbed Kevin's jacket while Baz waited his turn for Iris's attention and embraced her warmly.

"Day or night," he told her. "Anything you or Candace need."

"Thank you, Baz. I'm sorry to get to know you under these circumstances—"

"Likewise."

"—but I look forward to knowing you better." She kissed his cheek, then Regan's. "Drive carefully."

"Love you," Regan said. "Talk to you tomorrow."

As they strolled down the sidewalk, Baz spontaneously slid his hand around Regan's. It felt warm and strong, leaving her lightheaded and giddy. She couldn't help hoping that, once they got settled in the car, he might repeat the action.

Baz turned the key ... shifted into gear ... tuned the radio ... adjusted the mirror ...

It's like I'm back in high school awaiting the first lame excuse for contact with the cute quarterback.

A beat after the completion of the thought, the cute quarterback rewarded her by taking her hand. She almost wanted to tell him something about how it made her feel, but she resisted. No need to actually *prove* how lame she actually could be, right?

They pulled into the loading zone in front of Kevin's office building, and Baz squeezed Regan's hand before letting it go and snatching the jacket off the back seat.

"Sit tight. I'll run this up and be right back."

"Don't take too long," she warned. "You might come back and find your radio buttons completely reprogrammed. Wild things happen when I'm bored for too long."

"I'll run."

The grin he shot her before sliding out from behind the wheel sent an arrow of warmth straight through her. She traced his lean silhouette as he headed for the building, measuring his long strides, skimming the strength of his muscular shoulders, smiling as the crisp night breeze mussed his already-messy hair. She wanted to squeal for no other reason than the sheer cuteness of him.

She dug into her bag and produced her cell phone, choosing Abby on the speed dial.

"Hey," she answered. "What are you doing?"

"Sitting in Baz's car. What are you doing?"

Abby chuckled. "Sitting in Nate's."

"Nate's what?"

"Very funny. Are you calling for a purpose, dear Regan?"

"Sort of. I just wanted to tell you how adorable I think Baz is."

"I see."

"What about you? Want to giggle about Nate?"

"I kinda do."

Regan laughed. "Okay. Lay it on me."

"We're getting married."

Thump. Thump. Thump.

Something solid blocked her windpipe, and all her breath funneled instead through her ear canals, no other sounds to be heard beyond the incessant pounding of her own heart.

Thump. Thump. Thump.

"Regan? Did you hear me?"

"I don't think so."

Abby giggled. "You heard me right. Nate proposed and I accepted."

"Seriously?"

"Serious as the stroke you're having right now."

Regan chuckled. "Are you sure?"

"Sure that I'm serious? Or sure that I want to get married?"

"Both."

"Yes. I'm sure."

"Abby, you know I think you two are great together," she said. "But you've only been dating for about forty-five minutes."

"I am aware."

"Do you think you're being a little ... *hasty?*"

"Probably. But I'm still sure."

The rush of wind in her ears began to whistle softly, and Regan's eyes pooled with tears.

"You know ... it's not like I'm an expert on marriage or anything ... but ... I mean, I'm nothing if not a *cautionary tale*. And I was just thinking that maybe ... the decision to not sleep with someone until after marriage might ... you know ... make you want to hurry things up."

She almost heard the ping of Abby's silent Cheshire grin bouncing off the nearest cell phone tower.

"I do want to hurry things up," she replied. "But not for that reason."

"Do tell."

"I want to hurry and marry Nate, Regan, because I love him. With everything inside of me, I love him. He's the miracle I'd given up on. And when a miracle drops right in front of you, you don't walk around it and move on."

Regan sighed. Granted, she didn't know a lot about falling miracles, but she sure knew conviction in the voice of her best friend when she heard it. She wiped away one lone escapee from her tear duct.

"Well, I'm not wearing a cheesy maid of honor dress. So don't ask me."

Abby giggled. "I promise."

"So when are these speed-of-light nuptials taking place?"

"I'm not sure. I want to give Iris time to start breathing again. We actually were just talking about eloping, and then having a big party after she's—"

"You are not eloping without me."

"Maybe you and Baz could come along and be our witnesses," Abby suggested. "Hey, we might be on to something here."

"What, like a quick flight to Vegas or a drive to Tijuana or something?"

"Regan. Do I strike you as a Vegas or Tijuana type of bride?"

"You do not."

"But a destination wedding on a beach somewhere might be ..."

Abby's speculations about white sand and sunshine trailed away as Regan caught sight of Baz emerging from the office building like a flying bullet, the jacket clutched in his fist, and Kevin—disheveled and barefoot—hot on his trail.

"Abby, can I call you back? Something's going down."

"What's going down?"

"I'm not sure. I'll tell you when I call you back later."

Simultaneously disconnecting the call and lowering the passenger window, Regan watched and listened as Kevin grabbed Baz by the arm and roughly turned him around.

"Just wait a minute, would you?" he shouted.

She thought of a cornered wildcat as Baz straightened and shifted to a solid, unmoving posture. If Baz had hackles, she knew they would be standing rigidly on end just then. She jumped as he suddenly threw Kevin's jacket on the ground between them. She couldn't make out the words, but the intent—deliberate, short, and unsweet—made perfect sense before he turned around and stalked away. Behind him, Kevin picked up the jacket and just stood there watching him go.

When Baz reached the car, he seemed to throw himself into it, and he pushed out a low, guttural growl as he slammed the door behind him.

"What on earth?" Regan said, looking back at Kevin, still standing there outside the glass doors.

"I've defended him … unknowingly covered for him … all this time …"

Regan's attention darted back at Kevin. No shoes. His perfect dark hair now tousled. As realization dawned … "Oh, no."

"Oh, yeah," he exclaimed.

"He's not working tonight, is he?"

"No. It sure didn't look like work to me."

Regan's heart dropped. Then it rose again on sheer adrenaline. "Celia's going to murder him."

"I might beat her to it."

A petite blonde with short, perky curls emerged from the building just then, and she slipped both arms around one of Kevin's as she spoke to him softly. After a few exchanges between them, Kevin spotted Regan in the car beside Baz and dropped his shaking head.

Busted.

A moment later, he draped his arm around Perky's shoulder, turned, and the two of them strolled back inside.

"He's out of his mind," Regan said. "If I was a guy, I'd be scared spitless to cheat on Celia. You're sure she's not just somebody he works with, right? I mean, maybe they were just …" She actually couldn't think of what innocent thing they might have been doing.

"I'm pretty sure what I walked in on can't be explained away so easily," he said, and all thoughts of an innocent explanation evaporated. "It took her so long to get down here because of all that time it probably took to *find her clothes.*"

"Oh." Regan blew out a puff of air on a barrage of noisy frustration. "He's a brave, brave moron."

Baz groaned and tossed his head back against the seat. "I believed every lie he fed me, Regan. I told Celia to get some *therapy.* All the time, she was just acting on intuition. She knew, and all I did was tell her what a psycho she is."

"We have to tell her." Regan laced her fingers with Baz's and jiggled his hand.

"Don't we?"

He turned toward her, his eyes on fire with flames of dread.

"I mean, we can't really keep it from her."

"No. But ..."

"I know. The fork in the road boggles the mind." Regan sighed. "The bottom line being that she's one of my closest friends, and her suspicions about him have been killing her. She has to know she wasn't imagining it all, Baz. We have to tell her."

"We do," he said. "At the same time, you know Celia. She's going to tear up the messenger like a hungry shark following fresh blood in the water."

"Oh, yeah. No doubt about it."

"Thanks." He groaned. Then an idea sparked. "Go with me?"

"Not a chance."

When he reacted, she laughed. "Relax. She's my friend. I'll rally the girls and we'll tell her together. In a safe environment."

"Like a locked cage?"

"At least."

Chapter 21

Lynette propped herself against the kitchen sink. She stared blankly out the window to the backyard in an effort to ignore the too-loud hold music between her and the delivery of an Oriental feast in time for the girls' arrival. Trevor stepped up behind her and circled her waist with his arms, but when he moved in to kiss her neck, he immediately withdrew again.

"What *is that*?" he exclaimed. "Who are you talking to?"

"Oh, it's hold music. I'm holding for Jing-Jing Palace. The girls will be here in less than an hour."

He groaned with disappointment. "You're getting Jing-Jing?"

"When we meet at Iris's house, she spends half the day cooking for us. My good intentions flew straight out the window with the laundry list of things needed for Margaret's science project. So it was this or pizza."

"Get me an order of bourbon chicken with rice?"

"I thought you already ate."

"I did. But if you loved me like you say you do, you wouldn't have mentioned it."

She smiled and leaned her head back to his shoulder. "You're right. That was wrong."

"And be sure to ask for almond cookies, Love," he said, kissing her throat. "They won't put them in unless you ask."

"Don't you want to know what it's going to cost you?"

"There's cash in my desk drawer."

"Oh no you don't," Lynette growled. "If you want bourbon chicken and almond cookies, you're going to have to pay in other ways."

"Happy to," he whispered. "Get the girls to clear out early and we'll tuck in together, maybe watch that dirty video we made in the back seat at the school lot."

"You better be right about having the only copy. If that thing is floating around out there—"

"It's not. So is it a date?"

"Yes. But I have a higher currency in mind," she told him. "Although I'm not opposed to your suggestion, I also need you to take care of the kids tonight.

Anything and everything that comes up, from homework disasters to crises with the boy or girl of the hour. All of it. I have my own chaos to deal with, and in this case I'm going to be all full up. No room at the inn."

"Are you going to tell me what happened?" he asked, releasing his hold on her and moving to a stool at the counter.

"Yes." He perked, ready for the details behind that rather frantic late-night call from Regan and Abby. "But not until after everyone leaves. There's someone who needs to hear about it first."

"Must be wicked," he assessed with a sly grin.

"Well, it ain't good," she replied. "You'll want to keep everyone upstairs if you can." After a moment's thought, Lynette reconsidered. "Baby, Kevin's stepping out on Celia. She doesn't know yet."

"Do you have proof? I mean, you're sure about this?"

"Absolutely. Baz and Regan got the drop on him by accident."

"And you're going to tell her? Do you have some protective gear?"

Lynette groaned. "This is going to be a long night."

Trevor sauntered toward her, grinning. "And if you ever have any doubts about me—"

"I never do," she breathed.

"Okay, that's good. But if you ever find yourself sitting here on a rainy night, thinking about our marriage and the stray thought crosses your mind ..." He massaged her hips with both hands and she moved closer to him. "... just remember what I'm telling you right now. The vows we made to each other are written in stone somewhere deep within me."

"Ahhh," she cooed, closing her eyes and pressing her face into the curve of his neck.

"I will never stray."

"And I'll make every effort," she teased.

He slapped her behind before making his way back to the counter as the hold music ceased.

"Jing-Jing Palace. What's your order?"

With a nod to Trevor, she leaned against the counter. "I need a delivery, please. A ten-pack of the vegetable eggrolls ... a quart of shrimp lo mein ... a quart of sweet and sour pork ... a quart—no, *two quarts* of bourbon chicken ..."

Trevor gave her a thumbs-up before he stood and headed for the hall. Lynette covered the phone with her hand. "Wait." He turned around and she half-whispered to him. "We're going to need wine. Will you bring some in from the cabinet?"

"Red or white?"

"Yes."

He laughed and resumed his departure.

"Madame? You still there?"

"Yes, sorry. What did I say last?"

"Two quarts bourbon chicken."

"Right. Also, a quart of the boneless spare ribs ..."

If nothing else, all that Chinese food was sure to create a certain level of lethargic apathy that might help anesthetize the bad news about to be delivered to Celia.

Lynette couldn't help wishing Iris felt up to joining them, but she hadn't even invited her. Time with Candace seemed like the only thing appropriate for her grieving friend at the moment. They'd catch her up on the details later, when the time was right.

Still. Handling such a major situation felt odd and unbalanced without knowing Iris's wise and calming influence sat at the ready. Not to mention ... no big pot of something scrumptious and homemade with the intent to cure whatever ailed them. And in about an hour's time, Celia would have a lot ailing her. Lynette hoped she, Regan, and Abby were equipped to do what Iris's kitchen could not.

"Oh, yes," she told Jing-Jing's representative with a start. "Sorry. I'd like to pay by credit card. Oh, and can we get some extra almond cookies?"

An hour later, the food had been delivered. Trevor retrieved a heaping serving of bourbon chicken and two almond cookies, and Jamal escaped up the stairs with an eggroll and a handful of fortune cookies just as the front doorbell rang.

The containers had been arranged neatly down the length of the kitchen counter alongside a stack of plates and utensils, and Lynette opened the door to find that Celia had arrived first. Thankfully, Regan and Abby trotted up the sidewalk behind her.

"Come on in," Lynette told them.

"*Ay*, I didn't think I was going to get away from the restaurant in time to get here," Celia chattered as she passed. "I have a standing night off on Thursdays when we meet at Iris's house, but what was so important that we had to meet on an off day, heh? Regan say it's urgent we all be here. So now we're all here. What's so urgent, heh?"

Abby, Regan, and Lynette exchanged meaning-filled glances behind her as they followed.

"Abby has some news," Regan announced. "And we all had to be here for it."

Abby elbowed her, and Regan winced. "What? We had to tell her something, and your good news will cushion the blow. Besides, you sure don't want to tell her *after she finds out about Kevin*, do you?"

Abby shrugged as Lynette caught her arm. "You have good news?"

"Ooh, this looks *deleeshus*," Celia crooned when she saw the food. "You get it from Jing-Jing? I love their almond cookies." She'd already started spooning food onto a plate when she asked, "So tell us. What's your news, *novia?*"

Abby groaned and glared at Regan before throwing her left hand on the counter with a thud. She wiggled her fingers wildly before Lynette spotted the ring and squealed.

"Let me see that," she cried, snatching Abby's hand.

"Abby!" Celia exclaimed. "*Es sorprendente.* When did this *hoppen?*"

"Just before Dean's service," she told them. "But don't tell Iris. I want to tell her myself after she's had a chance to absorb everything, you know?"

"Is a beautiful ring. We're so *hoppy* for you," Celia said, embracing her.

"Thank you. We're over the moon about it."

"Regan, you're very quiet," Lynette observed. "Are you concerned because it happened so soon?"

"I can't lie," she replied. "It does concern me. But our friend is brimming with happiness, and that's what really matters."

"Wow," Abby said dryly.

"*Si.* Wow," Celia chimed in.

"Why don't we all get something to eat and relax in the family room," Lynette suggested. "We want to hear all about Abby and Nate's plans. And we do have some other business to discuss as well."

"We do?" Celia asked, already digging into the lo mein on her plate.

Regan touched her arm and nodded. "We do, Celia."

"But let's get some food and pour some wine," Lynette interjected. "Or there's chilled bottles of water in the fridge."

Once they'd all been served, they moved to the family room. Lynette and Celia took the sofa while Regan and Abby sat on the floor across the coffee table from them. After several bites, Celia looked from one of them to the next.

"So? What's this other *beezness?*"

Lynette looked to Regan. "You're up."

Regan set her fork on the corner of her plate and pressed both palms to the rug behind her, leaning heavily back on them. "The thing is," she began, then stopped.

"Has someone else died?" Celia asked seriously.

"Not exactly. You know how you asked Baz and me to bring Kevin his jacket last night?"

"*Si.* He came home wearing it, so I know you found him."

"Yeah. We found him."

"Okay." Celia's confusion contorted her face. "So ...?"

"Well, when we found him, he ... wasn't ... exactly ... alone."

She set her plate on the coffee table, folded her legs beneath her and sat erect. "Go on."

"Baz walked in on him," Regan said with a sigh. "Them."

"*Chez.* And?"

"He wasn't ... well ... clothed."

Like that favorite old toy of Shaaron's when she was little—the one where the clown popped out of the box without a millisecond's warning—Celia blasted from fanny to feet and glared down at Regan.

"I want every detail."

"Celia, sit down, honey," Lynette urged, tugging on her hand. "Take a breath and sit down."

Instead of breathing, she threw herself hard against the back of the couch and muttered—in supersonic Spanish—for a full minute or so. Then something happened that Lynette did not expect. Not out of Celia anyway.

Without any forewarning at all, Celia went eerily silent, her entire face falling like a wax mask under the heat of a torch, and she burst into soft, silent tears. The moment Lynette opened her arms, Celia threw herself at her, almost knocking the wind out of her lungs. It took a moment to recover.

"I know, honey. I'm so sorry."

Lynette held her and rubbed her shoulder while exchanging prolific glances with Regan and Abby. She had to look away, however—to keep from laughing right out loud—when Regan used both hands and an animated expression to communicate her mind being blown.

Celia pulled away slowly and backed into the corner of the sofa, her eyes wide and glossy, her posture still and erect.

"You're freaking us out, girl," Regan finally said. "What's going on in that Latina mind? Should we call the bomb squad or something?"

"Regan," Abby chastised with a light smack to her knee.

"Celia?" Lynette said, touching her arm. "Can I get you something?"

"I want to hear all the details," she said. "Don't leave any of it out."

Before Regan could complete the timeline—from their arrival in the parking lot to Baz going inside alone—an explosion of voices erupted from upstairs.

Lynette groaned as Trevor reprimanded the kids and commanded, "About face! I told you, you're staying upstairs."

"We won't interrupt," Shaaron whined. "We just want to get some snacks."

"You just ate an hour ago," he reprimanded, his British accent peaking the way it did when he became agitated. "You don't need snacks. Now march."

Except for Celia, they all had pressed pause on the current situation and turned their attention in the direction of the stairs. When doors slammed, they redirected their gazes to Celia, still sitting eerily still.

"Sorry," Lynette breathed. "Welcome to my world."

Again without warning, Celia slid forward and stood. "Okay," she declared, "I'm going now."

"What?" Abby cried. She and the others all got to their feet as well. "Celia, stick around. Let's have some dessert … or something to drink … or … coffee. Do you want coffee? I can make some. Lynette, you don't mind if I go make coffee, do you?"

Lynette knew she'd asked a rhetorical question and didn't bother to answer her. Instead, she took Celia's hand and looked her straight in the eye. "Honey, you're in shock. Let's just sit and talk it over before you light a fuse and explode into something you can't take back."

"Don't *hondle* me, Lynette. I do not need to be *hondled*."

"Celia," Regan interjected. "You kinda do."

"No. I don't. I'm going home now so I can hear what *Keffin* has to say for himself. I can't really do anything until I talk to my husband."

"Do you … I don't know …" Regan said, looking to Lynette and then to Abby. "… want one of us to go with you?"

"I do not."

"Celia, we don't mind," Abby said, hurrying to grab her bag. "Come on. I'll go with you. We can talk to Kevin together. Or … or I can sit in the other room while you do, just in case you need me afterward. How does that sound?"

Celia's deceptively serene composure turned stormy as she stared Abby down. "I'm going home now. And I'm going alone. Thank you for the dinner, and *felicitaciones* on your engagement to Nate, Abby. *Adiós*."

She turned on one heel, grabbed her purse, and clomped down the hall and out the door.

"Well," Regan said as she collapsed to the sofa. "That went well."

"Until we see the eleven o'clock news," Abby added as she joined her there. "It's all fun and games until a Colombian woman faces down her cheating husband."

Lynette grabbed three stemless glasses and a bottle of wine before joining them. "I don't know about Celia's culture," she said, "but a black sister confronted with this kind of news … there's pretty much a guarantee of a lot of noise and some broken glass."

"I think that might be a universal guarantee among women in general,"

Abby pointed out as she sipped her wine. "Why confine it to ethnicity?"

"True dat, honey."

Regan stood. "I'll call Baz and tell him the deed is done."

"He might want to offer Kevin some protection," Abby suggested.

"I'm not sure he wants to stand in Celia's way at this point."

Nate had balked a little when Abby invited him to join her at the cooking class she'd enrolled in weeks prior, but once they got into it she could see that he'd gotten into the spirit.

"Now that your spinach mixture is prepared," the instructor said from the front of the class of twelve, "let's move on to the phyllo dough."

Janice Bronson wore her raven-black hair pulled back into a tight mess clipped with a rhinestone barrette and, when she smiled, a surprisingly large gap showed between her two front teeth. A navy bibbed apron bearing the logo of her business, NOW WE'RE COOKIN', protected a long-sleeved gray Henley and baggy black jeans.

"Phyllo is a little tricky to work with," she said. "For purposes of your first foray into the world of spanakopita, we're going to double up on the layers, but ideally you want to use one sheet at a time."

"I've never heard of spanakopita, have you?" Nate whispered.

Abby nodded. "It's a little spinach pie. They serve it at a Greek tappas bar Regan and I like to go to sometimes."

"Gently unfold two sheets of the phyllo," Janice instructed them, "and lay it out on the boards and brush it with the melted butter. Then unfold two more sheets and repeat."

Abby noted that she and Nate worked well together. He laid out the phyllo, she brushed with butter, he laid out the next layer, she brushed it. It continued that way through cutting the strips, spooning the spinach and feta filling, creating the triangles, brushing with more butter, and placing them on the baking sheet.

"Once you place your trays into the oven," Janice told them, "choose what you need—glasses, plates, and utensils—and pour yourself some wine or water and let's all gather at the table."

The group of them filed through the line and to the rustic rectangular wood-planked table and chairs at the far side of the room. Each student of the class set their place settings with charming hunter green mats, clean white appetizer plates, crisp white linen napkins, and heavy sterling silverware. As Abby arranged their two places, Nate fetched two goblets of sparkling water and joined her at the table, which was already flanked with the other students, Janice at the head.

"For this first class," she told them, "I chose a Greek appetizer. But next week for the first course, we'll go Eastern European with a soba salad and fresh hearth bread. We'll tackle a new region for a main course and a dessert. Then in the sixth week, we're going to invite our friends and family and—for a nominal fee—we'll cook and serve them a full Tuscan feast."

Abby looked around the small space and quirked a brow. "How? I mean, where?"

Janice grinned. "Weather permitting, we'll have a lovely white tent with long tables set up in the parking lot out back. It's pretty spectacular, and people genuinely seem to love it."

"Do you do that for every cooking class?" someone asked. "It seems like you'd charge a lot more for that."

"We do it at the end of every six-week session. It's fun for the students, and it brings us a pretty healthy percentage of repeat customers for the classes once they taste the food."

"Fun," Abby commented, looking to Nate for his reaction. She sighed when he appeared to share her enthusiasm.

"You know, it might be something Iris could enjoy. A change of scenery. What do you think?"

"Why don't we stop over after class and take some spanakopita to her and Candace," she suggested. "Pave the way for the invitation in a few weeks."

He nodded. "It's a plan."

An hour later, the group—eight women and four men—had sampled the appetizers they'd made, gotten to know a little more about each other, and spoken an appropriate amount of *ooohs* and *ahhhs* over Abby's diamond engagement ring.

"You're so lucky," one of the women told Abby on their way out the door. "I don't think my husband would take this class with me if I paid him while wearing nothing but the apron."

Once they were on their way, a plastic container of their delectable spinach triangles on Abby's lap, she touched Nate's arm.

"She's right, you know."

"Who?" he asked.

"That woman on the way out. Judith? She said I'm lucky. I see it as blessed, but the idea's the same. I can hardly believe I actually found you."

Nate grinned. "I'm pretty sure *I* found *you*."

When they pulled into Iris's driveway, the downstairs lights still glowed, and a wash of yellow lamplight illuminated the front porch.

"It looks like they're still awake," Nate said.

Abby glanced at the clock on the dash. "Nine o'clock. Do you think I should try calling her first?"

At just that moment, the front door opened and Iris peered out at them. When she spotted Abby, she drew her sweater tighter and strolled toward the car as they got out.

"Is it too late?" Nate asked as he hugged her.

"We were just getting ready to head upstairs. Come on in. I'll make some coffee." Abby and Iris embraced, and Iris kissed her cheek warmly. "You look so pretty."

"Well, hold on to your hat," Abby joked. "We started a six-week cooking class tonight. *Meals of the Globe.*"

"Oh! Over at Now We're Cookin'?"

"Yes," she exclaimed. "You've been there?"

"I know the woman who owns the place. Janice—"

"That's our instructor," Nate told her as they walked inside.

"Oh, she's wonderful. We met at a food pantry a few years ago." She peered at the plastic container in Abby's hands. "Did you make that?"

Abby nodded. "Spanakopita. We thought you and Candace might like some."

"She's not doing so well with anything outside of cereal and milk at the moment," she said, and she smiled at Nate. "The woes of the first trimester."

"Well, how about you?" Abby asked. "Want to try our first dish together?"

"I'd love to. Let me just start the—" A diamond-tipped needle seemed to screech across the moment, and she fell silent and her jaw dropped open. "Abby. Sweetie. What is ... *that?*"

Heart racing, Abby instinctively yanked her hand back and jerked toward Nate. He gave her a reassuring smile, and it soothed her on contact.

"We have news," he told Iris.

She tenderly took Abby's hand and held it in both palms. "I can see that."

"I wanted to tell you," Abby gushed immediately. "It's just ... with everything you're going through ..."

"Don't be ridiculous. If you have news of this magnitude, I want to hear it." She stroked the diamond and smiled before looking up at her. "So you're engaged?"

She nodded, and Iris looked at Nate for confirmation.

He grinned. "If you can believe she would say yes to a guy like me, yes, we're getting married."

"Of course I can believe it," she beamed, surrounding him with both arms.

"If it was anyone else, I might lecture you about rushing into things. But you two just seem … right. I couldn't be happier for you." She turned around and kissed Abby's cheek. "Dean knew this, you know."

"He did?"

"The day he met Nate for the first time, he told me, 'That boy is Abby's match in every way.'"

Abby felt as if she'd been injected with pure adrenaline. "He said that?" she whimpered, and tears sprang to her eyes, spilling out over her cheeks.

"He did." Iris moved to the counter and busied herself with making coffee. "So when will the blessed event take place?"

"Oh, we haven't gotten that far yet," Abby told her with a glance toward Nate. "We don't want it to interfere with your … process. You've been through so much and—"

"I'll be grieving Dean for the rest of my life," she said casually. "That doesn't take away my joy for you. So you two plan your wedding. Just tell me what I can do to help and when to be there."

"My feeling is I want to marry her as soon as humanly possible," Nate said. "But Abby really wants you to participate."

"We were thinking we might elope, and then just have a big reception after—"

"How long have I known you?" Iris interrupted, spinning around to face Abby. "You don't think I've known you long and well enough to know how much you want a church wedding? You'll pry an elopement out of my cold, dead hands, young lady."

"Iris, I—"

"Nothing else to say," she barked, and she turned back to the coffeemaker. "Now let's taste those spinach pies of yours, and you tell me what else I've been missing. How's Regan? And Celia?"

Abby and Nate exchanged glances before she sighed. "Well, Iris. There is some news about Celia."

"Don't tell me she's invested in night vision goggles and tracking devices."

Nate snickered, and Abby elbowed him. "Stop it."

"What?" Iris exclaimed, looking back and forth between them. "What's happened?"

Chapter 22

"What is that?"

The alarm in his voice caused Regan to gasp before she looked up. Baz steered them to the turnout in front of Celia and Kevin's place.

Something strange … on the front lawn…

In the next moment, an upstairs window flew open and a mound of shirts, pants and jackets burst through and fluttered downward; the last to hit the ground, a light cotton shirt, had its sleeves flailing as a man might if falling overboard.

"Oh, no," Regan exclaimed as they came to a stop out front. She ducked down to get a closer look and—as she half-expected—spotted Celia leaning through the open window emptying a bureau drawer of socks and underwear and t-shirts over the side. She gasped, half laughing and half horrified, as a pair of boxers caught on the corner of a border shrub like a sideways beret on the head of a Frenchman.

Regan flew across the yard and planted herself on the sidewalk beneath the window. "Celia," she called out. "What are you doing?"

"Oh. Hi, Regan. How are you?" she asked. "Watch yourself." A large gathered sack came over the side of the window and narrowly missed hitting her.

"Celia. Stop it right now."

Baz took long strides across the yard behind her and stood next to Regan without speaking a word.

"Celia, do you hear me? We're coming in."

She led the way to the front door, but just as her fingers touched the knob, a squeal of brakes drew her attention to the street. Kevin exploded out from behind the wheel of his Mustang and raced across the grass.

When he reached Baz, he did a double take. "What are you doing here?" But before Baz could reply, Kevin pushed forward and nearly knocked Regan over to barge through the front door.

"Celia," he shouted. His footsteps stomped up the stairs, not much quieter than bombs detonating.

Regan set out to run through the door, but Baz snatched her by the waist and pulled her back outside. "Whoa there. Let's hang back a minute."

"Baz, they're going to kill each other."

"No. They're not. They're going to argue. Noisily. Let's start picking up his clothes and getting them into his car."

"You're kidding." She could hardly believe he thought she would lift a finger to help Kevin Hake. The guy who'd been lying to one of her best friends for she didn't know how long. "I'm not helping him."

"Fair enough," he replied, and she breathed a sigh of relief.

But the solace lasted a fraction of a second before Baz turned away and started picking up articles of clothing off the grass.

"Are you joking?"

"What," he said as he tossed a t-shirt over his shoulder. "Now *we're* going to fight?"

"No." She stalked toward him and tore the shirt away from him and threw it on the ground. "Unless you pick that up again."

Baz stared her down, then casually picked up the shirt and folded it without a word or a second glance.

The upstairs shouting match hurtled through the open window like a thunderstorm of imperceptible insults and accusations. The roar dulled, ebbing and flowing, then finally waning as Kevin made his way down the stairs and Celia stood at the top.

"… made me think I was *demente*. A crazy person."

"Oh. I guess I was wrong about that," Kevin shouted back at her. "You're *not* bat-waste crazy." Passing through the doorway and stepping outside, he muttered, "All evidence to the contrary."

"How many, *Keffin*? Heh? How many has there been?"

"I'm a little curious about that too," Baz said, and Kevin glared at him. "Really. Has it been going on all along? That girl at the Padres game, was she one of them? How many times did you scam me into covering for you?"

Regan marveled at the even keel of Baz's queries. He didn't raise his voice, didn't even come off as accusatory, simply posed the questions as if he truly wanted to understand and hear the answers.

"Come on, man," Kevin snapped as he collected his belongings off the grass and shrubs. "What are you even doing here?" When Baz didn't respond, Kevin aimed his anger at Regan. "You had to tell her, didn't you? You just couldn't stand it until you went and puked it all out for her. It wasn't up to you, Regan."

"Yeah," she said. "You're right. It wasn't my place at all. It was yours. But since you didn't follow through, I figured it was about time somebody put Celia out of her misery."

"Please," he spat, returning his attention to removing the apparel sprouting throughout the garden. "You couldn't wait to dump out the details. And you know what gets me? You call yourself her friend, and you knew how she would react. You *knew it*, Regan. You and those friends of yours ... you've never been anything but a pack of cronies."

Baz straightened, the muscle of his jaw spasming like a tight wire. "You're going to want to stop talking now, my friend."

"Why? Because this ... this ... *person* ..." He spat out the word like a bite of rotten lemon. "... that you've known for all of five minutes is now your new best friend?"

"Well, it appears I was in the market for one, even before I knew it."

Kevin turned toward Regan, and the look in his eyes sent a sharp knife of fear slicing straight through her. He grabbed her forearm and closed his fingers around it. She gave one sharp yank, but she couldn't break free of his grip.

"Get your hands off me," she insisted with a boldness she didn't actually feel.

And that was all that needed to be said. Baz somehow pried Kevin loose and—with one hand, no less—backed him up nearly five feet in a single flash of movement, sending him smoothly down into the border of shrubs. Kevin looked up at him from the ground, obviously stunned, as Baz stalked to the front door and motioned to Regan.

"Go inside with Celia. I'll help our friend pack up his car." When she didn't move from the spot, he softened and repeated, "Regan. Go inside with Celia."

She rushed past Kevin—just starting to get to his feet—and hurried through the front doorway.

"Lock this door," Baz said, and he squeezed her wrist before she did as she was told.

When she turned to look for Celia, she found her folded cleanly in half on the stairs, withered and utterly broken.

Regan sat beside her and encircled Celia with her arm. Lowering her head to Celia's shoulder, she said, "Listen to me. Do you remember what you said to me when Craig trampled all over our marriage?" She didn't reply beyond one sharp sniff. "You said finding out the truth is awful, but it's so much better than living in the deception."

"I know."

Barely a whisper but—unconvincing as it was—Regan tried to smile at the sheer progress of it.

The hum of Kevin and Baz's raised—yet restrained—voices appeared to buzz around Celia like a poisonous insect, and Regan tried to make out the words on the other side of the locked door to no avail.

"Do you want to tell me what happened?" Regan asked her, and Celia dug her fingers into her hair and tugged. "I've been trying to call you since you left the other night, and we finally just decided to drive over and check on you in person."

She stood, stalked toward the door, and pressed her eye to the peephole.

"Can you hear them?" Regan asked. "What are they saying?"

Celia shook her head and turned around, collapsing against the door, distraught torment contorting her exquisite face.

Regan had never seen her like this. "Have you two talked about it?"

She shook her head. "No. I came home from Lynette's ready to have it in with him—"

Oh. Have it out *with him.*

"—but he wasn't here. And he never even came home. Worse, he sent my calls straight to the voicemail, and he wouldn't call me back. Finally, I went to his job, but they said he was out on a shoot. I know this isn't true because of his beloved Mustang parked in the parking garage."

"So what led up to his arrival today?"

"Another night and still he doesn't come home, so a couple of hours ago I call his office and have them connect me to his voicemail there. I leave him a message and say I know why he is avoiding, and he better hurry up and come over to our house to pick up his things because at three o'clock I start throwing it all out on the lawn. And by tomorrow morning there will be an ad placed to sell that precious motorcycle parked under the awning on the side of the house."

"Well ..." Regan gulped around the dry spot at the back of her throat. "It worked."

"Yeh."

A sudden *pound-pound-pound* at the door behind her propelled Celia away from it, undiluted panic in her eyes as they locked into Regan's.

"Celia," Kevin bellowed. "I need the keys to the bike."

"Where are they?" Regan asked, standing.

"On the peg in the kitchen."

She scurried down the hall and spotted them right away by the door to the garage. Grabbing them, her heart thumped in time with her quick footsteps on the ceramic tile floor.

"I can give them to him," she offered upon her return.

"No." Celia took them, unbolted the door, and yanked it open.

She and Kevin stared at each other for several beats before he broke the silence. "Are you going to talk to me? We need to—"

Without a word, Celia threw the keys with full force, and Kevin winced as they struck him directly in the middle of his chest. Before he recovered, she slammed the door and bolted it again.

A moment later, he yelled at her through the barrier. "You've got to talk to me, Celia. You can't just—"

Mid-sentence, he went quiet, like an actor on the screen when the television is turned off.

"Baz, she's my wife. She has to talk to me. What's she think? I'm just going to disappear into the horizon without making a ripple in the water?"

"If you had any sense," Baz said, "that's exactly what you would do. Now go get the bike, and I'll drive the car."

"Where?" he shouted. "Where am I gonna go? Your place?"

"Not a chance. Pick a hotel and we'll go there."

Pride pumped through Regan's veins like surges of thick, hot blood.

Celia's lips tilted into a partial smile. "I kind of love Sebastian right now."

Me too.

"Check us out, Mom. We're having lunch out. Like normal people."

Iris looked up from her salad. Waiting, she supposed, for her daughter to expound. When Candace saw her expectant expression, she told her, "It seems foreign, doesn't it?"

"I guess it does."

"I mean, we've done it a thousand times before. But we always had Daddy to go home to, you know?"

Was she supposed to answer? Did Candace think she'd forgotten for one millisecond that Dean wouldn't be there when they returned?

"I'm glad you suggested it," she continued. "I didn't know if we were ready to do something normal, but I think it's good. Don't you?"

She nodded as she poked a cucumber chunk with her fork. "I do."

"How's your salad?"

"It's good."

"My soup tastes funny. I don't know if it's the soup, or if it's Michael."

Iris's heartbeat fluttered, and she narrowed her eyes and stared at her daughter. "Michael?"

"Oh. Yeah. I just have this feeling," she said, making circles on her little pouch of a stomach with the palm of her hand. "I think it's a boy, Mom. And I thought I'd name him after Daddy."

Dean Michael Kramer.

"I thought naming him Dean would be too on-the-nose, you know? But taking Daddy's middle name. He might like that, don't you think?"

She balanced her fork on the edge of the bowl. "I think he'd be honored." With a sigh, she asked, "What if your instincts are off and the baby turns out to be a girl?"

Candace pretended to think it over. "Michelle?"

The two of them shared a laugh, and Iris realized the simple act caused her cheeks to ache. Her heart as well.

"No," Candace said, shaking her head and filling her spoon with pumpkin soup. "I'm sure of it. I'm having a boy. It won't be long before the doc can confirm it for us. I have my next check-up in a couple of weeks." After slurping the soup from her spoon, she asked, "Do you want to go over to the baby store with me after this? I thought I'd get registered."

"Oh, can you wait on that? I'd love to do it with you, but I've got book club tonight and I have a lot to do."

Candace's pretty face seemed to freeze, and she held her spoon awkwardly, suspending it in the air. "Really?"

Iris sighed. "I thought it too soon also. But I had a change of heart after speaking with Celia this morning. We all seem to especially need each other right now. You can join us if you'd like."

"I'll swing in and say hello. But I don't think I'm ready for all the sympathetic eyes on us. Maybe I'll get into an early bath and watch some television."

"We can go through your registry together another day?"

"Sure."

"I need to stop at the grocery store on our way home. Hungry for anything special?"

Candace giggled and brushed back her blonde hair, her blue-green eyes shimmering. "It changes from moment to moment. I thought this pumpkin soup was going to change my life, and now I don't even think I can finish it. I might get a BLT to go and eat it in the car while you're in the store."

Iris chuckled, remembering her own love affair with bacon that lasted throughout the duration of her pregnancy, abruptly ending after Candace's birth.

"Well, we need the basics at least," she said, scribbling a short list on the back of an envelope from her purse. "Milk, eggs, bread, cheese."

"Oooh, cheese. Maybe I'll get a grilled cheese instead."

She added bacon to the list anyway. For that inevitable late night when this bacon craving came back to roost.

Iris walked into the store with no inspiration whatsoever about cooking for the girls and hoped that a stroll down the grocery aisles might spark an idea.

Lasagna? *Too heavy.*

They all really loved her stuffed pork chops. *Too much work.*

Soup and salad? Iris's chin quivered as her heart found its way to Italian Wedding Soup. *No. Maybe never again. But certainly not this soon.*

Somewhere around the produce section, she realized a little comfort food might be in order and she shifted into a gear she didn't know still existed in her.

Macaroni and cheese. The go-to comfort food for every occasion.

As she collected the ingredients—adding a large package of bacon nodding at her from the far end of the dairy section—the rest of the menu came into focus.

Balsamic and Dijon glazed ham. Green beans with toasted hazelnuts. Parmesan bread knots. And her signature macaroni and cheese with sharp cheddar, asiago, and sage. Involuntary salivation told her she'd made the perfect choice.

The next three hours confirmed it. With flour on her face and a wooden spoon clasped in her hand, Iris hadn't felt like crying even once. In fact, relief washed over her as she put the final touches on the meal because she realized she'd lost herself for a stretch of time; and with it, she'd shed the cloak of pain for a while as well. Even though food equaled family in so many ways, for the first time since they'd gotten Dean's diagnosis, the idea of family wasn't diluted by grief. She couldn't imagine how that had happened but decided too much thought might take away the beauty of it.

Not until the doorbell rang did she even think about the bereavement side of what her life had recently become. As she walked toward opening the door to her closest friends, unanticipated dread pressed in. Would they look at her with those glossy, sympathetic gazes? Had she become Poor Iris to them now that part of her had gone missing? Regan had once written in her blog that they'd become IreneAndFamilyMan to her, like one word. *IrisAndDean.* Who would she be now that AndDean had been severed off like a casualty of war?

But as soon as she opened the door to them, all apprehension fell to dust and blew away in a cool breeze comprised of Lynette's familiar smile ... Regan's hug ... Abby's soft touch ... Celia's self-containment. In the same way that bread, milk, eggs, and butter became the staples of her meal planning, these four women provided the essentials needed for Iris's healing.

"I'm so glad you're all here," she told them warmly. "I needed this so much."

"Wait until you see the dessert I brought," Abby exclaimed as she set the large bakery box on the table and untied the string.

But Iris's attention had been caught by Lynette as she plopped into her usual chair and dabbed the perspiration on her neck with a wadded paper towel.

"Are you okay?" she asked her quietly, to which Lynette simply blew out an exhale in a sharp puff.

"Prepare to hit your knees," Abby declared, opening the lid and stretching out her arm like Vanna pointing to the letters she'd unveiled. "And thank the Lord for the beauty that is *cinnamon apple cake filled with brown sugar cream.*" The obligatory moans seemed to appease Abby's expectations, and she grinned at them. "A friend of Nate's owns that bakery in the Gaslamp Quarter by all the galleries. We stopped in for some coffee and a cookie, and I gained twelve pounds just walking through the door."

"We need to fetch some plates and let's get into that thing," Celia announced.

Iris handed Abby the stack of dessert plates, forks, and large knife she'd set out on the counter.

"What smells so good?" Regan asked, following her nose as it appeared to lead her across the kitchen and straight to the oven door.

Iris announced the menu to mass appreciation. "It's all ready when we are," she told them, following Regan to the nook table where Abby sliced the cake.

When five plates—each bearing a portion of the delectable dessert—had been set into a line, Regan said, "It's going to be tough to decide who gets the first dessert tonight. We've got some real contenders at this table."

Abby chuckled. "Well, leave me out of the running. My life is pretty stellar right now. I vote for Iris."

Celia clucked out a blunt, "Ha!" Folding her arms across her considerable chest, she added, "Really?"

Abby winced. "And Celia. Iris and Celia."

"Yeah," Regan agreed. "It's a tie. I've got nothing. How about you, Lynette?"

All eyes turned to her as Lynette dabbed her drenched forehead. "It's official. I'm in menopause," she stated dryly.

Iris let out a laugh in a single syllable. "Well, it's not widowhood or a cheating husband. But I say we give it to her, girls."

Iris, Regan, Celia, and Abby—as if synchronized wait staff—simultaneously pushed a plated chunk of cake directly before Lynette.

"Yeh," Celia said with a nod. "You go, honey."

They all shared the amusement as Lynette unceremoniously accepted the gesture, dug her fork into the cake, and devoured the first bite. The others joined in and, as Iris took her first taste of the dessert, the muscles around her heart ached, but not painfully; instead, as the manifestation of a degree of relief that indicated it had been far too long since she'd let go and had a really good laugh.

"So Celia, now that you've had a minute to digest everything that's happened," Abby said, "what are your plans?"

Without a moment's thought, she announced, "I'm going to divorce the *vee-sil.*"

Abby squinted as she considered her words.

"Weasel," Lynette translated.

"Oooh." Abby nodded. After swallowing, she said, "Just a thought, but ... do you feel like that's a little ... impulsive?"

Regan swatted at her, and Lynette glared.

"Certainly not," she barked. "He's been cheating from the very beginning, Abby. Lying and sneaking around with women, telling stories and making me feel like a psycho wife for suspecting ..." Shaking her head, she focused on moving cake around with her fork without actual purpose as she transitioned into disgruntled Spanish.

They all exchanged glances, but when Celia looked up at them—not missing a beat of her indecipherable tirade—each of them nodded as if they understood every word.

"Okay," Abby conceded. "You're right. It's horrible what he's done."

"*Si*, horrible. There's no recovering from this, Abby. Especially when he has no ... no ..." Looking to Regan, she asked, "What's the word?"

"Remorse."

"*Si*. He has no remorse. I'm finished with him. I don't want to ever hear his name again. None of us will speak his name again, *chez*? Like Regan's blog, if we have to speak of him again, we call him Pretty Boy. But I don't think we should speak of him ever again. He is ... how you say like the man in the movies? ... He is *dead to me*."

"At least she didn't send him sleeping with the fishes," Regan cracked, and Iris suppressed the snicker with an immediate forced cough.

"What about you?" Celia asked, startling Iris. "What are your plans to continue, heh? Next steps, I mean."

"Oh," she said with a sigh. "I don't really know. I can't think beyond a few hours lately."

"Well, there's nothing wrong with that for a while," Lynette chimed in. "You need to take whatever time you need."

"Cooking our dinner tonight was the first time I've felt normal. If I could just stay in the kitchen day and night, I might have a real shot at ..." Her words trailed away as she considered how to say it. "...recovery? Although I don't know if I'll ever really recover."

"Of course you will," Abby said, and she stroked Iris's hand. "Look at Regan. After she was blindsided by Craig leaving—"

"I don't think we should speak his name either," Celia interrupted. "He is dead to us too, *chez*?"

"Okay," Abby said with a grin. "After *40-watt*, she eventually found her way to something that felt normal. She started blogging."

"Eh, Iris," Celia said, "maybe you could blog about food."

She smiled. "I'm not much of a writer. I'm more of a one-to-one people person."

"Then you should start a cooking school or something," Celia said.

Regan lifted her nose and inhaled the savory fragrance of their upcoming meal. "Speaking of food, let's eat."

"I'll help serve," Abby said, and she and Iris headed into the kitchen.

"*Chu* know what I like about your blog, Regan," Celia asked. "I like when you do those little videotaped segments where you talk to the *comera*." Looking to Iris, she added, "Maybe you could do some videotape cooking."

The suggestion seemed to pique Regan's attention and she quirked a brow. "You know, that's not a terrible idea."

"And if she want to have guest chef once in a while, I could do it. Maybe have her in at the restaurant."

"That's such a good idea," Regan exclaimed. "And you know what else she—"

"Would you all stop pushing her?" Lynette exclaimed. "She's just lost her husband. It's too soon to shove her into the next phase of her life when she's not finished with the last one yet. Give her some time, would you?"

Iris mouthed her thanks to Lynette and they shared a smile.

"For tonight, let's just focus on this amazing meal she's made for us."

"You know, I learn a lot about American cuisine from eating at your house *effry* week, Iris. Growing up in Colombia and then working at an ethnic restaurant, I kind of stick to what I know. But you help me appreciate the diversity."

"You're in our country now, lady," Regan teased. "You're the diversity, not us."

"*Si.* I guess that's right. Me and Lynette," she pointed out.

Lynette chuckled. "What's on the menu, Iris?"

"*Whateffer* it is, it smell a little like heaven, heh?"

"Oooh," Regan cried, hopping to her feet and closing the gap between herself and the ham Abby sliced. "Glazed ham?"

"What's it glazed with?" Lynette asked, joining them around the island.

"Balsamic something," Regan deduced. "I can smell that."

"Balsamic and Dijon," Iris told them, the revelation greeted with hums of appreciation.

Regan turned back to the oven and squealed. "Macaroni and cheese?"

"I thought we could all use a little old-fashioned comfort."

Regan shoved her hands into oven mitts and removed the cheesy delight. "Now you're speaking my language. This looks amazing."

"There are also green beans," Abby told them.

"With toasted hazelnut," Iris clarified. "And parmesan bread knots."

"Hurry. Let's load up our plates," Regan encouraged. "It's time to eat, right? My stomach is growling like a lion."

Lynette placed her arm loosely around Iris's shoulder. "Good to know you're not unappreciated, isn't it?"

"As long as your love isn't confined within the walls of my kitchen."

"Of course not," she replied.

"We like swimming in your pool too," Regan quipped, and she dipped her fork into the steaming casserole to steal a first bite.

Chapter 23

"That's sixty-one, even."

Regan handed over the cash and the clerk, in turn, extended a large paper shopping sack, the handles of which bowed under the weight inside. "Enjoy your reading."

"I'm sure I will."

Baz took the bag from her, and she slipped her hand inside his free one as they strolled along the wide avenue created by rows of booths on both sides. She hadn't missed the annual literacy book fair in a decade—at least—until a couple years back when she'd begun to casually dismiss it ... but couldn't quite remember why.

"Are you hungry?" she asked at first scent of fresh-baked cookies. Checking the oversized watch hanging on her wrist, she added, "We have about thirty minutes before we want to find seats for the reading." She spotted the food tent and gave his hand a tug. "Wait until you taste these cookies. You've never had anything like them."

He yielded to her change of directions before asking, "What reading?"

"Huh?"

"You said we're going to a reading. What is it?"

"Oh!" she exclaimed with a grin as she hustled him to the open table. "Two of the chocolate macadamia, please."

"That'll be six dollars."

Baz beat her to it and paid the woman with a nod. "Thanks." Once they moved away, he leaned toward her and remarked, "Three bucks for a cookie?"

"Wait'll you taste. You'll know what a deal you got. Besides, look at the size of them."

They found spots across from one another at the end of a long picnic table and settled down to enjoy the treats.

"Ah, man," she whined. "We should have gotten iced lattes."

Baz chuckled and shook his head as he did. "Where do you put it? You should be twelve hundred pounds the way you eat."

"I know, right? Good genes, I guess."

"I hope you call your mother and thank her for that."

"I'll do that as soon as I get home." Impatient for him to get on with it, she urged, "Will you eat your cookie, please? I'm dying to see your face when you do."

He appeased her by taking a significant bite, but tormented her with his slow, deliberate reaction.

"Well?"

He nodded slowly before he—finally!—said, "Yeah. It's pretty good."

"Pretty good? You're a moron."

A stream of chuckles rolled out of him before he turned serious. "It's the best cookie on the planet Earth. Really. Not even my grandmother made anything better."

"Well, now you're just insulting the cookie."

He spoke over the next bite. "So … the reading?"

"Oh, right. Every year, they have a banned book reading where celebrities read from books that have been banned from schools, libraries, churches, that kind of thing. They're mostly local celebrities, but there's a special guest this—"

Regan's heart stopped, and the words flash-froze with her thoughts as she saw … *him* … standing there behind Baz like he belonged there or something. Like he should be allowed anywhere near a man like Baz, his opposite in every way.

Smiling his dull, forty-watt smile, Craig greeted her. "How are you, Regan?"

Where was her voice when she needed it?

She cleared her throat before standing and glaring down at Baz. "Let's go. We'll be late for the reading."

Confused, Baz stood. But instead of making a move to run away with her, he turned to Craig and extended his hand. "Baz Jordan."

"Craig Sloane," he returned, and Baz's gaze darted to Regan for a fraction of an instant. "You must be the carpenter chef … or whatever she calls you in her blog."

He reads my blog? He has no right to read my blog. It's none of his business. It's private.

Well, of course it wasn't private. But it should have been kept private … *from him.*

"We're headed to a reading event or something," Baz said as he casually picked up Regan's bag of books. "Good to meet you."

I hope you're lying.

In the history of introductions, there had never been a meeting less good than this one.

"Well, before you go … I'd like to introduce you, Regan, to my fiancée,

Stephanie." He turned to the bleached-blonde with too-red lips and ridiculous fake eyelashes. "Steph, honey. This is Regan." He glared at Regan. "My ex-wife."

"Oh." She lifted her hand and offered it to Regan as if she half-expected her to kiss her ring, which she couldn't help but notice held a rock twice the size of the one he'd given his *first* fiancée. "Nice to meet you, Regan."

She couldn't summon anything beyond a curt nod before she turned and stalked away, not even caring whether Baz kept up with her. Or that she had just been uncharacteristically rude. Besides, she didn't have the time or inclination to stand around meeting fiancées with too much makeup and the stupidity to wear heels to a book fair.

Baz didn't say anything when he reached her. He just enveloped her hand with his as if continuing their previous walk from booth to booth without interruption. When they reached the tent with the BANNED BOOK READINGS sign over the entrance, Baz released her hand. He dropped the bag of books to the ground right between their feet and placed his hands on her shoulders.

She tried to avoid his gaze with no success. When he knew he had her, he enunciated, "You okay?"

"Sure. Why wouldn't I be?" she snapped.

"Yeah, you're right. No reason. Now that *that's* settled ..."

She deflated under his touch and wound toward him, stepping into his embrace with a whimper. "I just ... wasn't prepared to ... I haven't *seen him* since ..." Instead of using her words, she simply planted her face against his chest and growled.

Baz seemed to understand though. He just stroked her hair and held her there until she made the first move to separate.

"I can't believe I ever thought I loved him. But at least he was a good lesson for me. People wonder why I'm never getting married again? All they have—"

"You're never getting married again?"

"No. I am not."

"Ever hear how you should never say never?"

"In *this* case, I can safely say never. I just ... can't ... stand him ... *so much*," she seethed.

"I know."

"No, you don't know. Because you don't know *him*. He's just so ... so ..."

"Unlikeable."

"Yes! That's it. *Unlikeable.*"

"Do you want to go home?" he asked her.

"What? No. I want to listen to people read from banned books. Okay?"

The corner of his perfect mouth twitched, and he scratched the stubble on his jaw as he nodded agreeably. "Of course. Let's go hear stuff we're not supposed to."

"That's the spirit."

They made their way into the tent and found two folding chairs on the end of a row not too far back from the front table. A disc jockey from a local contemporary country radio station—Selma Keller, known as The Satin Voice—greeted the crowd of about fifty.

"When I was a kid, my favorite book was *Winnie the Pooh,* by A.A. Milne," she told them. "I must have read it a dozen times over the years. In fact, my mom thought I could probably recite it without benefit of the pages. Don't we all have certain books like that one? The ones that get into our souls and help shape how we look at things?"

She picked up the book from the table and displayed it for them. Without cracking the cover, she quoted a passage from memory. "Well," she added with a smirk, "you can see my mother sort of had a point."

Chuckles popped throughout the tent, but Regan couldn't reach down far enough for an amused reaction. Acid pooled at the back of her throat, leaving it burnt with the familiar aftertaste of … a 40-watt ex-husband. She hadn't even noticed the tears rising in her eyes until they sprang out and rolled down her cheeks.

Wait. Winnie the Pooh was a banned book?

"…in 2006, about the time I had a five-year-old daughter and wanted to share my memories of my old friends in the Hundred-Acre Wood. It seems talking animals seemed to some like an insult to God, and the book was banned in various parts of the United States."

Baz broke the thread of concentration she'd managed to find by touching her hand and leaning forward until their eyes met. "Are you okay?"

And with that, the fountain of tears pushed through its last bit of barrier.

Clutching her hand, he stood. "Come on."

She followed—not that he'd given her a choice—down the open aisle between rows of chairs and through the tent flap. Still, they didn't exchange a word until they reached a concessions area, and even then it was only about her preference between diet Coke and lemonade.

"Lemonade," she said, and it sounded like a croak.

A few minutes later, two frozen lemonades in hand, they found the farthest spot from other people and sat next to each other on a long bench. Baz handed her a wad of napkins, and she dried the last of her tears.

"Seeing the ex," he said. "Threw you for a loop, didn't it?"

She nodded.

"Are you still in love with him, Regan?"

"What?" she said with a laugh. "No. Of course not."

"Then why are you crying?"

"I wish I knew," she replied, and stopped to take several draws of the frozen drink while collecting her thoughts. "The thing is ... I never saw it coming."

"Well, how could you?"

"No, I don't mean seeing him today. I mean ... when he left me. We'd been trying to have a baby for the longest time. A really long time. He was away for a few days, and he finally came back. I was in the kitchen, and I heard him wheeling out his luggage. When I asked him if he was being sent away on another trip, that's when he told me."

"What did he say?"

"He said he'd rented an apartment. Somewhere with good light. And oh, by the way, our marriage is over."

Emotion bubbled and sputtered inside her, stealing her words, even her thoughts. All she had left was the warm and comforting look in Baz's blue-gray eyes. They reminded her of steel. Bracing, supporting steel.

Abby stood behind a lavender velvet curtain with her arms stretched out and her body stiff while a total stranger knelt behind her with a strange contraption created to speed up the process of fastening thirty rhinestone buttons on the back of the dress. On the other side, Regan lounged on a deep-purple chenille chaise, chattering on as if no curtain separated them.

"You should see this chick he's with now, Abbs. She's like a caricature. I mean, seriously, who looks like that?"

"But what about Craig?" she asked.

"He looked the same as always. Even wearing jeans and a sweater, he looked like he was in a four hundred-dollar suit."

Abby gazed at her reflection in one of the four mirrors surrounding her as Regan jabbered on.

"It's lovely, isn't it?" the clerk asked her reflection as she peered over her shoulder. "Empire waist with a fitted French lace bodice and illusion cap sleeves, sweetheart neckline ... and this is Chantilly tulle on the mermaid trumpet skirt. It's very becoming on your figure."

She sighed. *This is it.* Only the third dress she'd tried on, and this was the one. No doubt about it. Just like with Nate, she simply *knew.*

"I love it. This is the dress."

"Would you like to show your friend?"

Abby nodded, and the clerk pulled back the velvet curtain standing between Abby and Regan.

"My gosh, I'd forgotten how exhausting it could be trying to be married to someone like that. That's why Baz is so—" Regan stared at her—wide-eyed, her mouth gaping open, and her voice immediately dried up—until she finally breathed, "Abbs. You look …" When words failed, she just sighed and shook her head.

"Enchanting," the clerk completed for her.

Regan got to her feet and moved toward her for a closer look.

"Okay, so I won't have my hair all messy and twisty and pulled into a side braid," Abby told her with a chuckle. "I don't know what I'll do with it, maybe an up thing. I'll have to find the veil first to know, but—"

"Stop it," Regan said softly, taking both her hands. "Stop picking it apart. You look exquisite. You're going to be the most beautiful bride Nate could even imagine because you're *you*. … And this dress? Well, it sure doesn't hurt."

Tears pooled in Abby's eyes, and she laughed while squeezing Regan's hands. "Thank you."

"You're welcome. Now don't cry on the dress."

Laughter popped out of Abby in the form of a stress reliever. Regan and the sales clerk joined in.

"Good suggestion," the clerk agreed. "How about we try some veils to see what you like with this beautiful dress of yours. Do you have an idea of what you'd like? For a church wedding, you can go long *or* short."

"The lace on the dress is so pretty," Abby replied as Regan released her hands and retrieved a tissue for her. "I don't want to cover it up. But I was thinking a veil with a little sparkle to it might be nice."

"I think a fingertip length would be lovely with your dress. And if you plan to wear your hair up, we could choose one that slips right into your updo at the back of your head, right here. I think I know just the one. It has a border of small crystals. Let me go and get it."

The helpful woman hurried across the floor, leaving Abby and Regan alone for a moment.

"This is the dress," Regan said, and Abby's heart fluttered.

"It is, isn't it? I came in with no idea what I wanted, but before the buttons were even fastened and I got a look at it, I already knew."

"Speaking of buttons," Regan said, "there's a whole lot of them on the back of that dress. As your Maid of Honor, is it my job to make sure they're all buttoned up?"

"They have something for that," Abby replied with a grin. "I'll be sure and have her show you."

Regan ran a finger along the ruched cap sleeve. "So … Hey. What am I supposed to wear?"

"Let me take care of the veil and the shoes, and then we'll move on to you. I was thinking about this color for your dress," she said, stroking the lavender dressing room curtain. "What do you think?"

"It's pretty."

"And for the flowers, lavender and green hydrangeas with some roses?"

"Sure. That sounds … Sorry. What's a hydrangea?"

Abby chuckled. "First me. Let's get me suited up, and then we'll move down the list."

"You have a list?" she asked, then smiled. "Wait. You're Abigail Strayhan. Of course you have a list." After a moment, she asked, "When does choosing the cake come on the list? I don't want to miss that part, okay?"

"Yes, Regan."

"No, seriously. I don't want to miss that part."

Celia ran the roll of packing tape over the seam of the last box before pushing it to the wall and adding it to the pile in the corner. She grabbed a Sharpie and wrote *ugly ties & shoes* on the flap.

"That's the last of the closet," she told Iris, and the two of them sat side-by-side at the foot of the bed.

"What you didn't already throw out the window, anyway."

Celia chuckled and lifted one shoulder in a shrug.

"I don't know why you're doing all this for him," Iris remarked. "I'd think he should—"

"He is not setting foot inside this house ever again," she barked.

"Okay. I get it," she said, gazing over the boxes and bags she'd packed up. "You definitely give a project everything you've got. I've never seen someone's life packed up so quickly."

"Too bad I put my everything into *Keffin*, heh?"

Iris placed her hand over Celia's and rubbed it. "I'm so sorry, Sweetie. Is there any chance you two can work it out?"

"The working it out part of our marriage had a good run, Iris. I tried, I really did."

"I know you did."

"Now we enter the ending it period." They sat there in silence for a minute or so before she admitted, "I just wish I knew how to do that."

"You'll figure it out. Why don't we go downstairs and see if Lynette and Trevor need help finishing the garage before I have to go?"

"Okay."

Celia stood and led the way out of the bedroom, willing herself not to look back. She didn't want to see the other half of her life neatly labeled and stacked against the wall, ready to go on its way.

As she reached the door to the garage and set her hand on the knob, the good-natured banter between Lynette and Trevor stabbed as cleanly as her favorite Japanese steel knife in her restaurant kitchen. She stood and listened to them for a moment, wondering if she and Kevin ever sounded so comfortable together. She tried to look back on their relationship, but she couldn't manage to scale that huge brick wall just a few days old.

"Honey?" Iris said softly, and she placed her hand on Celia's shoulder.

"Yeh." She pushed open the door to the garage. "How's it going in here, heh?"

She didn't really need them to answer; she could clearly see their progress. Trevor had moved her car out to the street so that everything Kevin owned could be moved to one side of the garage. She suspected it had been Lynette behind the handle of the broom that had swept the garage floor. She hadn't seen it so pristine since the day they'd moved in.

How many toolboxes does he have? she wondered, checking out the orderly mountain of them stacked on one side of the garage next to the big red rolling thing with all the drawers and various buckets and containers marked with words like SPACKLE and EPOXY.

"Hey, Love," Trevor greeted her with a warm—and somehow comforting—smile. He pushed back a stray lock of black hair that fell across his forehead, and his very blue eyes sparkled as he motioned toward the mountain. "You'll want to have a look to make sure we haven't given him credit for anything that belongs to you."

"There's nothing in here I want," she stated.

"Well, we left you a few things, some extension cords and—"

"And the cute little pink toolkit we found," Lynette chimed in. "We assumed it's yours."

Celia lifted both hands and shook her head. "Can you believe that was one of my Christmas gifts last year? Like I know how to use any of the doo-dads inside of it. *Ay carumba*, the man is an *idiota*."

"We assumed the air compressor and the like go to Kevin."

Lynette interrupted Trevor. "No, honey. We're not saying his name."

"Oh. Then what? We'll just call him *He*?" He seemed confused.

Iris chuckled from the sidelines. "That's much better than the other names we've heard him called recently."

"Shall we phone and give him the 'all clear' to come pick up all this stuff?" Lynette asked.

"I *yust haff* to move the boxes from the bedroom down here, and then I'll ask Sebastian to do that. He's been amazing through this whole *lío*. Ever since he found out. I think he feels just awful that he missed the *seagulls* for such a long time."

Trevor looked to Lynette, and she translated. "The signals. He missed the signals."

"Regan says he's pretty torn up over suggesting you get some therapy instead of considering you might be right," Iris said.

"He's more than made up for that," she replied. "Sebastian and Regan have been such a great support to me."

"I won't be surprised if Regan goes the way of Abby someday soon," Lynette told them, and Celia released a guttural groan. "I know, I know. You're not in the mood to hear such things," she told Celia. Slipping her arm around Trevor's waist and sinking into him, she added, "I'm blinded by marital bliss."

When Celia's eyes narrowed and her expression went sour, Trevor quickly kissed Lynette's temple before pulling away. "I'll go up and start bringing down some of the boxes before she takes it out on me. Watch yourself, Baby."

"Will do," she said with a laugh. Once Trevor went inside, she moved to Celia and took her hand. "You're going to be fine. We'll get you through this and to the other side of it, and you'll be fine."

"Promise?"

"I do." Turning to Iris, she added, "You will too."

The three of them moved into a circular group hug, and Celia's heart squeezed with gratitude for such wonderful friends.

"What do you say," Lynette said before the circle had broken, "we leave Trev here to finish up and the three of us go out for a late lunch?"

"Won't he want to get a bite with us?" Iris asked as they separated.

"No, he has office hours this afternoon. He has to get to the university within the hour."

"It was so nice of him—of all three of you—to come and help me today," Celia told them. "I don't know what I'd do without my friends right now."

"So what's the next move?" Iris asked. "Did you call the lawyer?"

"I did. I have an appointment early next week to make the ball going."

"Rolling," Lynette said. "Get the ball rolling."

She shrugged. "Eh. However you say it."

"And ... you're sure you want to end it."

"*Sí*. Sebastian say he thinks it's been going on for a long time. And you know ... I just want to be done with it instead of feeling like the *stupido* jealous wife he's convinced everyone I am. No, I think I want to slice off the ties around the smock, you know? Quick like a bunny."

They both looked at her strangely for a moment before Iris inhaled sharply. "Ohh. Cut the apron strings."

"*Sí*, this is what I say. Just be done with him."

"As long as you're sure," Lynette replied. "Now where do we want to go for lunch? How about something over near Balboa Park? Abby and Regan are bridal shopping over there. Maybe they can join us."

"Oooh, let's try out the new place," Celia said. "I read about it in the newspaper on the weekend. They say it's to San Diego's American cuisine what my restaurant is to Spanish food. Something like Grill-on-the-Park? Or maybe Parkside Grill? I can't remember it."

"We can look it up on the way. I'll go tell Trevor our plans. Iris, can you drive?"

"We'll meet you out front in my car."

Celia didn't want to tell them she didn't think she could bear hearing about Abby's wedding plans. She'd just hope ... maybe they wouldn't be able to make it. Chastising herself as a terrible friend, she finally said it. "Do we have to call the girls? Can't we go, just us?"

Instead of the shock and disgust she half-expected, Iris and Lynette both took her questions in stride. If that didn't provide enough of a relief for her, Iris stroked her arm and Lynette nodded, smiling one of those fully understanding smiles of hers.

"That sounds like a plan," Iris said.

"*Gracias, mis dulces amigas*," she told them, relieved.

"We get it," Lynette told her as she passed on the way into the house. "Three's company, five's too much wedding talk."

Celia and Iris shared a giggle in her wake.

"Thank you," Celia whispered.

"We've got your back, honey."

"*Gracias al Señor por encima de.*"

Welcome to VERTICAL MAGAZINE
Moments-of-Truth.net

BLOG POST: REGAN SLOANE

The winds of change are blowing, readers. Family Man's funeral is behind us, and Irene is struggling to find her way in the world as one half of a whole. My "crazy nuts" friend Maria—you know the one with delusions of jealousy-fueled suspicions about her husband, Pretty Boy? Well, it turns out she's not so crazy after all. The whole story is still unfolding, but it looks like he may have had as many women throughout their marriage as I have books on my newly-built shelves. And that's a lot.

As for Gabby ... times are a-changin' for her too. I think I labeled it the No-Win Circle in an earlier blog. Gabby's pledge to give up sex until after she found someone to marry seemed pretty futile given none of her dates called again for a second or third date once they realized getting lucky wasn't on the agenda any time soon. She'd given up on dating at all for a while. But then she met him. He shares her faith, understands her desire to wait, even supports it.

As hard as it is for me to wrap my head around this fact, I happily share the news with you today: Gabby's Bradley Cooper has proposed.

Yep. You read me right.

He's already surrendered the diamond, they've set a date, and Gabby has chosen the dress. It's official. They seem like a natural match, and I've never seen my friend so stupidly happy.

I'm still in the getting-to-know-you portion of our program with my Carpenter Chef, but I can see a decision time of my own galloping over the horizon. Will we or won't we? And if we do, what will that mean? More importantly, what will it mean if we don't? The thought of giving that much of myself to a man again—any man!—after all those years under a 40-Watt thumb is a little overwhelming. But then again, not giving myself to CC feels like a deprivation I've never entertained before; unmatched by any other type of hardship. The desire is clearly there, but the follow-through gets bogged down, frozen in the flashbacks of the former life. The one where my deepest trust was trampled and broken. I don't think I could bear it again.

I have to admit I've started to wonder ... Maybe there's something to be said for Gabby's new kind of abstinence. What do you think?

Chapter 24

Regan kept musing about the great big laugh Abby had gotten over her last blog post. Regan had simply called to let her know she'd made the appointment for the final Maid of Honor dress fitting, but they'd spent nearly two hours on the phone reviewing wedding plans ... with Abby inflicting various jabs about the whole abstinence debate Regan had provoked on her blog. Her readers were women with opinions as diverse and polarizing as a run for public office.

"You do know I made that choice because of my faith, right?"

"Yeah. But I vividly remember you saying you couldn't find anyone who would keep dating you because of that choice, and then—"

"Look," Abby interrupted. "I'm all for you considering a chaste lifestyle. But you might want to consider the God who instructed us in that direction. That's all I'm saying."

It wasn't that Regan didn't think there might be a God out there somewhere. As much as she envied Abby for her set-in-stone convictions, though, she just couldn't manage to suspend belief enough to embrace the whole born-of-a-virgin and rose-on-the-third-day wives' tales.

"I think I'd need one of those burning bush experiences," she'd told Abby. "And the truth is ... even though I joke about it, I have no intention of refraining from ravaging Baz as soon as the time is right."

She'd imagined Abby covering her ears when she said it. Perhaps clamping her eyes shut and reciting, "La la la la."

Instead, she'd replied quite simply. "It's your choice to make. Only you can decide what feels right and what makes you truly happy."

And so when Baz phoned to say he had some work to do after closing his store, Regan wondered if the time had already come. It took about thirty seconds of creative imagining before she set her plans into motion. From shaving her legs to moisturizing all the places that had been neglected for so long—telling herself all the while that the final decision hadn't yet been made, but knowing full well that it had—she readied herself to commence the ravaging.

Wearing her favorite jeans and the navy top Baz had remarked on—*"Only you could make a Henley look so hot"*—she picked up a pizza on her way over, timing it so that she arrived just as Devin turned the key in the lock of the front door.

"Baz is in the back," the clerk told her as she left.

"Thanks. Have a good night."

Admiring the craftsmanship of Baz's furniture designs, she strolled the length of the store and inhaled sharply before reaching the office. The door stood open, and Baz slumped forward slightly, working at the computer. She watched him for almost a minute before taking another bracing breath.

"Hi," she sang as if she'd just arrived on the scene. He looked up and brightened at the sight of her. "I thought you might be hungry."

"Come on in," he said, standing. "I didn't expect to see you tonight."

"I know." She set the pizza box on the corner of his desk and smiled. "I could lie and tell you it was a spontaneous decision, but I've kind of been planning it ever since you called."

"You have?"

Regan moved toward him and slipped her arms over his shoulders. Tangling the fingers of both hands into the long hair at the nape of his neck, she brought his head closer … closer still. When their lips touched, she wasted no time coyly leading up to anything. She deepened the kiss immediately and growled as she wound her arms around his neck. He responded by sealing the distance between their bodies, pulling her toward him at the waist.

When they parted, Baz looked at her sleepily. "Really?"

"It's time, don't you think?" she replied.

"Oh, it's way past time as far as I'm concerned. But I was under the impression you were considering all the options and trying to make sure you're ready to move on."

"You read my blog again, didn't you?"

He chuckled. "Guilty as charged."

"Baz. I'm not proposing or anything, but … I want this."

"You don't have to tell me twice," he said, kissing her until she found herself breathless.

Baz lifted her, and her feet left the floor as he spun around and deposited her onto the corner of the desk. Just as his hands traveled upward—

A shrill siren sounded.

They flew apart, flames of panic crackling in both their eyes.

"What is that?" she cried.

"It's the alarm on the front door."

Baz flew out of the office, leaving her sitting there on the desk swimming around in the complexity of her tangled emotions, her heart pounding from shock, still slightly breathless.

When he returned a few seconds later, Baz held his cell phone to his ear. "Yes, I understand. No, I won't touch anything. Thank you." He disconnected the call and pushed the phone into his pocket. "Somebody tried to break in. They smashed the lock on the front door. The police will be here right away."

Regan blinked several times before the severity of the situation set in. "They ... broke in?"

"I'm sorry," he said, moving toward her. "For the interruption, I mean."

She had no words, so she just sighed.

"I need to go out front and meet the police."

"Sure. Of course."

Once again he left her there, sitting on the corner of his desk, her hair and clothes disheveled, her pulse racing.

Although the police arrived quickly, they tarried for an hour asking the same questions and creating black smudges all over the front door and windows. After they finally left, Regan helped Baz clean up the mess while they awaited the locksmith, and by the time they opened the pizza box, they were met with a cold, congealed, and unappetizing development.

"I usually like cold pizza," Regan said, "but that looks ..."

"Yeah. I can nuke it in the microwave to heat it up," he offered.

"That's okay. I think I'll pass." She smiled at him. "Want to follow me home?"

Baz kissed her lips softly. "You don't think maybe the moment has passed? At least for tonight?"

But I shaved my legs and everything.

"Can I get a rain check?" he asked.

"Maybe."

"What do you say we take a couple of days and head to the ranch?"

"Really?" she asked hopefully. "That sounds so good."

"The wedding is on Saturday?"

"Yes."

"Let's plan on leaving Sunday, and we'll come back Tuesday?"

"I think I can make that happen," she said, and she felt herself beaming like a stupid lighthouse.

Dial it down, loser.

"It's a plan then."

"It'll be fun." She picked up her purse. "Call me tomorrow?"

"Will do."

Regan sidetracked—half starved—to the Wendy's drive-thru for a double, fries, and a Frosty. Eating fries out of the bag on the drive home, she found herself wondering if her intent to sin had been thwarted by Abby's go-to God, and she grinned at the picture of a giant head shaking at her from overhead, pointing its disembodied finger in her direction and calling her a heathen.

"It's just a little sex," she told the gloomy night sky before popping another fry into her mouth. "It's not like I'm out doing it with guys every night of the week and twice on Sunday. I just wanted this one little rendezvous with a guy I really, really like. Did you *have* to send someone to rob the place? Seriously, I'm not amused."

A clap of thunder sounded and the dark clouds parted as a bolt of lightning lit up half the city out in front of her. An instant later, buckets of driving rain poured out of the sky.

Regan winced. Apparently, He wasn't amused either.

"Mom, can we talk?"

Those words had been sending a rush of dread through Iris since Candace was old enough to utter them.

"Certainly."

Candace set down her glass of tea and slipped into the chair across the table from her mother, fidgeting with her glass, staring down into it.

"You're scaring me a little," Iris told her.

"Sorry." She leaned back in her chair and sighed. "It's kind of weird to me that you and Daddy never asked me about ... *Michael's* daddy."

A mist of nervous perspiration rose on Iris's upper lip and the back of her neck. Where was this leading?

"You said he was a one-nighter. I think that tells me everything I need to know about him. Why are we discussing him now?"

"He called me last night."

Iris didn't say a word; she just stared at Candace and waited for more.

"He left a message and said he heard from my friend at school that I'm pregnant."

"And?"

"He offered me money."

"Well ... that's ..."

"For an abortion."

Candace's blue-green eyes found Iris's and held her gaze with a tight, steady vice.

"Well, that confirms it," Iris said after several beats of anticipation. "He's no one we need to think about."

"He's headed to med school next year, and he said he doesn't want kids anyway."

"Charming."

"So I guess … that's that. It's just me and Michael."

"And Michael's grammy."

Candace grinned, and a single tear dropped out of her eye. Wiping it away, she nodded. "And his grammy."

Iris reached across the table and took Candace's hand. "We're going to be all right, honey. We're in this together, you and me. I was thinking about it last night, and I realized what a blessing it is to have a brand new little life ushered into this house just when we have such a huge gap without your dad."

"I guess I didn't think of it like that."

"It just makes little Michael … *or Michelle* … all that much more of a blessing, doesn't it?"

She nodded. "Thank you, Mom."

"So don't worry about anything. We've got this."

"I wasn't planning on telling him," Candace said. "But I guess I hoped—if he found out about it—maybe he'd be excited, or want to get to know him or something."

"Maybe he'll come around later."

"I don't think so."

"No?"

"He's planning his wedding."

Iris's heart dropped. Not because of the news itself, but because of the disappointment and heartbreak she saw churning in Candace's expression.

"Did you have feelings for this young man, honey?"

Candace looked away the moment their eyes met. "No."

"No?"

She sighed. "Well, I don't know. I hoped he would ask me out all semester, so when he came over and started talking to me at a party, I thought … you know."

Iris squeezed her hand. "Can I give you a wonderful piece of advice my mother gave to me the first time my heart was broken?"

"Sure."

"Your grandmother was a woman of very few words," she said. "But she held me as I cried, and she looked me straight in the eye."

"Yeah? And what did she say?"

"She said … 'Sweetheart. Boys … *are stupid.*'"

Candace burst into a fit of laughter. "That is so not what I expected you to say."

"I warned you. A woman of few words."

"Boys are stupid," she repeated, nodding seriously. "Very wise."

"I like to think she passed some of that wisdom on to me."

"Oh, she did," Candace teased. "I see the similarities."

They shared a chuckle, and Iris blew her daughter a kiss across the table.

"You know, Mom, I think you need a project."

Iris arched a brow at her daughter and glared. "You mean beyond this whirlwind wedding of Abby's and preparing for my grandchild to be born?" Changing gears, she softened. "By the way, you're going to be my date to the wedding, aren't you?"

"Yes," she replied. "Don't change the subject. I think you need to do something *just for you*. A foreign concept to you, I realize. But I'd love to see you focus on something completely … *selfish*. Just once."

"What, like a spa day?"

"No. Like a career."

Iris clucked out a laugh. "A career? Like selling real estate or taking an administrative job? No, thank you."

"No. I mean doing something that really means something to you, that fuels your passion."

Iris waited to see where Candace might be headed, more for the entertainment value than for the actual suggestion. Finally, she sighed. "I think my days of passion might be over, honey."

"Don't say that. Mom, you're so good at so many things. But in particular, you're an amazing cook."

She laughed. "Now you sound like the girls."

"Why? What did they say?"

"Oh, nothing really. Just trying to fill a hole in my life that's shaped like your father, I think. It started with suggesting I write a food blog. Then when I said I'm not much of a writer, Celia said I should make some of those video blogs and have guest chefs on with me."

"What else? That sounds interesting."

"No. It does not sound interesting. I'm not a professional chef, Candace. I just like to cook for my family and friends. That's all."

"There's so much more to what you do," she insisted. "You turn food into … comfort. Into love and friendship. It's your *thing*, Mom."

"Well, it's good to know I have *a thing*. Everyone should have *a thing*."

"Mother."

"Candace. Really."

After a moment of silence, Candace gasped and flew to her feet. "You know what you should do, Mom?"

"Honey, please."

"No, wait. Just listen to me. You know how you and Daddy were going to refurbish the pool house for me and Michael. Well, now I'll be living here in the main house with you, so you'll still have—"

"Stop. Don't get carried away with this."

"—the pool house free and clear. You could still have Abby do her magic, but she could make it into a little studio with a kitchen, and a little dining room setup—"

"Candace."

"—where you could film a weekly vlog about cooking. It's genius."

"I am not going to—"

"Let's call Abby right now, Mom."

"Oh, yes," she said, the sarcasm dripping like bitter wine. "Let's call the bride the day before her wedding and talk to her about reconfiguring a pool house so I can start a new career I may or may not be starting."

"Okay. I get it. But we can at least run the idea by Regan. You know, in passing. Just to see what she thinks about it."

"I don't think so."

"Mom. Please. Will you at least just think about it?"

"Honey, we're still at the place where a lunch out of the house amazes us. You want me to start thinking about this kind of undertaking? Now?"

Without wavering, she replied, "Yes." Softening, she added, "For me. Will you just give it some thought, maybe talk it over with Regan? If it's not a reasonable course, we'll forget it. I'll never mention it again."

Iris sighed, and her tenacious daughter appeared to take it as some sort of agreement.

"Thank you," she cried. "And you know I'm really close to finishing my business management degree. If you did this, I could finish school while I work as your manager, keeping it all organized, taking care of the details. We'll be like Paula Deen."

"Paula Deen! Honey, I do *not* want to be like Paula Deen."

"Yeah, she works with her sons, you know. Together, they've built a whole family empire."

"An empire. From the pool house."

If nothing else, I could certainly learn a thing or two about hope *from this daughter of mine.*

"Maybe. You never know. I'll call Regan first just to feel her out and see what she thinks. You'll see, Mom. This is a brilliant plan."

"Candace, no. She's tied up with Abby's wedding ..."

In a flash, Iris found herself alone at the kitchen table, left in the dust of her daughter's brilliant plan.

"... at the moment."

"Oh, good grief." Regan stood in the doorway, clutching two bouquets of flowers, holding her breath. "Are you serious with this?"

She'd seen the dress already, but it seemed to have new light when the bride finished it off with a cascade of orange-red curls, shimmering make-up, and glistening diamond jewelry. The diamond choker and matching bracelet—simple but perfect complements to the dress—had been worn by Abby's mother on her wedding day, and by her paternal grandmother on hers.

"I've known you forever, and I didn't know you could come even close to looking this gorgeous. Where have you been hiding the supermodel?"

Abby smiled at her through the mirror's reflection. "Are those my flowers? Let me see."

Gloria Strayhan—Abby's mother—made a sound that reminded Regan of a car motor giving out. "Hold still until I get the veil pinned."

"Mom, my flowers."

"And they'll still be there in ninety seconds. Just hold your horses."

Regan chuckled and circled the twosome so that she could stand in front of the stunning bride formerly known as Abbs.

"I love them," Abby said on a sigh. "Mom, look what Shelley did with the bouquets."

"They're beautiful. Now hold still."

Abby reached for her bouquet—the larger of the two—and admired the arrangement of green and white hydrangeas, lavender and white roses, and crystal heart embellishments. She ran a finger over the stems, wrapped tightly in iridescent rhinestone ribbon. "Regan, aren't they amazing?"

"I don't think I've ever seen a prettier bouquet. Your cousin did a wonderful job."

"There. All done." Gloria used a ginger touch as she embraced Abby from behind and smiled at her reflection. "You're exquisite."

"Thanks, Mom."

Regan twirled her own bouquet and watched the prisms of light play off the crystals. When she looked back at Abby, a strange and urgent inclination to cry washed over her. She couldn't help but wonder what it must be like for a woman to stare into the eyes of her perfect match, and just *know*—without a sliver of doubt creeping in, without an instant of wondering if her neglected hormones had lifted their powerful arms and simply convinced her of the solidity of something that ultimately could never stand.

"You're sure," Gloria stated, as if she'd read Regan's thoughts and decided to voice her own concern. Two sets of familial eyes—both of them brown, both with gold flecks—locked together through the reflection of the standing oval mirror, and Abby smiled at her mother. "I just need to ask one last time."

"I'm sure," Abby stated.

Regan found herself nodding at the reply. When Abby grinned at her, she shrugged. "I know. But I'm surprisingly sure too."

Abby brightened suddenly. "Hey. Where are the girls?"

"They'll be back any minute. Lynette and Celia are both helping Iris and Candace with the reception room. You know how Iris is with the last-second details."

Abby beamed as her mother squeezed her one last time. "Iris has done a magnificent job helping to pull things together."

"Wait until you see it," Regan confirmed. "It's spectacular."

"I have no doubt."

"Shall I wait, or just see you out there?" Gloria asked.

A rap at the door stopped Abby from answering. When it slipped open, Lynette's was the first face they saw, followed by Celia and Iris.

"The replacements are here," Gloria teased, and she kissed Abby's cheek. "I'll see you on the aisle."

"I love you, Mom."

"I love you too."

Gloria touched Lynette's arm on her way out and asked them, "Take care of my girl until Nate gets the job?"

"Always," Iris said.

The moment the door closed behind Gloria, Celia rushed to Abby and took both her hands, speaking in rushed Spanish. Regan marveled—and not for the first time—at the way such accelerated and lengthy conversation in a foreign tongue came off so easily understandable when expressed by Celia. Her face and inflections simultaneously told the whole story.

"I agree," Regan said when she'd concluded. "There's never been a prettier bride."

Iris fluffed the veil as Lynette straightened the rhinestone comb holding it in place. "*Sí*," Lynette said with a chuckle. "Agreed!"

"Oh … no!" Abby exclaimed, drawing surprised attention from her friends.

"My nail. I chipped it. And it's my ring finger, for crying out loud. I can't leave it like this."

Regan grinned, grabbing her bag and pulling out an emery board. "Relax and come over to the table and sit down. I can take care of that in nothing flat."

Abby did as she'd instructed, pushing her hand toward Regan. As she filed down the ragged edge, Iris took the chair next to her.

"Listen," she said. "About that call you got from my daughter..."

"What call?" Abby interjected.

"Oh, Candace has this crazy idea—"

Regan cut her off. "It's not so crazy. In fact, I think she's right about you needing a distraction that isn't all about doing for other people, but thinking about yourself for a change."

"But really, a video blog?"

"Oh, like you and Celia were talking about at book club," Abby said with a nod to Regan.

"Except Candace came up with this really good idea about converting the pool house into a little studio where she could tape them. In fact, she wants you to work with them to convert it when you get back from Cabo."

"Oooh, I'd love to do that."

Iris groaned. "Can we please table any more talk about this? And maybe just enjoy Abby's wonderful day?"

"I think it's a *wunnerful* idea, Iris. Candace, she's right," Celia chimed in.

"Enough," Lynette said with a chuckle. "Let's have a wedding."

Chapter 25

A thunder of flapping butterfly wings tickled the inside of Abby's stomach as she stood at the back entrance of the church, fidgeting with her beautiful bouquet. Perhaps she should have given it more thought when she decided—with her father no longer alive to escort her—to walk the ten-mile aisle alone. She hadn't considered how comforting it might have been to have an arm to balance her. Maybe it wasn't too late to invite her mom to—

The first chords of Mendelssohn's traditional *Wedding March* sliced her doubts apart. The church attendant pulled open the double doors, and her line of sight went straight to Nate where he stood at the altar. Not even fifty guests filled the first few flower-draped pews on both sides of the aisle—a white carpet glistening with metallic threads—and like fragrant little breadcrumbs, lavender rose petals led Abby's march on the path toward Nate.

Instead of a tuxedo, he'd opted for a dapper black suit, and he looked amazing. In fact, she swooned slightly when she saw him. Their eyes met, and he held her gaze all the way up the aisle where she sent a silent prayer of thanks upward when he took her hand.

"I've known Abby for several years," Pastor Tim told the gathered guests, "and I've seen her grow in her faith in significant ways. When she told me she wanted to marry Nate, I had the same concerns and questions many of you had when you first heard. It seems a little rushed, doesn't it?"

Nate and Abby shared a smile as intermittent chuckles popped throughout the chapel.

"And then I saw them together," he continued. "The way they interact, the way they look at each other, just the simple mannerisms they share; all of it validated for me that this is something very special. Unique. Even … divine.

"When I asked Abby how she could be so sure," he went on, "she smiled and said, 'Pastor Tim, I imagined if I waited for the right man, it would be someone amazing, but Nate exceeds even my greatest hopes and expectations. I guess when you know … you just know, Pastor.' When I asked the same question of Nate, his answer was the same. Word for word. He said his grandfather had taught him that."

Abby's pulse quickened, and the butterflies took flight again.

"And so," the pastor continued, "as I went to our Lord in prayer for this young couple, I came away with one indelible thought. *When you know, you just ... know.* These two are meant for one another, and I thank each and every one of you here today for seeing that and supporting them in this step of faith."

Regan stroked Abby's arm, and she thought she might cry at her friend's simple, supportive touch.

"Abigail and Nathan, please join hands."

Abby handed off her bouquet to Regan before placing both of her hands into Nate's.

"The bride and groom have prepared their own vows."

She gulped around the huge dry lump at the back of her throat, but when she gazed into Nate's exceptional blue eyes, the nerves calmed, and her heart felt ... soothed.

"Nate," she said, "the scripture verse that comes to mind nearly every day since you asked me to marry you is from the apostle Paul's letter to the Ephesians. 'Now to him who is able to do immeasurably more than all we ask or imagine, according to his power that is at work within us.' You certainly weren't what I planned for, but you're far beyond anything I dared even hope for. Not only do I marry you without reservation, but I also commit—without a single doubt—my love and loyalty to you for the rest of my life."

Nate shook his head and sniffed. "Thank you," he said. "My heart is so full today, to the point that it's on overload. Unlike you—who avoided me at every opportunity—I knew from the instant we met that you were the woman I'd marry. Have children with. The woman who had just walked onto my job site and unknowingly pressed PLAY when I hadn't even realized I'd been on PAUSE. I'm so thankful to God, so completely filled with humbled gratitude, that He finally spoke loudly enough into your heart that you would actually want to marry me. You're the love of my life, Abby. And I'll spend every day showing you how grateful I am for this chance to spend my life with you."

A tear ambled down Abby's cheek, leaving a path of heat all the way to her chin.

"Abigail Strayhan," the pastor chimed in, "do you take Nathan as your husband, promising to love and honor him alone above all others, and do you promise to live a life of service to God and each other, following the example of Jesus Christ as set forth in the gospel?"

"I do."

"And Nathan Cross, do you take Abigail as your wife, promising to love and honor her alone above all others, and do you promise to live a life of service to God and each other, following the example of Jesus Christ as set forth in the gospel?"

"I do."

"And do you have rings to exchange as a symbol of the unending circle of love and commitment to the sanctity of your union?"

"Yes."

Nate and Abby placed matching platinum bands on one another's fingers—Abby's former chipped nail completely unnoticed as they did—the inside of both rings engraved with a verse from the Song of Solomon; the one they'd mutually agreed was the most important declaration either of them would ever make.

I AM MY BELOVED'S, AND MY BELOVED IS MINE.

Sections of pale green chiffon draped from the ceiling to create the effect of a tent, concealing their real purpose—to hide the inelegant overhead lighting throughout the church's small fellowship hall. In the center, a beautiful crystal chandelier held flickering flameless candles like those set into the floral wreath centerpieces on each of the nine round tables. The linens, flowers, and candles all reflected Abby's chosen color scheme of pale lavender and green with white and platinum accents. Mismatched vintage china, glasses, and tableware highlighted the atmosphere perfectly.

Despite her reservations about it, Iris and Abby's mother had worked very well together. Knowing Gloria had been a party planner in her youth made Abby's request that Iris collaborate all the more puzzling. Perhaps she'd just wanted to assign one of those necessary projects everyone seemed to feel she needed so much.

Baz returned from the coffee bar loaded down with cups balanced on his forearm and in his hands, squatting at the knees for Regan to help remove them.

"Cappuccinos for Iris and Celia," he announced. "Lattes for Lynette, Regan, and me. Espresso for Trevor, and decaf for the mother-to-be."

"Well done," Trevor said with a chuckle. "If that carpentry thing doesn't pay off, you may have a solid outlook as a barista."

"I dare to dream," Baz replied with a chuckle.

When he joined them at the table—he and Regan sitting directly across from Iris—she couldn't help noticing the easy way they had together. She thought about her penchant for a certain country singer with long blond hair and sizzling blue eyes, and she smiled. Moving away from Craig and toward the Keith Urban picture-type seemed like a far better fit for Regan these days.

Baz picked up a napkin and used it to swipe foam from Regan's lip, and the gesture pinched Iris's heart. Not for the first time that day, she missed Dean at her side so much. They'd shared every event like this one for the last couple of decades, and it seemed unnatural to have Candace on one side, but no Dean on the other.

"I think I have to go home soon," Celia muttered as she leaned against Iris's arm. "I want to be here for Abby, but all the hearts and flowers are wearing skinny for me, *chu* know?"

Wearing skinny. The bumble tickled Iris.

"Yes. It's wearing *thin* for me too."

"Ah, yes. I suppose it is."

When the singer on the small stage—young in years, considering the classic music he sang—crooned Frank Sinatra's long-ago hit song *Always*, Candace reached over and took her mother's hand just as her heart dropped with a thud.

"Daddy loved that song."

Tears sprang up in Iris's eyes so that Trevor and Lynette appeared through a blur as they made their way to the dance floor. "Yes, he did."

A piercing pain snatched the air from her lungs at the lyric, and Iris forced a few easy breaths.

"Celia," Baz said suddenly. "Regan has no appreciation for the need to dance to music like this." He gave her a nod. "Give me a whirl?"

Celia shrugged before standing and going with him.

"Regan," Candace said after they'd gone. "He's hot."

She grinned. "Don't I know it."

"Mom, my bladder's on overdrive. I'll make a stop in the ladies room, then we can head out."

"They haven't cut the cake yet," Regan objected. "You're going already?"

Candace touched Regan's shoulder as she rounded the table. "She's had a long day."

Once she headed toward the exit, Regan jumped up and took the chair Candace had occupied. "I'll bet you miss him even more at events like this."

Iris nodded, and the tears standing in her eyes found their moment of escape.

Regan wrapped her arms around Iris and tugged closer. "I love you," she whispered. "So, so much."

"I know. I love you too." When they parted, Iris used her napkin to dry her cheek. "You and Baz look very comfortable together. I'm glad to see you so happy."

"Thanks. He's pretty great. We're headed up to his ranch for a couple of days, by the way. We're leaving in the morning."

"Oh." Iris's eyes popped open a little wider and she looked at Regan. "I didn't realize you two had … progressed so quickly."

She chuckled. "We tried to progress quicker than this, but as soon as we headed in that direction, an alarm went off."

"Anxiety is natural, especially—"

"Oh. No. I mean an actual alarm. We were in his office at the store, and somebody tried to break in. The alarm literally went off."

Iris burst into laughter, and the levity still felt so alien that it almost ached. "I see."

"I figured it was Abby praying we wouldn't," Regan joked, and Iris chuckled. "So while she's off on her honeymoon, otherwise occupied, we're going to have another go at it."

She sniffed away her amusement. "I see. You're sure you're ready?"

Regan nodded. "We're so good together, Iris. I'm feeling things for him that I didn't think I remembered how to feel."

"That's lovely," she said, stroking Regan's hand.

"Did I tell you we ran into Craig at the book fair the other day?"

Startled, Iris exclaimed, "No."

"It seems he's getting ready to marry a Barbie doll."

"Oh. I'm sorry."

"No. She suits him. They'll go live in a Barbie Dreamhouse and drive Ken's convertible sports car … which he already has, as I recall."

Iris shook her head and laughed. "Regan, you're one of a kind. He never deserved you."

"Neither does Baz, but does anyone, really?" she said dryly before breaking out in a full, broad grin.

Regan had planned on inviting Baz in when he dropped her off after the wedding, but she'd forgotten they'd picked up Celia on their way to the church and she needed a ride home. Instead, she'd used the time for a good night's sleep, and spent the morning packing—and unpacking, and packing again—for their trip to the ranch. What did a girl take along for her first weekend away with a man since her divorce, especially when she wanted to travel light enough for him to think it was no big deal?

After landing—at last!—on her choices and zipping shut the rolling overnight bag that had been gathering dust in the garage for, oh, something like three years, she dragged it into the kitchen and ran a damp rag over it. No sense letting him know how unaccustomed she'd become to weekend getaways.

Steve toddled after her and stood there staring at her like the traitor he obviously thought she was.

"Don't look at me like that. You're coming with us."

Regan produced the large doggie travel tote that looked like a soft-sided picnic basket—she hadn't been able to resist it during one of their joint adventures to PetSmart. She swiped it with the cloth as well before loading the plastic food containers built into the side flap with Steve's favorite kibbles and a handful of biscuits. With his squeaky ball and plush cow toy still packed from their first trip to Baz's ranch, she retrieved his leash and laundered blanket from the utility room and tucked them inside.

She jumped when the front bell rang, and Steve waddled toward the door, barking. She followed him and tugged open the door to find Baz's smiling face there to greet her. Strange how much comfort that smile brought her after such a short time of familiarity with it.

"Time to hit the road?" he asked.

"All packed and ready. I just have to get the bags in the"— She started to turn away, but Baz took her by the arm. "What? Something wrong?" Her heartbeat skipped. "You haven't changed your mind, have you?"

"No," he said with a chuckle. "I just wanted to give you a chance to."

"To change my mind?"

"If you're not ready for this…"

"Put my dog in the car, will you? I'll wheel out the bags."

"I'll take that as an affirmative," he said. "Let's go, Steve."

The dog followed him down the sidewalk without hesitation as Baz sang a funny version of *On the Road Again*.

Regan giggled, fetching the bags and rolling them behind her to the door. Baz reappeared just in time to take them the rest of the way and open the passenger door for her.

As they merged onto Interstate 8, Baz flipped on the stereo and Keith Urban serenaded them out of all six speakers.

Regan looked over and their eyes met, Baz grinning like a Cheshire cat.

"Really? You like him too, do ya?"

"Yeah, he's fine. Thought I'd let your crush put you in the mood."

As Baz sang along with *A Little Bit of Everything*, Regan lifted both feet and propped them on the dashboard, wiggling her Coral Blush, sandal-ready toes as she closed her eyes and hummed along with Keith.

"I hope you brought better shoes than those," Baz said, and she gazed at the sequined straps of her flip-flops.

"What, you don't want me to go horseback riding in these? What a shame. I guess I'll have to skip the horses this time around."

"Regan."

"Chillax, horse guy. I packed them. These are just my getting-there shoes."

But getting there proved much easier in concept than in the actual doing of it. Just a few minutes after they turned off to Japatul Valley Road, another great big barrier blocked the way. First, there was a quick turn of the wheel that transformed Regan's seatbelt into a torture device, followed by a sort of explosion—the violent detonation of airbags, the noisy escape of steam, bumping and jostling reminiscent of airplane turbulence she'd once experienced—all of it accompanied by Steve's howls of warning that something unusual had happened. By the time the initial chaos settled and Baz had steered the car to the side of the road and stopped, white dust filled the air and Keith Urban turned irritating as he continued to croon at them.

"You all right?"

"Yes. You?"

"Yep."

Regan removed her seatbelt and turned completely around in her seat to peer through the back window. "What *was that?*" she cried, breathless. "A dog?" she added in a whisper, cupping her hand to shield the question from Steve.

"Bobcat, it looked like. I'll have a look under the car and check the damage."

"Is it dead?"

He ducked and looked into the side-view mirror. "Oh, it's dead," he stated as he climbed out.

"Stay, Steve," she commanded, imagining her dog would look like quite a hefty snack if any other bobcat friends still lurked about. In fact, she herself might make an appetizing main course with all that musky fear probably permeating every one of her pores. "Mind if I stay in the car?"

"Nope. Stay put."

Once Baz closed the door, Steve made two attempts at scaling the seat before he finally made it over with Regan's assistance. She gathered him to her with both arms and held him there, rocking him to the rhythm of her attempted breath control.

"It's okay. It's going to be okay."

Baz leaned through the half-open driver's side window and scowled.

"Oh, no. What?"

"We've lost the muffler, and the exhaust is hanging by a thread."

"What does that mean?"

"It means we call a tow truck. Get it repaired."

"How long will that take?"

"No telling," he said. "But long enough that we're probably not getting to the ranch until late tonight at best. Hand me my phone?"

She grabbed the cell from the storage tray between the seats and handed it to him. As Baz dialed and strolled away from the car, Regan tossed back her head and groaned.

"I'm guessing Aunt Abby's working overtime praying for hurdles to keep Uncle Baz and me apart," she told Steve as she scratched his ear. "What do you think of that, huh?"

Even blaming Abby and her celibate beliefs for the continuing obstacles, Regan still found it difficult to ignore the apparent neon blinking sign that validated her every fear about moving on from her past. Even with a guy who appeared to be able to give her every confident assurance Craig had never been able to provide. Maybe Abby knew something she didn't?

Baz leaned through the window. "I have a buddy up near the ranch who can fix it while we're there, but we have to wait for the tow truck."

"How long?"

"Well ... that's the bad part."

Regan closed her eyes and bounced against the headrest. "Of course it is."

Baz produced a large towel from the back and used it to sweep the airbag dust from the driver's seat. After climbing behind the wheel again, he offered it to Regan.

"I'm good." Steve was another matter. "Wait, yeah. Can I have it?"

As she dusted the dog, he sneezed. Then sneezed again.

"I know, buddy. Sorry."

It took Baz and Regan both to help Steve into the back seat where he circled twice and flopped down for a nap.

Baz leaned on the headrest and closed his eyes too. "Not exactly the day we had planned."

"No. Not so much. ... I blame Abby."

He lifted his head and gawked at her. "Abby? What did she do?"

"She's all ... celibate and proud of it."

Baz laughed heartily. "And?"

"And I'm pretty sure she's praying we won't ... you know."

With that, he laughed even harder. After a moment, he looked at her as if she'd sprouted another head. "You're serious."

"No. Not really." But was she? "She made this decision a while back about—"

"Yeah. I know. Did you forget I read your blog?"

"Right. So you know. And I think she's praying for me to ... you know."

"Wait until you get married again?"

"Yeah."

"But you're not getting married again. Isn't that what you said? *Never?*"

"Yeah."

"So you're not ever having sex again?"

"Well, not at this rate."

"It's only the second attempt, Regan."

She lifted one shoulder in a shrug. "Yeah."

The relative silence between them ticked past in time with Steve's stinky-breathed panting.

"I might have a solution," he said.

Regan turned toward him. "Really?"

"Yeah."

Realization dawned. "Oh. Sure. But … right here? On the side of the road?"

"No," he seemed to chastise. "That's not what I mean."

"What then?"

"Once the tow truck comes, we could switch gears and change our plans a little."

"Not go to the ranch?"

He shrugged. "We could catch a shuttle to Vegas instead."

"Vegas," she repeated, a cacophony of questions bouncing around her brain. "I don't get it. What's in Vegas?"

"About fifty wedding chapels."

Regan did a double-take and, when their gazes met, she burst into a fit of laughter and smacked his arm. "That's not funny, Baz."

But he didn't laugh with her. "I'm not joking, Regan."

"Seriously. Not funny."

He turned in his seat and folded his leg as he faced her. "And I am not joking."

She hardly felt her jaw drop open but, after several seconds, she realized it had.

When she finally felt ready to speak, her voice came out raspy and dry. "Just to be clear … you just proposed to a chick who said she was never getting married again."

"Yes." After a moment, he smiled. "But I also proposed to a woman in a holding pattern after being devastated, who wouldn't admit to being ready to try again if her life depended on it."

Her heartbeat thundering in her ears, Regan tried to catch her breath.

"This is …" She paused to swallow hard. "… a joke or something, right?"

"Nope. It's love. I love you. What's more, I'm pretty sure you love me too."

Love.

Regan admitted to herself that she had feelings for him, sure. In fact, she'd never met another man like him, who treated her the way he did, who treated her with the same thoughtfulness and amiable kindness. And sure, the first time she'd opened her front door to him, that unique spicy scent of his crawled up her nostrils and had never left again. But ...

Love? Please.

"You're thinking about it, aren't you?" he said, interrupting the dialogue going on in her head. "You're going over every detail of every moment we've spent together, trying to analyze it for some hint of actual love."

"No," she objected, knowing it had come out as completely unbelievable.

Oh, hush up.

Regan couldn't help herself from wondering if Abby's God might have something to say to her too, if He'd been carefully orchestrating events the way Abby so believed He had. Had He sent Baz—via Kevin, via Celia, via her desperate and pressing need for shelves—into her life for a greater purpose? Were they as meant for one another as it felt to her in the quiet moments when she let down her guard ... when she replayed things he said, moments they shared, the feelings he evoked in her?

Love?

Thoughts and plans to ravage and be ravaged aside, her efforts to discount the deeper things, the meant-to-be-ness of it all, had been hounding her since that first day when he'd come to her house. Somehow ... she'd known it even then. Something more than shelves and mutual friends seemed to have formed a foundation that existed before they'd even met.

Love.

"I think you are. You're thinking about it. So tell me what you've come up with. Is it love?"

"No." Her adamance ached. Why did breathing seem so difficult all of a sudden? "Maybe. I don't know."

He grinned at her. "I'll take that. And I love you too."

"Hush."

Baz nodded. "Okay." He shifted, facing forward, and she did too. "I'll just hush then." After a long, ear-splitting silence, Baz looked over at her again and asked, "So ... Vegas?"

"Yeah, okay."

Welcome to VERTICAL MAGAZINE
Moments-of-Truth.net

BLOG POST: REGAN SLOANE

The plan this morning, readers, was to come here and give you all the beautiful details of Gabby's wedding. And oh, what details there are to tell! A small church wedding with bushels of flowers and candles and style ... the most beautiful bride you could imagine ... swoon-worthy vows that would stop your hearts. It was one of the most romantic things I've ever seen.

Fast forward twenty-four hours, and you'll find me sitting on the side of the road with my Carpenter Chef waiting for a tow truck, talking about the possible hand of God, the one that moves things around like chess pieces, creating connections and moments of truth without our knowledge or foresight ... and that's when I had a Moment of Truth all my own.

He told me he loved me. And I had to admit that I've fallen in love with him. Another twenty-four hours, and we were on a flight to Las Vegas ... applying for a marriage license ... planning the most outrageous, fun and unexpected wedding we could find. He thought a quickie get-it-done wedding might be best, all things (like my fear factor) considered, and then we can have a more serious and heartfelt one with our friends in a month or so.

That's right, readers. I come to you this morning a married woman. Again. I'm not sure when it happened, but I know for sure it wasn't one specific moment. It was a series of them, from the one where he walked through my front door and my heart stopped ... to the one where I came face-to-face with 40-Watt, this new man at my side, the comparison stopping me dead in my tracks ... to the one where I looked over at him with airbag dust in my eyes and realized I don't just love him. I can't live without him.

So we chose an outrageous wedding venue (video link below)... on a roller coaster on the Las Vegas strip. What better representation of my love journey, right?

The girls were shocked (to say the least) and a little peeved when we invited them out for pancakes this morning (with Gabby on Skype from her tropical honeymoon) and laid the news on them. But forgiveness eventually settled in when we told them our plans to have another one (a "real one" according to Irene) in a month ... up on a ridge at my HUSBAND's ranch.

"Yes, Gabby, we'll shop together for the dress. I promise I won't even start looking until you get back."

"Of course, Irene. You'll be the one to put it all together and make it beautiful. Why would I ever ask anyone else?"

"Okay, Maria, we'll be sure to have food that's spicy and not bland. No, never bland! That would be a crime against marriages everywhere."

"Certainly, Annette. I've thought it through, and I'm absolutely certain he's the one. And you're right. I think you were the first one to predict it."

And yes, readers, there will be pictures. Lots and lots of pictures.

Until later ...
MRS. Carpenter Chef

Moments of Truth
sponsored by these fine books:

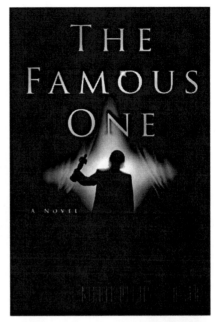

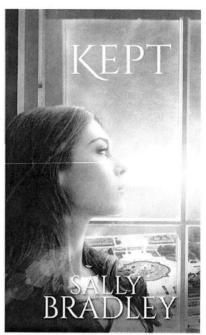

CPSIA information can be obtained at www.ICGtesting.com
Printed in the USA
LVOW07s1030280216

477034LV00006B/674/P